SEPTEMBER MOON

Candice Proctor

SEPTEMBER MOON

WHEELER
PUBLISHING, INC.
ROCKLAND, MA

★ AN AMERICAN COMPANY ★

Published in Large Print by arrangement with The Ballantine Publishing Group, a division of Random House, Inc., in the United States and Canada.

Wheeler Large Print Book Series.

Set in 16 pt Plantin.

Library of Congress Cataloging-in-Publication Data

Proctor, Candice E.
    September moon / Candice Proctor.
        p. (large print) cm.(Wheeler large print book series)
    ISBN 1-56895-917-6 (hardcover)
    1. Single fathers—Fiction. 2. Wilderness ares—Fiction. 3. Large type
books. I. Title. II. Series

[PS3566.R5877 S4   2000]
813'.54—dc21
                                                                00-040420
                                                                    CIP

For my husband, Tony, who hates dust and flies and ants in his pants more than Amanda ever could, yet went with me to the Flinders anyway.

And for Michele McDowall, Virginia Taylor, Kay Withers, and the other members past and present of the South Australian Romance/Popular Fiction Writers, with thanks for their generous assistance, and for the invaluable gift of their friendship.

PROLOGUE

Port Adelaide, South Australia

It was like an ache, Amanda Davenport decided, this need she had, this yearning to be back in England. Home, where she belonged.

She did not belong here. Even on a night such as this, when the sky above hung black and empty, and thick clouds obscured the unfamiliar southern stars, she still felt the wild, disturbing alienness of this place.

Tightening her hands around the smooth railing of the wrought-iron balustrade that wrapped the hotel's upper veranda, she gazed out over the port's dark, empty streets. At night, she couldn't see the unfamiliar colonial buildings with their peculiar blue-black stone walls and their deep verandas designed to keep out the hot Australian sun. She couldn't see the drooping leaves of the gray-green eucalyptus trees, or the dry, brooding hills in the distance.

Yet she had no need to see this place to know its strangeness. It was there, in the wattle and eucalypt-scented breeze, in the eerie cry of the kookaburra, in the indefinable aura of primitive mystery that hung in the air like an unseen presence.

A shiver coursed through her, causing her to hug her mantelet against the winter chill.

1

The sound of a strangling cough from inside the room brought her head around and she slipped quickly inside, folding her wrap over a wooden chair back as she crossed to the bed where her employer, Mrs. Blake, lay dying. Taking a glass of water from the bedside table, Amanda eased one arm beneath the older woman's shoulder. "Here. Drink this," Amanda said, raising the glass to Mrs. Blake's lips.

"I don't need more water. My lungs feel as if I'm drowning already." But the older woman drank anyway, her breath coming in short, wheezing gasps. After a few sips, she sank back against the pillows, her eyes closing.

Looking at her, it seemed to Amanda as if in the last twenty-four hours Frances Blake had shrunk in upon herself. Her cheeks had hollowed, her eyes sunk into gray, parchmentlike folds of skin. She was not an old woman—fifty, perhaps fifty-five. A life spent accompanying her botanist husband on his expeditions around the world had toughened her body and her outlook. But she had not been strong enough to survive the shock of seeing her husband murdered by the same thief who had left her virtually penniless. The doctor talked about tourniquets and foxglove, and said that with rest and proper treatment she might survive. Amanda doubted it.

In another day, a week at the most, Frances Blake would probably die. But by that time, the ship that was to have carried Amanda and her employers back to England would

2

have sailed. And there was no money to buy a new passage.

She sank onto the seat of the wooden chair, her gaze pulled against her will to the glazed veranda doors. Beyond their wavy glass panes she could see only darkness. Yet somewhere out there the *Prince Edward* lay at anchor, ready to catch the morning tide.

"It will be dawn soon." Mrs. Blake's raspy voice grated oddly in the still night air, echoing Amanda's own thoughts. "You must go."

Amanda turned to meet the other woman's pale gray eyes and shook her head. "I won't leave you here alone." *No one should have to die alone so far from home,* she thought, but she didn't say it.

Frances Blake's hand moved restlessly against the coverlet. "Jasper and I should have arranged things better," she said. "I am leaving you in an awkward situation."

"I'll get back to England somehow. Don't worry about me." Amanda leaned forward to take the other woman's hand. It felt alarmingly weightless and clammy, the thready pulse surging in slow throbs that sometimes missed a beat.

A peculiar smile twisted Mrs. Blake's bloodless lips. "I have worried about you for some time now, my dear. Even before we left England."

The casual term of endearment surprised Amanda even more than the peculiar words, for her relationship with the Blakes had always been one of respect rather than affection.

3

"Don't worry about me," Amanda said again. But Frances Blake's eyes had already closed, and in a moment Amanda heard the older woman's breath ease into the slow, even rhythms of sleep. Sighing, Amanda sank back in her chair and closed her own eyes.

Several hours later she was aroused by the piercingly sweet call of a magpie that lured her once again to the veranda. She slipped through the French doors, her heart slamming up against her ribs as she saw the brightening of the eastern sky. It was almost dawn.

She gazed out over the harbor. In the dim light she could just make out the dark spires of the ship's masts outlined against a bank of low gray clouds. In her imagination she could hear the rattle and creak of the anchor chain being hauled in, hear the snap of canvas as the sails filled with the salt-tinged wind. Feel the motion of the ship as it heaved with the swelling tide and set sail for England.

Tears burned her chest and clogged her throat. Swallowing hard, she turned away blindly and went inside.

Ten hours later, early in the afternoon of the third of July 1864, Frances Blake died, leaving Amanda alone and friendless in a strange, hostile land.

CHAPTER ONE

Amanda stood on the footpath, one hand anchoring her sensible hat against the tug of a chilling wind as she gazed up at the impressive bluestone facade of the house before her. She had no need to consult the clipped newspaper advertisement she had come to answer. She had read and reread those two sentences so many times, they seemed burned into her brain.

English gentlewoman required to act as governess. Interested parties may present their credentials to Mrs. Henrietta Radwith, 23 East Terrace, Adelaide, this Wednesday afternoon between the hours of two and four.

Amanda had never worked as a governess, but she was better educated than most men, and she was certainly an authentic English gentlewoman. She could only hope that might be enough.

It had been four weeks since the *Prince Edward* had sailed for home, and she had yet to find a new situation. Lately, simply staying alive was becoming more of a concern to her than getting back to England. She had taken to skipping dinner every other day in an attempt to conserve her dwindling resources. But time was running out.

Unconsciously pressing the fingers of one

white-gloved hand to her hollow midriff, Amanda mounted the shallow stone steps and tapped a polite tattoo with the brass door knocker.

"Miss Amanda Davenport," she said to the lanky, craggy-faced manservant who answered. "I have come to—"

Her voice trailed off as the man jerked his head toward the depths of the house, inviting her to enter. "Take a seat. Mrs. Radwith'll see ya in the library when it's yer turn."

Amanda stepped inside a vast, marble-floored hall at least sixty feet long and ten feet wide, and felt her hopes plummet down to the pointed toes of her high-topped shoes. A miscellaneous assortment of tapestry and brocade-covered chairs, settees, and miners couches had been shoved against the paneled walls between the fluted pilasters, decorative plasterwork arches, and handsome cedar doors that marched the length of the hall. And every seat but one was already occupied by an aspiring respondent to Mrs. Radwith's advertisement.

"Thank you," murmured Amanda. Perching on the edge of the hard wooden bench near the front door, she folded her cold-numbed hands over her bag in her lap and steadfastly resisted the urge to twist her fingers together in nervous agitation. English gentlewomen did not betray their emotions.

And so she sat, cold, nervous, but unmoving as, one by one, the other women were escorted to the paneled library door at the far end of the hall near the grand cedar staircase, then shown out again. One hour stretched into two until, finally, Amanda was the only woman left.

"Next."

She rose and followed the strange butler to a large, well-proportioned room of green velvet and darkly paneled, book-lined walls. A fire snapped and flared on the wide hearth, filling the room with welcome warmth. She found it an effort to shift her attention from those lovely flames to the handsome, dark-haired woman enthroned behind the massive mahogany desk.

The woman was expensively dressed in a gown of lilac alpaca trimmed with black velvet braid. In age, she might have been anywhere in her late thirties or early forties. She made no effort to rise but simply stared at Amanda over the top of gold wire-framed spectacles she wore pushed down to the end of her nose.

It had been more than five years since the death of Amanda's father had forced her to seek employment, yet she still resented these interviews, still hated being scrutinized like a rental horse in a cheap livery stable. She had to force herself to stand demurely and endure the rude scrutiny.

"How old are you?" demanded the woman.

Amanda's chin jerked up. "Twenty-seven."
And how old are you, she thought with an irreverent ripple of private amusement.

The woman sniffed, her gaze again traveling from the ugly, unfashionable hat Amanda used to hide the flamboyant blaze of her hair, to the simple mantelet that covered her prim and plain brown fustian gown. Mrs. Radwith held out an imperious hand. "Your credentials."

Amanda passed them over.

"Pray be seated."

Amanda took the straight-backed chair facing the desk and once again folded her hands in her lap. The ticking of the heavy bronze clock on the marble mantle counted the passing of the minutes.

"Given your background," said Mrs. Radwith without looking up as she flipped through the pages, "I would have expected you to seek employment as a private secretary, rather than as a governess."

"I tried, ma'am. No one in Adelaide appears to be interested in hiring a female secretary."

"It is an unusual occupation for a female." The pages flipped again. "And exactly what is your experience as a governess?"

Amanda's fingers tightened around the strap of her bag. "My father was a doctor of divinity at Oxford, so I received an excellent education. I am able to—"

"I didn't ask about your education. I can see from your references how extensive it is." Mrs. Radwith tossed Amanda's credentials onto the leather desktop and peeled the spectacles off her face to fix Amanda with a steady stare. "I am asking if you have ever actually served as a governess."

Amanda rose with calm dignity. "Please accept my apologies for wasting your—"

"Sit down."

"I beg your pardon?"

"I said, sit down."

Amanda sank to the chair edge.

"Tell me something, Miss Davenport. Did you by any chance count the number of females waiting in my hall this afternoon?"

She had, of course. She didn't see any point in denying it. "I believe there were twenty-three."

"And how many are still waiting?"

"None. I am the last." Amanda met the woman's brilliant blue stare, and felt a peculiar combination of hope and alarm surge through her. "Why is that?" she asked boldly.

Mrs. Radwith leaned back in her leather upholstered swivel chair. "First of all, let me explain that the advertisement was placed on behalf of my brother, Mr. Patrick O'Reilly. Mr. O'Reilly owns a large run to the north of here, near the township of Brinkman."

Amanda's forehead crinkled. "A run?"

"A pastoral property, named Penyaka. It consists of some one and a half thousand square miles of saltbush and Mitchell grass country, stocked with approximately twenty thousand head of cattle and one hundred thousand sheep."

Not the outback, Amanda thought, swallowing a flash of panic. *Please not the outback.*

At her silence, Mrs. Radwith raised her eyebrows. "Still interested?"

Amanda's empty stomach growled, drowning out the clang of warning bells in her brain. "Exactly how far to the north is it?"

"It's in the Flinders Ranges, on the very fringe of the colony's habitable area. To be frank, it is frighteningly isolated. Living conditions are primitive, one might even say dangerous."

Her words sent hideous, half-remembered tales of bushfires and black savages, of floods and snakes and poisonous spiders, chasing one another through Amanda's head. She thought of the endless miles of raw, untamed wilderness they had sailed past on their way to Adelaide, of the drunken, uncouth bushmen she had occasionally seen on the streets of Adelaide, and decided that if she were the type, she would probably have shuddered.

Instead, she asked, "Precisely how much is your brother prepared to pay?" The question was only a formality; Amanda was so desperate, she'd take almost anything.

"Sixty pounds a year."

Sixty pounds! It was all Amanda could do to keep from grinning with vulgar delight. Governesses in England had been known to work for fifteen pounds a year. With sixty pounds, she would be able to purchase passage back to England and still have a tidy sum on which to live while she searched for a new situation at home.

She carefully schooled her features into a serene expression. "And how many children does your brother have?"

"Three. Two girls and a boy, ranging in age from eleven to six."

"I believe myself capable of handling their instruction."

A disconcerting gleam of amusement flashed in Mrs. Radwith's eyes, then disappeared. "I am delighted to hear that, Miss Davenport. I should warn you, however, that the cost of sending you north is so high that if you accept this position, you must undertake to remain for a period of at least one full year. If you leave before the first twelve months are up, you will be required to pay your own way back to Adelaide. And if you leave within the first six months, the cost of sending you up to the Flinders will be deducted from your salary."

"And what is the cost?"

"Ten pounds. One way."

Amanda bit back a startled exclamation.

"Which means," Mrs. Radwith continued, "that if you stay less than four months, you will find yourself back in Adelaide with less money than you have now. And before you commit yourself, I think it only fair to tell you that one governess my brother hired left after two weeks. The longest any woman has lasted was six months."

Amanda smiled. "One might almost suspect you of trying to dissuade me."

"Perhaps I am. I see no point in sending you to my brother if I am not convinced you will be able to deal with the conditions you will find there."

Amanda felt her smile slip. She wasn't convinced she was capable of dealing with the conditions, either; she simply didn't see that she had much choice. Still, she felt compelled to ask the obvious question, "Exactly why did the other women leave?"

For the first time in the course of their interview, Mrs. Radwith looked vaguely uncomfortable. "Doubtless the isolation and harsh environment were partially to blame. Nevertheless, one cannot deny that my brother's children are—how shall I put it?—difficult. It is not easy for a man to run a station and raise three children at the same time."

"Your brother is a widower?"

"No."

"I beg your pardon. From what you said, I assumed the children's mother—"

"The children's mother is not discussed."

A pregnant silence descended upon the library while Amanda digested this statement. In the distance she could hear the familiar clip-clop of horses' hooves and the harsh, exotic screech of a cockatoo.

"Well?" demanded Mrs. Radwith. "Are you still interested, or not?"

Amanda tightened her hold on the bag in her lap. "If I could have some time to think about it? Until Friday, perhaps?"

Mrs. Radwith rose majestically to her feet. "As you like. If the position is still available by then, you will be welcome to have it. I'll call Roberts to show you out." She reached for the velvet bellpull hanging beside the mantel.

Raw panic gripped Amanda. *"Wait."*

Mrs. Radwith turned, one eyebrow lifting

haughtily. "I cannot hold the position open for you, if that's what you wish to ask."

Amanda's heart thudded wildly. She hated to make snap decisions. But in this instance, there was no time to do anything else. And what choice did she have, anyway? She could commit herself to spending the next year trying to teach three unmanageable children in the wilds of the Australian outback. Or she could starve in a gutter. It was that simple.

She sucked in a shaky breath, then pushed it out in a long sigh. "I'll do it."

Patrick O'Reilly lay flat on his back in Mary McCarthy's rumpled bed, the fingers of one hand clenched in her hair as the thick dark mass slid enticingly across his belly.

"Ah, Mary," he said with a gasp, his head arching back against the pillow, his eyes squeezing shut. "You're good."

Suddenly, that wonderful moist warmth left him and he felt her weight shift upward. He opened his eyes and lifted his head to look at her. "Why did you stop?"

She rested her chin on his chest, her fine dark eyes sparkling up at him, and he was struck again by what a handsome woman she was. She was older than he by at least five years. A lifetime spent in the bush had darkened her skin and sharpened her features and etched fine fans around her eyes. But her bone structure was good, and there was strength and character in every line.

He watched her smile. "I don't see any point in startin' somethin' again when we won't be able to finish it," she said.

"Hell, woman; you already started it." He ran his hands down her bare back to cup her buttocks as he lifted his hips. "And why won't we be able to finish it?"

"Oh no you don't." She slid sideways to lie naked beside him. "You seem to be forgettin' that the reason you came into town in the first place was to meet your new governess."

He grunted, rolling onto his hip so that they lay face-to-face, breast to chest. "I haven't forgotten. But I haven't heard the mail cart come through town yet." He took her mouth in a long, hot, sucking kiss. "Have you?"

She laughed into his mouth. "I don't think we'd have heard it if Saint Peter had blown his trumpet and called all the souls to Judgment Day."

"Aw, come on now. We weren't making that much noise, were we?" He traced her lips with his tongue. "Then again," he said softly, moving on to nibble at her neck. "Maybe we were."

She rolled onto her back and bracketed his cheeks with her hands, guiding his head lower. Mary wasn't the least bit shy about letting a man know what he could do to please her. "Besides," she said, lifting her chin, "what you plannin' on doin'? Pullin' on your boots and trousers as you run down the hill to meet the cart when you do hear it comin'? That oughta impress the new governess, all right."

O'Reilly let his nibbles ease down Mary's collarbone to her small, firm breasts and heard her sigh. "That's assuming this Miss Amanda Davenport is even on the cart," he said. "The last governess Hetty was supposed to be sending chickened out before she even left Adelaide."

"What's this one like? Did your sister say?"

"Nah." He swirled his tongue around one of Mary's dusky nipples and watched it harden. "Her message just told me the woman's name and when to expect her. Which means she's probably some dried-up, fifty-year-old spinster who's as rigid and unyielding as her whalebone stays. I just hope to God she's not another one of those damned English gentlewomen Hetty loves."

"I feel sorry for governesses."

Something in Mary's voice made him glance up at her. "Why?"

"Their lives are so narrow. So...empty."

O'Reilly shrugged. "I've always thought people make and miss their own opportunities in life." He brought his hand up to cup her breast.

"You need to find someone who will stay, Patrick. Your children need a woman who's around long enough that they can learn to trust her—maybe even develop some affection for her. Especially the girls. I know you spend as much time with them as you can, and you're a wonderful father, but..." She paused. "You really ought to think about marrying again."

He went utterly still. If it'd been any other

woman talking, he'd have suspected her of angling for a proposal. But he knew Mary, he knew the names of at least two other men who spent time in Mary's bed, and he knew she had no intention of marrying any of them. He began moving his hand again, slowly caressing her breast. "I still have a wife, remember?"

"Only legally."

"When it comes to wives, it's the legalities that count, I'm afraid."

She rolled onto her side again to look at him. "You could always divorce Katherine for adultery."

He flopped back on the pillow, one bent arm coming up to shade his eyes. "Oh, that would be lovely. I stand up in court and call my children's mother a whore."

Mary rested one hand on his chest. "Not a whore, exactly. How about a wandering wife?"

"Huh." He closed his hand over hers and swiveled his head to meet her gaze squarely. "Why don't *you* remarry? George has been dead four years now."

She scooted close enough to rest her head on his shoulder. "No one can ever replace George; you know that. Not in my heart." He heard a smile creep into her voice. "In my bed is a different matter."

He laughed softly and tightened his arm around her shoulders. "You know, Mary; that's what I like about you. You've got to be the most forthright, honest woman I've ever met. A man always knows exactly where he stands with you. What you want."

She let out a huff and skimmed her fingertips over his lower belly, smiling at the inevitable reaction she aroused. "You like me because we both want basically the same thing from each other. You want your lovin' fun and easy, and you know I'm not lookin' for complications any more than you are."

"I like you for a lot more than that, Mary, and you know it."

She twisted her head to look at him again. "Yes. I know it. And you're a good friend, Patrick O'Reilly."

He framed her face with his thumb and fingers. "Then you ought to know I have no intention of ever getting legally tangled up with another woman. One mistake like that was enough."

"We all make mistakes when we're young."

He sat up. "Bloody hell, woman. Why are you so anxious to marry me off?"

She sat up beside him. "Because I don't think you're really happy."

He stared into her wise woman's eyes, horrified to realize she saw that deeply into him. Reaching out, he pulled her onto his lap. "Hell, Mary. Why should I be happy? I've got a thousand square miles of scrub ready to dry up and blow away in this damn drought. I've got a good hundred head of sheep dying every week, and in another month I'll probably be losing that many every day."

"And if it rains tomorrow and the creeks run

17

again and the grass grows tall and sweet, would you be happy then, Patrick?"

They faced each other. "Are you happy, Mary? Really happy?"

She rolled away to pluck his pants off the floor and throw them at him. "Go meet your governess."

Amanda trudged up the dry, rutted track, her high-topped shoes kicking up little eddies of red dust as she walked. Her arms ached from the strain of carrying her writing desk, but it had been her mother's and she hadn't wanted to leave it with her other things in the broken-down cart that had been forced to stop at the blacksmith's shop on the edge of town.

Breathing heavily, she topped a small rise, then paused, conscious of an inner spasm of dismay as she gazed out over the township of Brinkman. According to the driver of the cart that had brought her here, Brinkman had been founded in the late 1850s; yet the settlement was still unbelievably raw. Constructed mainly of crudely cut sandstone blocks or upright saplings, it was not so much a town as a haphazard scattering of hovels flung amid the red rocks and dry scrub of the Flinders Ranges. Apart from the blacksmith's shop and the buildings of the copper mining company that had given the town birth, she could see only a squat store, a handful of cottages with bark or thatched roofs, and a one-story stone hotel with a weathered sign pro-

18

claiming "Brinkman Inn, Ichabod Horn-bottom, Proprietor."

Amanda walked on, puzzled. Beneath the harsh glare of the winter sun, the town seemed deserted. A team of bullocks hitched to a loaded wagon stood in front of the store, but it was a crude equipage, hardly the sort one would expect the brother of Mrs. Radwith to drive. Flies buzzed in the still air. As Amanda approached, one of the bullocks flicked its tail and shook its head, rattling the yoke, before subsiding back into somnolence.

There was no one here to meet her.

She blinked back a ridiculous urge to burst into tears. As the motherless only child of a scholar, Amanda had been alone most of her life. But she didn't think she had ever felt as alone as she did at this moment, standing in the deserted street of this strange town on the edge of nowhere.

Her entire body felt sore and unutterably weary after countless days of being thrown around on the hard seat of the cart as it rattled over a series of impossibly primitive tracks. Fine dust filmed her skin and clothing, and it had been so long since she'd been able to bathe properly that she was embarrassingly convinced that she *smelled*.

An icy breeze kicked up, swirling the dust around her. The bright sunlight stung her eyes, and she started thankfully toward the slice of deep shade offered by the veranda of the hotel across the street. As she climbed the high step to the stone flagging, a chorus of ribald

19

cheers and hearty male laughter erupted through the only one of the hotel's two doors that stood partially ajar. She hesitated, then pushed open the door and stepped inside.

The sharp scent of cheap alcohol pinched her nostrils. Through a haze of cigar and pipe smoke she could see a rough bar supporting some half a dozen men in red or plaid flannel shirts and rugged trousers. As Amanda's narrow-heeled shoes clicked over the bare floor, voices stopped in midsentence. Heads pivoted. Glass-filled hands arrested their progress toward open mouths. The atmosphere in the small, airless room fairly crackled with mingling shock and masculine outrage.

Conscious of having unwittingly committed a severe social solecism, Amanda took a step back over the threshold. But she didn't retreat any farther. "Pardon me for disturbing you, gentlemen," she said, her precise, Oxford-bred vowels sounding terribly out of place in this rough bush bar. "I am looking for a Mr. Patrick O'Reilly."

Half a dozen pairs of squinting eyes stared at her. Just when Amanda had decided that no one was going to answer her, a thin, stooped man with a graying fringe of hair stepped out from behind the bar. "O'Reilly ain't here," the man said, shifting a wad of tobacco from one sun-darkened, whiskered jaw to the other as he looked her up and down. "You that new governess he's been expectin'?"

"Yes." Amanda watched the old man purse his lips to let loose a stream of golden-brown tobacco juice that landed with a sickening, malodorous plop inside the brass cuspidor on the floor. She wrinkled her nose. It was impossible to imagine any brother of Mrs. Radwith frequenting this crude establishment, but she asked anyway. "About Mr. O'Reilly..."

"He was here for a wet one a bit ago," said one of the men near the bar. "He's probably off with Mary now."

A couple of the men exchanged grins. Someone tittered, and someone else muttered, "Now that's the kind of wet one I need." Everyone laughed except for Amanda.

"Mary?" repeated Amanda.

"Mary McCarthy," explained the grizzly old man with the wad of chewing tobacco. "The widow what owns the shop."

"Thank you." Amanda turned to stare at the squat stone building across the road. Her gaze fell on the bullock-drawn wagon she had noticed earlier, and for the first time, it occurred to her that this rough equipage might actually belong to Mr. O'Reilly. Her already depressed spirits sagging even lower, Amanda crossed the dusty track to push open the shop door.

She found herself in a long, narrow room crowded with big bins sporting hand-printed labels proclaiming their contents. *Flour. Oatmeal. Rice. Sago. Barley. Sugar.* Shelves of groceries and dry goods climbed the entire height of three walls, while through the door at the back she could see a storeroom filled with bags of bulkier items—potatoes and onions, jumbled together with caskets of nails and drums of kerosene and enormous wheels of wire and stout hemp.

There were two long wooden counters running along opposite sides of the front room, and against one of these lounged a tall, dark-haired boy, all arms and legs and bony shoulders. He stood hunched over an accounts book and seemed oblivious to Amanda's presence until she cleared her throat and said, "Excuse me? I'm looking for Mr. O'Reilly."

The boy's head came up, showing her a fierce, closed expression. "He ain't here."

"I was told he was with a Mrs. Mary McCarthy. Is she—"

"Who said it?" the boy demanded, sudden, angry color flooding his face. "And what else did they say about my mother?"

"Nothing," said Amanda quickly, backing up. "Nothing at all. Thank you." She swung about, shifting the weight of her writing desk to her other arm as she went to stand in the lee of the shop's meager veranda and wonder what she was supposed to do next.

A movement at the edge of the settlement drew her attention. Squinting against the bright sunlight, she realized that a man had appeared on the stoop of a sandstone cottage that stood in the shadow of a dusty red bluff. Digging his fists into the small of his back, he stretched and yawned, his long, beautiful body curving into a graceful arc, his unbuttoned waistcoat and blue serge shirt hanging open to reveal a lean-muscled expanse of naked, sun-bronzed masculine flesh.

Straightening, he lifted his hat to catch the chin strap, and the stark Australian sun glanced on golden hair bleached every shade from ochre to the color of ripe wheat. He settled the hat back on his head, stretched again, then turned as a woman appeared in the open doorway behind him. A woman with long dark hair that tumbled unbound and rumpled about her shoulders, as if she had only just come from her bed.

As Amanda watched, the man caught the woman around the back of the neck with the crook of his elbow and pulled her to him. Even at this distance, Amanda could hear the woman's delighted laugh, see her fingers splay, then clench at the man's shoulders as he bent his head and covered the woman's mouth with his own. He kissed her long and hard, his hands roving familiarly over her body. Unable to tear her gaze away, Amanda watched, conscious of an uncomfortable heat that was part shock, part a desperate, unnamed longing that flooded through her.

Releasing the woman with a familiar pat to her posterior, the man hopped off the stoop to land lightly, easily, in the barren yard, his open shirt flapping freely about his lean hips. Tucking his chin against his chest, he went to work on the buttons as he strolled down the hill.

Amanda watched the man come at her. She assured herself that this could not be Mr.

Patrick O'Reilly. He was too young and attractive, too casually sensual, too *Australian.* But he kept coming. Just short of the shop where Amanda waited in the shadows, he stopped and tucked his shirttails into white moleskin trousers so well worn that the cloth looked almost like supple leather. A very large, lethal-looking knife hung in a sheath strapped to one hip.

A sudden gust of wind caught at Amanda's skirts, rustling the stiff fustian and starched petticoats and billowing them out around her. The man paused with his hand still stuffed halfway down the waistband of his trousers. His head fell back and a pair of startlingly blue eyes stared at her from beneath straight, dark brows. She heard him mutter something beneath his breath, something that sounded suspiciously like "shit."

He yanked his hand from his waistband and doffed his hat. "Miss Davenport?"

Amanda's voice seemed to have stopped working. All she could do was nod.

A beguiling set of dimples appeared in his lean, tanned cheeks as he flashed her a devil's grin. "G'day," he said. "Welcome to the Flinders."

CHAPTER TWO

Thin and drab and as stiff-backed as a corpse in its coffin, the governess stared at O'Reilly from beneath the shelter of the store's veranda.

She had on an ugly, old-fashioned bonnet that covered every hair on her head and poked out to shadow her pale, tight-lipped face. Her mantelet was dull and shapeless, her brown dress even drabber and more plainly cut. He didn't think he'd ever seen a woman more obviously determined to make herself unattractive.

Shit, he thought again, although this time he was careful not to say it out loud. Settling his hat back on his head, he reached for the wooden case she held clutched in a death grip against her chest. "Here, let me take that."

"You—" The word ended in a squeak. She swallowed hard and hugged the box tighter. "You are employed by Mr. O'Reilly?"

English. O'Reilly froze, staring at the woman before him. Bloody hell. Hetty had done it to him again—sent him another one of her damned English gentlewomen.

He squeezed his eyes shut, momentarily indulging himself with the mental image of his hands closing around his big sister's neck and shaking her. Shaking her until she said yes, she understood that English gentlewomen didn't get along very well in the outback at the best of times, let alone in the middle of a killing drought. Yes, she understood that the last thing he wanted was for Hannah and Missy to start acting like a couple of precious little Englishwomen. For Christ's sake, what did he have to *do* to Hetty to make her understand that, after Katherine, if he never saw another bloody Englishwoman in his life, it would be too soon? *Damn* Hetty and her meddling, know-it-all ways.

He sucked in a deep breath and opened his eyes to find the new governess peering at him strangely. "You're English."

She squared her already rigidly held shoulders and proudly elevated her thin nose a bit higher into the air in a way that immediately reminded him of Katherine. "Naturally I am English," she said in her painfully precise diction. "Mrs. Radwith's advertisement specifically required the respondents to be English gentlewomen."

"Oh it did, did it?"

She gave him a supercilious look calculated to let him know she'd decided he must be a bit thick or something. "Surely, Mr. O'Reilly—"

"I am Patrick O'Reilly," he said testily. "Now if you'll let me have that case—"

"You?" An expression somewhere between disbelief and horror flooded into her face. "But you...you are *Australian*."

"Yeah." He gave up trying to get her to let him carry her bloody lap desk and just stood there, looking at her. Jesus, she was a tiny thing. The top of her head didn't come up any higher than his chest. She was fine-boned, too, and underfed looking, which gave her a worrisome air of fragility. As if the least hint of adversity would flatten her.

Against the harsh reality of the Flinders and the active animosity of his three hell-born brats, he thought, she didn't stand a chance.

As he watched, her gaze veered uncomfortably away from him, as if she'd decided her outspoken comment on his colonial birth might have sounded rather rude. He knew from experience that Englishwomen always made it a point to be painfully polite. Even when they were metaphorically sinking a knife into your back.

"I beg your pardon," she said stiffly. "It's just that your sister... That is, I assumed Mrs. Radwith was born in England."

"Oh, she can sound like a bloody pom when she wants. But she was still born out here, same as me."

At the words *bloody pom*, a band of indignant color leapt to Miss Amanda Davenport's fine, high cheekbones. Looking at her again, he realized she was younger than he'd taken her to be when he'd first seen her. She was even surprisingly easy on the eyes—or rather, she had been, before she'd pinched her lips together in one of those sour, censorious expressions English gentlewomen invariably assumed whenever someone said *shit* or *bloody hell* in their rarefied presence.

A gust of cold wind swirled around them, anointing them both with a fine layer of dust

27

and the bitter, pungent scents of the dying bush. He watched Miss Davenport stiffen her already rigid back to keep from flinching, and he almost felt sorry for her. She was so—so *English*.

He looked at her, standing there in her prim white gloves and stiff crinoline, with her formal manners and rigid outlook, and it occurred to him that everything that made her an English gentlewoman, everything that enabled her to move comfortably and surely through the world she'd known up until now, was useless to her here. Worse than useless: a liability. And she wasn't even aware of it.

He watched her chin come up, her thin nose quivering, and he knew, without being told, that this woman didn't want to be here in the Flinders any more than he wanted a woman like her out at Penyaka. But he needed *someone* to teach his children, and he needed someone now, not in another six months— presuming he could even coax Hetty into sending a replacement, which would be doubtful if he turned this one down flat. As for Miss Davenport, he figured she must be pretty desperate herself, to have come all the way up here for a job. The way he looked at it, they were stuck with each other.

Beside him, one of the bullocks shifted its weight, rattling the harness. O'Reilly scrunched his hat down lower on his head and glanced around, looking for the governess's trunks. "If you'll tell me where you left the rest of your things, we can get goin'."

As if she, too, had come to some kind of a decision, Amanda Davenport put one gloved fist up to her mouth and discreetly cleared her throat. "The mail cart was forced to stop at the blacksmith's shop to repair a broken wheel. I left my trunk and satchel there." Her gaze flicked to his wagon, and that brief appearance of color faded from her cheeks. "This—this farm vehicle is yours?"

O'Reilly's eyes narrowed. So a supply wagon was a touch beneath her ladyship, was it? "Yeah," he drawled. "But I'll be drivin' in the seat, not walkin'."

She looked at him strangely, as if she didn't even understand what he meant. But she did step down into the sun-washed, dusty road and let him take her precious lap desk. He went to stow it in the wagon bed. When he came back around she was still standing in the middle of the track, eyeing the wagon as if it were a toad or something.

"What's the matter?" He rested his hands on his hips. "Never ridden in a farm wagon before?"

She shook her head. "No. The seat is rather high, isn't it?" Her gaze shifted to him, and he realized that what he read in her face was not affronted arrogance but uncertainty, mixed with a touch of what he thought might be fear, although she was doing her best to hide it.

Swearing under his breath, he started toward her. "Here, let me help you up."

She sidled nervously away from him. "No."

29

Her voice almost squeaked with panic, surprising him so much, he stopped in his tracks. "No, thank you," she said more calmly. "I can manage."

He doubted she could, but he leaned back against one of the veranda posts, folded his arms across his chest, and watched.

Reaching as high as she could, she stretched one hand up to grasp the edge of the wooden seat. She was so tiny, she could only just wrap the tips of her fingers around it, and had to strain to get a grip on the front board with her other hand. She stood like that for a moment, her arms flung wide, so that she reminded him of a martyr, nailed to a cross. A well-endowed martyr, he thought irreverently, his eyes narrowing as he studied her profile. For such a tiny, sour-tempered thing, she sure had a nice pair of breasts. What a waste.

He had to hide a grin as he watched her lift her foot, then glance down uncertainly. Her full skirts hid her feet from her view, so she fumbled blindly to stick the toe of one shoe between the spokes of the wheel, using it as a step. She brought the other foot up, then took a hopping little jump that made her feet lose the wheel but wasn't enough to do more than propel her halfway up to the seat. Her hands clenched frantically at their grips, but she was stuck there, her stomach on the edge of the wagon, her feet kicking in the air, her little derriere poking out most invitingly.

She was lucky her crinoline was flexible

and unfashionably narrow, he thought, or she'd be giving everyone in Brinkman a good eyeful of whatever she wore under her skirts. He watched her wiggle a moment, then lie still, panting like a banked fish. O'Reilly eyed that upthrust bottom thoughtfully. He knew she wasn't going to like what he was about to do, but he couldn't see any other way around the problem.

Pushing away from the veranda, he came up behind her. "Want some help?"

He didn't quite catch her muffled response.

"What's that you said?" he asked.

She twisted her head around and stared at him, her face livid, her fine gray eyes snapping with an unexpected display of temper. "I said, *yes, please.*"

"All right, then." Reaching up, he cupped the round cheeks of her buttocks in his spread hands. She went rigid and let out an incoherent gasp of shock, but he ignored it. Tightening his grip, he lifted her up and into the wagon.

Amanda stared out over endless stark slopes of withered grass, sparse, scrubby trees, and brittle red rock.

This country was so wild, she thought; wild and harsh and brutal. A sense of dread had been building steadily within her, with every mile she traveled north of Adelaide. Now she felt a hollowness in her stomach that she recognized as fear. The township of Brinkman had been bad enough, but she was afraid Penyaka

31

itself was going to be worse—worse by far than she'd imagined possible.

She bit back a startled yelp as the man beside her cracked his whip and shouted something unintelligible at the bullocks pulling the wagon. They had spoken little since he had collected her things from the cart at the blacksmith's shop. Yet she remained acutely conscious of his rough, male presence beside her on the wagon seat. He was close enough that every time she breathed, she was aware of his scent—a mingling of leather and tobacco and a distinctly masculine essence that was not unpleasant. He had one of his scruffy brown leather boots planted beside her patent leather shoes, his knees spread wide so that his long, lean thigh pressed too close to her skirt. He made her feel hot and uncomfortable, and she didn't like it.

She stared down at his big, tanned hands, holding the reins with a laziness that did nothing to disguise the hard strength of that grip. She remembered the heat of those hands, intimately cupping her bottom, and she barely stopped herself from squirming with embarrassment.

She knew it had been unforgivably foolish of her not to let him help her into the wagon when he'd first offered. She could not understand, even now, why she had so absurdly shied away from the prospect of his touching her. She could only suppose it was because he had turned out to be so very different from the man she had expected.

She had pictured Mrs. Radwith's brother as

a proper, middle-aged gentleman, living in reasonably comfortable circumstances. She was still struggling to reconcile that image with this handsome, aggressively virile young man, who leapt half-naked from widows' porches and lived in the midst of such heart-stopping desolation.

It seemed to Amanda, suddenly, as if they had been driving forever. "How long will it take us to reach your run?" she asked, breaking the long silence. "That is what you call these properties, isn't it? Runs?"

The question came out sounding condescending and a bit supercilious, although she hadn't meant it that way. He swiveled to look at her. "We're on Penyaka now. But if you mean how far is it to the homestead itself, it's about an hour from town by horseback. The wagon's slower, but it shouldn't be long now."

"What do you mean by the homestead?"

There was a pause filled with the rattling of the harness and the howl of the cold wind. "That's what we call the big house on the main station. A homestead."

She turned to survey the horizon. Squinting against the dazzling sun, she noticed a few head of rangy cattle, and a distant herd of sheep under the watchful eye of a lone shepherd. Nearer at hand she spotted two emus, their necks stretching out as they minced away with unhurried, single-file grace. Yet the landscape still seemed empty, almost devoid of life. She wondered how anyone could survive in such a harsh place.

"It feels as if we're in the middle of nowhere," she said, surprised to hear herself speaking the thought aloud.

He let out a small huff of laughter. "Oh, it's not so bad anymore. When I first drove a herd up here from Victoria twelve years ago, the nearest town was a couple of days away."

"That must have been very difficult for your wife," Amanda said without thinking.

All trace of amusement vanished instantly from his face. She saw the thrust of his cheekbone beneath his taut skin as his expression hardened, and knew she had inadvertently touched a raw nerve. "My wife stayed in Victoria with her parents for the first few years," he said tersely. "She didn't come up here until Hannah was almost a year and half."

Amanda found herself staring at his sharp-boned profile. She decided he couldn't be much more than thirty now, she thought— thirty-two at the most. Twelve years ago he would have been young. Young to be driving a herd through wild, unexplored country to set up his own run. And very young to have already married and fathered a child.

Surprised by the wayward and decidedly improper direction of her thoughts, Amanda cleared her throat and said, "Tell me about your children. What they're like."

She sensed an easing of the tightness within him, a letting go of the hostility her words had so unexpectedly provoked. He pushed his hat brim up with his thumb. "Well, there's Hannah. She's the oldest. Then comes Liam, who's nine, and Melissa. She's the baby. But as to what they're like..." His lips curled up, his cheek creasing with his smile. "I think I'll let you make up your own mind about that."

She was so preoccupied with looking at him that when one of the wagon's wheels lurched into a deep rut, it almost sent her toppling from her perch on the high seat. She clutched at the board's rough edge and braced her feet wide against the bouncing and rattling of the wagon as it clattered down a steep, rocky incline. They were moving into more open country now, she noticed, the higher reaches of the Flinders Ranges looming to the north and west behind them. The land here ran mostly to undulating, tawny-colored hills and bold red tablelands, cut deeply by creeks lined with box trees and white-stemmed red gums and dense thickets of lignum. But the creeks were all dry, the trees and bushes dust-covered and dying.

"Your first time in the bush?"

O'Reilly's voice intruded upon her silence. "Yes," she said.

"How long you been in Australia, anyway?"

"Four months."

"If you don't like it, why'd you come out here?"

She glanced at him, disconcerted to discover her reaction to this wild, forbidding place so obvious. "I did not actually come here intending to stay. I came with Mr. Jasper Blake, the botanist, and his wife, Frances."

He peered at her from beneath his hat brim, his eyes flaring a bit in surprise. "You a botanist, then?"

"I am not formally trained. But my classical education enabled me to serve as secretary and assistant to Mr. Blake." She couldn't help it if she sounded proud; she *was* proud of her education, her accomplishments. "It's unusual for a woman to hold such a post, but Mrs. Blake preferred to travel with a female companion, so I was fortunate enough to secure the position."

"And these Blakes left you here?"

Amanda shook her head, a surge of grief squeezing her chest. "Originally, we were to be in Australia for a year. Mrs. Blake and I remained in Adelaide and cataloged the material, while Mr. Blake collected samples."

"So what went wrong?"

Amanda stared out over the strange, hostile landscape. Those secure, comparatively pleasant days with the Blakes seemed so long ago now, it was as if she spoke of another lifetime. "Shortly after our arrival, Mrs. Blake became ill—something to do with her heart. She wanted to stay, but Mr. Blake decided to return to England on the *Prince Edward*, in July. Only the very day we were to board ship a thief broke into our rooms at the hotel."

She hadn't meant to tell him all this, but the words just came spilling out of her. "We were on our way to breakfast, when Mr. Blake forgot something and turned back. He surprised the thief, and the man...killed him." She swallowed hard. "He also got away with every-thing of value—all the Blakes' money, my own savings, even our tickets."

"The tickets must have been in your names. I wouldn't have thought anyone else could use them."

"Oh, the shipping line said they would still let us have our cabins. They simply refused to refund the cost of the passage unless we could surrender the actual tickets."

"So why didn't you sail?"

She smoothed the ugly brown cloth of her skirt over her knees. "Mrs. Blake was too ill. She died several hours after the ship sailed."

There was a pause during which Amanda felt his eyes on her. "And you stayed with this woman until she died?" he said.

"Yes." Anxious to change the subject, she gazed out over the swaying black and brown backs of the plodding bullocks, and said quickly, "I'm glad that if I had to be stranded in the colonies, at least I ended up in South Australia."

"Why's that?"

"Because it was set up as a free colony, of course. There are no convicts here to worry about, like in the rest of Australia."

There was an uncomfortable silence, filled only with the crunch of stones beneath the bul-locks' plodding hooves and the sound of the wind howling around them, cold and dusty and lonely. "Convicts," he said. "They're a worry, all right."

The words were easy enough, but they carried an underlying, almost terse note that made her turn to look at him. He was still wearing that lazy smile, but his eyes had narrowed.

"You don't agree?" she said.

The smile tightened into something unmistakably nasty. "Course I do. Why, I was born in Tasmania, and the convicts there were a real worry." He drawled the words out, deliberately emphasizing his colonial twang, as if to mock her. " 'Specially my grandpapa. He was transported for stealin' a horse back in 1803, you see, and my mama, she always kept a nervous eye on him. Course, he claimed he was just borrowin' the horse. It was the *sheep* he was stealin'."

She stared at his dark, handsome face, with its bad-boy smile and glittering, challenging eyes. "You are making that up."

"Not a bit of it," he said, his attention flicking back to his team.

They were running now beside a dry creek bed, and the lead bullock slowed to eye the withered bush at the edge of the track with undisguised longing. O'Reilly cracked his bullwhip so close to Amanda's head that she flung up her hand to make sure her ear was still attached. "Gedup there, Mallee-boy," he called. "You ball-less bastard."

His raw language sent a shocked rush of color to Amanda's cheeks. If he was telling the truth—if his grandfather really *had* been transported as a convict—then she supposed she ought to apologize for her unintentional insult. Instead, she said tartly, "I take it you acquired your impressive vocabulary from your illustrious grandfather. Did he teach you any of his other skills?"

He turned his head and met her gaze. She looked into his disturbing eyes and, for a moment, forgot to breathe. She saw a flare of something hot and dangerous and exciting, something that reminded her that this man was no gentleman, that he was as wild and untamed as this land he made his home. "Skills, Miss Davenport?" he said, his voice rough and low. "Which of my skills were you interested in?"

For some reason she could not explain, his words brought back to her the image of Patrick O'Reilly as she had first seen him, his open shirt flapping in the breeze, his strong man's hands roaming familiarly over a woman's body. She felt a peculiar flutter in her stomach, a flutter that intensified as she realized she'd allowed the silence between them to drag out far too long.

"All of my livestock is legally acquired," he said, his lips twisting unexpectedly into a grin. "If that's what you meant."

She found she could no longer meet that intense blue stare, and swung her head away to look out over a land so lonely and primitive, it made her ache inside. She could not understand the feelings this place provoked in her. It was more than strangeness and fear. It was a restlessness, an edginess that was like a stirring of something she didn't want.

Something she didn't even want to name.

Patrick O'Reilly's main station consisted of some dozen or so sturdily constructed sandstone buildings that lay scattered seemingly at random along the side of a dry, rocky hill overlooking a broad valley.

Except this was not the kind of valley Amanda knew. This was no gentle English dale, knee-deep in clover and rich, sweet-smelling grass. This was a desolate swath of rocks and dusty, golden-brown vegetation that cut between the rugged, blue-green folds of the Flinders Ranges.

As the wagon lurched and swayed down the steep track, she noticed the drooping, gray-green leaves of a line of white-trunked gums that curled around the base of the hill. She knew the trees marked the site of a watercourse. But like all the other creeks they had crossed, this one was nothing but a tumble of dry rocks and widely scattered water holes.

High above the creek, at one edge of the compound and upstream from the other buildings, she could see the homestead itself. It was a low, one-story building, shaded on three sides by deep verandas. Massive, carefully shaped blocks of rosy-tinged, golden sandstone braced the house's corners and framed the openings for the doors and long windows. But the walls themselves were formed of rough stones, crudely plastered with some ochre-colored mortar. It gave the house the look of something ancient—primeval, even. The homestead couldn't have been here more than ten years or so, she thought, but already it looked as much a part of this harsh, sun-baked landscape as the cracked hills and raw red earth.

Yet if the house was a part of the land, the garden that surrounded it was not. Amanda stared in delighted astonishment at the flourishing oasis of green enclosed by a low stone wall. Within its boundary, rows of artichokes and carrots and tomatoes shared space with thyme and *Alchemilla mollis* and all the best-loved herbs and flowers of an English garden—roses and hollyhocks, pinks and ranunculus, stocks and plumbago.

"Whoa there, boys," called Mr. O'Reilly, reining in the bullocks beside the front gate.

Dust swirled around the cart, then drifted away, blown by a breeze scented with apple blossoms and lavender and the sweet, exotic fragrances of jasmine and honeysuckle. Before she could stop herself, Amanda caught her breath in delight. "Your garden is lovely. However do you keep it so green?"

"Chow rigged up a system with a windmill that draws from a water hole in the creek bed," he said, wrapping the reins around the brake handle.

She looked at him, puzzled by his curt tone. "Why did you plant it, if you don't like it?"

His head snapped back, his intense blue gaze slamming into her. For a moment, she didn't think he was going to answer her. Then he said, "I planted it for Katherine," before turning away to brace his arm on the back of the wagon seat and leap nimbly to the ground.

"You there, Campbell?" he shouted, staring at the silent, walled compound. *"Bloody hell,"* he muttered under his breath, and came around to help Amanda down.

Feeling terribly self-conscious, she primly held out the tips of her gloved fingers—

And had to bite back a gasp as his rough hands closed on her waist to lift her bodily off the seat. For one strangely exhilarating moment, Amanda soared through the air, held only by the strong grip of his hands at her sides. Then her feet touched the ground, and he released her and swung abruptly away.

"Campbell!" O'Reilly took off his hat and whacked it against his thigh, sending up a cloud of fine red dust. "Where the hell are you?"

Amanda stayed where she was, her fingertips pressed against her waist. She had the oddest sensation, as if she could still feel the warmth of his hands, burning all the way through the protective barrier of her dress and corset. She rubbed her fingers back and forth, trying to reclaim control of her own wayward flesh.

An abrupt noise jerked her around, startled. She saw the door of one of the smaller buildings within the compound fly open. A tall, skinny man staggered out onto the stoop and stood wavering back and forth in the breeze, an unkempt scarecrow with loose, tattered clothing and a massive black beard. He took one lurching step forward and grabbed the post supporting the small porch roof just in time to save himself from falling.

"O'Reilly?" He peered at the wagon as if it were a great distance away, rather than a matter of only a few yards. "Ya back already?" The man belched, filling the air with the unmistakable scent of rum. "I weren't expecting ya back so early." He shook his head slowly from side to side.

O'Reilly jammed his hat back on his head and planted his hands on his lean hips. "Campbell, just how the hell do you expect to unload this wagon, let alone see straight enough to record the supplies?"

"No worries, mate." The man—Campbell, she reminded herself—let go of the post to bat at a fly hovering around his nose. He lost his balance and tipped over face first into the dirt.

"Mr. O'Reilly," said Amanda in a carefully lowered voice. "This man is shockingly inebriated."

O'Reilly swung to face her. "Inebriated? Who, Campbell? Nah. He's only drunk." Walking over, he wrapped one hand around the man's arm and hauled the fallen bookkeeper to his feet. "See if Mallory and Ogden are in the barn, and bring them back to help unload the wagon." He gave Campbell a gentle push that almost sent him sprawling again. "And if that new chum, Lewis, is there, bring him along, too. He can do the writing."

"Papa."

O'Reilly spun about as a little girl of five or

six, with matted golden hair and an unbelievably dirty face, burst through the open front door of the house, ran across the veranda, and hurtled herself at him.

"Missy, darlin'." He crouched down to scoop the small child up in his arms. His blue eyes flashed and the dimples appeared in his cheeks, and Amanda felt her breath catch. The man might be foul-mouthed, low-bred, and immoral, but there was no denying that he could be quite dangerously attractive when he smiled.

"You been helping Sally clean out the chook houses?" He plucked a feather from the little girl's hair and took a second look at her grubby face. "Or was it the pigsties?"

Missy giggled and wrapped her arms about his neck as O'Reilly swung her up and around. "Nope. We's gettin' the room ready for the new gov'ness." Suddenly solemn, she stared at her father with an expression Amanda recognized as part of a practiced repertoire of incipient feminine wiles. "I don't want no new gov'ness, Papa. Please say we don't need one. You know they never stay anyway. And they're all mean and sour."

O'Reilly let out a peculiar huff that might have been a laugh as the little girl slid down his long body, her bare feet landing in the dirt. "You better hope she didn't hear that," he whispered as he seized the little girl's hand and swung her around to face Amanda. "Miss Davenport, may I present Miss Melissa O'Reilly? We all call her Missy," he added, his

44

obvious love for the child lighting up his face. "She has a hard time getting her tongue around Melissa."

Amanda knew a flash of pure panic as her gaze dropped from the man to the now sullen child. She had so little experience with children. Ignored by her scholarly father, her own mother dead, Amanda had known a childhood of lonely hours spent curled up with a book in the corners of silent, empty rooms. Now her lack of knowledge seemed to press in upon her, making her feel awkward, almost stupid. Plastering on a stiff smile, she stepped forward and held out her hand. "How do you do, Melissa?"

Melissa was small enough that she had to tilt back her head to stare up at Amanda. Stony-faced, the child thrust her filthy fingers into Amanda's proffered hand.

She felt her smile slip. "Now it is your turn, Melissa, to say, 'How do you do,' " Amanda prodded gently.

Melissa dropped Amanda's hand and whirled to take off for the house at a run. "Hannah!" she called, her bare feet slapping across the veranda. "She's here! The new gov'ness is here. Do come and see her."

Surreptitiously wiping her hand on her skirt, Amanda stared after the departing child. "How long has it been since these children had someone to look after them?"

O'Reilly fished a pipe and small leather pouch from his pocket. "If you're askin' how long it's been since they had a governess, it's been about five months." He opened a pocket-knife and used it to cut a slice off his tobacco plug. "But it's Sally who looks after them. She always has."

"Sally is their nursemaid?" Amanda asked, eyeing the preparation of the pipe with frigid disapproval.

"Sort of. She's an Aborigine."

Amanda's gaze flew to his, her hands coming up to form a tent before her mouth. "Do you mean to tell me that these children are being raised by some black savage?"

"Well, she's black, all right." He held a match to the bowl of his pipe, his cheeks hollowing as he sucked on the stem. "But I don't know if I'd call her a savage."

Amanda saw her then, a black woman in a faded blue dress, standing in the shadow of the veranda. How long had the woman been there? Amanda wondered with a vague twinge of discomfort. Had she heard what Amanda said? Would she have understood if she had heard? It was impossible to tell by looking at the woman's face.

Unlike the few sadly degraded natives Amanda had seen hanging around Adelaide, this one was upright and well proportioned, although small. Her dress must originally have been intended for someone both heavier and shorter, because it ended several inches above her ankles and hung loosely about her body. Like Missy, the woman wore neither shoes nor stockings and, judging from the way the thin cotton of her dress lay against her hips

46

and thighs, Amanda doubted that she wore anything at all beneath it. It was really quite
shocking.

More shocking still was the woman's face.
She was an older woman, probably middle-aged,
with gray-streaked hair and heavily wrinkled
skin. But what drew Amanda's fascinated
gaze was the woman's nose. The septum of her
nose had been pierced, and now held what
looked very much like a bone.

So intent was Amanda on studying the
woman that it was a moment before she realized,
much to her chagrin, that Sally was regarding
her with the same intense scrutiny as she was
regarding Sally. And Sally didn't seem
particularly impressed with what she saw.

"Whad for boss sister send dis one?" she said,
throwing back her head and curling her lip as
if she'd smelled something foul. "Dis one, no
good." She turned on her heel and disappeared into the house, leaving Amanda sput-
tering with outraged indignation.

Beside her, Patrick O'Reilly leaned against
the veranda post and practically doubled over
with loud laughter.

CHAPTER THREE

"Hannah? Liam? You there?" Carrying
Amanda's trunk, Mr. O'Reilly pushed in the
front door of the homestead. Amanda fol-

lowed him, trying to shake off the ridiculous sense of nervous foreboding that seemed to have settled over her.

The entrance opened directly into a large, dimly lit space that looked as if it must serve as a rugged version of an English drawing room. Her first impression was of battered settees and old chairs haphazardly covered with woven throws, of scattered tables half-buried beneath piles of papers and opened books, and a worn carpet with several large rents in it, as if someone had caught a spur in the threadbare nap.

But as her eyes adjusted to the softer light, she noticed that the faded carpet had once been fine. The corner fireplace bore a marble mantel, and the front door surround was an exquisite series of stained-glass panels depicting the brilliantly colored birds and flowers of the bush.

An unexpected wave of entirely unwanted emotion washed over Amanda as she watched Patrick O'Reilly's broad back disappear through a doorway to the left. He might come across as irreverent and almost ostentatiously casual, she thought, but at one time he had gone through a great deal of effort and expense to make this isolated house in the wilds of the outback into a comfortable home. Yet neither the house, nor the lovely English garden surrounding it, she thought, had been enough to keep the woman he had called Katherine here with him.

"Your room's in here," he called, and Amanda hurried after him.

The house seemed to have no halls or passages at all, for when she followed him through the doorway, she found herself in a bedchamber. It was large and airy, with two sets of French doors, one facing the front of the house, the other the side, that had been thrown open to the cool, late August air.

O'Reilly dumped her trunk at the foot of an old-fashioned cedar bed and headed back out to the cart. Amanda swung off her mantelet and draped it over the footboard of the bed. Then, still in her gloves and bonnet, she did a slow pirouette, assessing what would be her room for the next twelve months. Her gaze flicked from the high-fronted cedar chest of drawers and wardrobe to the tiled washstand to the cushionless, straight-backed chair beside a round table with a water-ring-marked top.

Another strange room in another strange house. In the five hard years since her father's death, Amanda had slept in everything from a cramped, stuffy attic to a crowded ship's cabin. At least this was private. The walls were newly whitewashed, the plain wooden floors looked freshly swept, and the carved cedar mantelpiece, when she walked over and ran one finger along it, free of dust.

"Something wrong with the housekeeping?"

Amanda whirled about. A tall, slim boy stood just outside her room, on the veranda. He wore the white moleskin trousers, heavy shirt, and leather waistcoat that seemed to form the standard male attire in outback Australia.

A wide-brimmed hat, low-crowned and pulled low over the eyes, obscured half his face.

"Hello," she said, flustered to have been caught so obviously questioning the cleanliness of her accommodation. "It's a nice room."

No trace of a smile lightened the boy's features. "It's haunted. Anyone tell you?" He sauntered into the room and began to walk slowly around her, insolently looking her up and down. Unwilling to be inspected, Amanda pivoted with him, so that they circled each other, like a couple of fighting cocks.

"Sally says it's the ghost of an Aboriginal woman raped by the man who built the house."

"I don't believe in ghosts. But I do believe that young men need to learn there are certain subjects not discussed in the company of ladies, and the type of incident you just mentioned is one of them."

"The governess before last said she didn't believe in ghosts either," confided the boy, ignoring her strictures. He had a fine-boned, almost effeminate face, Amanda noticed, with almond-shaped, deep brown eyes and thick, black lashes. His skin was tanned dark, and what she could see of his hair was dark, too. He looked nothing like Patrick O'Reilly.

Leaning in close, he dropped his voice to a whisper. "She used to hear a strange, haunting noise, like the droning of the wind, or the mournful cry of some unearthly creature. Early in the evening, mainly, around sunset. That was the time of day the Aboriginal girl is said to have died, you see."

The faded chintz curtains beside the open sets of doors moved restlessly in the wind. Amanda smelled eucalyptus and an exotic, lemony pepper scent blowing up from the broad valley below. Everything here was so wild, so strange, so...otherworldly. It frightened her simply being here. But she wasn't about to let this boy see her fear.

"Sunset I don't mind," Amanda said calmly, "as long as this noise doesn't awaken me at night. I do so dislike having my sleep disturbed."

The boy frowned, but he wasn't about to give up yet. "Oh, she heard it at night, too. And then, one morning, she didn't come to the schoolroom for lessons. We went lookin' to see what'd happened to her, and we found her here. In that bed." He gestured toward the big old cedar bed beside the door. "Sitting right up, she was, and staring straight ahead, her eyes opened wide like she'd seen something awful. Her mouth was open, too, like she was trying to scream. Only she couldn't scream, of course, because she was dead. Scared to death, the doc said."

Amanda realized she was clutching the lace collar of her dress and let her hand slide back down to her side. Mrs. Radwith hadn't mentioned any *deceased* predecessors. "How many governesses have you had?" Amanda asked, still turning in slow, measured circles with this unnatural, unpleasant child she was expected to teach. She was getting dizzy.

"Nine," he said. And this time, he smiled.

A slow, sly smile that was pure nastiness. She imagined he must have derived considerable enjoyment and satisfaction from the process of driving all nine of her predecessors away.

Except, of course, for the predecessor who had died in this bed.

Amanda stopped circling and determinedly held out her hand. "Allow me to introduce myself. I am Miss Davenport. And you must be...Liam, isn't it?"

A giggle sounded and Amanda turned to find Miss Melissa O'Reilly peeking around the door from the parlor. Someone—Sally?—had washed the child's face and brushed her hair and tidied the thick golden ringlets with a pink-checked ribbon. But she was still barefoot.

"That's not Liam," Missy said, her dimples peeping. "That's my sister, Hannah. She's a girl. She only dresses like a boy."

The girl in the moleskin trousers and broad-brimmed hat spun about and gave a very feminine hiss. "Mind your own business, you little—"

"Watch your mouth, young lady, or I'll tan the seat of those trousers you're so fond of wearing." Mr. O'Reilly, carrying Amanda's satchel and writing desk, appeared in the doorway behind Missy. Dumping Amanda's satchel on the floor beside her trunk, he set the writing desk on the table and pivoted to glare at his daughter. "You hear me, Hannah?"

Instead of dropping her eyes demurely and

murmuring *yes, sir,* Hannah glared right back at her father. "You always stand up for Missy," she said, her pointed little chin thrust aggressively forward.

"This has nothing to do with Missy." He planted his hands on his hips and stood with his legs braced wide. "I'm talking about your language."

"Yes it does have to do with Missy!" Hannah's voice cracked with emotion. Amanda saw unshed tears glitter in the girl's eyes, and felt a faint tug of unexpected sympathy for this strange, complicated girl. Hannah's thin chest rose as she sucked in a deep, shuddering breath. "You never tell Missy off when she does something to me. You love her more than you love me, and you know it."

"Now, Hannah," he began, reaching for her, but the girl whirled and dashed through the open French doors. "Damn it, Hannah!" O'Reilly bellowed. "Get back here."

Hannah never wavered. Hopping off the veranda, she darted down a lavender-edged, flagstone path, vaulted over the low stone wall that separated the house from the rest of the station, and disappeared behind an outbuilding.

Patrick O'Reilly stood in the open doorway and stared after her. "Bloody women," he muttered, as if the peculiarities of the female sex explained Hannah's behavior.

"Mr. O'Reilly," said Amanda, crossing her arms beneath her breasts. "May I have a word with you, please?"

He swung around to face her, and she knew from the expression on his face that, for a moment at least, he had essentially forgotten her presence. After five years as a servant, she should have become used to being invisible to her employers. But for some reason, this time it hurt.

"Yeah?" His gaze dropped to her crossed arms. "What's on your mind?"

For some reason, she found she had to clear her throat before she could trust herself to speak. "I am concerned by your threat to use physical violence on that child. I do not believe in it."

"Physical violence?" He leaned against her bedpost, a puzzled frown line appearing between his straight, dark brows.

It was oddly unsettling, having him in her bedroom, actually touching her bed. "I am well aware of the fact that my attitudes on this subject fly in the face of current pedagogical theories." She hoped he didn't notice that her voice was quavering, and pressed on resolutely. "However, as long as I am employed to instruct these children I would appreciate it if you would endeavor to avoid chastising them in the manner to which you are obviously accustomed."

He hooked his thumbs in his belt, a lazy smile curling the edges of his lips. She had expected to anger him, not amuse him. But she was beginning to realize that most things amused Patrick O'Reilly. "Let me get this right," he said. "You've got a problem with the idea of me walloping these children?"

"Precisely."

He straightened up and came toward her, not stopping until he was disconcertingly close. "You won't."

Her hand fluttered up to clutch at the ribbons of the bonnet she still wore. He was such a large man. He seemed to fill her room, with his size, and his pulsating energy, and his masculine scents of leather and tobacco and the dusty essence of the Australian bush. "I—I beg your pardon?"

"I said, you won't object to it. In fact, I'd bet anything you like that inside twenty-four hours you're actually going to be glad to have me *physically chastise* them."

She didn't realize she was backing up until her bottom bumped into the bedside table. "I do not believe in gambling." Her voice sounded breathless, unlike her own voice at all.

A dimple appeared beside his sensuously curved mouth, and she found herself staring at his lips, watching them as he spoke. "No," he said slowly, leaning into her. "I don't suppose you do, Miss Davenport."

They stared at each other, the moment heavy with implications Amanda only dimly understood. Then he turned suddenly away. "Missy?"

Amanda hadn't realized Missy was still there until the child's head reappeared around the corner. "Yes, Papa?"

Sauntering toward the little girl, he reached out to tweak one of her golden curls as he passed through the doorway. "How about showing Miss Davenport around the station?"

"Oh, there's no hurry," said Amanda, who wanted nothing so much as to be alone, to sort through the day's developments and try to come to terms with the hideous situation in which she had found herself.

O'Reilly shrugged. "Might as well get oriented before you start lessons tomorrow. Besides, you'll want to find Liam. You haven't met him yet."

His words brought an uncomfortable hollowness to the pit of Amanda's stomach that she recognized as dread. Her encounter with the other members of this household had been traumatic enough. She was not looking forward to Liam.

O'Reilly took the track that ran south along the bleached rocks of the creek bed, heading toward the woolshed. He walked slowly, his gaze narrowing as he studied the drooping gums, the cracked, desiccated mud of a vanished water hole, the clouds of dust that kicked up and blew away on the cold dry wind.

Beside one of the paddocks he paused, his forearms resting on the rough top rail as he squinted beyond the dried-up watercourse to the barren, undulating plains that stretched to the blue-gray shimmer of Wilpena Pound.

After a good rain, these slopes were covered with waving Mitchell grass scattered with wild parsnips and parakeelya. Cormorants, gray teal, and white-faced herons flicked over the glistening surfaces of water holes hedged with coolabahs and clumps of white and purple flag iris. After a good rain...

But they hadn't had a good rain for more than a year now. A summer of searing hot winds and burning blue skies had given way to a winter that was cold and hard and dry. Grass withered and died, dust lay thick on the flat scruffy leaves of the saltbush, hills turned stark. If the rains didn't come soon, summer would be upon them again. And then anything still left alive would die.

Looking out over the dying land, O'Reilly felt an ache in his heart. He loved this country. Loved its merciless grandeur and brutal beauty, its magnificent vast emptiness that made a man feel insignificant and yet vitally alive, all at the same time.

Which made it so bloody ironic, he thought, that he had contributed to this tragedy, with his sheep, and his cattle, and his ignorance.

He knew better now. Knew the land better. Knew not to overstock the range, knew that the rains could fail. He'd do a lot of things differently in the future.

Hell, he thought bitterly. If the rains didn't come soon, he wouldn't have a future. Everything he'd spent the last twelve years working and sweating and sacrificing for would be gone.

He pushed away from the rails. They'd be starting to shear soon, and the woolshed and shearers' quarters needed to be inspected. Normally he'd have put off shearing for

57

another six weeks or more, to avoid the danger of a late cold snap coming through and killing the shorn sheep out on the range. But not this year. This year he'd be killing the sheep himself, as soon as he took their wool.

He planned to cull his herds hard, cutting them down to the fittest and the best. But if the rains didn't come soon, even that wouldn't be enough. Soon the brush would be gone as well as the grass. The few remaining water holes would dry up. And then the animals on the range would die of thirst as well as of starvation. Eventually even the hay in the barns would be exhausted. Which meant the saddle horses and breeding stock would die, too, adding their bones to those of the tens of thousands of sheep and kangaroos and emus bleaching out on the ranges.

He stooped to pick up a twig, breaking it over and over again in his hands. He'd send the children south, to Hetty, before things got to that point, he decided. He wouldn't want them to have to watch it happen.

Hetty had been after him for years now to let her have Hannah and Missy. "A station in the wilds of the outback is no place for two motherless girls," she was always saying to him. The last time they'd gone to visit her, she'd tried to get him to leave the girls behind in Adelaide. Go back to Penyaka without them.

She'd come upon him in the stables, when he was inspecting one of the horse's hooves, and started in on him about it. "Hannah and Missy belong with their father," he'd told her, trying hard not to get angry with her, trying hard to remember that she meant well.

"Patrick." She laid her hand on his shoulder, her voice gentling. "I know how much you love those children, and I know what an important part of your life they are. But can't you see that what I'm suggesting would be better for them?"

"No, I don't see it, Hetty." He let the horse's hoof drop and straightened up. "Katherine hurt those children terribly with what she did six years ago. What kind of an effect do you think it would have on them if their father were to abandon them, too?"

"You wouldn't be abandoning them."

"As far as they're concerned, I would be. They love Penyaka. It's their home. They love their brother, and they love me. We belong together."

Hetty tightened her jaw, causing two long lines to appear, bracketing her mouth. "I can understand why this is hard for you, feeling the way you do about family. You were so young when Mother left—"

"*Bloody hell.* Leave her out of this." He spun about, startling her so much, she took a quick step back. Seizing a curry comb, he went to work on the chestnut's broad back. "I can take care of my own children."

"Can you? Then why won't any of the governesses I send up to you stay?"

"Because you're always hiring some damned Englishwoman who can't take life in the bush."

"I hire English gentlewomen because I believe that if you insist on raising those children in the outback, the least you can do is provide them with a genteel governess. And while I've no doubt that such women find the conditions at Penyaka trying, the truth is that the main reason they leave is because your children are totally undisciplined and unmanageable, and you know it. You indulge Missy shamelessly. Liam you treat more like one of your roustabouts than a nine-year-old boy, and as for Hannah—"

"Now, don't start on me about Hannah," he warned, shifting around to the horse's far side. "She's never been an easy child, even when she was little, and you know it."

"And now she's growing up, Patrick. She needs a woman's guidance and understanding."

"So, she'll have this Miss Soursides I just hired, or Sourbottom, or whatever her name is."

"Sourby," Hetty corrected, crossing her arms to cup her elbows in her palms. "Unfortunately, Miss Sourby resigned ten minutes ago. Someone filled her teapot with—well, let's put it this way, it wasn't tea."

"Shit." O'Reilly tossed the curry comb at the tack box.

"Yes, that's probably what it was," Hetty said, surprising him by cracking a smile. "Diluted to the proper color and consistency, of course."

At that, they'd laughed together. After another ten minutes, Hetty had given up trying to get him to leave the girls, and even

60

agreed to find him another governess. Miss Westbrook, her name had been, and she'd been from New South Wales, not England. She'd stayed five months.

He closed his palm around the broken lengths of twig in his hand, then tossed them away, wondering how long this new governess would last. She was a queer one, he thought. So ostentatiously virtuous and genteel and rigid that she made him want to shake her up, just for the sheer joy of watching her get rattled.

Yet he couldn't quite figure her out. Because while she might come across as an insufferable, dried-up old prude, the truth was that she was still fairly young. Even pretty, when one took a second look at her. Only the way she dressed and acted seemed to be precisely calculated to discourage any man from taking a second look at her.

And that made O'Reilly wonder why.

Amanda had never thought of herself as one of those people who considered wealth more important than birth and breeding. Yet, she had to admit that she was quietly impressed by the extent of Mr. Patrick O'Reilly's holdings.

In addition to the main house, storeroom, and office building, the walled garden compound also enclosed an outdoor kitchen and, beside that, the rooms of the two Chinese men Missy told her served as the household help.

"They're called Ching and Chow," volunteered Hannah, reappearing suddenly as Missy led Amanda along the cobbled alley that ran the length of the southern side of the house. "They originally came to work the Victoria gold fields, but Chow is afraid of small spaces. He says he gets to where he can't breathe."

Missy glared at her big sister. "Han-nah. Papa said I was apposed to take Miss Davenport around."

"Well, excuse me all to Melbourne and back," Hannah said, shoving her hands into her pockets and scowling.

Amanda expected the older girl to wander away again. Instead, Hannah stayed with them as Missy led the way down the hill to a scattering of outbuildings. She showed Amanda the workers' huts and men's kitchen, took her on a tour first through the stables and barns, then the cart shed and dairy, the smokehouse and pigsty and "chook" houses—which turned out to be chicken coops. The winter sun shone dazzlingly bright out of a clear blue sky, but the wind was raw and cold. Cold enough to chap Amanda's cheeks as it kicked up little eddies of red dust. She began to think longingly of the washstand in her room.

"I had no idea there was so much to see," she said, drawing the back of her gloved hand across her gritty forehead.

"There's still the woolshed and shearers' quarters." Missy tugged on Amanda's arm. "They're this way."

"I think she's tired, Missy," said Hannah with unexpected sensitivity. "And the woolshed's miles down the creek yet." She turned to give Amanda a smile that was dazzling in its brilliance. "If you like, you can just walk to the top of that bare hill there, and you ought to be able to see them."

"But—" Missy began.

Hannah clamped her arm around Missy's shoulder and smiled again at Amanda. "Can you see them?"

"No. Where?" Amanda took a few incautious steps forward, her gaze firmly fixed on the distant line of white-barked gums and dry, tumbled stones.

"There." Hannah backed away, her arm still tightly wrapped around Missy's shoulders.

Amanda lifted her hand to shade her eyes from the glare of the sun and squinted, but she could still see nothing except dry hills, blue sky, and dust blowing in the wind.

Something tickled her leg, then her arm. It was a curious sensation. An uncomfortable feeling, as if something were crawling on her. Amanda glanced down.

And screamed.

Scores of big, black *things* swarmed over her. They were so big, in fact, that it took her a moment to realize what they were. Ants. She was crawling with ants. Only these were unlike any ants she had ever seen in England. These were as long as her thumbnail and almost half as wide.

"Oh, my goodness," she cried in barely controlled terror, twisting this way and that, slapping frantically at her arms, her bodice, her skirt. "They're all over me!"

She was dimly aware of Missy staring at her, her hands clapped over her mouth, her eyes wide with horror. But the two older children were laughing so hard, they had to hold each other up.

Yes, there were three of them, Amanda realized suddenly. Liam had finally put in an appearance.

"Help me," she called, swatting madly at her skirt. But for every one she brushed off, it seemed as if there were another dozen to take its place.

She glanced toward the children again. They hadn't moved, and she noticed they were being very careful to keep well back from the circle of bare earth. Suddenly, she knew why. The mound was bare because every trace of vegetation had been worn away by the passing of millions of tiny feet.

The children had tricked her into standing on an anthill.

Still wriggling and brushing frantically at her clothes, she staggered toward her tormentors. But a sudden, sharp pain shot up her leg, stopping her in her tracks. "Agh!" she screamed again, louder this time. The ants weren't just crawling all over her, she realized with horror; they were biting her.

She felt another bite on her inner thigh, then two more, on her bottom. *Oh, the pain.* She had never dreamt that ant bites could hurt this badly. A dozen more sharp stabs brought tears to her eyes.

In a pain-hazed frenzy, she realized the ants had crawled up her legs and were now trapped by the scores in her drawers. And there was only one way to get them out.

Heedless of the children or anyone else who might be watching, Amanda whipped up her skirt, petticoat, and crinoline, and clawed frantically at the fastening of her drawers.

CHAPTER FOUR

O'Reilly was coming back from the woolshed when he heard the woman scream. Curious, he left the track and topped a nearby rise to squint toward the homestead.

He spotted her right away. She was spinning round and round like a whirling dervish, batting this way and that, hopping first on one leg, then on the other. His gaze focused on Liam and Hannah. He knew exactly what they had done.

Miss Davenport screamed again, only this time he heard pain in her voice. "Shit," he muttered, and took off at a run.

He was almost to her when she threw up her skirts. He saw shapely legs clad in black cotton stockings and chaste cotton drawers with only a modest edging of lace. Her crinoline was predictably conservative, but over it Miss Davenport wore a flamboyantly red satin petticoat. *Well, well, well,* O'Reilly thought, grinning to himself. Who'd have suspected such a painfully proper, plummy-voweled spinster of hiding a red satin petticoat beneath those drab, respectable skirts of hers?

Then she dropped her drawers.

She whirled, and he caught a glimpse of a triangle of auburn-colored hair, then a pert, nicely rounded little bottom that looked every bit as good as it'd felt in his hands that afternoon.

He skidded to a halt at the edge of the bare earth. "Damn it, woman," he yelled. "You're still standing on the edge of the bull ant nest. Move away from it."

She was beyond hearing him. "They're all over me," she said in an oddly tight, controlled voice. "Get them off me. Get them off."

"Bloody hell," he swore under his breath, and sprinted toward her.

He scooped her up in his arms and took off at a run for the nearest water hole. She was such a tiny thing, she didn't weigh much. But she was jerking this way and that, tormented by the ants, and he got an elbow in his midriff and another in his eye before they reached the creek. He could feel the damn things on him now. One bit him on the stomach. Another got him on the thigh.

"I'm going to kill those kids," he vowed, scrambling over the rocks that edged the water hole. "Let go of me."

"What?"

"I said, let go." And with that, he threw her into the creek.

She screamed once, a scream mingling shock and outrage, before sinking like a bucket of rocks, the hoop of her crinoline billowing out behind her. An ant bit him on his arm. He swore again and with a flying leap jumped in after her.

"Christalmighty," he yelled when he hit the icy water. It was deeper than he'd expected, and a hell of a lot colder. He shut his mouth just in time as the water closed over his head. Kicking off the bottom, he clawed his way back up, gasping when his head broke the surface.

Treading water, he shook the hair out of his eyes and looked around for that damn fool governess. He'd about decided he was going to have to dive down and haul her out when she reared up on his left, her flailing hand grabbing an overhanging rock.

She was coughing and choking something fierce. He paddled over and helpfully pounded her on the back.

She swung around, her elbow almost catching his eye again. "Don't you touch me!" she sputtered, water streaming down her face. Her nice, full breasts rose and fell with her heavy breathing; her gray eyes glinted like honed steel. She'd lost her bonnet and most of her hair had come down, so that it floated around her like a silky, weightless aura of glorious fire.

O'Reilly stared at her, at her wet, fine-boned face and trembling mouth and flame-colored hair so unexpectedly, sinfully vivid that it was like a siren call to temptation. And he was tempted, damn it. Unwillingly, even resentfully.

But tempted, nonetheless.

It was a pity, Amanda decided, that one could not actually die of humiliation.

After what had happened to her today, even death seemed preferable to facing the O'Reillys again. She glanced toward the western window and saw that beyond the closed curtains, the light was already fading. She let her breath out in a sigh. It would be dark soon. Hopefully she wouldn't need to see any of them again until morning.

She dug her finger into the bowl of thick white paste and held her wrapper away from her body. Twisting around, she strained to dab some of the mixture on each of the dozens of angry red bites that decorated her white buttocks and thighs.

She had no idea what the concoction was, but it brought soothing relief. She had mixed it herself from the white powder in a small blue bag Patrick O'Reilly had brought to her door.

"My grandmother always used it," he'd told her, his warm gaze lingering first on the hair that flowed loosely around Amanda's shoulders, then on the open neckline of her sapphire-blue silk wrapper. "Just add water to it, and it'll take away the sting. I'd offer to help you put it on, but—"

Snatching the bag from his hand, she'd slammed the door in his face.

Remembering the incident now, Amanda was shocked at how rude she had been. But then, they both knew where most of her bites were. Amanda straightened. Just the thought of that man's sparkling blue eyes seeing her like this, of his strong, tanned hands touching her so intimately, brought a fresh wave of hot embarrassment washing over her and caused an alarming fluttering sensation, way down low in her belly.

She let her wrapper fall back into place and went to the washstand to rinse her finger. She was reaching for the towel when it occurred to her that Patrick O'Reilly had already both seen her and touched her. Intimately.

She brought her hands up to her hot cheeks. "I want to die," she said aloud to the darkening room. "I just want to die."

She didn't really want to die, of course. She simply wanted to get away from here—far, far away from this wild land and that impossible man and his three fiendish children. She should never have taken this position, she thought despairingly. If she could leave tomorrow, she would.

She raked her loose hair back from her face and groaned. The problem was, she couldn't leave. She didn't even have the ten pounds she needed to pay her fare back to Adelaide. And what would she do when she got there, anyway? Unemployed, homeless, and impoverished, she really would die. Or sink to selling her body on the streets.

Shivering, she hugged her wrapper closer. She was stuck here. Stuck with that vulgar, ill-bred, foul-mouthed man and his detestable, unnatural children. At the thought, a sick, panicky feeling pressed in on her, making her heart beat wildly. Her blood thrummed in her ears, repeating the words like some kind of crazy refrain. *Stuck here, stuck here, stuck here.*

Gritting her teeth, Amanda pushed away from the washstand and went to rummage through her opened trunk for some dry clothes. She was trapped here all right. For twelve months. But Amanda Davenport had no intention of being defeated by three half-grown children, a convict's grandson, and an ants' nest.

Throwing off her wrapper, she yanked on a clean pair of drawers and a chemise. She might be stuck with the O'Reillys, she thought, wrapping her corset around her waist and sucking in her stomach so she could do up the hooks. But the O'Reillys were also stuck with her.

She buttoned on her camisole, crinoline, and petticoat, and shook the wrinkles out of her second-best gray dress. Patrick O'Reilly had hired her to teach his children, and teach them she would. She would teach them how to behave like proper, well-mannered children, not heathen savages. She would teach them to respect their elders. And she would teach their father—

A knock at her door brought her head

around. "Who is it?" she called, fumbling with the hooks at the back of her gown's high neck.

There was no answer.

Turning the faceted crystal handle, she yanked open the door to find herself confronting nothing but the gloomy silence of the empty parlor. It wasn't until she started to close the door that she noticed something had been left on the floor outside her room.

Bending down, she picked up a chipped blue pottery pitcher stuffed with ranunculus, lavender, and a small yellow flower she recognized as a native wildflower. Beneath the pitcher, someone had left a folded piece of paper. Amanda set the flowers on her bedside table and opened the note.

I is sory the ants bited yu, read the large, wobbly letters. *I holp yu feel beter soon. Missy.*

It was so unexpected, so touchingly sincere, that Amanda had to squeeze her eyes shut for a moment to keep back sudden tears. She reached out almost blindly to close her door, only to pause again at the low murmur of male voices drifting from the far end of the house.

"I don't like having to do this, Liam," she heard O'Reilly say. "You know that, don't you?"

"Yes, sir."

"Let's get it over with, then."

The unmistakable snap of a leather belt cut through the still night air. Amanda quietly shut her door and leaned against it, smiling.

She didn't care that it had been only a matter of hours since she had scornfully rejected O'Reilly's suggestion that closer acquaintance with his children would change her attitude toward corporal punishment. She didn't care that she honestly did object—in theory—to spanking. She only knew that at the moment, the sound of such energetic chastisement being visited upon the back-side of one of her tormentors was sweet music to her ears.

It was about half an hour later, when Amanda had almost finished her unpacking, that another knock fell on her door.

"One moment, please," she called. Lowering the lid on her trunk, she went to open the door, expecting to find someone with her supper tray. Her gaze fell on Liam O'Reilly and she said, "Oh."

He stood just outside her room, a skinny, sharp-featured boy with light-brown hair and unusual hazel eyes that glittered strangely. For a long, intense moment they stared at each other, each taking the other's measure, each remembering the ant incident and the beating it had earned Liam, each issuing and accepting a peculiar, wordless challenge.

The edges of his lips curled up into an unpleasant smile that showed a missing eye-tooth. "Father says to tell you supper's almost ready."

"Supper?" She glanced beyond him to the dining room, where a Chinese man wearing a knee-length cotton jacket and baggy blue trousers was holding a taper to a branch of candles. The lamps had been lit and fires kindled in both the parlor and the dining room. And judging from the number of places laid at the table, it appeared that not only did Mr. O'Reilly follow the unusual custom of eating meals with his children, he also expected her to join them.

"I thought..." She cleared her throat. "That is, I assumed a tray would be sent to my room." It was the usual procedure in England, where governesses were effectively lost between two worlds. Considered too genteel to eat in the servants' hall or kitchen with the rest of the "help," they were nevertheless not good enough to be invited to sit down at table with the family, as a chaplain might.

"Father always has the governess eat with us." Liam's sneer turned into a snicker. "He says it helps our manners."

"How nice," said Amanda. "I can assure you, I am very much looking forward to improving your manners."

In reality, she was mortified at the thought of having to face them all so soon after publicly dropping her drawers on that ants' nest. But she kept her voice bright and her smile in place, and she had the satisfaction of watching Liam's smirk slip slightly.

"Like that, do you, mate?" crooned O'Reilly.

In response, Liam's kelpie stretched out his neck and thumped his tail enthusiastically against the side of the battered old settee. O'Reilly laughed and shifted his attentions from one upright ear to the other. Barrister shivered his delight.

The sound of Miss Davenport closing her door brought the dog's head around. O'Reilly glanced up and watched as the new governess advanced stiffly toward the small group gathered around the fire.

She was wearing a high-necked gray dress almost as ugly as that brown thing she'd had on earlier today. She'd pulled her beautiful hair into a chaste spinster's bun, but even such a severe style couldn't dim its brilliance. She had some head of hair, he thought as she came into the halo of light cast by the fire. No wonder she hid it. Hair like hers gave a man ideas. The kind of ideas that scared women such as Miss Amanda Davenport.

She was trying to look serene, but the high color riding her normally pale cheeks betrayed just how mortified she was by what had happened that afternoon. He bet she'd have given almost anything—up to and maybe even including her precious, rigorously guarded virtue—if she'd never had to see any of them again. Yet here she was, facing them all with her shoulders back and her chin up. He wondered, idly, if she realized that holding her backbone as stiff as a mast on a Royal Navy vessel had the effect of making her magnificent breasts even more noticeable. He doubted it.

As she came up to them, Barrister lifted his

nose and sniffed, his tail wagging faster. He took several tentative steps toward her, then a few more. "Barrister," O'Reilly commanded, surprised by the dog's lack of discernment. "Sit."

Too late. Three bounds brought the dog close enough to rear up on his hind legs.

O'Reilly expected Miss Davenport to shrink back in revulsion, maybe even shriek in terror. Instead she brought up her hands and neatly caught the dog's paws before they landed on her gown. "Well, hello," she said with a smile, returning Barrister to all fours but softening the rejection by stooping to scratch him behind the ears much as O'Reilly himself had been doing. "The enthusiasm of your greeting is welcome, but not the form." She shifted her attention to the dog's neck, and Barrister sighed with ecstasy. "What's your name? Hmm, pretty boy?"

It was the first time O'Reilly had seen her smile, and he was surprised by the way it transformed her. It brought a sparkle to her sober gray eyes and called attention to her mouth, which was wide and full lipped and intriguingly sensual looking.

"His name's Barrister. I didn't expect you to like dogs," Liam said, with so much disappointment in his voice that it was obvious Barrister's presence had been another scheme to harass the new governess—only this idea hadn't worked.

"I had a dog when I was a little girl," said Miss Davenport, still faintly smiling. By now

Barrister had rolled over onto his back so that she could scratch his belly; his tongue lolled out, until he was staring up at her with such idiotic devotion that Liam snorted in disgust.

Chow appeared in the doorway, put his palms together, and bowed. "Supper ready."

Miss Davenport snapped to her feet, so obviously flustered by the fact she'd forgotten her precious formality and dignity long enough to stoop down and scratch a dog's belly that O'Reilly might have smiled—if it hadn't suddenly struck him as sad.

Watching her, he was surprised to find himself trying to picture the little girl this painfully repressed woman must once have been. He tried to imagine her as a child, with copper-colored ringlets falling around her shoulders and her pinafore dirty from wrestling with her dog...

Except the image wouldn't form. If that little girl ever had existed, he decided, she was so far lost in the past as to be beyond recall.

"I must wash my hands," she said stiffly. "I shan't be a moment."

When she came back she was wearing such a prim, lady-fallen-amongst-the-swine look that it was obvious she severely regretted whatever impulse had led her to relax enough to pet the dog. Worse, it was soon clear to O'Reilly that she considered them a bunch of degenerate colonials, and had decided to embark on a mission to civilize them all. Sinking into her dining chair with carefully calculated grace, she spread her napkin over her lap with such ostentatious gentility that he was tempted to tuck his own napkin into the neck of his shirt, just for the perverse pleasure of watching that snooty little nose of hers quiver in disdain.

Only Miss Davenport wasn't looking at him. She was staring at Hannah. "Didn't you have time to change for supper, Hannah?"

In the act of reaching for a bread roll, Hannah stiffened and threw her a sulky look. "What do you mean? I changed my shirt."

"I thought perhaps you might put on a dress," said Miss Davenport.

Liam sniggered. "Hannah never wears a dress."

"But..." Miss Davenport's brows drew together in a frown as she stared at Hannah's hair, which hung as short and ragged as if it'd been lopped off by a drunken American Indian on a rampage with a tomahawk. "Whatever happened to your hair?"

Hannah concentrated on buttering her bread.

"Hannah," said O'Reilly. "Miss Davenport asked you a question."

"She cut it herself," said Missy hastily, glancing from his frown to her sister's mulish profile. "Last year. It was as short as Liam's when she first did it. Papa wanted to kill her."

"I could trim it for you, if you like," Miss Davenport said, swiveling to select a slice of meat from the platter Chow held for her.

Watching her, O'Reilly wondered if she

77

realized that what she'd picked was kangaroo. He was about to tell her when Hannah said in a pseudosaintly voice, "Papa made me promise never to cut it again. And of course I would never go against my papa's expressed command."

"I'm sure your father didn't mean to include judicious straightening as part of that prohibition."

O'Reilly's eyes narrowed as he stared down the length of the table at the new governess. For a minute there, he actually thought he'd heard a quiver of amusement in her voice, but he decided he must have imagined it. "Of course it's not what I meant." He helped himself to a couple slices of roast lamb and several pieces of kangaroo. "But she's as stubborn as an Irishman in a beer-drinking competition, and twice as ornery."

Caught in the act of swallowing a mouthful of water, Miss Davenport choked. She frowned down the length of the table at him, then picked up her own fork with a great show of elegant forbearance. "What time do lessons begin in the morning?"

"Ten," said Liam.

She swung her head to look at him in surprise. "Ten? Goodness, that is late."

O'Reilly chuckled. "Let this serve as a warning to you, Miss Davenport. Liam here can spin a tale taller than anything you ever heard, and still manage to keep his face as solemn and sanctimonious as a bishop's at a baptism." He reached for the mashed pota-

78

toes. "Lessons begin at eight and run until one. Then again from two to three."

Miss Davenport transferred her frown from Liam to O'Reilly himself. "Surely that is not all the time these children devote to their studies?"

"I'm afraid so," he said, whacking a dollop of potatoes on his plate. "Here in the bush, children have a hell of a lot of things to learn that don't come out of books."

"But...six hours a day?" She stared down the length of the table at him. "That barely allows enough time for the basics, such as English and mathematics, and history and geography. Surely you would like Liam to be given a grounding in Greek and Latin as well?"

She sounded so genuinely upset about it that he almost warmed to her. Then she spoiled it all by giving him a tight smile. Not the smile he'd seen before, but a prim curling of the edges of her lips that did nothing to soften them. "I presume that even here in the colonies a classical education is considered important?"

She had a way of saying *the colonies* that really set up his back. As if *the colonies* were synonymous with dung heap, or the nether reaches of hell.

"Do you know Greek and Latin?" Hannah asked, looking at the new governess with grudging respect.

Miss Davenport smiled at her. "Yes, I do. My father was a scholar, so my classical education was unusually extensive."

"Aw, no," groaned Liam, scooting down

lower in his seat. "Don't I already do enough Greek and Latin with Whittaker?"

"Whittaker?" asked Miss Davenport.

"Christian Whittaker," O'Reilly clarified. "He's a bookkeeper with the Brinkman Mining Company. But it doesn't take up much of his time, so he rides out here every Thursday afternoon and spends a couple of hours teaching Liam classics."

"Oh."

She sounded so disappointed that for some reason O'Reilly couldn't name, he said, "But I'm sure Christian would appreciate it if you could spend some time working with Liam, too."

Liam sat bolt upright. *"Father."*

"Did you say this man's name is Whittaker?" Miss Davenport asked.

"Yes. Why?"

She leaned forward, her face becoming unexpectedly animated. "I wonder if he is related to the Whittakers of Oxfordshire? Have you heard of them? It's a very old family. The late general Anthony Whittaker served with Wellington during the wars with France."

It was one of the things O'Reilly disliked most about English gentlewomen—this idea they had that who a man's grandfather had been was more important than what a man had managed to make out of himself. Katherine had been like that, and so had O'Reilly's mother. "Well," he said dryly, "I don't know if Christian is related to *the* General Whittaker, but I think he does come from Oxfordshire. You'll have to ask him. He'll be out here day after tomorrow. Maybe you two can have tea together on the veranda. Talk about Home and your mutual old friends."

"That would be lovely," she said with a smile. Not that brittle, supercilious tightening of her lips he hated, but a wide, genuine smile that reminded O'Reilly that when she wasn't being a sanctimonious pain in the rear, she could be a damn fine-looking woman.

For some reason he couldn't explain, he felt a sudden need to wipe that smile off her face. Picking up the platter Chow had left on the table, he handed it to Liam. "Here, why don't you pass this down to Miss Davenport. She seemed to like that kangaroo meat."

He watched the muscles in her slender throat tighten as she swallowed. *"Kangaroo meat?"* she said, so horrified her mouth fell open in a most ungenteel expression.

"Didn't you know that was 'roo meat you've been eatin' there?"

"No."

Pale and wide-eyed, she set down her fork and groped wildly for her water glass. In fact, she looked so stricken that he almost—*almost*—wished he hadn't told her.

The night was clear and crisp, the familiar scents of jasmine and honeysuckle laced with the wild, exotic undertones of eucalyptus and lemon. Amanda stood beside the open French doors of her room, hugged her shawl-covered shoulders, and gazed out across the strange, undulating hills.

For the next twelve months this would be her home. She swallowed hard, fighting to keep back the feelings of aching aloneness, of vulnerability that threatened to swamp her.

She hadn't felt this isolated, this desolate since the months immediately following her father's death. She squeezed her eyes shut, blocking out the harsh, unfamiliar landscape as she tried to recapture the images of her childhood. *Cobblestoned streets glistening with wet in a spring rain. The golden light of a coal fire, warming her father's book-crowded study. Her father's rich, ringing baritone, telling his students wonderful stories of brave warriors and proud goddesses and wise, learned men of old—while Amanda sat outside the door, and listened, and wanted...*

She tried so hard to remember. But all she could hear was the wind whispering through the gum trees. And when she opened her eyes, it was to see an alien, unfriendly pattern of stars sprinkled across the purple heavens.

"Why, Papa?" she whispered aloud. "Why did you do this to me?"

She tried to tell herself he hadn't let her down deliberately. Angus Davenport had been so wrapped up in his lectures and texts and study tours that he'd never had time to think about what would happen to his only daughter if she were never to marry. Death had come to him quickly and unexpectedly, stopping his heart in the night. He probably never realized just how inadequately he'd provided for her. Or at least she told herself he hadn't realized. Better that than to admit that he hadn't cared. That he'd never cared.

A dog howled far off in the distance. Amanda lifted her head and listened, but the homestead around her lay still, quiet. That disturbing Australian and his misbegotten brood were asleep. Yet in a few short hours it would be morning, and she would have to face those monsters in the schoolroom.

A knot of apprehension twisted Amanda's stomach at the thought. It wasn't that she doubted her knowledge. Her father had taught her well, and she had been so eager to please him, so desperate to grasp a few more precious moments of his attention that she'd devoted herself to her studies with the same enthusiasm and energy most children reserved for their play.

It wasn't her knowledge but her pedagogical skills Amanda feared would be found lacking. She knew so little of children. How to interest them. How to handle them. In the course of her life, Amanda knew, she had met only a few born teachers. She was very sure she was not one herself.

The thought brought her back, inevitably, to her father. Angus Davenport had been that rare combination: a brilliant scholar who was also a gifted teacher. A master who could inspire even the most indifferent and jaded of the gentlemen's sons regularly sent up to Oxford.

Even such a wild, irresponsible young man as Viscount Mansfield's son, Grant.

Her treacherous memory resurrected Grant's image, his flashing dark eyes and charming grin warm with the promise of love and laughter and the forbidden delights of the flesh. But it was a lying image, shadowed by the pain of heartbreak and humiliation, and she pushed it away.

Yet her body remembered. She closed her eyes again and felt the wild wind lift her hair like a lover's caress. She touched her finger to her lips—slowly, softly, the way a man kisses a virgin, and the old, familiar ache trembled within her. The ache that was like an emptiness, deep inside. Empty womb. Empty arms. Empty heart.

Her hand slid down over her breasts. Freed from the constraints of her corset, her body trembled beneath the fine, worn linen of her nightdress. Ten years. It had been ten long years since she had felt a man's touch, known a man's kiss. Felt a man's hard heat press against her.

Her eyes flew open and she gasped as she realized what she'd been doing. Whirling back into her room, she banged the doors shut against the dangerous, seductive night, jerked the curtains together, and sought her bed.

But as she drifted off to sleep, her dreams were troubled by a haunting masculine presence. She tossed restlessly in her strange bed, feeling again the pleasure of a man's soft lips

84

and sure hands. Gaining from his hard body an exquisite release from that secret, shameful need that burned so deep within her.

It wasn't until the next morning that she realized the man in her dreams had laughed with eyes that were blue, not black. That the hands that touched her flesh with fire had been callused and strong.

And that when she arched with desire and clutched his head to her bare breast, his hair had glinted gold and amber in the hot Australian sun.

CHAPTER FIVE

Early the following morning, Amanda paused in the doorway to the deserted schoolroom and forced herself to take a deep, steadying breath. "You can do this," she told herself aloud. Then she added wryly, "You must do this."

The morning air was cold; she clutched the edges of her shawl together with one hand as she wandered around the room, studying it. High, dusty bookshelves took up all of one wall and part of another, while in the center of the room stood a large cedar table, its nicked and gauged surface giving mute testimony to the O'Reilly children's lack of enthusiasm for study. Sighing, she went to rummage through the drawers of the desk positioned between the French doors to the veranda and the fireplace, and realized that the room was so cold because no one had kindled the fire.

In England, every household had a servant whose duties included the routine sweeping of hearths and setting of fires. But when Amanda had awakened that morning to a cold hearth in her own bedroom, she'd realized Penyaka had no little maid who crept around at dawn, adding coal to the household's fires.

Still, she didn't want the children to have to face their first day's lessons in a freezing schoolroom. She would have to find someone to lay a fire.

Unlike Amanda's room, which opened off the parlor and faced the front of the house, the schoolroom, children's rooms, and the guest room all opened directly off the dining room. She went to the doorway, hoping to see Ching or Chow. And found Patrick O'Reilly instead.

He stood with one hip cocked against the table while he sipped a cup of steaming coffee and stared thoughtfully out the glass doors at the dry valley below. He wore the supple moleskins and leather waistcoat she'd first seen him in, with a cream-colored heavy shirt open at the neck. His broad-brimmed hat rested on the table beside his thigh, and she noticed his hair was damp, as if he'd wet it while washing. Water-darkened golden curls lay plastered against his suntanned forehead and hung over his collar in the back.

Memories of her dreams from the night before slammed into her, bringing an embarrassed heat to her cheeks and making her want to squirm. She had no control over her dreams; she knew that. But how could she—how *could* she have thought about this man in that way?

She must have made some sound, because his head swung around. "Miss Davenport." He took a slow sip of his coffee, his eyes on her face. "What you frowning about so early this mornin'?"

"Frowning? I wasn't— That is to say—" *What is wrong with you?* she told herself sternly. *You sound like a blithering idiot.* "It's the schoolroom fire. I'd like it kindled."

He paused in the act of raising the coffee cup to his lips again and looked at her. Slowly, deliberately, he swallowed and gave her a lopsided smile that brought one of those beguiling dimples to his cheek. "Go ahead."

Amanda's jaw went slack. "*Me?* You want *me* to light the fire?"

He took another slow swallow from his cup. "This is the bush, Miss Davenport, not England. I'm afraid you'll find we do things differently here. We're not ashamed of getting our hands dirty or workin' up a sweat. I work out there with my men every day, mustering cattle, dippin' sheep, whatever needs doing. I'm teaching all of my children, including Hannah and Missy, to be able to do everything there is to be done on a station. And we all light our own fires."

He threw down the rest of his coffee and reached for his hat, then paused to look at her

87

consideringly. "But if you don't know how to do it, I could ask Chow to show you—"

"No thank you," she said crisply. "I can handle it." Spinning about, she marched up to the schoolroom fireplace...and stared down at it, fighting back a ridiculous swelling of panic. She'd thought her life for the past five years had been difficult, but at least no one had expected her to do anything like light fires. Until now.

She glanced uncertainly at the basket of twisted, oddly shaped wood on the hearth. In her experience, fires were made with coal. She bent down, gingerly selected the largest piece, and thrust it into the middle of the ashes.

Ten minutes later, she lay sprawled out flat on her stomach, blowing on the silly thing for all she was worth, and the only reward she'd received was a face full of ashes and smoke. Her hair was coming down, her cheeks felt hot, she'd burned her little finger, and she'd decided she most definitely, most viciously, *hated* Patrick O'Reilly.

A low chuckle behind her brought her head around. Thank goodness it was Sally, and not one of the children. Wiping her stinging eyes, Amanda scrambled up into a more dignified position. "I seem to be having some difficulty getting the fire started."

For a long moment the black woman simply stared at her, as if debating with herself whether to help or to leave Amanda to her humiliation. Evidently she decided Amanda had suffered enough, because she padded forward on her bare feet, her movements oddly loose-limbed and agile—like a deer, Amanda thought, or a well-bred greyhound.

"Big wood nod make you fire, 'less maybe you lightning. You lightning?" She chuckled at her own joke and pushed Amanda's log to one side. Selecting a handful of wood scraps from the basket, she squatted down before the fireplace and in a ridiculously small amount of time managed to coax forth a promising blaze. Then she leaned back on her haunches and regarded Amanda through narrowed eyes. "Liddlest pickaninny in camp know how do start fire."

It was on the tip of Amanda's tongue to point out that she was not a pickaninny. But she gritted her teeth and said, "Thank you," instead.

"Come on, Hannah!" called a child's voice. "She's here already."

Amanda glanced up to see Missy swinging back and forth on the door frame. And in that brief instant, Sally disappeared out the doors to the veranda. It was oddly disconcerting, the way the woman could come and go so quietly. One moment she was there; the next, she was gone.

Hannah came slouching into the room, a sullen look on her face, a boy's trousers and shirt on her thin frame. Wordlessly, she slid into one of the chairs around the scarred cedar table.

"Good morning, Hannah."

Hannah chewed a ragged fingernail.

"You should say, 'Good morning, Miss Davenport.' "

Hannah threw her a dark look and resumed her study of her nail.

Amanda suppressed the urge to sigh. She seemed to be sighing constantly these days. "It's called courtesy, Hannah. Even gentlemen find it useful."

Missy hopped into the seat opposite her sister. "Mornin', Miss Davenport."

Amanda smiled at the little girl. "Good morning, Missy. And good morning to you, Liam," she added as the boy dragged into the room.

He murmured something indecipherable, but at least he answered her.

With any new job, first days were always the most difficult, Amanda reminded herself. "Well, now we can begin," she said, giving her three charges a smile.

Three unsmiling faces stared back at her, their expressions ranging from blank (Missy) to openly hostile (Hannah) to derisory (Liam).

Amanda decided to try not smiling, and changed her tone to brisk instead. "First I'd like to find out what you already know. That way, I'll have a better idea of what we need to concentrate on in the future. Shall we start with the globes?"

The responses ranged from a sigh (Missy) to dead silence (Hannah) to a groan (Liam). Amanda felt like groaning herself, but she reached for the globes.

Twenty minutes later, she was convinced the O'Reilly children were the most appallingly uneducated, slow-witted pupils it had ever been any governess's misfortune to attempt to teach. They seemed to know nothing, not even the most rudimentary principles.

After another half hour, she knew they were having her on.

"All right," she said, setting aside her grammar book. "You can keep pretending you don't know anything, and waste your time and mine for the next twelve months by forcing me to go over things you already know, or you can cooperate with me."

Three blank faces stared back at her. No wonder her nine predecessors had fled—probably screaming—back to the city, Amanda thought. She remembered how naively triumphant she had felt at securing a position paying sixty pounds a year. Sixty pounds. Ha. She deserved twice that amount.

She passed a hand over her forehead. She felt hot. The rising sun added to the roaring fire on the hearth had heated the room uncomfortably. She walked over to the French doors and opened them.

She stood for a moment, her hands resting on the door handles, and let the cool, jasmine-scented air from the garden bathe her hot cheeks. She could see Ching (or was it Chow?), leaning on a hoe over by the wall and talking to Patrick O'Reilly. The Australian sat perched on the top of the garden wall, his arms braced at his sides, his head thrown back as he laughed. Sunlight glazed the tanned features of his face with a golden glow. She could hear the deep, rich sound of his laughter floating to her across the garden.

For some reason, the sight of him—so carefree and vital—caught at her strangely. She felt a hollowness inside, like a longing, a longing for something she'd lost. Except she was very much afraid that what she'd lost was herself. The woman she used to be. A woman who could laugh and tease.

And attract handsome, virile young men.

What a ridiculous thought, she chided herself. Taking a deep breath, she swung away to face her tormentors once more. "Now. Shall we try it again? With cooperation this time?" She picked up a collection of Wordsworth's poems. "Hannah, would you please read the selection on page eight?"

Hannah wasn't even looking at Amanda. Grinning, the girl poked Liam with her elbow and leaned over to whisper something in his ear. Liam craned around in his seat, staring at the glass doors.

"Hannah," snapped Amanda. "Would you please pay attention?"

"Miss Davenport, look!" said Missy, round-eyed. "There's a goanna crawling in through the doors you left open."

"Missy, I do not appreciate—" She broke off as some noise—a slither, a scratching of reptilian claws—sounded behind her. She whirled around.

Terror, primitive and instinctive, shuddered through her at the sight of something so hideous, so strange, her breath left her body in a whoosh. With an enormous effort of will, she did not scream. But the hand grasping the book tightened until her fingers hurt.

The Thing, whatever it was, took a slow step forward, its muscular legs dragging its heavy body across the worn wooden floor. It had an elongated head patterned like wire netting, and dark-edged yellow spots running down its body to its long tail. She estimated it must be four feet long, maybe five. Its claws looked long and savage, and sent revolting stories of crocodiles swallowing unwary Englishmen flitting through her brain.

"What is it?" she asked in a strangled voice, backing up against the bookcase. She felt the hard edges of the shelves digging into her back and legs.

"It's a goanna," said Liam. "Lord, it's a big one, ain't it?"

He sounded delighted. Amanda pressed her hand to her chest in an effort to quiet her galloping heart. "Don't panic, children," she said, although she herself—and, to a lesser extent, Missy—was the only one who appeared alarmed. "Stay behind me. If we slowly back out the door, perhaps it won't attack."

At that moment, the monster's mouth gaped open and its long tongue flicked out. It was too much. A startled shriek escaped Amanda's lips before she could bite it back. Then the beast took three scrabbling steps toward her, and she dropped the book and screamed.

She snatched Missy out of her chair and backed toward the door to the dining room, the child balanced on her hip. "Hannah, Liam. Come away quickly."

She heard a shout. Booted feet pounded across the veranda and Patrick O'Reilly burst into the room. He looked so big and strong and, well, *capable,* that Amanda had to resist a weak, feminine urge to run to him and fling herself against his broad chest.

"What the bloody hell have you children—" His gaze fell on the goanna, and he let out a grunt of satisfaction. "Ha. There you are, you fat, chicken-stealin' bastard. We've been lookin' for you." Turning toward the open doors to the garden, he called, "Chow! It's in here." He glanced at Amanda, still clutching Missy and cowering in the doorway to the dining room. "Bet you've never seen a lizard this big, have you, Miss Davenport?"

"A lizard?" she croaked. "That thing is a lizard?"

"A chicken-eating lizard. It musta crawled into the garden last night and not been able to find its way out again. Chow found its tracks this mornin'." He began to edge his way around the side of the room. "Liam," he said. "I want you and Hannah to wait till Chow's ready, then help me chase it back outside. I don't think Miss Davenport would thank us for slaughtering this grandpa on her schoolroom floor." He threw her a quick grin. "Would you, ma'am?"

Amanda cleared her throat. "I suggest we

94

have a short break from lessons, children. We shall reconvene in, say, twenty minutes?" She didn't wait for an answer. Still hugging Missy to her, Amanda spun about and staggered from the room.

That night at the supper table, O'Reilly found Miss Davenport noticeably subdued.

Oh, she told Liam off for slurping his soup, and reminded Missy to sit up straight. But the crusading fire with which she'd set out to reform them all that first night was absent, and she took little part in any of their conversations.

Lounging at the head of the table, O'Reilly sipped his wine and thoughtfully eyed the auburn-haired, fine-boned woman across from him. He'd spent most of the afternoon making repairs to the shearing shed paddocks and worrying about how he was going to channel in enough water to wash the wool. But several times during the day he'd been surprised to catch himself looking forward to tonight, to seeing her, to watching her flush when he teased her. He was a bit disappointed now to find her so distracted, so drawn in upon herself. As if the last forty-eight hours had simply proved too much for her.

She excused herself right after dinner, saying she wanted to do a few things in the schoolroom before she retired. O'Reilly wandered outside to smoke his pipe, then read Missy a story and tucked her in bed. After that, he brooded on the sofa in front of the parlor fire while he watched Liam trounce Hannah at a game of chess. They were setting up for a rematch when O'Reilly finally followed the promptings of an uncharacteristically guilty conscience and visited the schoolroom.

She'd lit a small, clear glass coal oil lamp and set it near the end of the battered cedar schoolroom table. The flickering flame cast a pool of golden light over the bookshelf-lined wall but left the rest of the room in shadow. The night was cold and the fire on the hearth had long since gone out, but she hadn't tried to relight it. She'd thrown a tattered shawl around her shoulders and was awkwardly holding it in place with one hand while she ran the fingers of her other hand along the spines of the books on the shelves.

"Lookin' for somethin' to read?" he asked from the doorway.

With an audible gasp, she jumped and whirled to face him, her eyes dark with wariness, her full lips parted in sudden alarm. The book she'd just pulled from the shelf clattered to the floor, and the hand holding her shawl spasmed at her breast. "I beg your pardon. You startled me."

"I can see that." He sauntered forward and bent to retrieve the book she'd just dropped. Turning it over in his hand, he realized it was a slim volume of erotic love poems by Sappho.

"Interesting selection." He held it out to her. "Plannin' on practicin' your Greek?"

He enjoyed watching the color flood her cheeks, and the way her breasts rose when she sucked in a quick, hitching breath. Sappho's poems were very naughty. And the oh-so-proper Miss Davenport must have read them, or she wouldn't be squirming like this.

"I wasn't actually looking for something to read myself." She took the book but refused to meet his eyes. "I was simply—familiarizing myself with what is available. You have an unexpectedly impressive collection here."

He grunted. "Unexpected, is it?"

She wasn't listening. She'd been nervously fluttering the pages of the book between her fingers when she came upon his name, written in a boyish scrawl on the flyleaf. She stared at it. "This book was yours," she said wonderingly.

"That's right. I've had it since I was a lad. What's the matter? Did you reckon I was pretty close to illiterate or something?"

She had, of course. He could tell by the way her gaze flew to his, then flitted away.

He propped one shoulder against the bookcase and looked down at her. "When I was a boy, my father used to send me out to watch the sheep for weeks on end. I was used to having my sister and brothers at home, so those days out in the hills got pretty lonely. I don't know what I'd have done without books. I reckon you'd be surprised at how many I got through."

"I didn't have any brothers or sisters," she said quietly. "Books were my only companions. Always." She shoved the volume back into its space on the shelf. He saw her hand tremble noticeably, and she grasped the edge of the case as if to steady herself.

He didn't like this woman, and her attitudes irritated the hell out of him. But she looked so small and fragile and vulnerable, standing there in the golden lamplight, that he reached out and closed his fingers, lightly, around her slim wrist. "Did the children do something else to you today? Is that what's bothering you this evening?"

It was a simple touch, a spontaneous gesture of sympathy and support. But he was unprepared for the effect it had on him.

Her skin felt smooth and soft and sensuously delicious beneath his hand. He found he wanted to run his palm slowly, exquisitely up her arm. He wanted to lean in closer, to turn her in his arms and breathe in the fragrance of her hair, to explore the curve of her neck and learn the taste of her full, wide mouth.

He felt her go utterly still beneath his touch. Felt her pulse flutter. She cast a quick glance up at him, her eyes wide, her pupils seeming to dilate in the darkness. He sucked in a deep breath. And let her go.

"The children?" Her voice quavered, her head carefully bent away from him again. "No. Oh, no." He watched her rub her hand over and over the wrist he'd just touched. He wondered if she even knew she was doing it.

"Are you not telling me what they did because you're afraid I'll give them a whippin'? Because if that's it—"

"No." She turned, pressing her back against the bookshelves and bringing her arms up to hug herself as she stared off into the darkened corners of the room. "Truly, it's nothing to do with the children. It's..." She swallowed, and raised her chin in that arrogant gesture that had irritated him before, but now for some reason faintly amused him.

"If you must know," she said in a rush, "I find I am rather disappointed in myself. Because of the way I reacted to the goanna this morning. I had not thought myself such a pathetic creature. So...cowardly."

"You think you're a coward?"

"Yes."

"I don't."

She jerked. "Don't be ridiculous. My reaction was shameful. I even *screamed*." Her voice was rough with self-loathing.

He rested his arm along the shelf beside her head and leaned into her. "I doubt there's many people in this world who could watch a strange four-and-a-half foot reptile come slithering into the room with them and not get scared. After all, you didn't know it wasn't particularly dangerous—and believe me, you wouldn't have wanted it to take a chunk out of your leg, in any case. Yet you didn't run off and leave the children, or faint. You stood your ground."

He saw her jaw tighten. "I was terrified," she insisted, determined to flail herself with what she saw as her shortcomings. "I hate hysterical females, yet that's exactly what I acted like."

"You didn't look hysterical to me. Just scared. There is a difference." He watched her slender throat work as she swallowed, and knew an unwelcome tug of admiration. Here he'd assumed she'd been overset by everything that had happened since her arrival or by some new trick his children had pulled on her. Instead, she'd been berating herself for what she saw as her own lack of courage. And this from a woman who'd ended up stranded alone and penniless in a land she hated because she'd refused to sail for home and leave an old woman to die alone.

"Being brave doesn't mean not feeling fear," he said gently. "The way I see it, it doesn't take any courage to confront a danger you're not afraid of. It's when a man—or a woman—stands there and faces what terrifies them, that's what takes courage."

Her head swiveled so that she could look at him. He watched her nostrils flare in sudden surprise as she realized just how close to her he was. Close enough that his breath stirred the loose tendrils of flame-colored hair beside her ear. Close enough that he could smell her scent, a mixture of rosewater and starch and her own unexpectedly desirable, vibrant essense.

She stood, flushed and still, studying him in a way that made him wonder what she saw. She was so tiny, she had to tilt her head back to meet his gaze, and her neck arched invitingly.

It would have been the easiest thing in the

world to dip his head and kiss her. But no sooner did the thought flicker through his consciousness than he wondered where the hell it had come from. She was his children's governess, for Christsake. And the exact opposite of the type of woman he admired. She was too feminine and delicate, too straight-laced and corset-pinched, too ostentatiously virtuous, too *English*. Bloody hell, he didn't even *like* her.

Yet something about her piqued his interest, stirred his blood, and provoked his unwilling admiration. He looked into the dark gray shimmer of her eyes, watched her tongue creep out to wet her lips, and was almost lost again.

"There is so much here to fear," she whispered. "I don't know if I have the courage to face it all."

"You could always leave." Even as he said it, he knew he wanted her to leave. He needed her here, to teach his children. Yet for his own sake, he wished she would go away.

She shook her head, the movement causing the glow from the lamp flame to glance off the glorious wine-red highlights in her hair. "No. I won't leave until I've earned enough to get back to England."

"Then if it's that important to you, you'll do what you have to do." He shoved away from the bookcase and was half out the door before he turned. "By the way, how'd you like supper?"

Her eyes narrowed suspiciously. "Do you mean the pork? It was lovely. Why?"

It hadn't been pork, of course, but the goanna, and O'Reilly had just been waiting for the right moment to tell her about it. Only now that he had the chance, all he said was, "Yeah. The pork." He felt his lips twist into an odd smile. "Good night."

A piercing scream shattered the night.

Amanda sat up in bed, her heart pounding as she stared wildly into the cloaking darkness. She could see nothing. For a moment she felt disoriented, confused, unsure of where she was. Then memory returned, and she knew she was at Penyaka, in the Australian outback. And she realized that what she had just heard had been a child's scream.

She swung her feet out of bed, fumbled for her slippers, reached for her wrapper. Quickly knotting the sash, she jerked open her door.

The fire on the hearth had died down to a pile of embers that filled the darkened parlor with a reddish glow. She could see the vague, indistinct outlines of furniture, and the door to Patrick O'Reilly's room standing open, opposite hers. He was already up.

The flicker of a candle from the direction of the girls' room brought her head around. She saw a long, masculine shadow move across the wooden floor of the adjoining dining room and disappear. His voice came to her, a low-pitched, soothing murmur in the night.

She knew she should go back to bed. Instead,

she crept forward, hugging the wall and keeping her footfalls light. She could see him now, hunkered down beside Missy's bed. The flickering candle glazed his bare shoulders with a golden light, glinted on his tawny hair, showed his dark hand against the white swath of Missy's sheets.

"And what did the leprechaun find, Papa?" Missy asked, her hand clutching his, her voice tight with fear.

"Sure then, 'twas a pot of gold, right at the end of that rainbow, where he thought it'd be." O'Reilly's suddenly thick Irish brogue made Missy giggle. "And now," he continued, drawing the covers up beneath the little girl's chin, "if you close your eyes and lie very still, I'll sing you a song."

Amanda drew back, her fingers gripping the neck of her wrapper, her eyes squeezing shut as an old Irish ballad, sung in a mellow tenor, floated through the still house. It was a sad tale, of doomed love and hopeless striving and inevitable loss. But it was not the words of the song that brought the lump to Amanda's throat or the rush of tears that stung her eyes. It was the sight of this man, so loving and giving, so tender in his care of his frightened young daughter.

Amanda sucked in a deep, painful breath, shaken by half-buried memories of all the nights she herself had awakened as a child, disoriented, afraid, wanting the comforting nearness of someone who loved her, someone she knew would take care of her. But no one had ever come to her, no one had ever told her stories, no one had ever sung her to sleep. She had been left alone to stare wide-eyed into the terrifying blackness of the night, to shiver, and to start at each small sound. To ache with loneliness and need. And cry herself back to sleep.

Now a grown woman, Amanda stood alone in the darkness and listened to O'Reilly's soothing voice, so warm with love and tenderness and gentle concern, it made her chest burn with some strange emotion. And she realized that she was suddenly, achingly envious.

Of Missy.

CHAPTER SIX

After lessons the next day, Amanda escaped to the garden.

The cold wind that had made the last few days uncomfortable had dropped, leaving the afternoon unbelievably warm for late winter. She was strolling thoughtfully along a box-edged path when the clip-clop of a horse's hooves muffled by the thick dust of the track brought her head around. She expected to see one of the stockmen, or maybe Patrick O'Reilly, coming in from the mustering. But the man who reined in at the gate was no stockman.

He rode a big-boned roan with a broad back and a pronounced wheeze. Shuffling to a stop beside the garden wall, the horse gave a snort and hung its head pitifully.

"I fail to understand how you can be as exhausted as you pretend, Hermes," said the man in a precise English accent. His saddle leather creaked as he raised himself painfully in the stirrups. "Given that you steadfastly refused to be coaxed out of a walk the entire distance from town, I believe I have worked harder getting us here than you, my friend."

At the sound of Amanda's soft laughter, the man slewed around in his saddle, his fist tightening in the horse's mane as if to keep himself from falling off.

She found herself regarding a pleasant-looking young man of no more than twenty-five or thirty. He had soft brown eyes, a neat brown mustache, and the bloom of an English rose in his cheeks. His clothes were those of a gentleman: a modestly cut, brown wool frock coat lightly powdered now with dust from his ride, a conservative satin waistcoat, and a starched white shirt with its stiff collar buttoned up properly beneath his cleft chin.

At the sight of Amanda, he reached with one hand to doff his bowler hat and smiled, revealing even white teeth. "You must be Miss Davenport. Allow me to introduce myself. I am Christian Whittaker, keeper of accounts for the Brinkman mine, tutor of unwilling small boys, and unfortunate owner of a horse known as Hermes."

Amanda laughed again and came forward to offer him her hand. "How do you do, sir.

I had heard you were to ride out today, but I must confess I had begun to think you weren't coming after all."

Settling his hat back on his head, Mr. Whittaker leaned over perilously to take her hand. "It is a small man who blames others for his own shortcomings, so I shall not attempt to shift responsibility to this fleet-footed beast here." Hermes jerked his head up and whipped his tail back and forth, almost unseating his rider. Mr. Whittaker let go of her hand and made another grab at the mane. "I fear the problem is that I never did much riding before coming to Australia."

Amanda smiled at him. "Then do hasten to get down and come in. Liam is waiting for you in the schoolroom."

"With eager anticipation, I am sure." Mr. Whittaker gave an exaggerated sigh and rolled his eyes in a way that made Amanda want to laugh again. She suddenly felt very gay. It was so *good* to talk to someone from Home, to hear the rich, full vowels of her childhood. To be treated with polite respect rather than with a teasing, faintly suggestive familiarity that aroused all sorts of wanton, half-forgotten thoughts in one's head.

She watched in quiet amusement as Mr. Whittaker grasped his horse's mane with both hands and leaned forward. Levering his right leg up and over Hermes' broad back, he slid to the ground in a clumsy rush. He was not a big man, like Patrick O'Reilly, but small, and slightly plump. He did not tower over her, intimidating her with his size and his strength and his aggressive masculinity.

"There," he said, bending over to brush off his dusty clothes. "Safely to earth again. Now all I have to do is take care of Hermes here."

At the sound of his name, the roan laid down its ears and tossed its thick head. Discovering that Whittaker had released the reins in order to deal with his disheveled clothes, Hermes began to back.

Amanda's hand closed around the roan's reins just below the bit, stopping it. "Let me take him for you. You'd best go in before Liam disappears."

Mr. Whittaker looked up from straightening his waistcoat, his jaw slack with surprise. "You, Miss Davenport? Oh, but I could never ask such a thing—"

Amanda shook her head. "I don't mind. I'll lead him down to the stables and give him to one of the men."

A look of relief passed over Whittaker's features, although he still visibly hesitated. "If you are quite certain you can handle the brute..."

"Quite certain."

He smiled. "I don't know how to thank you."

"You can thank me by joining me on the veranda for tea after your lessons," said Amanda, shocking herself with her own boldness. "And talking to me of England."

The rosy color in Mr. Whittaker's cheeks deepened endearingly. "With pleasure," he said, doffing his hat one last time before unhooking his leather satchel from the saddle and hurrying off toward the house.

With her free hand, Amanda reached up to rub the big horse's velvety nose. "I think he's a very nice young man," she whispered softly in Hermes' ear. "And you have treated him abominably. So if you try any of your tricks with me, you ill-mannered, misnamed oaf, I shall thump you squarely between the eyes. Consider yourself warned."

The roan rolled his big brown eyes and stared consideringly at her. Then he hung his head in contrite obeisance and followed Amanda to the stables.

"Liam told me about your recent reptilian visitor," said Christian Whittaker, delicately taking a sip of his tea as he sat with Amanda on the eastern veranda. "It sounds as if it were probably a Gould's goanna—that's technically a *Varanus gouldii*," he added conscientiously. "Although it's difficult to be certain, since the remains have unfortunately been consumed."

Amanda's head jerked up. "Consumed?"

"Yes. I understand you had it for dinner last night."

Oblivious to her horrified, wide-eyed stare, he rolled on. "They usually grow to about four feet. The perentie—that's the *Veranus giganteus*, incidentally—can reach eight feet. But it is rarely seen north of Alligator Gorge."

"I suppose I should be thankful for that, at least," said Amanda, forcing a tight smile.

"Actually, it's not the goannas you need to worry about. It's the snakes that are poisonous— and the most deadly of all is the brown snake. If you ever see one of those, move away quickly."

"Brown snakes?" repeated Amanda, swallowing hard. She reached quickly for the teapot. "Would you like some more tea?"

"Please," he said, handing her his cup.

He was younger than she'd first taken him to be, she decided; surely no more than twenty-four or -five. Yet it was obvious that he had been born and raised a gentleman. He was so polite, so reticent, so delightfully *English*. A man like Christian Whittaker, she thought, would never be caught publicly cavorting with loose widows in the middle of the afternoon. He would never boldly put his hands on a spinster governess's derriere, whatever the circumstances. And he would certainly never look at her with such naked heat in his eyes as to make her imagine for one, breathless moment that he was about to kiss her.

Jerking her mind away from the thought, she carefully poured the tea. "Did you bring your family to Australia with you?"

"Oh, I am not married yet. Not that I would have exposed a gently bred Englishwoman to this place, even if I were," he added, reaching for the cream.

"Have you been here long?" she asked.

109

"Three and a half years. Which means I have six months left of my four-year sentence."

She laughed. "You make it sound like a prison term."

His mustache lifted in a shy smile. "It feels like it, at times."

"You mean to go back to England, then?"

"Goodness, yes. I only came out because my father is a principal investor in the Brinkman Mining Company, and he wished me to keep an eye on things from this end. I fear I am not cut out to be a colonist. Apart from the fact that I think constantly of Home, I find this land too harsh. Too wild."

"Yes. Its beauty is very stark, almost brutal, isn't it?" She stared off down the valley, over the barns and paddocks and stockyards of Penyaka. As she watched, O'Reilly came out of one of the stables and began to stroll up the hill toward the house. For some ridiculous reason, she felt her heart begin to beat faster.

"You find it beautiful?" said Whittaker in surprise.

"In a frightening, merciless way, yes. Don't you?"

"At times, perhaps. Before this drought, the wildflowers used to bloom in the spring, and it could be surprisingly pretty. You wouldn't credit it looking at this scene now, but I've seen these hills knee-deep in lush green grass and the valley a waving sea of heliotrope daisies and bush bluebells and wild candytuft. And that creek..." He gestured toward the twisted trail of dry rocks bleaching white in the sun. "It can run so full, you might think it a sizable river, if you did not know better."

"This drought is bad, isn't it?" Out of the corner of her eye, she noticed that O'Reilly had almost reached the entrance to the garden. With a peculiar sense of panic, she realized he was coming to join them on the veranda.

She hadn't seen him since their encounter in the schoolroom last night, and she found herself suddenly wondering how she would comfortably be able to meet his eye. Which was ridiculous, she told herself. Nothing had happened. And yet...and yet, something had.

Mr. Whittaker smoothed the ends of his mustache. "This drought will be the ruin of us all, I'm afraid, if it keeps up. Unless we get rain soon, all of the Flinders north of Melrose will be deserted except for the Aborigines and kangaroos—although I doubt there'll be many of them left either."

She swung her head to stare at him. "Do you mean to say that O'Reilly is threatened? Here, on Penyaka?"

His gaze flitted away from hers, as if he felt he'd said too much. "As to that, I don't know. Mr. O'Reilly is more fortunate than most in that his run contains a number of unusually deep water holes. The problem is the feed..."

His voice trailed off as they watched Patrick O'Reilly come at them, the spurs on his boot heels rasping over the flagged garden path. He had a lean, long-legged way of walking,

111

Amanda thought, that somehow managed to be both lazy and agile at the same time. His waistcoat hung open, and he had his shirt unbuttoned halfway down his chest so that she could see a swath of bare, sun-browned skin, tight with muscle, glistening with sweat. The man never seemed properly clothed.

Her hand crept up to tug at her suddenly too-tight collar. She felt her pulse beating, fast, in the hollow of her neck as she watched him pause just short of the veranda, his thumb pushing his broad-brimmed hat back farther on his head. His vivid blue eyes met hers and for one, intense moment, a frisson of awareness passed between them. An intimate, frightening connection that she didn't want.

Then he turned his head, and his gaze drifted to Mr. Whittaker and the very proper English tea she had laid out, and she saw a dimple crease his cheek. "Miss Davenport," he drawled, nodding to her. "Christian."

She inclined her head and said, "Mr. O'Reilly," in a prim, stilted voice while Mr. Whittaker hastened to stand up and bow politely.

O'Reilly sauntered over to the canvas water bag that hung in the shade of the veranda and reached for the tin mug dangling from its chain. "Warm this afternoon," he said over his shoulder as he let the water splash into the mug. "Too bloody warm for August." With one fluid motion, he raised the cup and threw the water down his throat, then reached over to draw more.

"Indeed," said Mr. Whittaker. "I shudder to think what it will be like in January."

O'Reilly murmured something unintelligible. Tossing his hat to one side, he lifted the mug of water and upended it over the top of his head.

He had his head flung back, his eyes squeezed shut. Amanda watched the water trickle down his lean, tanned cheeks to mingle with the sweat. More water darkened the tawny hair that curled against his forehead, and slid down the strong, taut curve of his throat. She felt something swell in her. Something secret and abandoned and painfully needy.

"You haven't experienced an Australian summer yet, Miss Davenport," said Christian Whittaker, breaking into her thoughts.

She jerked her gaze away from the raw, intensely physical man near the water bag. "No. I haven't."

"The heat is indescribable. And the dust storms! Did you know it's possible to actually see one of them coming? It looks like a great, dirty curtain, being pulled across the sky by some giant, malevolent hand." He swept his arm dramatically through the air.

"They'll be worse this year," said O'Reilly, coming to sprawl in the chair beside her, his long legs thrown out across the flagstones. He sat the way he walked, she decided: lazy, yet somehow exuding an aura of leashed energy.

"Would you like some tea, Mr. O'Reilly?" she asked, reaching for a clean cup.

"Tea?" He swung to face her, a gleam of

amusement lighting his eyes. "Why, yes please, Miss Davenport."

She could feel his teasing gaze upon her as she lifted the teapot and poured. She found it oddly disconcerting having him so close, knowing he was watching her. It was as if he radiated some sort of animal energy, so that even though she wasn't looking at him, she was still intensely aware of him, of his nearness, of his scent—the mingling of leather and hardworking man and the harsh Australian bush. When she passed him his tea, her hands shook so badly, the cup rattled in its saucer.

She could not understand her absurd fascination with this Australian's body. The man virtually reveled in being uncultured, rude, irreverent—everything she despised. She glanced from Patrick O'Reilly, with his worn moleskins and unbuttoned serge shirt, to Mr. Whittaker, with his neat brown suit, bowler hat, and faint, pleasant aroma of bay rum and hair tonic, and felt a renewed surge of pleasure in the young Englishman's company.

"I understand you ride out here to tutor Liam every week," she said, passing him a plate of sandwiches.

"Every Thursday."

"You must have tea with me again next week."

"That would be wonderful, Miss Davenport," said Mr. Whittaker.

She heard O'Reilly expel his breath in a little puff of air. She glanced at him sharply, but he had his hat pulled down low, hiding his face. If he were laughing at her, she couldn't see it.

Then he pushed his hat back, his eyes narrowing as he stared off into the distance. Amanda twisted around to look, but all she could see was a red cloud of dust hovering heavy in the air, dispersing slowly on the breeze.

"What is it?" she asked.

"Bullockies, probably," he said. "Taking a load to the Cox run. The track cuts through Penyaka."

She could see them now, two drays, each pulled by a team of eight bullocks. The drivers walked beside their loads, their enormous fourteen-foot bullwhips snapping as they called out to their teams. "Whoa back, Cranky. Come here, Blackie."

They rolled up in front of the homestead, and O'Reilly stretched to his feet and lounged out to meet them. "G'day," he called, tucking the fingertips of both hands beneath his wide brown belt.

"Will they spend the night here?" Amanda asked, watching O'Reilly walk up to the first driver, a tall, gangly man with a long, weatherworn face and protruding yellow teeth.

"Probably," said Mr. Whittaker. "They often do."

She could hear O'Reilly's voice, floating on the wattle-scented breeze. "...you can have all the water you want, and we've got tucker for you men. But we're mighty short on feed."

One of the drivers—bullockies, O'Reilly

had called them—worked his jaw and sent a stream of filthy tobacco juice shooting through the air to land with a splat in the dust. "No worries, mate. We're carryin' hay. Got to, these days."

O'Reilly reached into his vest pocket to pull out his pipe and tobacco pouch. "What's that do to your rate per ton-mile?"

"We've had to put it up to three shillings."

O'Reilly responded with a crude sexual expletive.

Amanda's gaze flickered involuntarily to Christian Whittaker. He glanced away, his ruddy cheeks reddening. "Mr. O'Reilly's language can be...colorful at times," he said awkwardly.

"Yes. I had noticed."

He looked at her then, his brown eyes warm with sympathy. "It must be very difficult for a lady of your obvious breeding and background to find herself in such primitive surroundings."

She knew she should have welcomed his compassion and ready understanding of just how stressful her position here was; instead, she found that it irritated her for some reason, and she didn't quite know why.

"*Gee up.*" A shout from one of the bullockies brought them both around. "*Gee up, Cranky.*" With a creaking of axles and a snapping of whips, the bullock teams moved off toward the creek bed. Amanda caught sight of Liam tearing alongside the lead dray, his head thrown back, whooping and laughing. His shirt was off, his young body lithe and brown

116

in the sun. The dog Barrister barked joyously, racing by his side.

"Oh, goodness." Mr. Whittaker started up. "There goes Liam, and I had a book in my satchel I meant to lend him."

"I'll give it to him, if you like," said Amanda, also rising, but slowly, for she was not anxious for the afternoon with her new friend to end.

"It's only a copy of Caesar's *Commentaries on the Gallic War.*" He reached into the worn leather case beside his chair and came up with a small blue book. "I thought it might appeal to a boy such as Liam more than Virgil."

He handed it to her and hesitated, seemingly as reluctant as she to end the interlude. "I suppose I must be off. The days are still fairly short and I don't like to ride in the dark." He settled his bowler hat on his neatly trimmed brown hair. "I shall see you next week?"

"Yes." She tucked the slim volume under her arm and held out her hand. "I shall look forward to it."

"As will I." He grasped her hand with gratifying warmth. "Good day, Miss Davenport. And thank you so much for the tea. It has been a pleasure."

Still smiling faintly, she leaned against the veranda post to watch him leave. One of the men brought up Hermes, and her smile broadened as she watched Christian Whittaker coax his broad-backed roan into a reluctant trot that kicked up little eddies of dust still vis-

117

ible long after both man and horse had disappeared over the crest of the hill.

Amanda lingered in the garden, enjoying the pleasant warmth of the evening until the hot ball of the sun sank toward the Flinders Ranges and a golden light drenched the valley, darkening the sky to a vivid indigo and throwing long shadows across hills bleached the color of ripe wheat.

When she entered the parlor, she was surprised to find Hannah seated at the pedestal-based round cedar table that stood in the center of the room, her slim young body hunched over a book as she tried to read by the light of single candle.

"You need more light, Hannah," Amanda said, closing the door behind her.

Hannah's head jerked up. Slamming the book closed, she thrust it beneath the apron of the table and glared at Amanda, her hostile stare both willing her to go away and defying her to stay and interfere.

"What are you reading?" Amanda asked.

A muscle jumped along the girl's tightened jaw as she continued, silently, to stare at Amanda.

Amanda walked over to the table and held out her hand. "Let me see it."

She wasn't sure what she would have done if Hannah had refused. But after a moment's hesitation, Hannah sighed, threw Amanda a look of pure malice, and tossed the book onto the table.

Amanda didn't know what to expect. A lurid romance, perhaps, which the child had somehow managed to acquire. The last thing she had anticipated was to find herself staring down at Liam's sadly abused copy of Virgil's *Aeneid*.

The old chair creaked as Hannah thrust it back. She leapt to her feet and had half turned to leave before Amanda's hand flashed out to catch the girl's arm just above the elbow. "No. Hannah, wait."

The girl's head whipped around. She stared at Amanda, a sneer on her lips, contempt flashing in her dark-brown eyes.

Amanda stared back at her, feeling oddly at a loss. She picked up the book and held it out. "Why did you hide this from me?"

Hannah glanced at the book but made no move to take it. "I'm not supposed to learn how to read it."

"Who says?"

Hannah laughed bitterly. "Miss Sutton. Miss Westbrook. Miss McDuff. Need I continue?"

"I take it these ladies were some of your previous governesses?"

Hannah nodded.

"And they forbade you to learn Latin?"

"Of course." She pinched her nose and raised her voice an octave in a vicious imitation of an English governess. "We women have delicate constitutions, weak spirits, and feeble mental abilities, my dear. It is not for us to go forth into the world, think great thoughts, and do great deeds. We leave that to the men, who are far better suited than us to a vigorous life. We females are destined for domesticity. The only education a woman needs is what is essential for her to please her husband, raise her children, and care for her household."

"Do you believe that?"

Hannah's hand fell slowly back to her side as she stared at Amanda in surprise. "No. Don't you?"

"It would be difficult to reconcile with the realities of my own position in the world, now, wouldn't it?"

Hannah paused, as if considering. "That didn't seem to bother any of the other governesses."

"Perhaps not." Amanda held out the book again. "Here, take it. If you like, I could talk to your father about having you join Liam in his lessons with Mr. Whittaker. Or I could teach you myself."

Hannah took the book, but only to drop it negligently back on the table and shrug. "No. Please don't. I'm not really that interested."

Amanda wasn't convinced, but she decided to let it go for now. The girl thrust her hands in her pockets and turned away.

"Hannah?"

She pivoted back around.

"Do you know where Liam is? I have a book Mr. Whittaker asked me to give him."

"He's probably hanging around the bullockies' camp. He usually does, whenever they come through. They don't let me stay because I'm a girl, but Liam likes to listen to their yarns. Sometimes they even let him have a sip or two."

Surely she wasn't implying— It wasn't possible that— "A sip or two of what?" asked Amanda suspiciously.

Hannah grinned at her. "Brandy. Rum. Whatever they've got."

Amanda studied the girl, but Hannah was like her father and her brother; her face never gave anything away. "You're saying that to shock me, aren't you?"

Hannah laughed out loud and turned away.

Amanda walked slowly back to her room, convinced that Hannah was having her on again. Except what if she wasn't?

With a muttered exclamation, Amanda grabbed a shawl and slammed out of the house.

CHAPTER SEVEN

The familiar scents of lavender and pinks rose up on the evening air to greet Amanda as she cut across the garden. But once she let herself out of the back gate to follow the dusty path toward the creek, she found herself in a different world.

Without the benefits of the Chinese gardener's ingenious irrigation system, the vegetation here was parched, dying. Dry twigs and leaves snapped and crackled beneath the leather soles of her high-topped shoes. Withered grass rustled as her crinolined skirts swept the sides of the path. The air smelled of dust and the strange, volatile oils of the giant eucalypts towering over her head.

She could see the bullockies' camp through the red gums down by the creek. The men had built a fire and rigged up a spit on which a side of mutton slowly roasted, sizzling and dripping fat into the leaping orange-and-gold flames. She heard the crackle of the fire, smelled the roasting meat on the tangy, eucalypt-scented smoke. She had half expected to find Mr. O'Reilly here, too, but she could see only the two bullockies and Liam.

At some point the boy had retrieved his shirt and a light jacket as the sinking sun drained the unseasonable warmth from the day. He sat on a fallen log, his legs sprawled out in front of him in a posture that reminded Amanda, strongly, of his father. Beside him, Barrister lay panting happily. When the dog saw Amanda, his tail began to thump in greeting.

It was still light, the sun only just slipping below the horizon to splash the high, wispy clouds with touches of gold and vivid pink. But the three human males by the fire were so absorbed by their pursuit of vice that no one but the dog noticed her approach.

"Shi-it," said Liam, drawling out the syllables in a perfect imitation of his father. "You should see the gen-u-ine, rarefied, corset-pinched lady my aunt Hetty sent us for a governess this time. I heard Father tell Mr. Campbell he wouldn't be surprised if she wears her corset to bed." The two bullockies laughed like a couple of braying jackasses while Liam wrapped his fist around the neck of a bottle and raised it to his lips.

"Liam O'Reilly. " Amanda's voice rang out as she stalked into the small clearing. Barrister stood up and trotted forward expectantly, but she only patted him absently on the head. "I hope for your sake that is not an alcoholic beverage in your hand."

Caught in the act of swallowing, Liam looked up, choked, and fell to coughing. The dirty, smelly, unshaven rustics by the fire guffawed again, one even going so far as to slap his thigh.

"And you." She whirled on the two men. "Have you no shame? Corrupting an innocent child?"

"Innocent?" One of the bullockies—a fat, middle-aged man with a balding pate and a bulbous nose—stared at her in confusion. Then his frown cleared and enlightenment dawned. "Oh, you mean Liam here." He snickered and elbowed his companion in the ribs. "Hear that, Sweeny? She thinks Liam here is an innocent." He gave her a broad grin that displayed a checkerboard of missing teeth. "Innocent. Tee-hee. That's a good one."

With an inelegant noise that came out sounding suspiciously like a snort, Amanda swung back to the boy. "Liam, put down that bottle and come away this instant."

"Why?" Liam sneered with a swaggering kind of bravado she suspected was half-false, half-rum. "Father doesn't mind. He's even taken me into Hornbottom's hotel."

It probably wasn't true, but at that moment, Amanda thought she wouldn't put anything past the wretched man. Wore her corset to bed, indeed. She lifted her chin and said loftily, "I am unaware of your father's sentiments on this matter. I, however, object to this behavior most strongly. And if I must, I will request Ching and Chow to accompany me here and physically drag you back to the house." It was an outrageous bluff, of course; she hadn't the faintest idea if they would do such a thing for her or not.

Liam's eyes widened in surprise, then narrowed in disbelief. "You wouldn't."

Amanda put her hands on her hips and stared down her nose at him. "I would."

She might be a small woman, but as long as he stayed sprawled on the ground like that, he had to tilt his head back at a painful angle just to look up at her. It put him at a distinct disadvantage. Yet for him to stand up would be to admit a small but nevertheless significant defeat.

He squirmed uncomfortably but stayed where he was.

"Liam," she began threateningly.

One of the bullockies—the thin, rabbit-toothed one named Sweeny this time—shook his head sadly and said, "Better go then, lad. We wouldn't want you gettin' in trouble with your new lady governess."

She thought for a moment the boy still meant to refuse. He glared up at her, his chest heaving with impotent indignation, fury, and what she feared looked very much like a promise of revenge shining in his hazel eyes. Then he levered up off the ground and took off at a run across the rocky stream bed, the dog at his heels.

A gust of wind eddied the fire, sending sparks shooting up into the sunset-streaked sky and billowing the blue smoke into her eyes. "Thank you, gentlemen." She turned away hastily, her eyes stinging from the smoke.

"Anytime, ma'am." Sweeny bit off a plug of tobacco with his prominent rabbit teeth. "Pleasure to have made yer acquaintance."

The other bullocky heaved to his feet and lumbered over to retrieve the bottle abandoned by Liam. "Sorry if we caused you any trouble, ma'am. We didn't mean no harm. We wouldna let him have more'n a taste."

"I am relieved to hear that, gentlemen. Good evening." Rubbing her sore eyes with a thumb and index finger, Amanda headed blindly back toward the homestead.

Behind her, she heard one of the ignoramuses make a lowly muttered, crudely worded sexual suggestion she only half understood. The other bullocky grunted. "Hell, I don't care what color hair she has. I know that type of female. And I'd rather try to poke one of those bullocks over there than get it on with a tight-assed old maid like that."

Both men chuckled. Amanda kept walking, her head held high, her back ramrod straight, and within her a fierce determination to find Patrick O'Reilly and tell him exactly what she thought of him, his friends, and the way he was raising his children.

An unseen magpie warbled its heartbreaking song as Amanda strode purposefully across the garden toward the small square stone office building where she'd last seen O'Reilly. In the distance, the sun disappeared behind a ragged peak, leaving the long, buckled line of the Flinders Ranges to stand out purple and fierce against the fire-washed sky.

Through the small-paned window to the left of the office door she saw a faint light that wavered, then grew stronger as someone set a match to an oil lamp. After the curtest of knocks, Amanda threw open the door and stalked inside.

Mr. Campbell, in the act of replacing the chimney on the lamp, started so violently, he almost dropped it. "Lord, Miss," he gasped, peering at her with bloodshot eyes. "You nearly scared me to death."

"I beg your pardon." The stench of rum and stale sweat emanating from the man hit her in the face, almost staggering her. She retreated back over the threshold to the porch and sucked in a clean breath of fresh air.

She supposed she shouldn't find it so surprising that O'Reilly allowed his son to drink, Amanda decided, when he openly tolerated such disreputable drunken behavior among his men. "I am looking for Mr. O'Reilly," she said in her best, most repressive diction. *And when I find him,* she thought, *I am going to tell him what I think of his bookkeeper as well as his bullocky friends.*

Campbell scratched his long, filthy black beard. "Well, he ain't here no more. You might try down by the cart shed. He were there a minute ago. Saw him talkin' to some of Sally's people."

"Sally's people?"

"Aborigines."

"Oh, I see. Thank you."

Her indignation rising with every step, Amanda left the office and marched downhill to the cart shed.

She could see him now, in the distance. Even in the gloom, his coiled, lazy stance was unmistakable. He stood with one hip cocked to the side, his arms crossed over his chest. She was so intent upon the man himself that it wasn't until Amanda was almost upon him that she realized the two dusky-skinned figures he was talking to were clothed only in the colors of the setting sun. One was male, the other female, and both were quite, quite naked.

Amanda gasped and would have turned to leave, only O'Reilly heard her and swung around.

"Miss Davenport. Come over here. There's someone you might be interested to meet. This here is Sally's brother, Pinba. And that's Gabby, his lubra."

Slowly, reluctantly, Amanda edged closer. She stood rigid, her hands clasped firmly behind her back. Somehow she managed to murmur a stiff, formal, "How do you do?" The problem was, she didn't know where to look. She could not look at the naked man; she found the idea of simply being close to one both mortifying and alarming. Yet she could not look at the naked woman, either. The Aboriginal woman was younger than her husband. Her healthy, upright breasts seemed almost to thrust out at Amanda. And while painfully conscious of Patrick O'Reilly standing beside her, she found she could not look at him, either. All she could seem to think was, *He can see that woman's naked breasts.* Amanda refused to think about what else was visible on the woman.

"When you have a free moment, Mr. O'Reilly, there is something I wish to discuss with you," Amanda said, staring determinedly at the tips of the mountains, turning black and mysterious now as evening descended upon them.

Pinba said something in his native tongue that Amanda could not understand. O'Reilly laughed, and Amanda's concentration wavered. Her gaze drifted downward. She realized the Aboriginal man was not entirely naked. He wore a brief loincloth fashioned of netting and tied

128

around his bare hips with something that looked like string.

"It's made from rushes," said O'Reilly, apparently aware of the object of her fascination. "They weave it into a kind of string, and use it for everything from nets and cradles to billy bags and..." He paused for emphasis. "Loincloths."

He's enjoying this. The thought exploded in her brain as her head snapped up, her gaze flying to his. *He knows I'm mortified by these people's nudity and he's deliberately tormenting me with it.* She saw the laugh lines beside his eyes deepen as a lazy smile curled the edges of his lips, and her own lips parted on a quickly indrawn breath.

Exposure to such brazen nudity was not only shocking, she decided, it was also dangerous. Why else would she suddenly find herself wondering what Patrick O'Reilly must look like without *his* clothes on? She remembered stolen glimpses of a hard, tanned chest and a flat stomach, ridged with muscle, and it was easy to imagine the rest. The lean line of his flanks. His long legs strapped with muscle. The taut curve of his buttocks.

Her heart pounded hard and fast, sending the blood coursing through her, making her painfully aware of her own body, normally so buried beneath layers of cotton, linen, wool, and whalebone that she scarcely gave it a thought. It was as if her breasts had swelled, pressing against the stiff bodice of her gown. She felt an ache, a familiar, dreaded need

129

way down low in her belly that made her want to gasp. Suddenly terrified that he might be able to read in her eyes the wayward direction of her thoughts, she turned away, her cheeks burning with mortification.

"We can talk now," he said. "If you like."

"What? Oh. Oh, no." Amanda's hands flew to her hot cheeks. "Later." She swallowed convulsively. "Later will be fine."

With a hastily murmured apology, she picked up her skirts and fled.

Too agitated to reenter the house, Amanda paced the flagstoned paths of the garden, her narrow-heeled shoes tapping a brisk click-click on the paving. From down the hill came the bleating of sheep and the lowing of cattle as O'Reilly's breeding stock settled down for the night; farmyard sounds, as unfamiliar to Oxford-bred Amanda as the screech of the cockatoos nesting in the creek-bed gums.

Suppressing a sigh, she tilted back her head and gazed up at the first stars glimmering out of the darkening sky. She told herself she was upset by her encounter with the naked Aborigines. It was shock that made her pulse beat rapidly, her breath come in quick little pants. Her maidenly sensibilities had been affronted. Anyone would believe that.

Or at least someone like Christian Whittaker would believe it, even if Patrick O'Reilly did not.

She caught a faint scent of tobacco smoke,

130

mingling with the sweetness of the garden's rose and honeysuckle. A pipe glowed red out of the darkness, and she knew he stood there, watching her.

She paused some ten feet from the house. She could see him now, leaning against a veranda post, one thumb hooked in his belt in a way that drew her attention to his lean hips.

"Nice evenin'," he said, blowing out a short puff of smoke.

She jerked her head up. "Yes."

"Somethin' botherin' you?"

"Bothering me? No."

"You left in kind of a hurry down there by the cart shed. I thought maybe you were frightened of Pinba and Gabby. I figured you might like to know you've nothing to worry about. They wouldn't hurt anybody on my run."

"I was not frightened," she said. *Not of what you think.*

His cheeks hollowed as he sucked on his pipe. "You looked pretty shook up to me."

"If I were overset, it was entirely due to the natives being—" She couldn't bring herself to say the word *nude* aloud to this man, and took refuge in obscurity. "In *puris naturalis.*"

"You mean buck naked?" She was too far away to see his eyes in the darkness, but she could hear the laugh in his voice.

"Yes," she said tersely, feeling her cheeks burn. She was glad it was dark.

"You'll get used to it."

"But I have no desire to get used to it—or to any of the other unsavory aspects of this

131

colony." She knew she sounded insufferably pompous and self-righteous, but she didn't care. It was as if she were using words as a kind of shield, a buffer, to keep as much distance as possible between herself and this disturbing man. "Circumstance might have forced me to live in Australia temporarily," she said loftily, "but I have no intention of forgetting that I am English. I will never surrender my gentility to your bush."

His lips curled away from his pipe. "Is that the way you see it? That if something's un-English then it must be unladylike? So while you might have to put up with life here—temporarily—you would never consider adapting to it?"

"Adapt to *this*?" She spread her hand in a wide arc, taking in not so much the pale, sun-dried hills and looming Flinders Ranges, but the very essence of life in Australia. "Of course I would never adapt to this. To do so would be to lose myself. My sense of who and what I am."

"Don't you mean *lower* yourself?"

She did, of course, but she wasn't about to go so far as to say it. "Even you must admit that there is a certain level of depravity and"—her lip curled as she remembered the bullockies—"vulgarity in the common Australian character."

"Depravity."

"That's right. Although I suppose it's hardly surprising, given the circumstances."

"Such as what, exactly?" He tapped his

pipe against the veranda post, knocking out the ashes that fell in a shower of sparks to be ground beneath the heel of his boot.

She found she could not continue to look at him and turned away, her arms crossed at her chest, to watch the rising moon. Big and round and quite breathtakingly lovely, it shone with an unearthly white light. She had never seen anything like it. "Well," she said slowly, searching for an appropriate example. The one she chose was unfortunate. "Take this continual exposure to native men and women in a state of complete—"

"Nudity," he supplied.

"Precisely. It cannot help but have a disastrous effect on the moral fiber of the colony's white inhabitants."

"Why?" he asked, his voice deceptively smooth. "Do you feel your moral fiber unraveling, Miss Davenport?"

"Me?" She swung back around, her arms dropping to her sides as she watched him step out of the shadows of the veranda and come at her, moonlight limning the hard planes of his face and causing the sun-bleached highlights in his tawny hair to glow like silver.

His hair was too long, she decided. It curled against his forehead and hung over his collar in the back, making him look rough and uncivilized. She noticed he had his shirt open at the neck, too; just a couple of buttons, but it was enough to show her the tanned, strong column of his throat. Enough to trigger dangerous tremors, way down low in her belly.

He came to a halt in front of her. "Why don't you just admit it?"

A wind blew up, flapping her skirts, wrapping them around the hard length of his leg. He was too close. She waited for him to step back, but he didn't. "Admit what?" she asked, her voice sounding oddly thick.

"That being here unsettles you. Only it's not for the reasons you try to pretend. It's because life here is too honest. Too fundamental. It strips away all those polite falsities you've always lived with, and now that you find yourself face-to-face with raw reality, you don't know how to handle it."

"No." She stared up into his lean, taut features. Against her will, her gaze fastened on his mouth, and she watched the dimples form in his cheeks as he spoke.

"Yes."

For one intense moment, they looked at each other. Then she sucked in a quick breath of air that was like a gasp and spun away from him. Away from the truth of what he was saying. Away from what she knew would happen if she let herself stay and be trapped by the moonlight and the heat of his big male body and the inevitability of her own unwilling response.

"Oh, God," she cried, hugging herself, unable to understand what was happening to her. "I don't belong here. Everything's too unfamiliar, too confusing, too wild. I wish I had never come here."

"So why did you? Why didn't you stay in Adelaide?"

134

"Why? Because I was desperate, that's why." She gave a harsh laugh that came out sounding suspiciously like a sob. "I've always worked as a private secretary. But most people seem to think impoverished gentlewomen should be governesses. So I thought I'd try becoming a governess."

She knew she shouldn't be saying these things to him, but at the moment she didn't care. "Only problem was, Adelaide is full of English governesses—*experienced* governesses. By the time I answered your sister's advertisement, I had begun to wonder if I was going to be able simply to keep a roof over my head, let alone earn enough to get back to England."

"Getting back to England is important, is it?"

She brought up her hand to dash her palm across her eyes, suddenly ashamed of just how badly she'd lost control of herself. "It's the most important thing in the world to me," she said quietly.

"Why?"

She turned to stare at him in surprise. "Because it's Home. It's where I belong. I could never be happy here."

He stood gazing down at her with a strange expression she found unsettling—as if he were looking inside her, seeing something she didn't want him to see. Something she didn't want to see herself. "I've always thought happiness is less a matter of where you are than who you are."

Amanda stared back at him, shocked by his wisdom and his understanding. She didn't want to let herself see this side of him. She wanted to go on thinking of him as uncouth and raw and ignorant. When he was like this—gentle and wise and compassionate, she realized just how dangerously attractive he truly was.

He reached out, unexpectedly, and ran the backs of his fingers down her cheek. She trembled with the disturbing feelings that his touch, his very nearness always seemed to arouse within her. She drew in a shaky breath that did nothing to ease the pressure in her chest. "I could never be happy here."

They stared at each other in silence for a long moment. The night air curled around them, unseasonably warm and heavy with the pungent scents of the Australian bush. "No," he said softly. "I don't suppose you could be."

This time, he was the one to look away. He turned toward the Flinders, lost now in the blackness of the night, and she thought she heard him sigh. "What did you want to talk to me about, anyway?"

For a moment she couldn't imagine what he was referring to. Then she remembered all she had intended to say to him about Liam and the bullockies and that bookkeeper, Campbell. Only, she didn't want to talk about it. Not now. "It can wait until later."

"You were bursting with righteous indignation about something when you tracked me down at the cart shed. Might as well get it over with."

"Very well. I have been wanting to talk to you about the children."

She sensed a subtle change in his attitude. "What about them?" he asked, his eyes narrowing. "Is there a problem with their lessons?"

"No. I think we're beginning to come to an understanding on that."

"Then what the hell's the matter?"

"Really, Mr. O'Reilly. I must protest this continued use of profanity—"

"Quit protesting and just spit out whatever it is you've got to say."

She felt her own irritation rise to match his. "Very well. Since you insist, I will." She sucked in a deep breath. "I do not believe it proper for these children to be constantly exposed to the men of doubtful character and reprehensible conduct who seem to frequent this station."

"Such as?" he asked in a dangerously silky voice.

"Your bookkeeper, for one." She flung her arm in the general direction of the office. "The man is a disgrace."

O'Reilly stared down at her. She could not begin to read the expression on his face. "So you think I should fire Campbell, do you?"

"Yes, I do."

He lifted his head, his gaze drawn toward something lost in the darkness of the night. "There's a small graveyard across the creek. Have you seen it?"

Amanda shook her head. "I've noticed it. But I haven't actually visited it. Why?"

"Next time you have a chance, I think you ought to go take a look at it. You'll see it contains three new graves. One's of a woman named Ellen Campbell, and beside her are the graves of her twin eight-year-old sons, Nathan and Mathew. They all died six weeks ago."

"Campbell's family?" Amanda said hoarsely.

"That's right. He came down with some kind of stomach sickness when he was in Melrose for supplies. Only instead of staying put, he came home so that Ellen could nurse him, and he ended up passing whatever he had on to the rest of his family. He survived it. They didn't."

"I didn't know," she whispered.

"No. You didn't." He swung his gaze back to her face. "Campbell's a good man. If he feels the need to drown his sorrow and his guilt in alcohol for a while, I reckon I can afford to give him the time and space to do it."

Amanda looked at the man beside her, seeing again a side of him she didn't want to see, didn't want to know about, didn't want to acknowledge. She cleared her throat and looked away.

"I can understand—even applaud your for-bearance when it comes to Mr. Campbell. But what of those two bullockies who came through this evening? Those men truly are degenerates."

He surprised her by laughing softly. "I don't know if I'd call Sweeny and Jessup degenerate, exactly. A bit wild and unwashed maybe. But not degenerate."

"Not degenerate? When they regale Liam

with tales totally unsuitable for one of his tender years—"

"Bullockies are famous for their yarnin'."

"—and allow him to drink intoxicating beverages?"

There was a pause. Then he said, "I don't expect you to understand this, Miss Davenport, but I happen to think it's better to allow a boy to taste alcohol, rather than forbidding him to touch it. Sweeny and Jessup might be a bit crude, but I don't think they'd ever let Liam do more than take a swig of whatever they've got."

"And you think a—*a swig or two* are acceptable?"

"Look, I know what drinkin' can do to a man in country like this. And it's precisely because I know it that I intend to make sure Liam grows up aware of what alcohol is like. That way, he's not going to build drinking up in his mind as something he can't wait to try, something he doesn't know how to handle, something he thinks he can use to prove he's a man."

"Is that why you took him into Hornbottom's hotel?"

"He told you that, did he?"

She had expected him to deny it. Now she almost gaped at him. "Is it true?"

"Yes." His mouth curled into a slow grin that let her know there was a lot more to this story than the little bit she'd been told.

"You're not going to explain it to me, are you?"

His grin widened. "Nope."

She stared up at his lean, handsome face and suddenly felt rocked by a confusing swirl of emotions she didn't understand and didn't want. The evening breeze fluttered his worn shirt against his hard chest and molded the sleeves around the work-toned muscles of his arms. He looked so big and strong and achingly, enticingly masculine, standing there in the moonlight, that she almost shuddered.

Suddenly desperate to reach the bright safety of the house, she swung away from him. "I don't understand you," she said. But what she meant was, *I don't understand myself. I don't understand what is happening between us. What almost happened here tonight.*

And I'm so terribly afraid of what will happen next.

Missy lay on her back in the hay and watched the dust motes floating lazily in a beam of late afternoon sunlight. The hay scratched her bare arms and sometimes gave her a rash, but she loved the way it rustled when she buried herself down in it, and she enjoyed the clean, dried-grassy way it smelled. It reminded her of long hot summer days and horses and secret meetings of the O'Reilly Raiders, as Hannah called them.

Liam thought they should be named the O'Reilly Warriors, but Hannah was bigger, and when Liam tried to argue with her about it, she punched him in the nose. So they called themselves the O'Reilly Raiders, and the hay barn was their secret headquarters, where they plotted new and awful ways to get rid of the latest governess. At least Liam and Hannah plotted. Missy mostly just listened.

"I finally got one," said Liam, sticking a straw in his mouth and pretending it was a pipe.

Hannah rolled over onto her stomach and kicked her feet in the air. "How big?"

"Ten feet."

"Get off it, Liam. How big?"

Liam threw his older sister a malevolent glare. "Well, five feet, at least." Then he grinned. "If she was scared of that goanna, wait till she finds this snake in her room at night."

"Li-am. You never caught no five-foot snake."

"Nope. Jacko caught it for me." Jacko was one of Sally's nephews who worked for Papa as a stockman. "It took him a few days, but he finally found one. He's got it in a bag in that big old hollow gum by the creek. When we're ready, I'll bring it up and hide it behind the kitchen. We'll turn it loose in her room after everyone's in bed."

Missy shifted uncomfortably. "I think it's mean."

Two similar sets of eyes, one brown, the other hazel, swung around to stare at her. "Of course it's mean," said Hannah, enunciating each word slowly and carefully, as if Missy didn't know English or something. "That's why we're doing it."

Missy hated it when Hannah talked to her in that tone of voice. Hannah thought that just

141

because Missy was little, she didn't understand things. Only Missy usually did understand; she just looked at things a little differently, that's all. "I don't think this gov'ness is as nasty as the other ones," she said stubbornly. "I think she's pretty. Especially when she smiles."

"When does she ever smile?" scoffed Liam.

"She smiles at me."

"Of course she does," said Hannah in disgust. "You gave her flowers." Hannah held her stomach and leaned over and gagged, like she was about to throw up.

"I felt sorry for her."

"Ha," said Liam. "You felt sorry for Miss Down, when we put sand in that cream she was always spreading all over her face."

"I did not! I never liked Miss Down. She used to thump me in the middle of the back with her knuckles whenever I pronouned a word wrong. It was Miss Macmillan I thought you were too hard on. She wasn't that bad. And after she stepped in that fresh cow pile you put beside her bed in the morning, she left."

Liam laughed. "That was a good one, wasn't it?"

Missy shook her head. She didn't like most of the governesses Aunt Hetty sent up from Adelaide; most of them were so pinched and sour and serious, they made everyone's life miserable until they finally went away again. But she didn't *resent* them, the way Liam and Hannah did.

Sometimes Missy thought maybe it was because of Mama. Missy had never known

Mama, so she didn't really miss her. But Hannah and Liam did. They didn't just miss Mama, they were angry with her for having gone away and left them. At least that's what Sally said when Liam and Hannah were mean to her. Sally said Missy had to try to understand that they hurt inside, and that's what made them try to hurt other people. But Missy wasn't sure she believed it. After all, Papa was never mean, and he must miss Mama, too. Although he never talked about Mama either. No one ever talked about Mama. And that made Missy sad, because she wished she knew more about her mama.

"Are you for us, or against us?" demanded Hannah, fixing Missy with a ferocious stare.

Missy sighed. "I'm with you."

Hannah nodded. "Good." She turned to Liam. "When do you want to do it?"

Liam smiled wide enough to show his missing tooth. "Tonight."

CHAPTER EIGHT

The flame of the coal oil lamp flickered and smoked, sending misshapen shadows dancing up the whitewashed bedroom walls.

It was late, and Amanda should have been in bed. But she felt oddly restless, unable to settle. Clutching her shawl close to her nightdress, she bent to adjust the lamp's wick.

143

Her gaze fell on the writing desk that had been her mother's, and she picked it up and sank into the chair, the desk held on her lap.

She hadn't used the desk since her arrival in Penyaka a week ago today. She had no botanical specimens to catalog, no letters to write. There was no one in England who would be looking for a letter from Amanda Davenport.

A melancholy sense of loneliness swept through her at the thought. She ran her fingers over the desk's surface, tracing the delicately inlaid design.

This desk and a few small pieces of jewelry were Amanda's only links to the woman who had died giving her birth. Her mother's death had left a void in Amanda's life, a sense of something lacking, something that would have made her more complete, more capable. Since coming to Penyaka, she had begun to think that if only she'd had a mother herself, perhaps she would have been better prepared for the task of taking care of the three O'Reilly children.

And they did need someone to care for them—not just teach them, the way their father seemed to think.

She knew O'Reilly loved his children fiercely; that wasn't the problem. She had watched him—surreptitiously—so many times this last week. Tucking Missy into bed at night. Playing chess with Liam or Hannah in front of the fire. Sitting out on the veranda with the three of them, laughing and talking as twilight descended on the surrounding bush. Yet she still sensed, somehow, that it wasn't enough. There was something wrong in this family. It seemed so strange that no one—not even the children—ever mentioned Katherine O'Reilly.

Sighing, Amanda set the desk on the round table and carried the lamp to her bedside. The night was cold, and she was glad to snuggle down beneath the heavy covers. But as she reached to twist off the lamp, it occurred to Amanda that without realizing it, at some point in the last week she had gone from wanting to control the children to wanting to help them. If she wasn't careful, she thought wryly, she might actually start to care for the little hellions.

Just the thought of it made her laugh softly to herself.

The fear penetrated her consciousness before the noise.

She sat up in bed, fuddled with sleep, blinded by the night. Her heart raced painfully in her chest, sending the blood pounding through her limbs so hard, they tingled. She sucked in quick, shallow breaths, her lips parted, her mouth dry. What was it?

She twisted wildly about, peering through the darkness at the door to the parlor, at the French doors to the veranda. Nothing. All were closed.

And yet something had awakened her. Something her body—or perhaps it was her unconscious—sensed as a threat, even if her mind remained unaware of it.

Then she heard it. A faint, rasping sound. A slither. She was not alone. Someone—*something* was in the room with her.

She fumbled around on her bedside table and found the matches. It took three tries before she managed to get one to strike.

Light flared, golden, wavering, dim. But bright enough to show her the long, fat brown snake slithering across her floor.

A brown snake.

She let out a quick, frightened gasp and almost dropped the match. Her hand shook so badly, she was afraid the flame might go out, but she managed to reach slowly, carefully, and light the lamp. It was difficult to do, since she didn't dare take her eyes off the snake in the process.

The lamp wick flared up, bright. As if startled by the sudden light, the snake halted in the middle of the room. It was so long, its body seemed to stretch halfway back to the door. As she watched, it swung around and raised its narrow, pointed, shiny black head to stare at her.

Amanda tried to swallow the choking ball of fear in her throat. "Mr. O'Reilly," she called. It came out as a hoarse croak.

He would never hear her. She edged to the far side of the bed, and tried again. "Mr. O'Reilly. Mr. O'Reilly? *Mister O'Reilly!*"

In the distance, a door banged. She heard a thud, and an instant later her own door flew open with so much force, it crashed into the wall behind it.

Patrick O'Reilly, big and naked, burst through the doorway. "What the hell?" His gaze swept from her to the snake. The snake reared up, its head swinging around to confront this new danger only a few feet from its flicking tongue. "Holy shit."

She didn't see the knife until O'Reilly raised his hand and sent the blade whistling through the air. She heard a vibrating *thwunk* as the tip bit into the wooden door frame on the far side of the room. The snake's thin body, minus its head, flopped onto the floor.

O'Reilly walked forward to stare down at the dead snake while Amanda, stunned, could only stare at him.

He had a magnificent body. Tall, lean, and broad shouldered, strong and yet graceful. Sun-bleached hair curled against a tanned neck. His back was brown, too, and strapped with muscles that rippled as he leaned over to inspect the dead reptile. His buttocks were taut, hard, and white, as white as his long, well-shaped legs. Amanda's breath left her body in a whoosh, and though the night was cold, she felt herself grow hot.

"I shouldn't have killed it," he said, and to her astonishment he actually sounded as if he regretted it. "It's just a black-headed python. They look like a brown snake, but it wouldn't have hurt you. They're harmless." He looked at her over his shoulder. "How did it get in here, anyway?"

She shook her head. "I can't imagine. All the doors were closed."

He straightened and turned to face her. She knew she should look away, but she could not. Against her will, her gaze roved over him. His chest was exquisitely defined by years of hard work, his stomach so hard, the ridges of muscle clearly delineated. And below that rose a large, proud male member that swelled even as she stared at it.

Her head snapped up and her gaze met his. A slow, lazy smile spread across his face and brought a gleam to his deep blue eyes. He didn't seem the least discomfited by his own nakedness. But he knew she'd been looking at him, knew she'd been admiring his body. Burning with embarrassment, she swung her head around and stared pointedly at the far wall.

"Mr. O'Reilly, your...your clothes."

"It doesn't bother me. Does it bother you?" She could hear the rich timbre of amusement in his voice.

"Yes, it does. There is a towel. By the washstand. If you would kindly..."

"Drape it around my strategic parts? All right." She heard a faint rustle. "Done."

She continued to stare at the wall.

"I'd lay my money Liam's behind this," he said.

She was so surprised, she forgot she had meant not to look at him. She swung around in time to see him bend over and pick up the dead snake. The towel lifted enticingly. "Liam?" she repeated in a squeaky voice.

"And Hannah, too, more than likely." He jerked his head toward the door as he bent again to retrieve his knife. "You don't see them, do you? Do you really think that under normal circumstances none of them would show up to see what all the shouting's about?"

Amanda glanced at the empty, darkened parlor. "Yes, you're right, of course. What a horrid thing to do. I suppose it was my reaction to the goanna the other day which gave them the idea."

"They'll decide it was a bloody stupid idea before I'm through with them," he said grimly.

"No." Heedless of both his virtual nakedness and her own nightdress, she swung her legs out of bed and stood up. "I do not want you to punish them."

One straight, dark brow quirked upward in silent amusement. "Why? Because you don't believe in *physical chastisement*? I'd have thought a week's exposure to my hell-bent brood would have modified your opinions on that."

"Of course not," she said haughtily, in blithe disregard of the vindictive delight she had taken in the physical punishment he had visited upon her tormentors after the ant incident.

He raised the limp, scaly body of the dead snake. "They deserve to have the seat of their trousers dusted good after a stunt like this, and you know it."

"Perhaps," she admitted. "But don't you see? They've done this to *me*. It's not right that you should be the one to punish them. I'm the one who should deal with it."

149

He took a step that brought him shockingly close to her. She stared up at him, her heart pounding in her chest, her lips parted. He was big and he was naked and he was in her bedroom in the middle of the night. If she reached out her hands, she could rest them flat against his bare chest. His face had taken on a peculiarly taut, heated look that she found oddly disturbing and yet fatally attractive at the same time. Her gaze settled on his lips. She'd never before realized how full they were, how sensual.

And it came to her in a hot, quivering rush of realization that she wanted to touch his sleek, muscled body. She wanted to hold his face between her hands and kiss his lips. She wanted to feel his arms around her, hear him whisper words of seduction in her ear. She wanted him. And it was only with an enormous effort of will that she kept herself from swaying toward him.

"So you want to handle it yourself?" he asked quietly. It was a moment before she realized he was talking about the children and their punishment.

She could not look him in the eye. Her hand crept up to her cheek and she turned away. "Yes," she somehow managed to say. "I must."

"All right."

She trembled, afraid he meant to close the distance between them once more, and not knowing how she would react if he did. Instead, he moved to the door. "Oh, by the way," he said, pausing half out the doorway.

She pivoted to face him. "Yes?"

He threw her a broad, wicked grin. "Your nightdress is unbuttoned."

"What?" She glanced down and saw to her consternation that he was right. The high collar of her nightdress often seemed to choke her at night, and unable to sleep, she had unfastened at least half the front placket. The nightdress might be modestly cut, with a high neck and long sleeves, but the material was worn and thin, and with the buttons undone it gaped open to reveal a shocking slice of her breasts.

Horrified, she gripped the edges of her nightdress together tightly in her fist. "Why didn't you tell me before?" she demanded. But when she looked up he was gone, leaving her towel, swaying slightly, on the door handle.

She heard his door shut across the parlor, but the house was not silent. There was a furtive whisper, the scuffling of small feet, then the sound of two more doors being carefully eased closed in the distance.

"Dear God," she whispered, lifting the towel from the handle and shutting her door against the night. "What is wrong with me? What is this place *doing* to me?"

She decided to punish the children for the snake incident by not punishing them at all. She wanted them to regret what they had done because they realized it was wrong, not because she had made them suffer for it.

In the schoolroom the next morning, they

watched her warily. They had obviously over-heard enough the night before to know that she had convinced their father to allow her to be the one to mete out their punishment. But beyond taking the edition of Frome's *Reptiles of the Southern Continent* down from the shelves and saying, "I thought we might study snakes this morning, since it seems to be a topic which interests you," she made no reference to the incident at all.

In the end, the Frome was probably a mistake, at least as far as Amanda was concerned. She had never realized there were so many poisonous snakes in the *world*, let alone that most of them were gathered together in the one continent upon which she had the misfortune to be temporarily residing.

"You're lucky it wasn't a carpet python," Christian Whittaker told her the following afternoon, when he joined her for tea on the veranda after Liam's lessons. "They can grow up to seven feet long."

"Yes, I know. That's the *Morelia bredli*, isn't it?" said Amanda, a quiver of amusement in her voice.

He slewed around in his seat to stare at her. "Why, yes. It is." His young face shone with enthusiasm. "Are you a student of reptiles, too, Miss Davenport?"

"Only reluctantly," she admitted, ashamed of herself for teasing him about a subject she was beginning to realize was his passion. "The children and I were looking at an edition of Frome today during lessons."

"Oh, Frome." He dismissed the expert with a wave of his hand. "He was well enough in his time. But I have been collecting and preserving specimens ever since I arrived and I have discovered a number of errors. What a pity Mr. O'Reilly decapitated your midnight visitor; with the head intact it would have made a nice addition to my collection."

"What a pity," agreed Amanda.

"In fact," he added, coloring endearingly, "I am considering contacting Frome's London publishers and offering to put together an updated edition for them when I return Home."

"That would be wonderful for you." Amanda smiled at him warmly. "H. B. Gibson and Sons, is it not? My father published his translations of Euripides with them."

There was a clattering of fine china as Mr. Whittaker set down his teacup and stared at her in astonishment. "Don't tell me your father was Angus Davenport?"

"Yes," said Amanda, flushing with pride. "You've heard of him?"

"But of course! I went to Cambridge myself, but who hasn't heard of Angus Davenport? A brilliant scholar. Absolutely brilliant."

Her smile broadened.

"I heard that in his will he endowed a series of lectures to be delivered annually in Oxford on the Athenian tragedians."

Amanda's smile disappeared. "Yes, he did." She turned to reach for the plate of scones. "Here, Mr. Whittaker; do have some more."

A skinny, slightly grubby brown hand closed over two of the scones before she could lift the plate. She glanced up and found herself staring into the swirled green-and-gold eyes of Liam O'Reilly.

Instead of snatching the plate away, she held it out to him. "Would you like some, Liam?"

He threw her a ferocious scowl but surprised her by murmuring, "Thank you," before he dashed down the long veranda and cut across the garden.

Amanda watched him go, and sighed. "I fear Liam bitterly resents the fact that I did not allow his father to punish him for putting that snake in my room."

"Resents it?" Christian Whittaker paused in the act of spreading strawberry preserves on his own scone to throw her a puzzled look. "I should think he would be grateful."

"But that's exactly why he does resent it." Amanda's gaze followed the boy as he tore up the sun-dried hillside, his dog at his heels. He looked so wild and free that, for a moment, she envied him. She smiled sadly to herself and turned to the man beside her. "It has given me an unfair advantage, you see."

Mr. Whittaker shook his head. "I'm afraid I don't understand."

She laughed softly. "That's because you're nothing like Liam O'Reilly."

Mr. Whittaker still looked confused. And it occurred to Amanda as she watched Liam disappear over the crest of the hill that she herself had more in common with the boy than she would care to admit.

Her eyes narrowed as she noticed a cloud of dust hanging heavily over the track to the northeast. "Someone is coming," she said, stepping to the edge of the veranda.

Christian Whittaker came to stand beside her and squint into the distance. "It's the bullockies," he said after a moment. "On their way back down to Port Augusta."

O'Reilly was in the office when he heard the crack of bullwhips and the clatter of iron-bound wooden wheels rattling over the stones in the dusty track. He sauntered out onto the stoop and watched Sweeny and Jessup pull up their teams, his gaze sharpening as he noticed the showy Englishman riding alongside them. Only it wasn't the man that interested O'Reilly so much as the bloodred Thoroughbred the man had on a leading rein.

"Whoa back, Blackie. Come here, Cranky." Sweeny looked up and gave O'Reilly a tobacco-stained grin. "G'day, mate."

"G'day." O'Reilly stepped out into the track, his attention focused on the dapper Englishman with oily dark hair and long Dundreary whiskers who was reining in his sleek black horse beside the lead cart. O'Reilly took in the man's dusty peg-top trousers and tight-waisted, full-skirted coat and let his breath out in a low whistle. "Who's the new chum?" he asked, nodding toward the stranger.

155

"Name's Lumley." Sweeny shifted his chew. "Some lord's son from Durham. Been staying with Cox."

O'Reilly's eyes narrowed as he focused on the big blood bay. That horse looked a hell of a lot like Hannibal Cox's bay stallion, Fire Dancer. Although O'Reilly couldn't imagine Cox letting go of a horse that could run like the New Zealand Thoroughbred.

"G'day," O'Reilly called, strolling forward to introduce himself. "You're welcome to a room in the house, if you want."

"That would be most sincerely appreciated," said Lumley as he swung out of the saddle and tried to shake the dust off his coat.

O'Reilly ran an appraising hand over the bay's withers. "Nice horse."

"Indeed he is." The Englishman slapped his tweed trousers, filling the air with more red dust.

"Reminds me of the colt Cox brought in from New Zealand last year."

"It's him, all right. Fire Dancer, out of Night Dancer."

"That a fact?" O'Reilly rubbed the big bay's nose. "The horse turn out to be touched in the wind or something? Last time I saw Cox, he swore he wouldn't trade this horse for an English earldom."

"He didn't trade him. I won him." The Englishman untied his bag from the saddle. "At cards."

O'Reilly's hand stopped its rhythmic motion. "Like cards, do you?" He grinned. "We'll have to have a game or two. After supper."

CHAPTER NINE

The Englishman was installed in the guest bedroom, while the bullockies pitched camp down by the creek again. As Amanda sat preparing the next day's lessons at her desk in the schoolroom, she could hear their laughter and good-natured swearing floating up through the gum trees.

Gradually she became aware of two other male voices, one low and controlled, the other high-pitched and raised in anger, coming from nearer at hand.

"Why not?" she heard Liam say. "You never complained about me spending time with them before. It's because of her, isn't it? I can't believe you'd do this."

Lifting her head, she glanced toward the bottom of the garden to see father and son standing just inside the lower gate. O'Reilly had his thumbs hooked in his back pockets. His stance was relaxed and easy, his response too quiet for her to hear. But she saw Liam hit out angrily, his frustrated swipe knocking the top off a nearby pink hollyhock. He spun about, still batting savagely at every offending piece of vegetation in his path, and stalked off toward the barns. Amanda smiled and went back to her lessons.

She hadn't met Mr. Lumley herself yet. Before the bullockies had reached the homestead that afternoon, she had deliberately said good evening to Mr. Whittaker and disappeared into the house. But she had heard about him, and she was very much looking forward to the presence of an English gentleman at supper this evening.

Conversation at the O'Reilly table usually ranged from such unsuitable subjects as the upcoming shearing season to the disgusting activities of the local swan hoppers, with the children encouraged to contribute or even interrupt without compunction. But tonight would be different. With someone like Mr. Lumley as a guest, she would be able to converse on a variety of genteel topics, such as regattas on the Thames, or the latest statements by the Opposition, or recent literary publications, such as Mr. Dickens's *Our Mutual Friend.*

Mr. O'Reilly, she thought with a smile of malicious satisfaction as she went to change into her best gown, would probably not enjoy the evening at all. She swiftly pinned up her hair and then added a delicate white fichu to soften the severe lines of her dress. The fichu was of real Horiton lace, and she rarely used it, since she would never be able to afford to replace it once it finally wore out. But tonight she was determined to look her best.

Smoothing the treasured lace, Amanda leaned forward to study her reflection in the plain wooden mirror that hung over her washstand. She was not particularly satisfied with the image that stared back at her. The problem was her hair, she decided. Frowning at it, she reached up and began to loosen it.

"The brandy is quite tolerable," said Lumley, smacking his lips and rolling the brandy glass back and forth between his thick fingers. "Especially when one considers where we are. It must be extraordinarily difficult to acquire good brandy here in the colonies."

O'Reilly tilted back his head against the tattered sofa and regarded the Englishman through narrowed eyes. "Sure as hell is." He reached for his own drink. "I've often suspected Hornbottom waters his liquor down with horse piss. But it adds a nice flavor, don't you think?"

Caught in the act of swallowing, Lumley choked and fell to coughing. O'Reilly grinned. He was just raising his own glass when he heard Miss Davenport's door open. She was later than usual coming out for supper. Probably getting all gussied up to meet her compatriot, he thought, his grin deepening. He was looking forward to watching her reaction to Lumley.

Then she moved forward into the circle of light thrown by the fire, and O'Reilly's hand stopped halfway in the act of bringing his drink up to his mouth.

Shit.

Her dress wasn't particularly attractive; the dull gray-and-white-striped satin was depressing and it was made too high at the neck. But she'd added a pretty lace thing around her shoulders, and she'd done something to her hair. She still had it pulled back into a chignon, but she'd loosened it somehow, so that it framed her face more gently. She'd even let a few wisps hang down to curl against her cheeks. The fire caught the loose strands and set them aglow.

He didn't like the effect that hint of softness and femininity had on him. He'd already noticed she was a damn fine-looking woman, but he'd never seen her like this, deliberately making herself attractive. Hell, she didn't even loosen her hair for her chummy little teas on the veranda with Whittaker. For some reason, it annoyed him all to hell that she'd gone out of her way to look attractive for a pasty-faced, pretentious pom like Lumley.

He set down his drink and stretched to his feet. "There you are, Miss Davenport. May I present Mr. Robert Lumley? From Durham."

O'Reilly watched her full lips curl into one of her rare smiles. She held out her hand and he thought, *Bloody hell, she sure didn't hold out her hand to me when I picked her up that day in Brinkman.* Beside him, Lumley also rose to his feet and had his own hand almost extended when O'Reilly added, "Miss Davenport is my children's governess."

"Governess?" repeated Lumley, his bushy eyebrows shooting up. "Well, imagine that. She joins you at mealtime, does she? How quaintly provincial." He touched her hand, but briefly, and gave her the curtest of bows.

O'Reilly watched the smile fade from Miss

160

Davenport's lovely lips, and he felt a spurt of anger. The anger didn't surprise him. The Englishman was a pompous ass. What puzzled him was the sense of protectiveness that welled up along with the anger.

But he should have known Amanda Davenport was capable of taking care of herself. She stiffened a moment, then relaxed, her forehead crinkling as if in thought. "Lumley, did you say? We had a butler named Lumley, once. I believe he was from Durham as well. I wonder if you are by any chance related?"

Mr. Lumley's eyes bulged. His magnificent Dundreary whiskers worked back and forth, but not a sound issued from his open mouth.

"Supper ready," announced Chow, bowing in the doorway.

The children scrambled for the table, and O'Reilly took advantage of the chaos to lean close to Miss Davenport and whisper under his breath, "Did you really have a butler named Lumley?"

Her candid gray eyes met his, and a deliciously mischievous smile he hadn't seen before curled her lips. "We never even had a butler."

Later that night, Amanda jerked her brush through her thick hair, her strokes quick and angry, her thoughts in turmoil.

She remembered the eager anticipation with which she had earlier dressed for supper, and felt like a fool. So much for an interlude

161

of polite, sophisticated conversation. Ha. Robert Lumley's position as O'Reilly's guest might have required him to sit at the same table as his host's governess, but it seemed that no power on earth could make him condescend to talk with her, or even look at her.

But O'Reilly had looked. All evening she had been conscious of his lounging in his chair at the far end of the table, a heated intensity to his gaze as he stared at her. He'd looked at her like that before, she knew, but briefly, and always when they were alone.

Tonight he hadn't been able to take his eyes off her. At times she'd had the distinct impression he was picturing her not as she was, sitting at table in her prim gray-and-white-striped satin, but as he'd seen her before. With her skirts thrown up around her waist or her nightshirt unbuttoned.

She felt her body grow warm and tingly just at the thought.

Her hand tightened around the brush handle and dropped. *Admit it,* she told herself. *You didn't dress so carefully or loosen your hair tonight for some unknown Englishman passing through.* That had been only an excuse. An excuse to make herself more attractive to Patrick O'Reilly. Because she had wanted him to look at her. She wanted O'Reilly to look at her the way a man looks at a woman.

And she had succeeded. Far better than she'd expected.

"Good Lord," she whispered to the woman in the mirror. "What have you done?"

And exactly what, she wondered, was she going to do now? Because there was no going back. Something had altered between them tonight. Something subtle and unspoken, but nonetheless real.

She flipped all her hair forward over her left shoulder and began braiding it for the night. The unexpected sound of male voices coming from the parlor made her pause, her head tilted, listening. She heard glass clink against glass. Someone laughed. A whirling sound, like a deck of cards being shuffled, followed, and a mysterious clacking, as if something were being stacked.

She told herself to ignore it, that it was none of her business, but she could not. She heard Patrick O'Reilly's rich, deep laugh, almost as if he were tempting her. She could resist no longer.

Quickly tying off her hair, she shrugged into her wrapper. She started to open the door, hesitated, and reached over to extinguish the lamp first. Back at the door, she turned the handle carefully and eased the door open a tiny crack.

The scene that met her eyes was like something out of a Bosch painting of sin and iniquity. Four men sat huddled around the cedar table in the center of the room. Smoke swirled slowly on an unseen updraft, giving an otherworldly, almost sinister cast to the dim lamplight. Brandy fumes hung heavy in the air; Amanda could see a glass half-filled with the thick golden liquid beside each man's elbow.

As she watched, the man with his back to her—Sweeny, she realized—emptied his glass and reached to refill it from the bottle that stood near at hand.

The other bullocky—Jessup, she thought O'Reilly had called him—was on Sweeny's left. On his right sat Mr. Lumley, his oiled black locks gleaming in the lamplight. O'Reilly himself faced her. He held a deck of cards in his hands, and as she watched, he sliced the deck in two and sent the halves whirling together and then snapping back in a startlingly professional shuffle.

"Draw poker, gentlemen?" he said, the stem of his pipe clamped tightly in his teeth. He never raised his eyes from the other men, never glanced her way. But she saw a dimple wink in his tanned cheek, and in the same, pleasant, even voice, he added, "Unless you'd care to suggest a different game, Miss Davenport?"

Amanda jumped and slammed her door.

O'Reilly reached his hands high over his head and gave a long, back-unkinking kind of stretch. The rising sun threw rectangles of clear, bright light across the floor of the adjacent dining room. Christ, it had been a long night. But profitable. Very profitable. Not only had he won the stallion, but a tidy sum of cash, too. He smiled and pushed back his chair.

"Good game," he said, stretching to his feet. "Thanks, gentlemen. We'll have to do it again sometime."

Lumley, his oily hair hanging in frantic clumps against his forehead, muttered something obscene and stumbled off toward the guest room. O'Reilly looked at Jessup and shrugged. The two bullockies stretched, belched, and farted, and took themselves off.

Whistling softly to himself, O'Reilly stacked the banknotes and coins that littered the table in front of him. The sound of a door opening made him look up.

Miss Amanda Davenport paused just inside the room, her glorious auburn hair scraped back once again into that uncompromising knot he hated. She held her shawl clutched around her thin shoulders, and she had her mouth screwed into that tight grimace he also hated.

Whatever impulse had led her to loosen her hair last night, she was obviously regretting it now. She looked determined to pretend it hadn't happened, determined to act as if he hadn't had a glimpse of that other Miss Davenport—what he'd come to think of as the *real* Amanda. It was as if she actually were two women, he decided, watching her now. One determinedly uptight and frigid: a disapproving and ostentatiously moral English gentlewoman. But the other...

It was the other woman who intrigued him and attracted him more than he wanted to admit. The repressed, hidden woman who wore a red satin petticoat and a gaudy Chinese silk wrapper and scratched dogs behind their ears. He could practically count the rare glimpses he'd had of her... That night in

165

the garden when she'd been so delightfully rattled by her encounter with the Aborigines. And again in her room, when he'd been as naked as a man could be, and her body had quivered and yearned toward him even as she forced herself to turn away.

Well, she wasn't quivering today. She was stiff with outrage. He saw her gaze travel from the pile of empty bottles to the splattered spittoon on the floor—Jessup and Sweeny tended to miss after a few hours of throwing down drinks—to the cards spilled across the tabletop. When she got back to his own unshaven and probably disheveled person, her lips were pressed so tightly together, he was surprised they didn't squeak in protest.

"Mornin', Miss Davenport." He gave her a big grin. "Hope we didn't keep you awake last night."

She took three steps forward, stopped, and threw a quick glance at the children's bedrooms, as if to make certain their doors were still closed. "*Mister* O'Reilly," she hissed, her voice low. He hated it when she called him *Mister* like that—as if she were according him an honor he didn't deserve. It really set up his back. "*Mister* O'Reilly, have you no thought for your children?"

Slowly, deliberately, he folded the pile of banknotes in his hand and stuffed them into his pocket. "Course I do. Why do you think we played in here, rather than in the dining room, where we might have kept 'em awake?"

She turned so white, he figured she must have

laced her stays too tight. "I am speaking, sir, of the example you are setting for them. You have been gambling and drinking *all night.*"

He ran his hand over his beard-roughened jaw. "Yeah. Well, it took longer than I figured."

"To do what? Fleece your guest?"

He really was in no mood for this. His head hurt like hell, and his mouth tasted as if a possum had died in it last week. "Come on," he coaxed, propping one hip up on the edge of the table. "I didn't *fleece* the Honorable Mr. Robert Lumley." He gave her a broad grin. "I just won his horse and beat some of the arrogance out of him. After the way he treated you at supper last night, I wouldn't think you'd make such a fuss."

She plucked at the fringe on her shawl. "In England, guests are not made to sit at table with the governess."

He knew she was acting so prickly because she regretted letting her guard down last night, but he could not believe she'd defend that pompous ass. "No? Well in the bush, they are."

She bent one elbow and propped her hand up on her hip. She had such nice, slim hips. And a great backside, too, as well as those full, luscious breasts he'd glimpsed through the open placket of her gown the other night. He smiled at the memory.

She couldn't know what he was grinning about—thank God. But she obviously knew it wasn't anything she liked. Her eyes narrowed. "Just as it is the custom in the bush to take nine-year-old boys into the local pub for a drink?" she demanded.

So they were back to that, were they? He blew out a long, exasperated breath. "Look, lady, I'm as drunk as a red-back spider in a whorehouse piss pot, and twice as ornery. Don't start on me."

He could practically hear the starch crackle and the whalebones stiffen as she drew herself up like an affronted prickly pear. "*Mister* O'Reilly. More profanity?"

He pulled back his lips in a smile that showed his teeth. "Why not? It goes with the gamblin' and the drinkin', doesn't it?"

"I would not know," she said in her loftiest, most insufferably condescending manner. "Not being addicted to vice myself."

"I reckon that's your problem right there."

"I beg your pardon?"

He pushed away from the table. "The way I see it, life must be mighty dull without a bit of vice livenin' things up every once and a while." He sauntered toward her and didn't stop until his thighs pressed against her crinolined gown. He knew it rattled her when he got too near her, and he did so love to shake her up, even though he knew it was a dangerous game he played, and one he couldn't clearly see the end of.

If he pushed her too hard, he knew she was liable to leave. But then, a part of him wanted her to leave. Wanted to scare her away from him.

"Tell me, Miss Davenport," he asked, drop-

168

ping his voice to a whisper. "Don't you find your life dull?"

She stared up at him, her lips parted, her breath escaping in a long sigh that left her body trembling. He let his eyes rove over the features of her face. Her large, clear gray eyes fringed with thick lashes. The high, wide cheekbones. The full mouth that was surely made for something besides censorious frowns and petty moralizing. A mouth like that was made for pleasure.

And it came to him that, as badly as he wanted her to leave, he also wanted to kiss that mouth—had wanted to kiss it for days. But he wanted more than that. He wanted to strip away this ugly old maid's dress of hers and reveal the vital, beautiful woman beneath. He wanted to shake her up, wake her up. He wanted to make her laugh, sigh, moan. He wanted this woman.

He saw the pink tip of her tongue peek out, and watched as it slid along her full lower lip. "If..." She stopped and swallowed, the muscles of her slender white throat cording with effort. "Even if my life were dull, I would not seek the remedy in vice."

When she wasn't preaching, she had a nice, husky voice that by itself would be enough to make a man hard, if he weren't already. A voice like that came from someplace deep inside a woman.

A voice like that could throb with passion.

He gave her a slow, lazy smile. "You know what I think, Miss Davenport? I think you're a fraud."

Her delicate brows snapped together. "A *fraud*?"

"That's right." He splayed his hand against the wall beside her and leaned into it. "I think that somewhere, buried beneath all that starch and whalebone and those prissy governess ways of yours, is another woman you don't want anyone to see."

"Don't be ridiculous," she said, twisting her head away. But he noticed the telltale blush of color that tinged her cheeks, and she would not look him in the eye.

He bent toward her, close enough to see the flecks of black that shot out from her pupils like sooty sparks in the gray of her irises. "A woman who's soft, not hard. A woman who's passionate, not prudish." His voice took on a silken edge. "A woman with a secret craving for vice."

"No," she whispered, her hand creeping up to grasp the meager lace collar of her prim gown. She sucked in a quick breath of air and her breasts lifted. God, she had nice breasts. He could imagine how they'd feel in his hands. Warm and heavy and full. He knew what they'd taste like, too. And he knew the kind of breathy, erotic noises she'd make when he sucked one of their dusky peaks into his mouth.

"Yes," he said.

His breath stirred a rebellious strand of hair that fell in an almost frivolous curl against her forehead. Her head swiveled back around to look at him, although she didn't say anything. They stared at each other for a long moment. He dipped his head. Close enough to kiss her, although he didn't try because he knew she wasn't ready for that yet. "Yes," he said again, his lips hovering over hers. "And I'm going to prove it to you."

Then he pushed off from the wall and left her there, clutching her shawl to her heaving breasts and staring after him.

CHAPTER TEN

Amanda stood with one arm wrapped around a veranda support, her gaze fixed on the Ranges turning blue and purple as the western sky whitened toward evening. She sucked in a breath of crisp, dry air scented with all the elusive fragrances of the bush, and let it out with a sigh.

It was as if the haunting beauty of this ancient land stirred her soul, she thought; as if it struck at some wild, lonely chord deep within her that she'd thought long dead. As if the sheer, humbling, frightening timelessness that pervaded this place were calling her, tempting her. The way O'Reilly tempted her.

I'll prove it to you.

His low, rough voice was there, whispering with the wind that rustled the dry leaves. Taunting her, exposing her for what she really was.

She squeezed her eyes shut, her grip on the post tightening. Oh, God, how had he known? What had she done, what had she said, how had she betrayed herself? Until coming here, she'd honestly believed she'd overcome her weakness, left it behind as part of the hidden, shameful past. She'd believed herself to have become exactly as she appeared to the world: prim, respectable, ruthlessly controlled.

Yet this uncouth Australian, this convict's grandson with his wild, irreverent ways and healthy, virile body had awakened what she'd thought long dead. Exposed her for what she really was.

A chorus of voices broke the relative stillness of the bush. Amanda looked up, her eyes squinting against the glare as she scanned the evening sky. It was a sound she had learned to recognize as the homecoming call of the great flocks of corellas that came flying in to roost for the night in the line of gums along the creek bed.

She always heard them before she saw them—hundreds of them, screeching and honking almost like geese. Suddenly, the sun caught the sweep of their snowy feathers and they appeared like a great, noisy white sail, billowing through the clear sky. Her breath clogged her throat with awe.

"Missy said I'd probably find you out here."

She whipped around to discover Patrick O'Reilly watching her from the corner of the house. She had not heard his approach. He could move as silently as Sally when he wanted, a trick she found unsettling.

He strolled forward to stand beside her at the edge of the veranda and gaze up at a sky now filled with thousands of the chattering, darting white birds. Side by side, they watched silently as the corellas fluttered and squawked around the graceful, white-barked limbs of the gums. She did not glance at him again, but she remained intensely aware of his body beside hers, of the heat of his nearness.

She was conscious of a disturbing sense of intimacy in the sharing of this moment of natural splendor and beauty. To break it, she said, "Did you wish to speak to me?"

He nodded, his attention seemingly focused on the gums down by the creek, their branches glistening white with row after row of jostling, preening corellas. "It's about this morning. I—"

"Please, Mr. O'Reilly," she said hastily, her hands gripped together in front of her. "I would rather not talk about it."

He swung his head to look at her. "No. Hear me out. I just want to say I'm sorry. I was out of line. I know I was drunk, but I still shouldn't have said what I did."

They stared at each other. She found herself oddly disconcerted by his words. Disconcerted, and... She tried to define what she was feeling and realized with a sense of shock that it was disappointment. Heaven help her, she thought with despair. She was in far worse straits than she'd realized.

"I should probably apologize for my own behavior this morning," she said stiffly. She had never found it easy to apologize. "We seem to bring out the worst in each other. I must have sounded insufferably hoity-toity."

He tilted his head to slant a glance up at her from beneath his hat brim, and she saw he was smiling. "Do you ride?"

It was the last thing she had expected him to say. "I beg your pardon?"

"Can you ride a horse?"

"Yes. Why?"

"There's a water hole a few miles from here that's fed by a natural spring the Aborigines say never runs dry. It's called Cadnowie. I was plannin' on ridin' out there later this week with Missy to take a look at it, and I thought you might like to come with us."

"Oh, but I couldn't."

"Why not?"

"I have lessons—"

"We'll leave after lessons. Take a picnic supper."

"My preparations..."

He grinned at her. "You can't really ride, is that it?"

"Of course I can ride," Amanda said indignantly, turning away with something perilously close to a flounce. "I shall be ready on the day of your choosing."

Alone in her room that night, Amanda shook out her old riding habit and held it up to the lamplight. It was a good seven or eight years out of fashion, with a narrow skirt and a jacket that closed down the front with small buttons. But the hunter-green cloth was unworn, the collar and cuffs of fine black linen, and there was even a jaunty black gros-grain cravat.

A thrill of excitement shot through her as she lifted the beaver hat with its slightly crumpled green gauze veil. She set the hat at a rakish angle on her head and held the riding habit up against her body as she twisted to face the washstand mirror. A flushed, animated stranger from out of the past stared back at her.

I'll prove it to you.

She spun away from the mirror, the dress crushed in her arms, her heart pounding hard and fast. She should never have agreed to this expedition. For one wild moment she considered telling O'Reilly she'd changed her mind. Except that Hannah and Liam had announced they were going, too, and Friday had already been set as the day. She couldn't back out now without losing face before the children. And she couldn't afford to do that.

She took off the hat and set it carefully aside. She was being ridiculous, she told herself. It was a simple family outing. She was excited to be given a chance to ride again, and she was curious to see this water hole.

She had nothing to fear.

The next day, Amanda decided she had postponed the inevitable long enough, and gave the girls their first piano lesson.

"I still don't understand why I have to learn to play the silly thing, when Liam doesn't," grumbled Hannah as she followed Amanda and Missy to the dining room, where a beautiful inlaid mahogany piano stood gathering dust in a corner.

Amanda stifled a sigh. "Hannah, we have been through all of this already, at least a dozen times. First of all, it is not a 'silly thing,' it's a piano, and a very lovely one at that. Secondly, you are a female, and whether you like it or not, wearing trousers and cutting your hair won't change the fact that, someday, you will be a lady. And ladies play the piano."

When Hannah answered her only with silence, Amanda turned to the instrument and carefully folded back the cover to reveal the gleaming row of ivory keys. "There. Let's hope it's in tune."

"Papa has Mr. Hornbottom from the Brinkman Inn come out once a year and tune it," said Missy.

Amanda glanced at the little girl in surprise. "Does your father play?"

Missy shook her head, her blond curls sweeping back and forth across her shoulders. "No."

A succession of clear notes floated through the room as Amanda ran her fingers lightly up and down the keys. The instrument certainly sounded in tune. But then, Amanda had never been a particularly musical person. She had always hated her own piano lessons, and practiced as seldom as she could get away with it.

"Why don't you play first, Missy?" She adjusted the stool and lifted a yellowing pile of sheet music from a nearby shelf. "What were you practicing when your last governess left?"

"That one," said Missy, reaching for it. "Aunt Hetty told me once that this was her favorite piece, when she was learning." Missy hopped up on the stool and set the music on the stand. "She learned on this piano, too, you know."

Amanda glanced up from the music she'd been sorting. "Oh?" she said, trying to sound casual. "This was your aunt's piano?" Somehow, this precious instrument—so much a symbol of any gentlewoman's claim to good breeding—did not fit with the image Amanda had formed of O'Reilly's childhood. But then, neither did the books in the library, she reminded herself.

Missy swung her short legs back and forth. "Well, sort of. It was my grandmother's. Papa brought it here from Victoria, after Grandfather died. It's because of Grandmother that Papa keeps it tuned and wants us to learn to play it."

The brittle pages in Amanda's hands crackled as her fingers tightened around them. She

177

knew she shouldn't ask, but she couldn't seem to help herself. "Your mother didn't play?"

It was Hannah who answered, her voice oddly low and harsh. "Oh, she played all right."

Amanda looked at the girl's tight, strained face. "Then I should think you'd be anxious to learn to play. Like your mother."

Hannah's head reared back, her nostrils flaring, and Amanda knew she had just made a serious mistake. "Why?" Hannah practically spat out the word. "So I can be like her? Don't you see? I don't *want* to be like her."

"Because she was a lady?" Amanda asked quietly, wishing she understood what tormented this strange, unhappy girl.

"Yes. And do you know what she is now? She's some Frenchman's mistress. His whore."

Amanda gasped. *"Hannah."*

Hannah slammed her palms down on the keys, the discordant crash shattering the taut atmosphere of the dining room as she flung herself away from the piano.

"Hannah, wait," Amanda called, starting after her. Then she noticed Patrick O'Reilly, quietly watching them from just inside the parlor doors.

He stood with his thumbs hooked in his belt, his hat brim pulled low over his eyes. Amanda faltered to a halt. She wasn't sure how long he had been there, but something about his coiled, controlled stance left her in no doubt that he had heard everything Hannah had just said.

Halfway across the room, Hannah herself drew up, her chest lifting on a quickly indrawn breath when she caught sight of her father.

A muscle leapt along O'Reilly's tightened jaw as he stared at his daughter. "You'll apologize to Miss Davenport," he said, his voice surprisingly calm and level.

Hannah faced him, her shoulders square, her head up. "Why should I? It's true. We all know it. Why shouldn't she?"

Amanda felt her heart pound uncomfortably in her chest. If she had ever spoken like that to her own father, he'd have struck her. But O'Reilly never raised his hand, just said quietly, "You'll apologize for your language."

They stared at each other, father and daughter, the air thick with the energy of their strong emotions. Once Amanda had thought this girl looked nothing like O'Reilly. Now she could see the resemblance all too clearly. It was there in the glittering intensity of their eyes, in the stubborn strength of their tightened jaws, in the fierce determination of their powerful wills.

"I won't apologize."

"Then I think your mouth has an appointment with a bar of soap."

"Yes, sir," said Hannah, and followed him to his room, her head still held high.

Left alone in the middle of the dining room, Amanda swung around to meet Missy's troubled gaze. "Do you still want to play?" Amanda asked, feeling oddly shaken and disturbed. "Or shall we leave it for another day?"

179

"I'll play."

"All right." Amanda went to stand beside the piano again, and turned Missy's music for her. She tried to keep her attention on the progression of the notes, on the positioning of the little girl's fingers as she hesitantly worked her way through the simple piece.

But Amanda's attention kept wandering. Partially, she knew, it was because she was so terribly aware of the drama that was doubtless still continuing between O'Reilly and his daughter in the other room.

But more than anything, she couldn't seem to forget Hannah's strange, awful words. Or the look on O'Reilly's face when his daughter called her mother a Frenchman's whore.

Two days later, the projected outing to Cadnowie took place.

By the time Amanda changed her clothes after lessons, they were waiting for her, the three O'Reilly children and their father, by the front gate.

The sun beat down warm and gay and oddly healing on the shoulders of Amanda's riding jacket as she walked toward them. She was so conscious of her unaccustomed finery that she felt nervous and shy and maybe just a little bit proud.

The three children were already on their horses: Liam on his roan, Hannah astride a nervous, white-socked black, and Missy on a white pony. O'Reilly himself stood with one foot idly propped on the mounting stone, his elbow on his bent knee, the reins of two horses dangling through his fingers.

At the tap of her boots on the flagged path he turned, his head coming up. She enjoyed the look on his face. The quick widening of his eyes in surprise, followed by a sparkle of admiration and a slow heat she recognized as desire.

Secretly, she had hoped for this reaction. Only now that she had it, she found herself oddly unsettled, and her step faltered as she reached the gate.

"Gosh, Miss Davenport," said Missy on an awed expulsion of breath. "You're *beautiful*."

Jerking her gaze away from O'Reilly, Amanda smiled up at the little girl. "Why, thank you, Missy." As long as the children were with them, she reminded herself, she had nothing to worry about. She ran her hand down the pony's nose. "Your pony's lovely. What's her name?"

"It's a he," said Missy. "His name is Ivory." She nodded to the two riderless horses. One was the big chestnut Amanda had often seen O'Reilly riding; the other, a sleek black, had been fitted with a sidesaddle. "Papa brought Calypso for you. He says she's a real sweet goer and she's so well mannered that you can't go wrong with her, even if you're as bad a rider as Mr. Whittaker."

O'Reilly swore under his breath and ducked his head, but Amanda knew he was hiding a

181

laugh. "Heck, Missy. You weren't even supposed to hear that, let alone repeat it."

Missy giggled while Amanda laughed out loud. She suddenly felt carefree, happy. She gathered the black mare's reins and went quite still as O'Reilly stepped behind her.

"Let me help you up."

He was so close, his big male body seemed to surround her. His breath brushed her cheek, moister than the wind, warmer than the spring sun. For one wild moment she let herself imagine what it would be like to feel his arms close around her. To turn and spread her hands against his hard, broad chest. To open her mouth beneath his kiss.

Shuddering, she inhaled the scent of the bush and the horses, and barely managed to answer. "Thank you."

She twisted sideways, expecting him to give her a leg up. Before she could raise her foot, his hands closed around her waist and he lifted her into the saddle as effortlessly as he had swung her down from the wagon that first day. She automatically held on to the reins and hooked her knee around the saddlebow, but her hands clutched at the tensed strength of his upper arms. And forgot to let go.

Her breath caught as she stared down at his lean, taut face. His eyes were so blue, she thought; as blue as the brutal Australian sky. She could see the creases in his cheeks where his dimples would appear when he laughed or talked. She watched him swallow, felt the tremor that ran through him. And for one

182

intense moment their gazes locked and an almost palpable tension leapt between them, filling the air with a hungering need that was nonetheless real for being unspoken.

And she thought, even with the children here, she still was not safe. Not from the effect he had on her. Not from this thing that was between them.

Then he dropped his hands from her sides and turned toward his horse, and she jerked her gaze away from him, adjusted her skirt, fiddled with the reins—anything to keep from looking at him again.

"Ready?"

She lifted her head to find him astride his big chestnut, his gaze obviously assessing her seat. "I'm ready. And you needn't watch me as if you expect to see me tumble off Calypso here at any moment. I told you I know how to ride."

His mouth relaxed into a grin. "I hope so. I'm afraid there's not a whole lot of grass left out there to cushion you if you do fall."

"Huh," said Amanda, and touched her heel to the black's side.

For some reason she had expected that they would ride along the creek bed. Instead, O'Reilly struck out almost due south, following a trail that climbed the ridge behind the house, then snaked across wild, undulating country of cracked red rock and bare earth and scattered, twisted trees. The sky above burned a blue more vivid than anything she'd ever seen in England, but the breeze blowing down off the mountaintops was cool and fresh.

"It's lovely riding out here," she said when the children trotted on ahead and she found herself alone with O'Reilly.

She watched a faint flicker of surprise pass over his features. "I've always enjoyed it. Unfortunately, it's damned easy to lose your way if you don't know the bush. You don't ever want to be out here by yourself." He cast an appraising sideways glance at her. "Where'd a woman with your background learn to ride so well, anyway?"

She was absurdly pleased to discover that he hadn't found her lacking as a horsewoman. "My uncle was the squire of a village not far from Oxford," she told him. "He kept a horse for me when I was young."

Thinking of the lush green dells of England, she felt a swift pang of homesickness seize her, almost taking her breath away. She shifted her gaze from the man beside her to the wild, desolate land stretching out around her.

"Are your parents dead, then?" he asked.

"Yes." She stared at the dusty ground visible between the mare's twitching black ears. "My father died five years ago. I never knew my mother; she died when I was born."

She expected him to say, "I'm sorry," which was the traditional, polite response. Instead, he said, "So why didn't you go to your uncle? When your father died, I mean."

"Even if charity is freely given," said Amanda quietly, "it's still charity."

184

"I can't imagine you as anyone's drudge. You might dress the part, lady, but you sure as hell don't act it."

She should have been offended. Instead, she was surprised into a laugh. "Actually, I was most fortunate in my previous employers. The Blakes always treated me with unfailing respect."

"And how long were you with them?"

"Four years. Before that, I had a position with Lord and Lady Preston."

Something in her voice made him look at her sharply. "You weren't as fortunate with the Prestons, I take it?"

A gurgle of laughter escaped her lips. "I was fired. I'm afraid I threw a pot of ink at Lady Preston." She sobered quickly, feeling her cheeks grow hot at the memory and wondering what had possessed her to tell him that. But when she risked a sideways peek at him, she found his lips curling up into a lazy smile that brought a quick heat to her belly. She jerked her gaze away and watched the three children trotting ahead of them.

"I'm glad you warned me." His voice was warm and teasing. "I hadn't pegged you as the violent type. And seeing as how you're my governess rather than my secretary, in my case it'd probably be a globe you'd choose to lob at me."

She felt the flush in her cheeks deepen. "I do not often lose my temper."

"Huh," he said, as if he didn't believe her. "So why'd you decide to work as a secretary rather than a governess? That's what most women who found themselves in your position would have done, isn't it?"

She swung her head to look at him. "It's...difficult to explain."

"Try."

She sucked in a deep breath, and let it out slowly. The answer she usually gave was that she'd known what governesses' lives were like, and she hadn't wanted that. But she could hardly say such a thing while she worked as a governess in this man's house. So she told him the other reason. "My education is better than that given to most men. I didn't see why my employment opportunities should be limited simply by the fact that I happened to have been born a female."

She expected him to laugh. Most men would have laughed. But he just looked at her in that still, silent way he had. And suddenly she was afraid that he saw too much, that she'd said too much.

After that they rode in silence except for the creak of saddle leather and the clomp-clomp of hooves and the swish of the horses' tails slapping at flies. They cut across rolling, sunburned tableland dotted with widely scattered red and white gums, belts of stringy barks, and a few sheoaks. Then they rounded a hill and suddenly Amanda found herself facing a jagged escarpment that thrust up from the arid plain, the red sandstone face buckled and broken and eroded by time. At its base nestled a still pool of glistening water shaded by the spreading branches of a big coolabah tree and a few ghost gums mixed with acacias.

By English standards, the vegetation was not lush. The trees and few scattered bushes were gray-green and scraggly, the grass golden and dying, the gums drooping. It only seemed verdant in contrast to the surrounding hills and the jagged red rock face rising above it. The effect was breathtaking.

Reining in beside the suddenly silent and subdued children, Amanda felt the strange power of this place creep over her. Its power, and its peace. It reminded her of the awe that always overcame her whenever she stepped inside an ancient Norman or Gothic church in England. Here was that same sense of holiness, of ancient mystery. Only more pure, more immediate, more natural. The very air seemed to vibrate with an inexplicable, transcendent spirituality.

"The Aborigines call it Cadnowie," said O'Reilly quietly, swinging out of his saddle and coming around to help her dismount.

She slid down into his arms. "Is this your land?" she asked in an oddly hushed voice.

"Yes. But I tell my shepherds to avoid it. It's a sacred place."

"To the Aborigines, you mean? Should we even be here?" She glanced around, suddenly nervous. Liam and Hannah were unsaddling the horses, while Missy was talking to Ivory and pulling up handfuls of grass to hold beneath his white nose.

"They don't mind us visiting. It's a happy, welcoming place. Don't you feel it?"

"Yes." She went to stand at the pool's edge. The water was so clear, she could see the rocky bottom far below. "Why did you want to come here today?" she asked.

She saw his reflection shimmering next to hers on the glasslike surface of the water as he came to stand beside her. She watched his image as he pushed back his hat and squinted up at the spreading limbs of a giant ghost gum. "If this drought keeps up, I'm going to have to use this water. I won't have a choice."

She heard the regret in his voice and she swung her head to look directly at him, surprised to realize that he, too, felt the pull of this place. And unsettled to realize that he appreciated its magic enough to wish he could preserve it.

The shadows in his vivid blue eyes caught at her. She swallowed hard, feeling something shift inside her. Here was one more side of him she didn't want to see. She wanted to go on thinking of him as insensitive and crass. She didn't want to have to face the truth: that her image of him was flawed, that she had manufactured it herself to keep from having to admit just how dangerously attractive she found him. Not only physically—although that pull was powerful enough. It was this man, Patrick O'Reilly—the essence of him, the soul of him—that fascinated her. Called to her.

His gaze caught hers and that instant in time stretched out, became something intimate. Something confusing and frightening but very real. Then loose stones and dirt rolled down

188

the slope to shatter the calm surface of the pool and the stillness of the moment as Liam slid to a halt beside them. "I'm hungry. Can we eat right away?"

O'Reilly held her gaze for one more pounding heartbeat, then turned toward the boy. "Sure thing."

They spread a rug beneath the big coolabah tree and ate the picnic supper Ching had packed for them. The ride had given the children hearty appetites and they ate largely in silence, only squabbling once over the selection of chicken pieces, and again over the division of the chocolate cake.

After that the children wandered away to clamber about the rocky edges of the pool while O'Reilly stretched out flat on his back on the rug, his hat tipped over his face as if he were sleeping. Amanda leaned back against the flaky trunk of the tree and felt the peace of this place envelop her.

But the peace had a jagged edge to it. She was too conscious of the man who lay beside her. Of the way his moleskin trousers drew tight across his hard thighs when he propped one boot up on his bent knee. Of the way his chest lifted against the worn blue cloth of his shirt when he breathed. She found herself imagining the shape of muscle and flesh beneath the cloth. She imagined her hands touching him there, where the neck of his shirt gaped open to reveal his tanned throat.

189

She jerked her gaze away. The older children had tired of the pool and were now running footraces out on the flat. Missy had taken off her shoes and stockings and hitched up her skirts so that she could poke around the lapping edge of the water with a long stick.

"Be careful you don't get wet, Missy," Amanda called.

O'Reilly eased back his hat and glanced at the water hole. "She'll be right. Don't worry."

Amanda watched the little girl shove the stick down into the pool's bottom, then lean forward, looking sharply. "What is she doing?"

"Huntin' for yabbies."

Amanda swung her gaze back to him. "For what?"

"Yabbies. Some people call them mud bugs. You eat them."

"*Bugs*? You eat bugs?"

O'Reilly let out a huff of laughter. "They're good. They taste like crayfish."

She raised her eyebrows in polite disbelief. "The way goanna tastes like pork?"

"Actually, I always thought goanna resembles chicken, myself." She saw his dimples peep. "But if you want a real treat, you ought to try a witchetty grub. The Aborigines dig them out of trees, and a good one will grow as long and thick as a man's finger. Course they tend to wiggle a bit as you let 'em slide down your throat, but—"

"Mr. O'Reilly," Amanda said calmly, picking up the remnants of the chocolate cake and holding it over his head, "I must ask you most respectfully to kindly be silent."

He eyed the suspended cake. "Very well, Miss Davenport. Since you ask me so respect-fully."

A shout and the thud of horses' hooves brought her head around. She set the cake down and almost gasped at the sight of Liam and Hannah mounted bareback on their horses, thundering across the plains, the horses' churning hooves kicking up dust and turf. Hannah's ragged hair streamed out behind her, while Liam's whoops drifted back on the warm breeze.

"What are they doing?" Amanda asked, raising one hand to shield her eyes from the glare of the sun.

O'Reilly lifted his head, then laid it back down again. "Looks like they're havin' a race."

"Without their saddles?"

He shrugged. "Why not?"

"Because it's dangerous."

"Nah. Those two children could ride prac-tically before they could walk."

Amanda watched the horses reach a distant tree and circle back toward the water hole. Hannah led by a good two lengths, her horse stretching out, its powerful haunches bunching as its flashing hooves ate up the distance until it seemed almost to fly across the barren ground. "That big black Hannah is riding is surely too strong for her," said Amanda, her teeth worrying her lower lip.

He swiveled his head to look at her. "Relax.

I've met very few natural horsemen in my life, but I've gotta say, Hannah's one of 'em. Hell, I had a big row with her before we left, because she wanted to ride Fire Dancer out here."

Amanda ducked her chin to hide her smile. She'd begun to realize that O'Reilly and his elder daughter had a "big row" at least every other day.

"Which of your horses is Fire Dancer?" she asked

A warm, sleepy look crept into his eyes. "The stallion I won off Lumley."

"Oh." She felt herself grow hot at the memory of that morning, and transferred her attention to Missy, who was now sitting on one of the weathered rocks rising up from the side of the water hole.

In the golden light of the late afternoon sun, the child's hair tumbled down her back in a riot of fair, baby-fine curls. She was doing something with a pile of pebbles between her feet and had her skirt and petticoats bunched up about her knees, her thin bare legs sticking out looking almost as tanned as any native's.

Watching her, Amanda tried to imagine what kind of mother could go away and leave this sweet, loving, giving child. Or Hannah, with her dark, needy soul. Or a wild, reckless, wonderful boy like Liam. And suddenly, Amanda was tired of trying to guess, of trying to understand without actually knowing. Keeping her attention fixed on the child,

Amanda asked quietly, "How old was Missy when her mother went away?"

She heard O'Reilly sit up quickly beside her, but she did not look at him. She did not want to see the expression on his face, did not want to know what he still felt for that mysterious woman who had been—no, she reminded herself; still *was,* surely?—his wife.

He was silent for so long that she didn't think he was going to answer her. Then she heard him suck in a deep breath and let it out on a long sigh. "Six months," he said. "Missy was six months old when Katherine left. Luckily I'd already found Sally to wet-nurse the baby. Otherwise, God knows what would have happened to her."

"Is she still alive? Your wife, I mean."

"She's still alive. Or at least she was, last I heard."

"Doesn't she keep in touch with the children?"

He shook his head. "She went back to Victoria at first. But about six months later...she met a Frenchman. An officer. She went to Paris with him."

Amanda watched a brilliant blue dragonfly hover over the still surface of the pool. "A Frenchman's whore," Hannah had said.

"I've never divorced her," O'Reilly said quietly. "Although I know a lot of people think I should. I just don't think it would be good for the children."

"Yes. I can understand that." She could no longer bear not seeing his face. She swiveled

193

her head and looked at him. He sat at his ease, one leg bent, his forearm resting on his upright knee. He had his hat pushed back on his sun-streaked hair as he stared as Missy. His dimples showed in his lean cheeks and the sun creases beside his narrowed eyes were etched deep, but not by a smile. It was as if he gazed far into the past. And whatever it was he saw brought him great pain.

"How could she do it?" Amanda asked, the words bursting unplanned from someplace inside her. "How could a woman go away and leave her children like that?"

He swung his head to stare at her. She saw his jaw tighten, saw the hard glitter of his eyes. And in that moment, Amanda thought, he truly hated her.

"I don't know. You tell me. I'll never understand women. Especially Englishwomen."

"She was English?" Amanda said with a gasp. "Your wife was English?"

"Didn't you know?" His lips pulled back into a sneer. "She was English, all right. As English as press-gangs and sumptuary laws and the fires of Smithfield. And she hated Australia every bit as much as you do." He levered up from the rug and swung away. "It's time to go," he said over his shoulder.

Amanda stayed where she was, her hands gripping together as she watched him stroll down the hill to where Missy's pony and the two remaining horses grazed peacefully.

The sun still beat down warm and friendly on her shoulders; the birds still chattered

194

cheerfully from the high branches of the surrounding trees. But the magic had gone out
of the golden afternoon, and she felt tired
and chilled and oddly alone. She knew she
should be gathering together what was left of
the picnic things. Instead, she sat and watched
O'Reilly's tall, lean figure as he saddled the
horses with swift, efficient strokes.

Her chest ached almost unbearably. She
wrapped her arms around her waist and
hugged herself, but the ache within wouldn't
go away. It was as if her heart swelled, filling
with something that was more than empathy.
Something she didn't want to feel again for any
man.

Especially not for this man. This Australian
who hated England and the English, and who
had a wife named Katherine to whom he was
tied for all time.

O'Reilly sat on the top rail of the split-wood
fence. The pale light of the waning moon
shivered over the dark-red hide of the stallion
loping in wide, useless circles around the
paddock. It was late, the night still enough that
he could hear the croaking of a frog from
down by the creek bed, and the rhythmic
thud of the horse's hooves, pounding cease-
lessly on the hard earth.

He set a match to his pipe and breathed in
the rich aroma of the tobacco, mingling with
the other night smells. The heavy, ever-pre-
sent tang of eucalyptus, the sweet scent of dried

grass, the warmth of healthy horseflesh. Tilting back his head, he gazed up at a white blaze of stars scattered across the blackness of infinity. He always thought the night sky looked so cold. Even on a warm night like tonight, the sky looked cold.

He could still remember staring up at the stars as a boy on those long, lonely nights when he'd been sent out into the bush with a mob of sheep. His father had worked them all hard—or at least he'd worked the three boys. But their mother had insisted that Hetty be raised as a young lady, no matter how rough the realities of life on a new station in the wilds of Victoria might be. And by the time their mother was gone, Hetty had been seventeen and already engaged.

O'Reilly had left home himself at seventeen, anxious for a new life, his own life. First he'd hired on as a jackaroo. But there was more money to be made in shearing. So he'd worked the circuit, saving his money, planning to buy a mob of sheep and cattle and drive it to the new country opening up in South Australia. Start his own run.

Then he'd met Katherine Barr-Jones.

He'd been just another nineteen-year-old shearer the day he rode onto the Barr-Jones station. He would never forget his first sight of that big stone house, surrounded by acres of carefully clipped and tended gardens. Most of the gentlemen's sons who came out to Australia were long on what they liked to call "breeding" and short on the money they needed to live in the manner they thought they deserved. But not Katherine's papa. Trenton Barr-Jones had made a fortune in India, and he'd decided to invest it all in Australia.

Katherine hadn't been too happy about her papa's plans to set up his own private empire in the colonies. She'd rather have stayed in England, and she made no effort to hide what she thought of Australia. O'Reilly would always remember the first time he'd seen her. She'd looked so proud and haughty and untouchable, sitting sidesaddle on that showy white mare of hers. But he'd known she was watching the shearers, watching *him*. Wanting him.

Vibrantly alive and strong-willed, Katherine might have been only eighteen and a virgin, but she'd always been the kind of person to take what she wanted. By the time the shearing season ended, Katherine was pregnant, and Trenton Barr-Jones had an Irish convict's grandson as a son-in-law.

Listening to a dingo howl now, out in the bush, O'Reilly thought about all the stolen hours he and Katherine had spent together that spring. About how he'd held her in his arms and told her his dreams of opening up his own run, of someday building a big stone house to rival her father's. It wasn't until later that he realized she hadn't even been listening. She'd been too busy weaving her own secret plans, which mainly involved O'Reilly going to work for her papa's shipping company and taking her back to England.

She didn't tell him about her scheme until after they were married, and she never forgave him for laughing out loud when she suggested it. Hell, it'd taken two years before she got over it enough to agree to join him in the new house he'd built for her at Penyaka. Yet he had still believed, then, that he could make her happy. And there had been some good times. Just not enough.

Shifting sideways on the narrow railing, O'Reilly let his gaze wander over the darkened buildings of Penyaka. He might not have a house as big as Trenton Barr-Jones's yet, but he was proud of his run, proud of what he had built here. And if he survived this drought, he planned to make it even better. Now that he was older, he could look back on those first days of his marriage and see that in his own way, he'd been as selfish and ungiving as Katherine. Yet, he still didn't think he'd made a mistake by not giving in to her. Penyaka might have been hard on Katherine, but a lifetime shut away in an office in England would have been slow death for O'Reilly. It was their marriage that had been a mistake. If it hadn't been for the children, he'd have said she'd been right to end it. But he doubted he could ever forgive her for the damage she'd done to their children.

A high-pitched neighing jerked O'Reilly's attention back to the far end of the paddock, where the big bay pranced, head up, neck arched, dark mane fluttering in the warm night air. They were planning to breed the stallion to one of the Thoroughbred mares tomorrow, and it was as if Fire Dancer could sense it, could smell the mare in heat.

O'Reilly grinned at the restless horse. "I feel the same way, old boy," he said when the bay trotted up to shove its nose against his chest. He rubbed the white diamond between the stallion's dark eyes, his thoughts drifting to Amanda Davenport.

He knew her now, knew enough to look past her starchy manners and plummy accent and see just how different from Katherine she really was. Unfortunately, the two women were different in almost every way but one—Amanda hated Australia, and she was desperate to get back to England.

He knew it, and yet... And yet, that didn't stop him from lying in bed at night and imagining what it would be like to have her naked and beneath him. He wanted to fill his hands with her full breasts, to taste her sweet lips and send his hard body pounding into her softness. He wanted to make her let go of all that prim and proper nonsense she wrapped around herself. He wanted to hear her laugh, and moan and scream with pleasure—

And quench this burning, untamed yearning within him.

After lessons the next day, Amanda retreated to her room and tried to lose herself in Cicero. But the print swam in front of her eyes and her mind wandered, so that she finally cast the book aside and went to throw open the French doors to the veranda.

She had thought the fresh air might help her concentrate. Only instead of returning to her book, she lingered, one hand on the latch, her gaze drifting over the neatly edged paths and flowering borders of the garden Patrick O'Reilly had planted for his English wife.

Amanda felt a strange, yearning kind of sadness steal over her as she realized how little she knew about him. About the life he had lived before that day she had met him on the streets of Brinkman. About the experiences that had gone together to make up this man, Patrick O'Reilly, that he was now. She tried to tell herself she was being common, indulging in vulgar curiosity and an atypical prurient interest in other peoples' affairs. But it was more than that, and she knew it.

She had just swung about to go back inside when the sound of his voice came to her on the afternoon breeze. "Steady, girl."

Amanda stopped, her head lifted, listening. There was a gentle, coaxing quality to his tone that she had never heard before. His words were gentle, too. Soothing words, words a man might use to calm a nervous virgin, to allay her fears as he positioned himself to enter her.

Shocked by the direction of her thoughts, she reached to shut the doors when the wind gusted again and she heard O'Reilly say, "She'll be right, sweetheart. Easy now. Hush."

Amanda hesitated, then stepped out onto the veranda.

CHAPTER ELEVEN

O'Reilly's smooth, seductive voice seemed to beckon her. Across the garden, down the hill to the stockyards.

It was late afternoon, and the sun shone bright and high in the sky. There wasn't much grass left on the hillside, just scattered dry yellow stalks that crumbled to dust beneath Amanda's shoes as she walked, sending insects whirling away from her. Beside the empty creek bed, the rows of white-trunked, gray-leaved gums drooped lifelessly in the dry, still air. She could see a kingfisher sitting on a low bare branch, his enormous head swiveling as he watched her pass. A kookaburra, O'Reilly had called it. Jackass of the bush. She saw its big beak open and heard its strange, raucous laughter float off down the valley. *Hoo-hoo-hoo-haa-haa-hoo-hoo.*

She was near enough to the stockyards now to notice the knot of men crowded around one of the yards. She strolled toward them, the sun hot on her hatless head. She recognized Campbell, and Jacko, the Aboriginal stockman. Liam and Hannah were there, too, hanging on the fence, their feet balanced on the bottom rail, their arms hooked around a post for support.

And then she saw O'Reilly.

He had stripped down to his shirt, which as usual hung half-unbuttoned, showing a tantalizing swath of muscled, sun-bronzed chest.

He had his low-crowned hat pushed back on his golden head, his attention focused on the skittish horse mesmerized by his crooning voice.

It stood in the center of the yard: a young chestnut mare, quivering but still, her head bowed, her hind legs spread, her tail up and lifted to one side, exposing her entrance to the purebred stud cavorting arrogantly around her.

Amanda paused with one hand on the fence's top rail, her breath catching in her throat as she took in the power and raw sexuality of the magnificent bay stallion. This could only be Fire Dancer. He pranced around his mate, his neck arched, each strutting stride bunching the powerful muscles that rippled beneath his sweat-sheened, bloodred hide. Then he threw back his head, his nostrils flaring, and the wind whipped at his dark mane as he closed on the quiescent, waiting mare.

Amanda could see his sex organ, proud and engorged, as he reared back and mounted the mare, biting her on the neck as he entered her. The mare shuddered and screamed.

Amanda's hand closed into a fist that she shoved against her lips. She could not tear her gaze away from the two animals mating before her. It was brutal and frightening and indescribably fascinating. The stallion, so blatantly dominating and conquering; the mare, submissive, subdued, accepting.

At long last, it ended. The stallion's hooves flashed as he thundered around the yard, neighing his triumph, kicking up a fine dust that shimmered golden in the sunlight. The mare stood where he had left her, forgotten, dismissed. Amanda looked away...

And found herself staring into the narrowed eyes of Patrick O'Reilly.

He had been watching her. She knew it by the intensity of his brilliant blue stare, by the taut, unmistakable look of arousal on his face. While she had been watching the horses, he had been watching her. And he knew. He *knew* that this animal display of sexuality had excited her. He knew that within her chest her heart pounded and that, even now, beneath the stiff bodice of her prim gown, her breasts felt full and her nipples had hardened into two erect nubs.

They stared at each other across the dusty stockyard, aware of each other as only a man and a woman can be. Physically aware. Aware of the possibilities. Aware of their desires.

Someone said O'Reilly's name. His gaze jerked away from her, breaking the spell. Amanda swung around, sucking in air as if she were winded, her back pressing against the high rails of the fence for support. The wood felt warm and rough through the cloth of her dress, the spring breeze fanned her cheeks. But inside, she was in turmoil.

She realized that one of the men had caught the stallion and was leading it toward the stables. The dust began to settle; the men, to disperse. Through the thinning crowd she saw Hannah again, saw the fascinated expression sharpening the girl's face as she watched the stud being led away. And Amanda thought, a girl that age should not have been allowed to watch such a spectacle. She would have to speak to O'Reilly about it.

But at the thought of confronting him about it, Amanda felt her stomach clench and she knew she could not face him. Not now. With something like a moan, she fled back to her room.

"Did Miss Davenport talk to you about this afternoon?" Liam asked when O'Reilly went in to say good night.

"No. Why?" O'Reilly asked, leaning against the footrail of the boy's bed.

Liam plucked at the edges of his white sheet. "She lit into Hannah and me right before supper. About us watchin' you breedin' Fire Dancer. She said it wasn't proper, especially for Hannah." He shot his father an appraising, sideways glance. "You're not going to let her talk you out of havin' us help around the station, are you?"

"Hardly." O'Reilly pushed away from the bedpost and went to twist off the lamp. He paused for a moment. "What do you think of her, anyway?"

Liam looked up at him in surprise. "I don't know. Why'd you ask? You never asked about any of the other governesses."

O'Reilly shrugged. "She seems...different from the others in some way."

"She's a lot smarter, that's all. It makes

her harder to trick. And she's got more grit than the others, too. You wouldn't think it from first lookin' at her, but it's true."

O'Reilly laughed softly. "Good night, Liam."

He wandered back out to the empty parlor. A log collapsed on the hearth, releasing a fanfare of sparks that shot up the chimney. He stood for a while, gazing thoughtfully down at the glowing coals. Then he adjusted the lamp on the table, picked up the book he'd been reading, and settled into a corner of the sofa. At his feet, Barrister thumped his tail, then lay quiet again.

About half an hour later he was surprised to hear Miss Davenport's door open. She usually scooted into her room right after supper and rarely poked her nose out again until morning. He kept his head bent, but he could see the hem of her drab skirt appear at the edge of the circle of light as she approached him. He rested the book on his knee and looked up.

She had her arms crossed over her beautiful breasts, her wonderful, fiery hair raked back in a rigidly controlled bun, and her luscious mouth cinched. But her eyes... Ah, her glowing, heated eyes betrayed her.

He felt desire, unbidden and unwanted, surge through him at the sight of her. He damped it down and gave her a lazy, teasing smile. "Evenin', Miss Davenport. Something on your mind?"

She hugged herself tighter. "If I could have a moment of your time?"

He stretched his boots out toward the fire,

linked his hands behind his neck, and slipped his rump a bit farther down on the old sofa. "Sure thing. Have a seat."

He watched in amusement as she hesitated. He could tell she'd much rather say what she had to say on her feet, probably so she could make a quick getaway. But she evidently didn't feel she could as long as he continued to sprawl at his ease.

He didn't budge, so she compromised by coming around to perch on the edge of the chair that sat at a right angle to the sofa. "It's about Hannah," she said, folding her hands together primly on her lap.

"What about Hannah?"

She sucked in a deep breath that caused her breasts to lift enticingly. "I have been meaning to speak to you about her for some time now. I think Hannah is reaching an age at which she should no longer be allowed to roam freely about the station, dressed like a boy and witnessing spectacles such as the one she was exposed to this afternoon."

Spreading his elbows wide, he tipped his head back and regarded her through half-lowered lids. "Well, I sure as hell ain't man enough to wrestle her into stays and a petticoat, if that's what you mean. But you're more than welcome to try."

"You could *forbid* her to wear trousers."

"I could, but I'm not that stupid. I make it a practice not to pick a fight unless I'm bloody well sure I can win it."

"What a peculiar way of putting it," she said,

her nostrils quivering with that disdain she was so bloody good at showing. "I would have thought it simply a matter of exerting your parental authority. Or is that too much to expect? Because when it comes right down to it, I frankly haven't noticed you paying much attention to Hannah at all—unless it's to quarrel with her. In fact, I suspect it's half the girl's problem."

He dropped his arms and leaned forward to shake his index finger beneath her thin, patrician nose. "Now, wait a minute here. Don't you go interfering between me and Hannah. We get along just fine."

She stared him straight in the eye. "I hadn't noticed."

"Bloody hell." He reared up onto his feet, knocking the forgotten book flying. "I hired you to teach my children, not to raise them. You leave the raising to me."

She rose gracefully to face him. "Perhaps if you were doing a better job of raising them, you would not have such a difficult time getting a governess to stay here and teach them."

Her words were such a close echo of something Hetty had once said to him that it flicked him on the raw. He thrust his fingers through his hair, raking it back off his forehead. "*Christalmighty*, lady—"

"And you can stop swearing at me."

Her gaze held his steadily, her voice quiet but unwavering. Slowly, his hand fell back to his side as he stared down at her. And it came to him that the only reason she was here arguing with him was because she cared about Hannah—genuinely cared about all of his children in a way that none of the endless procession of governesses before her had done. And he knew a stirring someplace deep inside that he did not want to feel.

He did not want to like this woman, although he'd been finding it more and more difficult not to. Teasing her, maybe even trying to kiss her, was supposed to be fun. *Liking* her introduced an element of earnestness into the process that he didn't want.

Beside them the fire crackled and flared, sending golden light dancing over the fine-boned features of her face and burnishing her hair with a warm red glow. The rest of the house stretched out dark and silent around them.

They were alone.

He watched her eyes widen with the knowledge of it. There were flecks of black in the gray of her irises, sooty sparks that radiated out like a starburst. When she was aroused, the gray seemed to shimmer and the black deepened to velvet.

He took the two steps needed to close the distance between them. Her pupils dilated wildly as she stared up at him and her delicate white throat worked as she swallowed. But she didn't back away from him.

"Amanda," he said softly. He reached up and began to pull the pins, gently, one by one, from her chignon. At his touch, she quivered. He watched her lips part, watched her eyelids flutter half-closed. He pulled out three pins. Four. Then her eyes flew open wide and her hand clamped around his wrist.

"Don't."

"Why?" He brought up his free hand and eased his fingers into the heavy coil, loosening it. She kept her fingers clenched around his one wrist, but she made no move to stop what his other hand was doing. "Why do you scrape your hair back like this?" he whispered, freeing her hair, sending it cascading in fiery waves around her shoulders. "To convince people that you're as passionless and unexcitable as you like to pretend you are?" He cupped his hand behind her neck. "Or are you trying to convince yourself?"

She stared up at him, her eyes wide and deep with thoughts he wished he could understand. "I am as I seem."

He shook his head. "No."

He eased his hands down to her shoulders and began to knead the tense muscles there. "Relax," he said. "I won't do anything you don't want me to do."

"I don't want you to do anything."

He expelled his breath in a low laugh. "I bet you got into trouble all the time for lying when you were a little girl."

"I did not." Her breath came thick and fast, parting her lips, shuddering her chest. "I...was a very truthful child."

"That a fact?" He brushed his thumbs back

and forth against the sensitive flesh just below her ears. "Well, you've grown into a very untruthful woman."

"No."

"No? Then why is your heart beatin' like crazy right now? And there's no point in denying it, because..." He slipped his hand down to place it, palm flat, fingers splayed, against her chest. "I can feel it."

She stared down at his hand, its fingers curled around the edge of her left breast. He could feel her heart thudding wildly against his palm, see her chest rising and falling with her unsteady breaths.

She lifted her eyes to his, and he fell into them. She had such beautiful eyes, like the rain-drenched, storm-swirled skies on the edge of all of his tomorrows. He saw her lips part. Heard the wanting, whimpering sound that escaped from her throat. And he bent his head and kissed her.

Her lips were soft and smooth and willing. But he kept the pressure of his kiss gentle, tender. He slid his hands down to ride her hips as he moved his mouth easily back and forth across hers, letting her get to know the taste of him, the feel of him.

He saw her eyelids slide shut, felt her quiver in his arms. Then her hand came up, slowly, to touch the nape of his neck in a way that sent desire ripping through him, hardening his loins, shortening his breath. He groaned, and her mouth opened beneath his as her fingers spasmed in his hair, clutching him to her.

Surprised, he deepened the kiss, his hands gliding to the curve of her spine, drawing her closer to him, pressing her breasts against his chest.

She had been kissed before. The knowledge of it exploded in his brain as his tongue tangled with hers and the kiss caught fire. This was no shy spinster's embrace. Some man, at some time, had taught Miss Amanda Davenport about desire and sensuality and the ways of the flesh.

For one wild moment, O'Reilly's blood pounded hot and savage and demanding through his body. He wanted to strip away her ugly governess's dress and fill his hands with her heavy naked breasts. He wanted to draw her nipples one by one into his mouth and taste their warm muskiness. He wanted to lay her down before the fire and ease himself between her slender white thighs and sate the aching, hungry, burning need within him.

But this woman was afraid of passion, and he knew it. He also knew that at any moment she was liable to realize where this was all going, and panic. He swirled his tongue around hers, nipped at her lower lip, tasted the tantalizing hints of what it could be like. And somehow maintained enough sense to raise his head and end it.

He watched her eyelids flutter open. He stared down into her deep, dark eyes, and while she was still too languorous to complain about it, he dipped his head again and gave her one last, lingering kiss. "Good night,

Miss Davenport," he murmured. Then he turned around and left her.

While he still could.

The washcloth grated roughly against the tender skin of Amanda's lips. She scraped harder, rubbing the cloth back and forth until her mouth hurt and the bitter taste of the soap stung her tongue. And then she scrubbed some more.

She told herself his kiss had been a vile, loathsome thing, that she scrubbed to remove any lingering traces of his scent, his taste, his essence. Only it was a lie. Because his kiss had been wondrous. Rapturous. A seductively exalting moment of enchantment and wicked arousal that she was desperate to erase.

She slumped against the side of the washstand, her head bowed in shame. She didn't understand how such a thing could have happened. How she could have allowed her fascination with that man to lead her to betray herself so blatantly. She pressed her hands to her heated cheeks and tried to imagine what he must have thought—what he must be thinking of her right now.

She had to find some way to make certain that such a thing never happened again, she told herself. Just remembering the hot, wet feel of his lips moving against hers, the strength of his man's body beneath her hands, the hard proof of his arousal pressed against her, was enough to trigger an onslaught of forbidden but delicious sensations that tightened her belly and made her hungry for something too frightening even to think about.

She let out a groan and dropped the washcloth to bury her face in her hands. What was happening to her? All the thoughts and feelings, needs and desires she thought she'd buried long ago had come back to torment her. Except it was worse, worse by far than she ever remembered it being.

She sank down onto her haunches, her arms wrapping around her knees to hug her legs tightly to her chest. In the distance, a dingo howled. She heard the wind come up, rustling the dry leaves and brittle branches of the gums down by the creek. She hooked her hands around her wrists and hugged herself, tighter and tighter, as if she were holding herself together.

Holding on to the woman she was determined to be.

He was stripping off his trousers and getting ready to go to bed when he heard the pounding on his door.

"Just a minute," he called, hitching his pants back up over his hips but not bothering to button them. "What the hell's the—"

He wrenched open the door and found himself confronting Amanda.

It had been a good half hour since he'd left her beside the fire, but she was still dressed. She had a shawl clutched against her breasts as if for protection, and she skittered back a few feet when he opened the door, her eyes widening as she took in his bare chest and unbuttoned trousers.

"Amanda?" He instinctively reached for her. "Are you all right?"

"Stay away from me," she said in a low, tightly controlled voice, her face white. "I have taken the unorthodox step of approaching you at this hour for one reason and one reason only: to remind you, Mr. O'Reilly, that I came to this miserable, inhospitable corner of the colonies to act as governess to your children. And as long as I am employed in that capacity, I must insist that in the future you refrain from ever again forcing your attentions on me in such a manner as occurred this evening."

"Bloody hell." He let go of the door and took a hasty step toward her. "I didn't force a bloody thing on you tonight and you bloody well know it."

She scooted sideways like a harried crab. "Nevertheless," she said breathlessly, refusing to be drawn on that point. "I must insist."

He opened his mouth to remind her of the way she'd explored his tongue with her own and rubbed her belly against the length of his erection. But then he thought better of it and clenched his jaw down tight on what he'd been about to say.

He never should have let things reach this stage between them, and he knew it. But he was damned if he was going to pretend that it had all been his doing. "All right, You've got it." He jabbed a finger at her. "Next time you want me to kiss you, lady, you're going to have to ask for it."

She sucked in an angry gasp. "As if I—"

Without even waiting to hear what she had to say, he stomped into his room and slammed the door.

"Do you know what I miss most about England?" asked Christian Whittaker as they drank tea together the following afternoon.

Amanda smiled and shook her head. "No. Tell me."

"Autumn. September in England. The brilliant pinks and yellows and oranges of the last roses splashed against redbrick cottages with thatched roofs. The sound of church bells, ringing out over a valley so lush and green and beautiful, it makes your soul ache to look at it." He glanced at her shyly, as if embarrassed by his lyrical flight. "What do you miss?"

She didn't even need to think about it. "The rain."

They laughed together. Like friends, she thought. She liked the idea of having Christian Whittaker as her friend. She'd had so few friends in her life. And Christian was so pleasant, so gentle and well mannered, so reassuringly *English*.

Lifting her tea, she studied him covertly over the rim of the china cup and wondered why she could never imagine Christian as anything more than a friend. He had a pleasant face, she decided. His cheeks were full and ruddy, his chin square and prominent, his eyes light brown and sincere. His brown hair was neatly cut, his mustache carefully trimmed and waxed, his clothes everything that a gentleman's clothes should be. She had no doubt that even the hottest days of midsummer would find him impeccably attired in jacket, waistcoat, and tie, his shirt virtuously buttoned up to its high collar.

Amanda suppressed a sigh. A woman would be safe with a man like this, she thought. Safe not only from the importunities of the cruel, materialistic world, but from herself. Safe from all the wild, sensual impulses that could so easily destroy her.

She studied his straight, thin-lipped English mouth, just visible beneath the bushy mustache, and tried to imagine what it would be like to kiss him. Cool, probably. And dry. She couldn't imagine Mr. Whittaker opening his mouth.

Or thrusting his tongue down her throat.

A long shadow darkened the pristine linen cloth she'd used to cover the tea table. "G'day," drawled a deep, lazy voice.

Amanda started violently. It was as if she had conjured the devil with her own wicked thoughts.

Mr. Whittaker hastened to stand and bow formally. "Good afternoon, Mr. O'Reilly."

Amanda looked up into a pair of intense blue eyes, glittering with the memory of everything that had happened between them last night. He pulled out a chair and sat down. She jerked her gaze away.

How *could* she have betrayed herself like that last night? she thought wildly. How could she have simply stood there, subdued and placid, while he loosened her hair and pulled her into his arms for his kiss? She had been as acquiescent as that chestnut mare in the paddock yesterday, waiting submissively for the stud to penetrate her.

Unbidden, an image flashed through Amanda's mind. An image of O'Reilly looming over her, soothing her with gentle, coaxing words as he spread her legs and prepared to mount her. Aghast at the wayward direction of her thoughts, she almost shuddered. She could *not* keep letting herself think of him like this.

"I am afraid Liam and I will have to miss a few of our sessions," Christian Whittaker was saying. "I have been asked by the company to attend to some business in Adelaide. I probably won't be back until next month."

O'Reilly pushed the brim of his hat farther back on his head. "No worries. We're going to start shearing in a few days anyway. Liam'll be kept busy enough with that."

Mr. Whittaker raised his brows in surprise. "Is it not too early?"

A grin that held no amusement twisted O'Reilly's lips. "Under normal circumstances, yes. Although it's always a bit of a gamble, whenever you decide to do it. Shear too late and a hot spell will scorch the sheep's backs

217

and let the flies get at them; shear too early and an unexpected cold snap can kill the lot. But the way this drought's going, if I don't shear soon, I won't have any sheep left alive to shear anyway. I plan to cull bloody hard this year."

"What does that mean?" Amanda asked, noticing the two creases etched by worry between his eyes. On the surface he seemed so carefree and easygoing. But he carried a lot inside him, this Australian.

He looked away from her, out over the dying hills. "It means that as things stand now, this range can't support the number of animals I'm running on it. So I can either let them all starve to death, or I can sell or slaughter half of them now and hope the ones that are left are strong enough to make it through till this bloody dry spell breaks." He pursed his lips. "If it ever does."

"If the drought doesn't end soon," said Christian Whittaker, "the mines are going to have to close. We'll never be profitable if we have to pay so much simply to haul our ore out of the Flinders."

Amanda turned to him in surprise. "Is there any real danger that might happen?"

"I'm afraid so. It's one of the reasons I'm being sent down to Adelaide. To see what kind of support there is for running a railway line up here."

O'Reilly expelled his breath in one of those little huffs she now recognized as a laugh. "Not much chance of that."

"No, but we need to try." He reached into his worn satchel and drew out a slim, expensively bound book. "If Liam has time while I'm gone, have him take a look at this translation of *Medea*. We'll be starting Euripides after I get back, and I thought it might be a good idea if he became familiar with the English version before we tackle the original Greek."

Amanda picked up the brown leather volume and ran her fingers over the embossed gold letters on the cover. "It's one of my father's translations," she said, her voice barely more than a whisper.

"Yes. Be sure to ask Liam to take care of it, would you? It means a great deal to me."

She glanced up to meet Christian Whittaker's serious brown eyes, and smiled. "I'll make certain he does."

Christian left soon after that. She expected O'Reilly to wander away, too, but he didn't, even though the atmosphere between them crackled with wary sexuality and residual anger. She busied herself stacking cups and saucers on the tray, painfully conscious of the man sprawled lazily in the chair beside her. Out of the corner of her eye, she saw him reach his strong, tanned hand to pick up the *Medea*.

"So this Angus Davenport was your father, was he?" He flipped through the first leaves of the book and grunted. "A big Oxford man."

"Yes."

"I would have expected a man like that to have plenty of money."

"Not as much as you might think." She reached for the teapot.

"But enough so's his daughter wouldn't need to hire herself out as a secretary or governess."

She could feel the heat of his gaze upon her as she moved to set the teapot on the tray, then just stood there, staring down at it. "My father loved Oxford almost as much as he loved the world of the ancient Greeks. It was always his dream to endow a series of lectures on the Athenian tragedians, so I..." Her fingers slid over the graceful curve of the fine china teapot she still held between her hands. "I try not to begrudge him the pleasure I know it must have brought him to be able to do that."

He let out his breath in a mirthless laugh. "Christ, why shouldn't you resent what he did? Seems to me, you're the one hurting because of it."

Amanda shook her head, her gaze still resolutely fastened on the pink-and-green floral design of the teapot, as if it were the most fascinating thing she had ever seen. "No. He left me what he considered an adequate sum for a modest dowry. Unfortunately, it wasn't enough for me to live on for the rest of my life, when I did not marry."

"And exactly who was he expecting you to marry?"

She looked up, feeling a sad smile tug at her lips. "The local vicar, of course. Mr. Smutley, his name was. He courted me for eighteen months. Since I enjoyed discussing literature and philosophy with him, I fear I never discouraged him as forcefully as I perhaps should have. My father assumed I meant to marry him."

She was surprised by the intensity of O'Reilly's gaze as he stared back at her. "A vicar?" His teeth flashed in a sudden grin. "Your father couldn't have known you very well."

How did you guess? she wanted to ask, but didn't. "No, my father didn't know me well at all." *He never bothered,* she thought, but she didn't say that, either.

She watched O'Reilly uncoil from his chair and circle the table, his gaze reckless and heated as he came at her. The westering sun slanted in beneath the veranda and glazed his strong, bare arms with gold where they showed beneath his rolled-up shirtsleeves.

"So who was he?"

She kept her gaze fastened on that beguiling hollow just above the juncture of his collarbone. "I don't know what you mean."

"Yes, you do." He was close enough he could have touched her, if he'd wanted. He always stood too close to her, as if he knew it rattled her. But then, of course he knew. He seemed to know far too much about her.

He leaned in even closer, until his face was just inches from hers. Her gaze settled on his moving lips as he said, "Who taught you to open your mouth beneath a man's kiss? And to fear the things you feel when a man touches your body?"

Her startled gaze flew to meet his intent,

burning one. He was like wildfire, she thought. Dangerous and unpredictable. And she did fear him, as any sane person fears fire. She feared him, and all the things she felt when he put his strong man's hands on her weak woman's flesh.

Swallowing hard, she tore herself from his hypnotic blue stare and turned to gaze out over the sun-parched hills. "I don't want to talk about it."

"All right." He rubbed the backs of his fingers with unexpected gentleness against her cheek. "You've told me most of what I need to know anyway."

Amanda had always thought of September as a time of falling wet leaves and gray, frost-nipped mornings, of crackling bonfires and plump orangy-red rosehips and sweetly scented haystacks. But here in the Flinders, the coming of September meant the passage from a warm winter into a hot, sun-seared spring.

With spring came the shearing season, and she saw little of O'Reilly in the days that followed. He spent most of his time visiting the outlying shepherds' huts, or supervising the digging of some channel down by the woolshed, or handling one of a hundred other tasks she only dimly understood. She told herself she was relieved he was too busy to approach her. She told herself a lot of things she knew weren't true.

At first she assumed that O'Reilly and his

222

men would shear the sheep themselves. But when she said as much one morning in the schoolroom, Liam and Hannah hooted with laughter.

"As if Father and the shepherds and jackaroos could muster, wash, and shear a hundred thousand sheep," snickered Liam, digging his elbow into Hannah's ribs.

Only Missy sat silent, staring solemnly at her older brother's and sister's grinning faces. She turned to where Amanda stood beside her desk, her shoulders rigid. "There's groups of shearers what travels around, Miss Davenport," she said quietly. "They goes from station to station. They're so good at it, some of 'em can shear more than a hundred sheep in a day. Papa used to work as a shearer once, before he married Mama, so he's pretty quick. But even he can only shear sixty."

"Thank you, Missy," said Amanda gratefully.

After that, Missy appointed herself as Amanda's unofficial Sheep Tutor. She told Amanda about how the sheep needed to be brought in from the scattered outstations, and about the loose-limbed, stoop-shouldered shearers, each at his own stand, who could clip the wool so close to a sheep's loose, kinky skin that it looked naked when they were finished. ·

Thanks to Missy, Amanda added a long list of new words to her vocabulary: strange terms, such as crutching and skirting, and endless names for sheep, from wethers and cobblers to overgrowns and wets. She learned that

Liam and Hannah—in fact, almost everyone on the station except for Missy and Amanda—would be called upon to work in the woolshed for the six weeks or more the shearing was expected to last.

"And when the shearin' is finished, Papa always holds horse races, and a dance in the woolshed," Missy told her one afternoon on the veranda, when Amanda was brushing the little girl's unruly hair during the break between lessons. "Folks come from miles around. They dance all night and then ride home when the sun comes up in the morning to light the way." She craned her head around to squint at Amanda's plain gray dress, and her forehead puckered in thought. "Do you have something to wear? Something pretty?"

Amanda smiled and shook her head. "Not really. Look straight ahead, please." She gathered the thick blond hair in one hand and divided it into three for a braid. "It doesn't matter. I won't be going."

"But you must! All the governesses do. And the children, too."

"Oh. Well, I suppose I must, then. But I shan't dance, in any case."

"Why not?" asked Missy, with all of a six-year-old's tenacious persistence.

"If you don't look straight ahead, miss, this braid will be crooked." Amanda's hands flashed in and out as she wove the three strands together. After a pause, she said, "It wouldn't be seemly for a governess to be seen dancing. Too frivolous."

"Aren't governesses supposed to have fun?" asked Missy, twisting around again.

"No, they're not."

"Then I don't think you should be a governess."

A gurgle of laughter escaped Amanda's lips. "Don't you? And what, pray tell, do you think I should be, Missy?"

"I think you'd make a nice mother."

Amanda's hands stilled as a long-buried pain wrenched at her heart. Once she had wanted children. Once she had dreamed of holding her own sweet-smelling baby to her breast, had imagined what it would be like to catch a child's first smile. To guide its first steps and watch its wonder at the unfolding of the beauties of nature around it. But she had put all that behind her long ago. Hadn't she?

She forced herself to finish tying off the braid. "I'm not married, child," she said quietly. "Remember?"

"Well, that shouldn't be too hard to fix." Melissa swung completely around and rested her hands on Amanda's knees. "There's lots of men around here that need wives."

"Missy—"

"There's Mr. Campbell." Missy's nose wrinkled up. "But he smells funny and he's always fallin' over because he drinks too much now, so I don't think he'd make a very good husband."

"Melissa, I do not think it is appropriate for you—"

"You *could* marry Mr. Whittaker," she continued irrepressibly. "He doesn't smell, and he's nice. But Papa says he has the worst seat on a horse he's ever seen and besides, Mr. Whittaker would take you back to England with him and I wouldn't like that. So I think it would be better if you married Papa. Then you'd be my mama and you'd never leave, would you?"

Amanda stared down into Missy's open face. She knew the speech wasn't as artless as it seemed, but that did nothing to lessen the impact of the longing and need that Amanda glimpsed in the child's big blue eyes.

"Oh, Missy," she whispered, and hugged the child to her. "You'll get a new mother someday. You'll see."

"I don't want just any mama. I want you."

"But Missy—" She broke off as a chorus of whoops and ribald cheers cut through the still noonday air. Turning toward the sound, Amanda heard the jingle of harnesses and the clip-clop of horses' hooves on the stony road.

"It's the shearers!" Missy cried, jumping up to grab Amanda's hand and tug her out of her chair. "Come and see!"

CHAPTER TWELVE

Melissa tugged Amanda around the side of the house and through the garden to the front gate. There Amanda stopped, amazed by the sight of the dozens of shearers filling the dusty track. Most were scruffy men, wearing patched moleskin trousers and dirty, floppy-brimmed hats and anywhere from two days' to two months' growth of beard on their faces. But some were dapper, almost dandyish in their fine peg trousers and nipped-in coats.

"The ones with the tall hats and kangaroo knapsacks are called Derwent Drums," Missy told her as they watched the cavalcade lumber off down the creek toward the woolshed and shearers' quarters. "They're from Tasmania. Papa says they might shear slow, but they're careful. You see the ones with the blanket swags? They're Sydney-siders. They're fast, but they can cut the sheep up bad."

Overhead, the sun shone dazzlingly bright in an achingly blue sky. Once again, Amanda realized, she had hurried outside without her bonnet. Her complexion would be ruined if she wasn't careful, she told herself, as a stiff spring wind buffeted her ears and tugged at her hair to send loose tendrils against her face. She brought up her hand to catch the way-ward strands and smooth them back behind her ear...

And knew O'Reilly watched her.

She could feel his gaze on her, like a tense heat. She turned, her elbow cocked skyward, her hand still on her hair, and her gaze tangled with his.

He'd been out mustering sheep and was just trotting his horse back to the stockyards. He sat tall and easy in the saddle, his beautiful, hard body swaying as if he were one with the big chestnut he rode. She saw him say something to the men riding with him. They all laughed. O'Reilly's dimples flashed, and something wanting and needy caught at Amanda's insides. She saw him turn the chestnut's head and spur toward the shearers. And her.

She stood on the verge of the dusty road and watched him ride toward her with an amused, disconcerting gleam in his narrowed blue eyes that he made no attempt to subdue, even when she forced herself to frown back at him.

An eddy of wind rich with the scents of horsehair and saddle leather and eucalyptus oil swirled around her, tugging even more of her hair loose. She flung up both hands, desperately trying to keep it from flying shamelessly about her head.

He was abreast of her now. And as he passed, he leaned toward her, close enough to say in a low voice, "You see? You can't keep it under control. No matter how hard you try."

And they both knew he wasn't talking about her hair.

The newly shorn ewe bolted across the yard, the warm, noontime sun shimmering over her naked pink back. She had a patch of black tar on her far shoulder, where the shearer must have nicked her.

O'Reilly whistled. A flash of brown and black streaked across the stony ground, toward the ewe. Barrister darted around her, turning her. *Baa*. The sheep's tongue lolled out and she bleated in terror. *Baa, baa*. She didn't know she was one of the lucky ones. She was young, strong, and healthy; she would be allowed to live.

O'Reilly swiped his sleeve across his sweaty forehead. "Move this lot on out, Grisham," he shouted. The shepherd nodded and whistled up his dogs.

O'Reilly swung his attention back to the pen of milling, bleating sheep. He picked out a dozen or so wethers and consigned them to the mob he planned to drive down to Port Augusta. They wouldn't bring much, selling just for their hides and tallow and glue, but it was better than sending them downwind to have their throats slit or their heads bashed in with a club.

Which was the fate of the old, the weak, and the very young.

He shoved away from the fence. "Take over for a while, will you, Jacko?"

The black man nodded and swung up to perch on the top railing. Jacko had worked on Penyaka for only three years, but the Aborigine knew animals. He could probably judge a sheep's chances of survival better than O'Reilly himself.

Moving away from the confusion, noise, and stench of the woolshed, O'Reilly struck out uphill, heading downwind, away from the creek. At the top of the rise he paused and turned to let his gaze wander over his land.

A hot, dry wind scoured the slopes, kicking up eddies of gray-red dust that half obscured the horizon. There was no green, only shades of gray, red, and gold. Stripped of vegetation, the earth lay cracked, the scattered rocks brittle and exposed to the sun like the desiccated carcass of a dead animal. Red rocks. Gray dust. Faded, dead grass.

Farther down the hill he could see a big old native black oak, half-dead now, its shade sheltering a family of wallabies. Ears alert, nose twitching, a mother with her half-grown young beside her raised her head and stared at him. O'Reilly stilled, but she bolted anyway, taking off with great, flying leaps. He could hear the thump, thump of her big feet hitting the hard dirt as the rest of the wallabies turned to follow her.

When he'd first come here ten years ago, the grasslands had teemed with wallabies and kangaroos and emus, and the flocks of gaily colored cockatoos and native swans had been so big, they'd darkened the sky. But the sheep ate the grass and shrubs that had once sustained the native animals, and now it wasn't just the sheep that were dying. The land was dying. O'Reilly had never been the kind of man to waste time on regret, but the knowledge of the part he'd played in killing it lay like something festering and painful in his gut.

He swung to the right, toward the dry rocky gulch he'd selected as his killing field. Before he heard it, he smelled it: the metallic tang of blood wafting sickeningly in the hot air. Then came the sounds: the panicked bleating of the sheep, the dull *thwunk* of wood striking skulls, the heavy thud of bodies falling on top of more bodies.

He crested the ridge. He could see them now. The doomed sheep bunched together, mindless in their terror, their little heads jerking frantically, their tongues hanging out, their tiny, trampling hooves kicking up a pall of dust that hung over the scene like a shroud.

Waddies flailing, knives flashing, the black men waded among them. He could have shot the mob, but that would have cost tens of thousands of rounds of ammunition and the time of men he couldn't spare. So he had hired some of Sally's people to do the work, and he was paying them by letting them keep as many of the sheep as they wanted.

He knew most white men would think he was crazy, letting Aborigines get used to the taste of mutton. But he couldn't see burning sheep carcasses when children were starving.

And the Aborigines were starving. They lived too close to the land. They were a part of it, like the kangaroos and wallabies and cockatoos. And like the kangaroos and wallabies and cockatoos, they were dying.

Pinba glanced up, a bloody waddy clutched in one fist, and smiled when he caught sight of O'Reilly. Killing sheep meant nothing to Aborigines. In their way of thinking, the sheep were not a part of this land, and therefore stood outside the circle of life as they knew it.

231

But these sheep were O'Reilly's life. He'd spent the last eleven years building up his herds. Now he was destroying them.

Gritting his teeth, he loosed his knife from its sheath on his belt and waded into the surging sea of pearly-pink sheep, black human skin, and bright-red blood.

Amanda sat on the veranda reading one of *Aesop's Fables* to Missy, who snuggled contentedly in the crook of her arm. "Can we read the next one?" Missy pleaded when Amanda finished.

"Probably not," said Amanda. "The others will be coming back soon."

Missy gazed up at her with big blue eyes so like O'Reilly's. "Why haven't you been down to watch the shearing yet? I'd think you'd want to see it."

Amanda found she couldn't continue to meet that intense blue stare. "Perhaps one day," she lied. Because the truth was that she had no intention of visiting the shearing shed, where O'Reilly and the others worked so hard during the day. It would be too forward, too suggestive, too much of a betrayal of just how she really felt.

She'd spent the last two weeks telling herself, over and over, that she wanted nothing to do with him. That she could overcome this weakness she'd discovered within herself. That she could conquer the dangerous, wicked feelings and impulses that the Australian aroused in her. And yet...

And yet all the while, her entire being had been straining for stolen glimpses of his handsome, suntanned face and strong body. For the distant sound of his soft, lazy drawl.

More and more she caught herself remembering that night before the fire. Dwelling on the hard strength of his shoulders beneath her touch. The soft, heady taste of his lips on hers. The way her body had trembled and soared and thrummed with vibrant, heart-pounding life when she'd stood in his arms. She had even found herself lying in bed at night, imagining what would have happened if he hadn't stopped when he did.

What if he had unfastened her dress and opened her chemise to put his strong, tanned hands on her breasts; would she have let him? Would she have let him, if he'd slid his hands beneath her skirts and up the insides of her thighs? Would she have let him touch her, there, where she ached to be touched?

Wicked thoughts, abandoned thoughts. Seductive thoughts.

Useless thoughts. For he had taken her at her word and remained true to his promise; he had made no further attempt to kiss her or even touch her. She should have been relieved. She wanted to be relieved. But the truth, she had come to realize, was that she secretly yearned for him to touch her again, kiss her again.

"There's Sally!" exclaimed Missy, wiggling off the bench. Amanda caught the book just before it hit the pavement. With an indulgent smile she watched Missy dart across the garden and down the hill to where the Aboriginal woman walked, strung out in a line between Liam and Hannah. Sally spent her days down at the woolshed working with the rest of them. She did the skirting, Missy said—which meant she picked the dirt-encrusted edges off the fleeces before passing them on to be classed and pressed into bales.

Liam reached the house first and paused to pour himself a drink from the water bag hanging in the shade of the veranda. Beside him, the dog Barrister circled three times, then flopped down and panted his exhaustion.

"Good evening, Liam," Amanda said, consciously making her voice as pleasant as she could. She was always wary of the boy, although she was careful not to show it. Liam had never forgiven her for talking his father into putting a stop to his carousing with the bullockies, and she knew it would be only a matter of time until the boy found some way to repay her.

He nodded to her, then flung back his head and guzzled the water. His face was shiny with sweat and streaked gray with dirt, his brown hair plastered dark against his scalp. Shearing must be messy work.

She started to open the book again, but stopped at the sound of a strange, distant noise. She lifted her head, listening. It was like nothing she had ever heard, an unearthly howl that echoed through the hills to assault Amanda's very soul. It was a wailing that was not a wail. A humming that was not a hum, but vibrated and rose and fell and at times almost twanged. The effect was eerie and disembodied and otherworldly, like the ghostly memory of some primeval echo that seemed to reverberate around the surrounding hills, coming from everywhere and nowhere.

"What is that?" asked Amanda, flattening her hand against her chest, where her heart beat hard and fast.

"What's what?" asked Liam, pouring himself more water.

"That—that peculiar noise."

He raised his cup and stared at her. "What noise?"

"That sound. Like a throbbing, or a whirling hum. Surely you hear it?"

He shook his head slowly, his face serious. "Why? Do you?"

Amanda opened her mouth to say something sharp, then thought better of it and pressed her lips tightly together.

Liam blandly sipped his water. "The Aboriginal women have a legend about a murdered girl who moans at dusk, although I thought only women about to die were supposed to hear it. It's secret women's business, so I don't know much about it. But Hannah could tell you."

"I think I've already heard this story," said Amanda dryly. "Where is Hannah?"

Liam nodded toward the garden. "There."

Amanda twisted around. Sally and Missy had disappeared into the house, but Hannah was just letting herself in the side gate. She looked as tired and dirty as her brother.

"Hey, Hannah," Liam called. "Miss Davenport says she hears a strange sound."

Brother's and sister's gazes caught and held. There was a barely perceptible check in the girl's stride before she continued up the flagged walk, her face a mask of intense concern. Was it a trick of the fading light, Amanda wondered, or had she seen a fleeting flash of amusement before the girl carefully schooled her features?

"Oh, dear. I hope it's not—" She checked herself and glanced pointedly away, as if reluctant to continue.

"Don't tell me, Hannah," said Amanda. "It's your resident ghost, come to haunt me. Right? What's she supposed to do? Foretell my own imminent demise?"

Brother and sister looked at each other again, but neither said a word. They were obviously masters at this game.

A movement from the shadows of the veranda drew Amanda's attention to Liam's dog. Suddenly alert, Barrister lifted his head, his ears cocked forward, his tail suspended in the air behind him.

"Look at Barrister," said Amanda. "He hears it, too. Don't you, Barrister?"

As if in response, the dog pushed to his feet. He stood still a moment, staring at the distant, moaning hills. Then he threw back his head and howled, a wild, lonely sound that reminded Amanda more of a dingo than a dog.

"Why is he doing that?" she asked, staring at the dog.

Hannah pursed her lips in a worried frown. "The Aborigines say that when a dog howls at nothing, it's because he sees a spirit."

Amanda looked from the children back to the dog. Without a word, she picked up Missy's book and went inside.

The memory of that strange, unearthly rhythm haunted Amanda long after the actual droning intonations finally stopped.

She felt restless, as if she didn't fit in her own skin. She retired to her room shortly after supper but she didn't remove her clothes. She tried to read a book but couldn't concentrate. Finally, smothering an exclamation of annoyance, she pulled open the doors to the veranda and stepped outside.

The day had been unbelievably hot. Frighteningly so, when one considered that it was only late September. Even now when the sun had long since slipped behind the distant hills, a hot wind still blew across the land, sucking the moisture from the earth and every living thing on it.

Pulled by the balmy night, Amanda ventured out into the garden itself. Above her a deep purple sky arced ruinously clear and so full of brilliant, glittering stars that it made her heart ache just to look at it. Near the western boundary wall she noticed a young English elm throwing silent shadows that stretched like long alien fingers across the pale silver of the dead grass of the hillside. Amanda could hear its leaves moving restlessly in the hot, exotic wind. It was as if the tree were talking to her, telling her it didn't belong here.

She didn't belong here.

She stared at the black mass of the high Flinders Ranges thrusting up jagged and mysterious against the star-spangled sky. The wind came from beyond those mountains, from out of the empty, unknown center of the continent. The pungent, dry smells of the desert rode with it, overlaying the nearer, sweeter fragrances of the English garden.

She saw him then, standing at the edge of the garden, his hands braced against the top of the low stone wall in front of him, his gaze fixed on the stark, surrounding hills. There was something rigid, brittle even, about the way he held himself. It was as if he radiated tension that shimmied in the warm air around him.

Missy had told Amanda about the slaughter of sheep that had begun. She'd thought it sounded terrible. But looking at O'Reilly now it occurred to her that she probably had little concept of how truly horrific it really was.

She hesitated to draw closer to him. But the pain she sensed in him pulled her, and the memory of that pagan cadence pulsated in her head, haunting her. The sound had stopped before O'Reilly had returned to the homestead for supper, but he must have heard it. He must know what it was.

She approached him quietly. She heard him expel his breath in a sharp, almost angry blast; saw the muscles work in his throat as he swallowed. She paused again, conscious of a sense of crossing an invisible boundary into something private, something intimate.

Once she had thought of him as a man who never took anything seriously. A man who ridiculed and scorned everything, especially the things she considered most important. Now, watching his strong jaw tighten as he gazed out over the dying land, she wondered how she could ever have so misread him.

"This wind is bad," he said without turning his head, and she realized he must have heard her walk up behind him.

"I'm not used to a hot wind coming out of the north."

"No. My mother never got used to it either." He swung to face her, his right hip resting on the top of the wall. It was one of his typically lazy stances, but something was different tonight.

"Your mother was English?" she said in surprise.

"Oh yes. She came over as a girl, when her father was put on half pay after Waterloo." He tilted back his head and looked down his nose at her, imitating Amanda's own plummy accent—or was it his mother's? "Colonel James Fitzroy Beaumont the third," he intoned.

"From Kent. He fought with Wellington, you know." He lowered his chin, his hard gaze slamming into her, his precise English accent gone. "Just like General Whittaker."

"I didn't mean that the way it sounded."

"Yes you did."

He was in a reckless, dangerous mood. She'd never seen him like this before. But then, she'd never seen him after he'd spent a week slaughtering his own sheep by the thousands.

"You were born in Tasmania, weren't you?" she said cautiously.

"Yes."

"I'd heard Tasmania is more like England."

"It is. But my father left Tassie shortly after I was born, to take up a new run in Victoria. It was bloody hard there at first, especially for a woman raised the way my mother was. And by the time he prospered, she was gone."

"She died young? I'm sorry."

He gave a harsh, bitter laugh. "Hell, no. She could still be alive now for all I know. When I was twelve, she decided she was tired of Australia and the Irishman she'd married and the four children she'd had by him. So she found herself a pom and went back to England with him."

Dear God, thought Amanda, staring up into his handsome, shadowed face. He'd said it carelessly enough, but she caught the echo of bitterness in his voice, caught a flickering glimpse of the hurting, abandoned little boy he'd

240

once been. She thought of his English wife, who had also hated Australia, and who had also left him. And for the first time in her life, Amanda felt ashamed of her own Englishness.

"No wonder you don't like the English," she said softly.

"Nah." His lips twisted into a wry grin that tugged oddly at her heart. "I'm Irish, remember? Hating the English is part of our national identity."

"But you're half-English." Not only was he half-English, she realized, but on his mother's side he was obviously far better born than he'd deliberately led her to believe. Once that would have mattered to her. It still should have mattered. But for some odd reason, she found that it did not.

He shook his head. "Don't remind me." She watched him twist around to look out over the valley again. "What did you want, anyway?" he asked after a moment.

She hesitated, the harsh wind buffeting her ears and whipping at the hem of her skirt.

"You obviously came over here to talk to me about something. So what was it?"

She went to stand beside him at the wall. Beside him, but not too close. "I heard a strange sound this afternoon. I was wondering if you could tell me what it was."

"A sound?" He glanced down at her. "What kind of a sound?"

"That's just it. I don't even know how to describe it. It was...uncanny. Like the howling of the wind, or the whimpering of an animal, only deeper, louder. And it went on and on and on. Don't tell me you didn't hear it?"

"No. But if you'd ever been in the stinking din of a shearing shed, you wouldn't wonder at that. When was this?"

"Near dusk, as Liam and Hannah were walking back up to the homestead. I'm certain they heard it. But for some reason they pretended not to. I thought perhaps they're planning to play some new trick on me."

She watched the wind flutter the shaggy ends of his hair against his neck, and she had an almost irresistible urge to reach out and touch him there. To feel the pulse that beat low in his throat.

"You want me to talk to them?" he asked.

"Oh, no. Please don't," she said hastily. "I just thought you might be able to tell me what it was, that's all. Thank you. Good night."

She turned to go back to the house, but his hand shot out and caught her by the wrist, stopping her. Heat sizzled up her arm and crackled in the air around them. She sucked in a startled breath, her gaze flying to meet his.

"Stay," he said, his eyes intent and serious. He slid his hand down to take hers and tug her toward him, wrapping his arm around her in such a way that his hand rested on the small of her back, his fingers still entwined with hers.

They were so close, his thighs brushed hers and her breasts would have pressed against his chest if she hadn't retained enough sense to flatten the palm of her free hand against the muscled wall of his abdomen and keep some distance between them.

Her head fell back as she stared up into his hard, shadowed face. They were so close, his energy seemed to flow over her, entrap her, arouse her at some primitive, subconscious level she could not even begin to understand. Simply being this near to him was enough to make her feel warm and tingly, to set her heart to beating faster, to start those treacherous, hungry tremors, way down low in her belly.

"Stay," he said again, dropping his voice to a whisper.

Her heart careened wildly. She found she could no longer bear the intensity of his brilliant, glittering stare and dropped her gaze to the buttons of the blue work shirt covering his broad chest. "You promised you wouldn't kiss me again," she choked out.

"I won't try to kiss you," he said, even as his thumb rubbed sensuously across the backs of her captive fingers.

It was a simple movement, but dangerously arousing. She knew she should not be letting him do it, but the sensation was too wonderful. And so she hovered, confused, wanting to be right where she was, wishing desperately she had the strength to run away from him and what he made her feel.

"I promise I won't try to kiss you," he repeated, his voice low and husky, his lips dangerously close to her ear. "Only...stay."

243

Keeping his fingers clasped with hers, he began to move his hand in slow, easy circles, his knuckles ranging sinuously up her back, down over her hips. She felt as if she were being swirled away in a moist pool of heat. She forgot to breathe. She forgot everything except for the sensation of his casual caress. In its own way, it was even more seductive than if he had kissed her.

Her eyes drifted half-closed as she lost herself in the wonder of his touch. Who would have believed that such a strong, rough man could be capable of such gentleness, such tempting tenderness. She ached, she trembled, she burned with the need to press herself to him, to join herself to him. She was practically shuddering with the effort required to stay upright and rigid in the circle of his arm. "I shouldn't have come out here."

"It's human contact, Mandy. We all need it. You need it." He paused. "I need it."

"But I don't want this," she said hoarsely. Although what she meant was, *I don't want what is happening between us.*

And it was as if he heard what she meant rather than what she said, because he answered, "Neither do I."

"Then why..."

"I don't know why." He brought his free hand up to touch her face, his fingers spreading gently over her cheek. She saw the hunger in his eyes. Hunger and anger and a shadow of confusion that matched her own. "But it's happening. I want you, Amanda. And you want

244

me. Only there's something inside you that's stopping you."

He ran his thumb along her lower lip. "What is it, Mandy? What happened to you in the past that's got you so afraid of letting go again that you charge through life with this beautiful, sensuous mouth of yours crimped down to a thin, sour line? What's made you so bloody afraid to feel anything, except maybe anger and contempt and disdain?"

For a moment, she couldn't answer him. They stared at each other, his brows drawn together as if in genuine concern, her chest lifting and falling as she fought to control herself.

"It..." She swallowed. "It has nothing whatsoever to do with anything that happened to me in the past," she lied. "What is stopping me is my maidenly modesty. Common sense. What the French call *pudeur.*"

One corner of his mouth quirked up in a smile. "At least you recognize that something is stopping you from doing what you want to do."

Her eyes widened in dismay as she realized he was cleverer than she'd given him credit for. She seemed to make it a habit of underestimating him.

At the sight of her discomfiture, his smile broadened. "You bring this down to a battle of logic, Mandy, and you're gonna lose. Because what I'm arguing for is a fundamental law of nature that keeps the human race going. Whereas what you're advocating is a mere

245

cultural embellishment, by no means universal and probably more observed in the breach than in the practice."

"That does not mean it is wrong."

"Maybe." He ran his fingertips slowly, agonizingly, down the tender flesh of her neck in a way that made her suck in an audible hiss of delight. "But what does this tell you? What does your body tell you now?"

"Please," she whispered. "You must stop."

But even as she spoke, her free hand stole up his hard chest to clutch at his neck, as if she would hold him to her, as if she could not bear the thought of letting him go.

"Shhh. Don't fight it, Amanda. Just let it happen." She felt the moist, warm rush of his words caress her ear, and a deliciously needy heat clenched deep in her being. Before she could stop herself, she arched against him, pressing the center of that need against him.

"But this is wrong," she murmured.

"No." His fingertips did unimaginably wonderful things as they danced down her throat, flicked open the top buttons of her high-necked dress so that he could trace the line of her collarbone. She shuddered, lost in a heated vortex of desire and pleasure.

Then his lean, strong hand slipped downward to close over her breast.

She gasped at a sensation so overwhelming she almost cried out. She bucked against him, but he kept his other hand entwined with hers at the small of her back, holding her pressed tight against him. "Tell me what you feel," he said softly, his lips temptingly near to hers. He rasped his thumb across her nipple, and even through the cloth of her dress and chemise, that traitorous nub immediately peaked with want.

She wrenched her head away from the seductive nearness of his lips and forced herself to stare unblinkingly out over the empty, moonlit plains. She heard an owl hoot in the distance, heard the dry leaves of the gum trees down by the creek whisper in the wind. Yet every fiber of her being remained agonizingly aware of the warmth of his hand on her breast, the power of his body so close to hers.

"Disgust," she said at last, her breath coming in hard, fast pants. "I feel disgust."

She heard his low chuckle as he moved his hand in a slow, gentle caress that sent waves of shivering, needy delight coursing through her. "Look at me and say it. If you can."

Her head swung around, his gaze riveted hers. "I feel...I feel..." Her tongue slipped out to moisten her dry lips. He gently worked his fingers, kneading the fullness of her breast, flooding her with fire. "I feel..." Her breath caught in her throat and she couldn't say it. If she said it, he might stop what he was doing, and she didn't think she could bear that.

He dipped his head and nuzzled her neck. "Pleasure," he said hoarsely. "What you feel is pleasure, Amanda. And desire. Feel it. Enjoy it. Admit you like it."

"No."

"Why not?"

She clenched at his broad shoulders with both hands, her fingers digging into the work-hardened muscles of his back. She realized dimly that at some point he had released her hand and was no longer holding her to him. But it didn't matter. She was hopelessly, helplessly held captive by her own wanton desire and the exquisite pleasure of what he was doing to her hungry body.

"Ah, Christ." His voice was a ragged groan. "I didn't mean— But I can't—"

She squeezed her eyes shut, lost, adrift in the sensation of his hands as they enflamed her tender belly, slid with delicious slowness beneath her skirt to run fire up her inner thigh to her—

With a cry of dismay, she flattened her palms against his chest and pushed, wrenching herself away from him. *"Don't touch me there."*

She backed away from him, one hand clenching the open collar of her dress. She realized that at some point he must have loosened her hair, so that it tumbled wantonly, betrayingly about her shoulders.

He stood quite still, his hips braced against the garden wall, his legs spread wide, his chest heaving as he drew in air. His eyes were fastened on hers, his face taut with arousal and frustration. "All right," he said. "Not there."

"Don't touch me anywhere." Her fingers fumbled with her buttons. "You promised you wouldn't."

He shook his head, his lips slanting into a smile that clutched treacherously at her heart. "I promised I wouldn't kiss you. I don't remember saying anything about touching."

"If you were a gentleman—" She tried to coil her hair back up, only she seemed to have lost most of her pins.

"But I'm not, remember?" He pushed away from the wall with a forceful heave that had her skittering backward. "I'm a bloody Australian. And that's exactly why you like me. Because I break all the rules so you don't have to. Which means you can kiss me and let me touch you, and you can get all excited and enjoy yourself, and then afterward you can blame it all on me and tell yourself it only happened because I'm so bloody uncouth and uncivilized and un-English."

She stared at him. At his work-broadened shoulders and tanned cheeks and sun-narrowed eyes. And she knew he was right. But only up to a point.

She prayed to God that he never guessed the rest of it.

Twisting sideways, he snapped a sprig of flowers from one of the plumbagos rioting over the top of the wall, its white blossoms glowing pale and beautiful in the moonlight. Holding the twig, he raised his gaze to hers, his eyes glinting with a teasing challenge. "You can't deny the fact you liked what happened here tonight as much as I did."

She couldn't, of course. She could only stare at him, wide-eyed and silent.

He stretched out his hand and she made to jerk back. He said, "No. Hold still." So she stood, trembling, breathless, while he tucked the spray into the loose hair above her ear, then trailed his fingers down her cheek.

"Ah, Mandy." He sighed. "I don't see the end of this. I wish I did, but I don't."

"We shall resist our desires, of course." Her voice quavered, but she held her chin determinedly high. "We are both mature enough and strong enough, surely, not to be overwhelmed by our physical inclinations."

A dimple appeared in one of his cheeks. "Problem is," he said, his hand falling back to his side, "it's not just physical and you know it. If it was, it wouldn't be a problem. For either of us."

She sucked in a quick, startled breath, although she couldn't have said what shocked her more—the discovery that he knew the dangerous tendency of her wayward affections. Or the implication that his own feelings were more involved than she'd ever imagined.

He held her gaze for a long, heart-pounding moment, then swung to face the moon-drenched valley below. "You'd better go inside now."

Tearing her gaze from him, she spun about to walk quickly back to the house. But when she reached the veranda, she couldn't keep herself from pausing, couldn't stop her eyes from darting back for one last look at where he still stood, tall and beautiful, at the edge of the garden.

She told herself she would make certain nothing like this ever happened again. She told herself she was morally strong enough to resist the obvious weakness of her flesh.

She had to be. Because there could be no future for them together. Because he was tied to this land, and she was determined to return to England.

And because somewhere out there lived a woman named Katherine O'Reilly, who was still legally his wife.

CHAPTER THIRTEEN

The ghostly sound returned the next evening, then not again until a week later, and then the week after that.

With everyone, even Chow and Ching, busy with the shearing much of the time, the homestead compound often stood deserted except for Missy and Amanda. During the day Amanda didn't mind the solitude. Sometimes, she and Missy saddled Calypso and Ivory and went for a ride, always being careful to keep to the trail that ran along the creek bed, so that they wouldn't get lost. Other times, they took Missy's lessons out onto the veranda and worked on the little girl's reading and numbers in the fresh air.

But when the light began to leach from the sky and shadows lengthened across the hills,

Amanda found herself growing nervous, waiting to see if that eerie thrumming would begin to vibrate through the air again.

She was standing on the edge of the veranda, her hand wrapped around a post as she watched faint wisps of clouds gather over the now silent, brooding hills, when something scraped against stone behind her.

She whipped around. "Oh...Hannah. You startled me."

The girl pulled out one of the veranda chairs and straddled it backward the way a man might do. "Somethin' wrong?"

Amanda leaned back against the post and gave Hannah a long, steady look. "As a matter of fact, yes. That is a decidedly improper posture for a lady."

Hannah's eyes narrowed. "I am not a lady."

"I won't argue with that," snapped Amanda, her temper worn thin by the intermittent menacing sound and too many nights made sleepless by unsated sexual tension. "But you are, whether you like to admit it or not, a female, and you are growing up. It's past time you learned to at least act like a lady."

"I told you, I don't want to act like a lady. Why should I? All they ever do is lie around feeling faint because their stays are laced too tight." She tossed her head, sending her loose hair rippling in thick waves around her shoulders. Amanda thought the girl must have washed it since she came up from the woolshed because it shone soft and clean and dark as polished jet. She was already a striking girl, with big brown eyes and a perfectly formed, heart-shaped face. It occurred to Amanda, studying her, that she would grow into a stunning woman.

"I want to be a stockman or a bullocky when I grow up," she announced. "And I don't see why I shouldn't be able to. I can ride better than Liam and I can crack a whip better, too."

Amanda stared down at the proud, defiant, miserably unhappy girl, and felt as if something were tearing within her, exposing an old wound. A wound that had scarred over, perhaps, but never entirely healed.

"My dear Hannah," she said, her voice breaking with barely suppressed emotion as she walked forward to sink into the chair beside the taut girl. "I'm sure you can. I'm sure you've worked very hard to be able to do everything better than any boy your age. I know I did."

Hannah's head snapped around, her eyes widening as she stared at Amanda in shocked silence.

"Oh, I don't mean chasing cows and cracking whips. The boys I grew up around didn't do those things. But they did study Greek and Latin, and read philosophy and history and other things considered inappropriate for young girls. Girls in families like mine were supposed to spend their time learning to be agreeable and practicing the piano."

"You don't play the piano very well," said Hannah, her lips twitching into a reluctant smile. Amanda had continued giving Missy and Hannah instruction at the piano whenever she thought about it. But she didn't think about it very often, and the lessons were usually short and decidedly lacking in enthusiasm on her part.

She ventured to place her white lady's hand over Hannah's slim brown one, where it rested on the back of the chair. Hannah's hand jerked, but she didn't try to remove it. "I wasn't as brave as you, I'm afraid," Amanda admitted, returning the girl's smile. "I never tried to wear trousers or act like a boy in that way. But I did study all the things I wasn't supposed to. I studied very hard. And I rarely ever practiced my piano."

"You wanted to be a boy, too?"

"I thought I did. It took me a long time to realize that what I really wanted was my father's love and approval. He barely seemed to notice my existence, you see. I thought, if only I'd been born a boy who could some day grow up to become a scholar like my father, then he'd have shown more interest in me. He'd have loved me."

Her voice threatened to break again, but she forced herself to go on. "Except, of course, it didn't work. No matter how hard I studied, I couldn't turn myself into a boy. And I couldn't make my father love me more than he loved his books and the cold stone buildings of his college."

"What about your mother? Did he love her?"

"I don't know," Amanda answered honestly. "She died when I was born. But I don't think he had any great passion for her. I've gradually realized that some men are simply incapable of loving anyone very deeply, and my father was one of them. It didn't have anything to do with who or what I was at all."

Even as she said it, Amanda knew it had been a mistake. For Patrick O'Reilly, surely, was a man of deep loves and great passions.

"My father loves Missy. He says he treats her different from me because she's younger and needs more attention. But it isn't true. He never treated me the way he treats her."

The pain of wanting in the young girl's velvet brown eyes was so naked that Amanda had to turn away from it to watch the shifting wisps of white clouds riding high in the sky. She didn't know what to say. She knew O'Reilly loved his firstborn daughter. But there was no doubt that their relationship was a troubled one.

"It's because I look like her," Hannah said bitterly. "My mother. Whenever he sees me, he remembers her, and so he hates me."

"Oh, no, Hannah. Surely…"

A sad, too-wise smile thinned Hannah's lips. "It's true. Here, I'll show you."

She pushed off her chair and disappeared inside, only to return a moment later, something clutched tightly in her fist. "Look." She laid an exquisite miniature on the table beside them.

A peculiar lump filled Amanda's throat as

she stared down at a portrait of a young woman painted on ivory and framed in a delicate filigree of gold. It was an expensive piece, worked by a skilled artisan. She glanced from the miniature to Hannah. "Your mother?"

"Yes."

Swallowing hard, Amanda leaned forward to study the woman who was O'Reilly's wife.

She was beautiful. Her lips full and deliciously curved, her nose straight and thin, her face as heart-shaped as Hannah's. Her eyes were a wide, clear brown, her skin a pale cream, her hair as dark as the night.

"Do you see?"

Amanda looked up into Hannah's beautiful face, framed by waves of ebony. Her chin was stronger than her mother's, and she had that intense, intelligent stare that marked all three of Patrick O'Reilly's children. But in every other way, Hannah was the image of Katherine.

Amanda dropped her gaze back to the miniature. "Your mother is a lovely woman."

Hannah picked up the miniature and stared down at it with a curious combination of longing and something darker, something fierce, that came perilously close to being hate. "She's even prettier in real life."

"Do you remember her?"

"Of course. I was five when she went away."

"And Missy was only a baby."

"So?"

"Did it ever occur to you," said Amanda, feeling her way carefully, "that it might be the reason your father treats Missy differently? Because he's raised her by himself, without her mother, from the time she was a baby? It can't have been easy for her, never having known her mother. Perhaps he's felt he needed to go out of his way to make up for it."

She could tell by the arrested expression on Hannah's face that the explanation had never occurred to the girl before. Her brown eyes practically glowed with a desperate kind of hope. Then it was as if something slammed shut, as she refused to believe it. "It hasn't been easy for me, either."

"No. I don't suppose it has. But you're very good at hiding your pain, Hannah. Perhaps your father never realized how badly you were hurting inside."

Hannah regarded her steadily, until Amanda had the uncomfortable sensation the girl saw more than Amanda had meant to reveal about herself. "You grew up without a mother, too, didn't you?"

Amanda sighed. "Yes. And you're right; it's never easy, no matter what your age. It's one of those things I suppose no one ever gets over."

For a moment they sat together in silence, but it was a companionable silence, born from the knowledge that they shared a unique bond, forged from their common pain.

Reluctantly, Amanda thrust back her chair. "I must hurry if I'm to have time to change for supper."

As she rose, she glanced over and noticed

Sally standing in the shadows, staring at her. Lately, Amanda often found the Aboriginal woman silently watching her when she was with the children. "Did you want something, Sally?"

Sally stared off over the desiccated hills. "Big kangaroos and possums all tumble down," she said, a faraway, almost frightening expression in her eyes. "No good for blackfellow. Soon blackfellow tumble down, too."

Disconcerted, Amanda glanced back at Hannah. "I don't understand."

" 'Tumble down' means to die," explained Hannah. "Are you going to let Jacko do it?" she asked Sally. "Are you?"

"Do what?" asked Amanda.

"Papa wants Jacko to do a rain dance. Try to break the drought. But Jacko said he couldn't unless Sally agreed. He's her nephew, you see, and she's considered a pretty powerful witch woman herself, among her people."

Sally nodded. "Jacko makum rain for O'Reilly."

Amanda smiled. "Surely Mr. O'Reilly does not honestly believe—" She broke off with something like a gasp as a hideous apparition appeared at the edge of the veranda.

It stood upright, the size and shape of a man. But its body glistened red and white in the sunlight, and it had *feathers*. A scream formed in Amanda's mind, but she managed to trap it before it erupted and embarrassed her. Because the apparition, she realized almost immediately, was actually Jacko.

He had stripped off his stockman's clothes and painted his naked black body with white clay and red ochre mixed with oil, and then covered himself with emu down. Beside him walked O'Reilly, carrying some kind of a bark vessel and a string bag.

"Where do you want to set up?" O'Reilly asked, hesitating in the center of the garden's small chamomile lawn.

"This looks good, I think," said Jacko, turning in a small circle. His English was considerably better than his aunt's. So good, in fact, that it sounded strange coming from his now naked, primitively painted figure.

O'Reilly set down the bag and the hollow bark basin that Amanda realized was full of water. Then he sauntered over to join them on the veranda, his step hesitating for a moment when he saw Amanda. "Why, g'day, Miss Davenport. You here to watch, too?"

Her gaze met his and for a brief instant the memory of everything that had passed between them the other night, with all the emotions it had aroused, shimmied in the hot air. She felt her cheeks grow warm, felt her breath hitch and catch in her throat. She stared at him, at his sun-streaked hair and straight dark brows and narrowed blue eyes. Then she saw his mouth curve faintly, and she jerked her attention back to the naked stockman.

"Surely you don't credit these native legends," she said.

He came to stand beside her, his body big and sun warmed and intimidatingly close.

"Why not?" He shoved his hat back on his head. "I've seen enough things in my life I bloody well can't explain by any of the natural laws or religious beliefs I was brought up to accept. Besides, when I think about it, it simply doesn't make sense to me that God would present all the keys to holiness and spirituality to a few million Europeans, and damn the rest of the world to a soulless wasteland."

"That's blasphemy," she said automatically.

"Maybe." He leaned in closer. "But I'd deck myself out in chicken feathers and dance down the streets of Brinkman buck naked myself if I thought it would save this land."

He looked at her in that intensely challenging way he had, and she suddenly felt somehow less than him. Less than what she wanted herself to be. She swallowed hard, her throat feeling almost too raw to let her speak. "Would you explain this ceremony to me?" she asked quietly.

His glittering blue eyes held her gaze for one pregnant moment; then he nodded to where Jacko had knelt on the ground to remove a collection of small smooth stones from the bag and carefully align them in a pile. "The rain stones are from Cadnowie," O'Reilly said as Jacko placed a clear, faceted crystal at the apex of the pyramid of red and gray stones. "Because it never runs dry, the water hole is considered a powerful link to the rain spirit."

As she watched, Jacko straightened and

lifted the water-filled bark vessel. "The water in the bark is from Cadnowie, too," O'Reilly continued as Jacko began to move, his body jerking in quick, rhythmic jolts. "And see that green twig he carries? It's from a needle-brush. Their roots are a good source of water if you're ever lost in the bush."

Suddenly, Jacko flung back his head and let loose a strange, animal-like howl.

"The dingo is Jacko's totem," O'Reilly explained as the stockman danced around the stones in slow, measured steps, his voice now rising and falling in a singsong chant. "It's part of what connects him to this land."

Jacko dipped the twig in the bark and flung a sprinkling of water over the stones, the drops glistening like diamonds in the late afternoon sun.

A cooling breeze skimmed across the garden. Amanda glanced up at the sky and saw that the scattered white wisps she'd noticed earlier had coalesced into one big cloud that seemed to hover over the garden.

Jacko twirled round and round, his body angled forward, his knees bent, his feet flat, his head jerking back and forth as if to some silently pounding music. The wind gusted again, shaking the high boughs of the trees and lifting the hair from Amanda's forehead with a breath of moist air.

And then it began to rain.

"It worked," squealed Hannah.

Big, scattered drops hit the ground, filling the air with the scent of dust and wet earth.

Amanda could hear the rain pounding on the roof, see the leaves of the trees and shrubs in the garden shivering beneath the impact.

But on the surrounding hills, the sun shone bright and hot and dry.

Jacko stopped dancing and slowly straightened. "It's raining," he said in disgust, glancing around. "But only on the bloody garden."

Sally shook her head as if to say, *I knew it wasn't going to work*. "Drought spirit no take rain stones oudda fire till all sheep tumble down," she said, and went into the house.

O'Reilly stepped out into the open. "Still skeptical, Miss Davenport?" he asked, letting the rain beat down on his hat and shoulders.

"It would have rained anyway," Amanda insisted, although she wasn't sure she believed it. "I noticed the clouds earlier."

O'Reilly held his hands out at his sides, his palms uplifted, his face turned toward the sky. Already the rain was easing off, the cloud dispersing. But to her surprise, his dimples flashed, and she heard the rich rumble of his laughter. "Well," he said, "at least Chow won't need to water the garden."

She looked at him. At the water splashing on the planes of his upturned face and trickling in rivulets down his lean cheeks. At the curve of his lips. At the bare column of his tanned throat and the strong, capable breadth of his wide shoulders. She felt the breath easing in and out of her lungs. Felt the moist air cool against her face. Felt time grind down and stop as she looked at him. Just looked at him.

She'd already known that over the course of the last two months, what had begun as simple physical fascination had turned into a deep, frightening desire. She'd known that what had begun as antipathy had gradually shifted to a grudging kind of liking that was deepening into affection.

But what she hadn't realized was that at some point, without her being aware of it—without her even wanting it—liking had turned to love.

She felt her love for this man swell within her until it burned in her breast like an ache. An ache that was never going to go away.

And was never going to be fulfilled.

Ten days later, Amanda was sitting on the veranda, darning one of her stockings and listening to Missy recite the times tables when the strange wailing sounded again.

"Four twos are eight," Missy chanted, hopping from one flag in the garden path to the next. At the edge of the garden behind her, the laundry that Chow had done earlier hung dry and still in the fading, late afternoon light. "Five twos are ten. Six twos are twelve and seven twos are—" She broke off, her small body stilling as the low-pitched, unearthly moan echoed once more through the shadowy hills.

Amanda set aside her mending and rose to her feet, her attention, like the child's, focused on the brooding, alien landscape now throbbing with an eerie, inhuman voice around them. "It's started again," she whispered.

"I asked Sally why someone keeps playing the didgeridoo," said Missy. "But she wouldn't tell me."

Amanda's startled gaze flew to the child. She had never discussed the moaning drone with Missy. She wasn't sure if it was because she hadn't wanted the little girl to see how troubled she was by it, or if she'd simply been unwilling to discover that Missy was a part of whatever trick her siblings were playing. "What's a dig...a dig..."

"Didgeridoo," repeated Missy, grinning as she always did whenever she discovered she knew something her governess did not. "It's a long, hollow, sticklike thing Aboriginal men play."

"You mean it's a musical instrument?"

"I guess so."

It was music of some sort, she realized now. Only so strange and atonal that she hadn't recognized it.

Missy stared at her solemnly. "Liam said he told you what it was, but that you were so scared at the thought that there were Aborigines in the bush, watching us, that you didn't want anyone to talk about it."

"He said that, did he? Clever."

"You mean he made that up?"

When Amanda didn't answer, the little girl's hands curled into two angry fists she held clutched against her sides. "That's mean. He

264

and Hannah did the same thing to Miss Sutton. They convinced her she was the only one who could hear it because she was about to die, and she got so nervous she couldn't eat or sleep. She jumped at the least noise and started talkin' to people who weren't there. And then one night she set her candle so close to her bedroom curtains that they caught on fire. Papa finally had to send her away."

"In other words, she went mad," said Amanda quietly. "Tell me, which one of your governesses died here?"

Missy shook her head. "None of 'em."

So the dead governess was just another part of Hannah's tale. The knowledge should have been a comfort to Amanda, only it was not. The idea of some poor silly creature driven out of her mind by the wind and the wild, wide-open spaces was infinitely more frightening than the thought of some spinster dying of a heart attack in her bed.

Amanda gazed out over the dusk-darkened hills, still vibrating with that strange, haunting music, and a shiver of fear ran up her spine. The ghostly moaning had been disturbing enough when she'd thought it a prank. Now she knew that somewhere out there sat an unseen, primitive man who was deliberately filling the air with this primeval beat. She listened to it echo on and on, until she imagined she could feel it seep into her, pound through her, become a part of her blood.

Then, as suddenly as it had begun, the dull wailing stopped. In the startling quiet, she could hear the butcher birds and wagtails chirping their evening songs from their nests down by the creek. She glanced nervously at the dark, empty house behind her. "Why is everyone so late tonight?" she said, half to herself. Not even Chow and Ching had returned yet, and Sally had been gone all afternoon. The atmosphere of the homestead suddenly seemed alien, as if the familiar had been invaded by the unfamiliar.

"Miss Davenport," said Missy, tugging at her skirt. "What's that?"

Amanda's gaze followed the child's pointing finger. A tall, black figure hovered at the far edge of the garden, outlined clearly against a splash of white-blooming roses. It was the figure of a man, unnaturally silent and menacing, his arms poised above his head, as if he held some strange weapon.

Amanda felt a ball of fear wedge in her throat, choking her. "Missy," she croaked. "Does your papa have a rifle?"

"Mm-hmm." The little girl nodded her head, her gaze fastened on the strange apparition at the bottom of the garden. "He keeps it on a rack over the door in his bedroom."

Amanda took the child's cold hand. "Come with me. Quickly."

Feeling paralyzed by fear, Amanda somehow managed to walk through the dining room and parlor and pull a chair over to the door so she could climb up and take Patrick O'Reilly's gun down from its rack.

"Now, Missy, this is important," she said,

carefully checking the gun's mechanism. It was primed and ready to fire. "I want you to go into my room and wait for me there."

"But I want to stay with you."

"No, darling." She rested one hand on the little girl's quivering shoulder. "Please, just do as I say."

Leaving Missy safely inside, Amanda forced herself to walk back through the quiet, shadow-filled house and out onto the veranda.

The dark figure at the edge of the garden waited for her.

Amanda raised the gun to her shoulder and carefully sighted it in. "Who are you?" she called, her voice quavering but strong.

An unexpectedly cool gust of wind fanned her cheeks and sent a scattering of dry leaves rattling across the flagstones. The man seemed to waver, then stood firm. He did not answer.

"Identify yourself," she demanded, using the traditional formula. "In the Queen's name, I call upon you to answer, or I shall fire."

The dusty, eucalypt-scented wind gusted again, moaning through the eaves. The man seemed to lurch forward. Amanda's sweaty fingers tightened around the butt of the gun. She wanted to scare him away, not shoot him. Sucking in a deep, steadying breath, she swung the rifle barrel until it pointed a good ten feet to the left of the man's upraised arms, and carefully squeezed the trigger.

The gun roared and spit fire. The recoil slammed the butt painfully into Amanda's shoulder, knocking her backward and bringing startled tears to her eyes. The man jerked and flopped over backward.

"Oh, my goodness," she gasped, lowering the gun.

"You killed him," said Missy in awe, sliding out from behind the dining room door.

"But I couldn't have. I didn't even aim at him. I am certain I..." Amanda chewed her lip. "Oh, heavens."

She did not know what to do. The man could be hurt and in urgent need of help. She couldn't just leave him down there alone to bleed to death while she went for help. Then again, he might not be hurt at all, but lying in wait for her, ready to grab her if she came near. Oh, God. What should she do?

The gun still gripped tightly in her hands, Amanda stepped cautiously off the veranda with Missy trailing silently behind her. Her full, crinolined skirt brushed the boxwood and lavender edging the path, filling the air with sweet, familiar scents so oddly at variance with the strange, shrill calls of the white corellas coming in to roost in the gums down by the creek.

Her footsteps slowed as she approached the end of the garden. Her heart pounded and her knees shook and she almost turned around and ran back to the house.

The light was fading fast, the setting sun staining the sky an unnatural shade of cerise. But there was enough light to show Amanda and Missy that there were no white roses blooming in this corner of the garden. Instead, the chemises, handkerchiefs, and pinafores Chow had washed and hung up that morning now lay tumbled ignobly in the dirt.

And in the midst of the ruined laundry rested Amanda's dark brown dress. It sprawled across the earth as limp as a corpse, its arms upflung, the cuffs still pinned to a clothesline now neatly severed by a well-aimed bullet.

CHAPTER FOURTEEN

O'Reilly lifted the tin cup and drank deeply, the water sluicing nice and easy down his parched throat. A surprisingly cool breeze had kicked up since the sun started slipping behind the Ranges. After so many stinking hours in the stuffy atmosphere of the woolshed, it felt bloody damn good.

"Reckon it'll only be a few more days, mate?" said one of the Derwent Drums, swiping the back of one arm across his freckled forehead as he strolled over to where O'Reilly stood, hip-shot, beside the water tank outside the shearers' quarters.

"Yeah, looks like it." O'Reilly reached to refill the cup, just as the crack of a rifle shot echoed down the hill.

His head jerked around. "Christalmighty." The tin pannikin hit the flagging with a clatter as he yanked his horse's reins loose from the nearby post. He had the chestnut stretched out

269

in a canter before his seat even hit the saddle.

His eyes narrowed as he scanned the distant cluster of buildings for signs of some unnatural movement. The shearing had ended for the day, but most of the men were still mingling around the shearers' quarters. A shot that close to the house could only mean trouble.

Raking his spurs across the gelding's sides, he urged the chestnut into a wild-eyed, foam-flecked run that sent a choking cloud of red dust billowing out around him. Bushrangers weren't as common in South Australia as they were in Victoria or New South Wales, but three of them had raped and cut up a woman at an outstation down by Melrose not very long ago. And although he got on pretty well with the blacks, one could never really be sure...

He reined the chestnut in hard by the garden, where he could see a few stockmen and a shepherd crowding around the side gate. Swinging out of the saddle, he threw his reins to one of the stockmen and pushed his way through the knot of men.

He checked for the briefest instant when he caught the sound of Amanda's laughter, floating to him from out of the gathering darkness. He'd never heard her really laugh before, but that deep, throaty gurgle could come only from her. It occurred to him for an instant that she might be hysterical, but there wasn't anything wild or mindless about that laughter. It was rippling and hearty, the kind of laugh that made you want to smile, just hearing it.

And then he saw her.

She knelt in a bed of creeping thyme. Snowy white handkerchiefs and dainty feminine underthings lay scattered around her like fallen flags of surrender. Her head was thrown back and her eyes squeezed shut, and she held her left hand pressed to her ribs, as if she'd laughed so hard her side hurt. He could see something lying across her lap. As he drew closer, he realized she held her ugly brown dress grasped in her arms like a dying lover. Missy leaned against her shoulder, giggling.

Neither the woman nor the child had seen him yet, and for a moment he let himself simply enjoy looking at this unexpected side of Miss Amanda Davenport. Her cheeks were flushed and streaming with tears of laughter, her hair tumbling half-down around her shoulders, her prim gray gown stained green around the knees. He thought she had never looked more beautiful, and something swelled within him, something sweet and aching and unwelcome.

And for a moment, it was as if the years had fallen away and he could see her as she must once have been—could imagine her as the child she'd left behind. An exuberant and rebellious child with her dog barking at her heels and her brilliant, flame-colored hair bouncing against her back as she ran, laughing, to escape the tedious disapproval of some stern piano teacher. And he could imagine her as a young woman, too; her eyes squeezed shut, her lips parted in rapture as she allowed some unnamed man to touch her body in ways she had been trying to forget ever since.

Missy glanced up then and saw him. "Oh, Papa! Guess what? I thought I saw a strange man, watching us from the bottom of the garden. So Miss Davenport got your rifle and shot at him, to scare him away. Only it wasn't a man at all, just Miss Davenport's dress, hanging on the line with the rest of the laundry!"

At the sound of Missy's voice, Amanda's head snapped around and her eyes flew open. The laughter died on her lips.

She scrambled to her feet, embarrassment deepening the flush in her cheeks. "Mr. O'Reilly! I...I don't know what to say. I am most dreadfully sorry to have caused such a disturbance." She reached quickly to retrieve something from the bed of thyme. When she straightened again, he realized it was his rifle. She handled it competently, if not comfortably, and it made him realize how little he really knew about this woman.

"Where did you learn to shoot?"

Her eyes widened in surprise. "I beg your pardon?"

"I said, who taught you to handle a gun?"

She glanced down at the rifle in her hands, then away. She did not meet his gaze. She was so obviously, painfully mortified by all the commotion she'd caused that he was hard put not to laugh. "My uncle." She swallowed. "The country squire I told you about."

He reached to take the gun from her slack

grasp. She released it immediately. "Who'd you think you were shootin' at, anyway?" he asked, automatically checking the rifle's mechanism. "Bushrangers? Or blackfellows?"

She shook her head. "I wasn't sure. Missy saw the man—or rather, thought she saw him—right after the didgeridoo stopped. I suppose—"

He saw her stiffen. Turning, he realized Liam had come up, his thin chest heaving with the effort to draw breath after his run up the hill. Her lips tightened at the sight of him, and O'Reilly knew she was regretting letting the boy scent her fear. Liam could be a bit like a shark: let him smell your blood and he'd go for the kill.

But the look the boy gave her was more one of surprise than satisfaction. "You found out what it was, then?"

Her cool gray eyes met Liam's turbulent hazel ones. "Yes," she said. "Ironic, isn't it, that I should prove to be more rattled by the reality than by your invention?"

"But you weren't really rattled, were you? I mean, when Missy thought she saw someone, you got Father's gun and you shot at him."

"Not at him, no. I shot wide and high. I could hardly aim at him when it might have been you, playing another one of your tricks."

Liam stared down at the neatly severed clothesline. A muscle worked in his tight jaw. He threw a considering look, sideways, back up at his governess. "For all you knew, it coulda been a bushranger or some renegade

273

black after you, yet you had the guts to come down here and check on him anyway, all by yourself? Not knowing if he was dead or just hurt?"

She drew in a shaky breath and O'Reilly thought he had some idea of what it must have cost her, to force herself to walk to the bottom of the shadowy garden and face the man she thought she'd shot. "Well," she said, obviously trying to make her voice light but not quite succeeding, "if I had hit someone, I could hardly leave him down here, alone, to bleed to death, now, could I?"

Liam didn't say anything, just gazed down at the clothesline again.

O'Reilly had spent the last six years watching his son make life hell for a succession of nervous, impotent gentlewomen. He had seen governesses thrown into rages, reduced to tears, even driven to near madness. And not once had he seen the boy betray the least sign of remorse for any of the things he had done to them.

Yet as he watched Liam's stare swivel from Amanda's composed face to the gun to the decimated laundry and back again, O'Reilly caught a glimpse of what might have been regret shadowing his son's sharp features. Regret, and something else O'Reilly recognized as reluctant, grudging respect.

O'Reilly shifted his gaze back to the woman beside him. She was so dainty and soft and feminine, he thought; yet she was tough. Tougher maybe even than she realized herself. He let his gaze drift over the flushed line of her cheek. The curve of her full lip. The blaze of her glorious hair where it caught the last rays of the setting sun. And he felt it again, that wild, sweet surge of emotion that took his breath away.

And scared the hell out of him.

O'Reilly held a match to his pipe, his eyes narrowing against the smoke as the tobacco ignited. He shook the match to extinguish it and then held it until it was cold. A man couldn't be too careful about fires in the bush.

Somewhere in the distance a boobook owl hooted its monotonous call and a dingo howled at the wide, uncaring, cloudless night sky. He tossed the cold match into the void of the darkened garden, then propped himself against a veranda post and stared across the creek at the endless expanse of hills, looking empty and dead in the silver moonlight.

Another two days and the shearing would be finished. Then they'd have the after-shearing races and the ball. And after that, he would be leaving to drive a mob of sheep south.

He'd decided to take only part of the sheep he'd selected to the slaughterhouses in Port Augusta. The rest he thought he'd try driving to the southern hills, see if he couldn't find some pasturage to rent near Melrose, or even Clare. Someplace far enough south that drought wasn't a problem.

He shifted his shoulders against the post. It was a risk, of course. He could lose the whole mob on the road or drive them halfway to Antarctica without finding any place to graze them. But if he was lucky and he did somehow manage to keep part of the mob alive, then he'd be in a better position to restock the station when the rains came next autumn.

Always assuming, of course, that the drought broke and the rains did come.

He cupped his palm around the bowl of his pipe, then realized it had gone out and grown cold. Shoving away from the post, he knocked the pipe against the weathered wood and slipped it back into his pocket as he wandered one of the garden paths.

He hated this garden. Oh, not the fruits and vegetables, of course. Out here in the bush, if you wanted things like grapes and pears and beans and tomatoes, you had to raise them yourself. What he hated was the stocks and forget-me-nots, the hollyhocks and Canterbury bells and lavenders and roses—all the useless, pretentious trappings of an English garden that Katherine had missed living here in the Ranges.

He could never figure out why Chow didn't just let the damn things die. But whenever O'Reilly tried to talk to him about it, Chow just blinked and nodded his head and went right on watering and pruning and deadheading.

Swearing under his breath, O'Reilly swung around to stare at his house. The house he'd built for Katherine.

If a man was smart, O'Reilly thought, he didn't waste his money building his wife a big fancy house and filling it with imported Italian marble mantelpieces and crystal chandeliers and lead-light windows that had to be hauled in over rough tracks at a ruinous cost. No, if a man was smart, he put his money into wells and tanks and fences, and built up runs in different parts of the country, so that he could move his stock when drought threatened one area or the local government suddenly started casting covetous eyes on the big leaseholds. If a man was smart...

If a man was smart, he kept away from gently bred Englishwomen with impeccable accents and refined habits and expensive tastes.

He kept away from women like Miss Amanda Davenport.

From here, he could see the French doors on the side of her room. She had her curtains closed against the night, but her lamp was still on and he could see her shadow moving around the room as she got ready for bed. The curtains were thin enough that he could even tell what she was doing. She was brushing her hair.

He watched her shadow elbows point to the ceiling, then sweep downward as she drew the brush through her long, thick hair. He could imagine the silky, flame-colored strands gliding over her shoulders, over the mounds of her breasts. He remembered the way she'd looked earlier that evening when he'd come upon her in the garden: her head thrown back, her eyes squeezed shut, her face flushed. She would look like that, he imagined, when a man took her.

At the thought, O'Reilly spun around on his heels and swore into the dark, empty garden. Christalmighty. Didn't he ever learn?

It had to be some kind of a family affliction, he decided, this penchant the O'Reilly men had for the wrong kind of women. Because like his father before him, it seemed all he had to do was meet a good-looking woman with a pommy accent and a snooty attitude, and he got hard.

Like his father before him...

He had a memory of his mother that haunted him always, a memory of a night only a week or so before she went away. He'd awakened in the still hours of the night to find her sitting at her piano. His father had bought the piano for her after Luke was born, the year wool prices were higher than anyone had ever seen them. It was the only thing like that Patrick could remember his father ever buying his mother; his father's money normally all went into building up his run.

His mother had loved that piano. She used to sit and play it by the hour, a peaceful, faraway look on her face. But over the years the piano had grown more and more out of tune. Without anyone to tune it, his mother had eventually stopped playing it. She hadn't been playing it that night, just sitting there, running the tips of her fingers up and down the keys, so lightly they didn't make a sound.

In the dim light cast by the foul-smelling slush lamp, she'd looked young, pretty. Thinking about it now, O'Reilly realized she couldn't have been more than thirty-six or thirty-eight at the time. Years of hard work and unhappiness had blurred her features and etched sad lines between her nose and mouth, but that night she'd been beautiful, her face relaxed, her eyes dreamy.

"Why don't you play anymore?" he'd asked.

He had to repeat the question twice before she turned her head. She stared at him oddly, as if she were looking through him more than at him. "It's out of tune," she said.

"You could still play it, couldn't you?"

"No."

"Then what are you doing?"

"I'm just listening," she said. And a week later, she left.

O'Reilly pursed his lips and blew out his breath in a long sigh. She'd been so unhappy. At the time, he'd blamed his father for it. His father, who had married a woman raised with music and books and gentle, cultivated conversation around candlelit dinner tables, and then made her live in a slab hut with a dirt floor and a calico ceiling that rippled eerily whenever a snake slithered across it. He'd made her scrub clothes in copper pots over open fires and butcher hogs and wash with harsh lye soap and birth her babies in a crude hide bed without even another woman there to help her through the pain and the fear. Often his father would go off for weeks at a time—mustering his sheep, branding calves—and leave her alone in that miserable hut. With only the wind and her fears and her ruined dreams for company.

She'd hated it, of course. And after a while, she got to where she hated his father. By the time she left, she must have decided she hated her children, too. She sure didn't take them with her.

Against his will, O'Reilly found his gaze drifting back to Amanda's room. The windows were dark. She'd gone to bed.

There was a time when O'Reilly thought he'd learned from his father's mistake. He'd learned that you don't marry a woman who's been raised to think that things like a comfortable house and close neighbors are necessary for her happiness, and then put her in a crude hut and expect to keep her happy.

So he'd taken the money that should have gone into sinking wells and buying more land, and he'd built Katherine the best house he could afford. He'd hauled his mother's piano up from Victoria so Katherine could make music, and he'd bought her fine china so she could set a pretty table, and gentle, rose-scented soaps to make her feel pretty and pampered.

But she'd left him anyway. Because the truth...the truth he should have learned from what happened to his father was that women like his mother, and Katherine, and Amanda Davenport, hate the bush.

It wasn't just the primitive conditions and the shimmering heat and the howling wind and the endless flies they hated. It was the stark, inescapable brutality of ancient, scarred ridges thrusting up bold and broken and bloodred against a hard blue sky. It was the endless, aching vistas of a land empty of all pretense, where everything was raw and vast and awe-inspiringly magnificent. A land as wild and wide open and untamable as a man's soul.

Everything he loved most about this land, they hated.

The next morning, Amanda awoke to find herself staring into Missy's solemn face, just inches from her own.

"Missy?" She sat up with a start and rubbed her hand over her eyes. "What are you doing here?"

"Sally's gone walkabout."

Amanda lowered her hand and swiveled her head to stare at the little girl. Missy was still in her nightdress, her hair a tangle. "She what?"

"She's gone walkabout."

"And what exactly does that mean?"

Missy shrugged. "It means, she's gone."

Amanda swung her legs out of bed and felt with her feet for her slippers. "What do you mean, gone? She's probably just slept late. What time is it?"

"No. She's gone."

Amanda reached for her father's old pocket

281

watch, which she kept on her bedside table. Six o'clock. With a groan, she shrugged into her wrapper. "Let's go and see, shall we?"

She took Missy's hand and together they walked through the quiet parlor and dining room to the back veranda, where Sally slept on a pallet near the corner of the house. Amanda had once asked why Sally didn't sleep in the house, or at least in one of the out-buildings, but Missy said Sally couldn't rest easy unless she was in the open air.

Amanda stopped. In the thin, crisp light of dawn, the pallet lay empty except for the pale blue of Sally's loose cotton dress cutting a swath across one end. "See," said Missy.

Amanda stared at the empty bed and abandoned dress. The woman must have walked off naked. "But why? Has she ever done this before?"

Missy shook her head. "No. Never. Jacko went walkabout once, last year. The other Aboriginal stockmen and shepherds do it, too, sometimes. But Sally never has. She always told me she'd stay as long as I needed her."

Amanda heard the catch in the little girl's voice and knelt down to wrap one arm around her thin shoulders. "I'm sure she'll be back," Amanda said, although it was only wishful thinking and they both knew it.

Missy rubbed her fist across her eyes. "It's because of the didgeridoo. I know it is. It was calling her and she had to go." Suddenly, the pinched little face crumpled. "Who's

282

going to take care of me? Sally always took care of me."

Amanda clutched the child to her, feeling the sobs that wracked the small body, feeling the little girl's pain and fear as if it were her own. "Oh, Missy." She pressed her cheek against the child's downy soft hair, breathing in her sweet scent. She remembered O'Reilly once telling her that Sally had first come to Penyaka as Missy's wet nurse. Which meant that in a very real sense, Amanda thought, Sally was the only mother that Missy had ever known.

Amanda's chest felt tight and she sucked in a deep breath, trying to ease it. "I'll take care of you, Missy," she whispered, hugging the child to her. "Don't worry."

Something stirred in the air, and even before Amanda looked up, she knew that O'Reilly was there.

Still kneeling with Missy clutched to her, Amanda twisted to find him standing in the open doorway, one arm braced against the frame. He wore his moleskin trousers and his boots and nothing else. His chest was bare and beautiful, his cheeks unshaven, his sun-streaked hair still ruffled from sleep. A strange, brittle light she'd never seen before glittered in his eyes as he stared at her.

She glanced away quickly, suddenly wary of what he might see in her eyes.

His attention focused on the child in her arms. "What's wrong with Missy?"

"It's Sally," said Amanda quietly. "She seems to have disappeared."

283

He straightened and took a step forward, his gaze sweeping from the empty pallet to the dry, endless plains. "Gone walkabout, has she?"

"She didn't tell you she was leaving?"

"No. But I can't say I'm surprised. It's this bloody drought. She has a husband and a couple grown kids of her own. I guess she decided they need her more than we do."

"But I need her," said Missy, her voice muffled against Amanda's shoulder.

Amanda tightened her grip on Missy's small body and stood up, bringing the child with her. "You have me." She shifted Missy's weight to her hip. "I think perhaps Sally knew that."

She straightened, achingly aware that she wore only a wrapper thrown open over her nightdress. She watched the heat leap into O'Reilly's eyes as his gaze traveled slowly over her, from her unbound hair to her bare ankles. Heat, and a resentful kind of anger she didn't understand. She expected him to make some provocative remark, but he didn't. He just stood there, staring at her, his big, half-naked, masculine presence disturbing her in a way that needed no words.

Missy lifted her head from Amanda's shoulder and looked at her, her tearstained face tight with misery. "Will you stay?"

An overwhelming feeling of tenderness rose up and caught at Amanda's heart. "I'll stay, darling," she whispered, turning toward the door.

O'Reilly stood to one side, silently watching her. But as she passed him, she thought she

284

heard him say something. Something so soft, it was little more than a thought breathed aloud.

"Yeah? For how long?"

CHAPTER FIFTEEN

The following morning, in an attempt to cheer Missy up, Amanda finally gave in to the little girl's pestering and walked down the creek bed to the woolshed to watch one of the last days of the shearing.

The ground around the woolshed was flat and crisscrossed with rough, weather-worn rail fences that divided the area into several large yards and numerous smaller holding pens crowded with milling, bleating sheep. Dust hung thick and acrid in the air, and the flies were hideous. One hovered around Amanda's mouth; another landed on her nose. She shooed them with her hand, but a moment later they were back again. Australian flies could be unbelievably, maddeningly persistent. She hated them.

Swatting absently at the hovering flies, she stared out over the undulating sea of woolly backs. She had always thought of sheep as white or pale gray. Surely the sheep in England were white? But not here. These sheep were a dirty red-brown. As she watched, an Aboriginal shepherd swept one of the bawling creatures off its feet and threw it to another man standing waist-deep in the water hole. The sheep hit with a splash, sending water spraying high up into the air. The men laughed.

"What are they doing?" Amanda asked, bringing up her hand to shade her eyes from the harsh sun. "One would think they're giving the sheep a bath."

"They are," said Missy, skipping along beside her. "Papa says fleeces keep better if the sheep aren't washed before they're sheared, but the poms pay more for washed wool, so Papa always does it. Only with the creek not runnin' this year, they had to dig a channel from the spring to the water hole. See?"

Amanda watched the man in the water dunk the sheep's head and shove it under a bar to a second pen, where four or five men took turns rubbing the sheep's fleece as they passed it down the line.

"It's not nice to call the English poms," said Amanda, her gaze following the waterlogged sheep as it staggered out onto a gravel bank and gave an indignant bleat.

"Papa does."

"I know. But you shouldn't do it." She glanced down in time to see the little girl's chin jut out rebelliously, and had to turn away to hide her smile. "Why don't you show me the shearing shed?"

The shearing shed was an enormous building with massive walls of rough, gray-pink stones mortised with lime. A great doorway on the eastern end opened into a central pen crowded with unshorn sheep. Down either side of the central pen stretched two shearing floors where the shearers worked in rows, each with his own stand. Behind them ranged the outer pens into which the shorn sheep were thrust until they could be counted to arrive at each man's tally.

Amanda hesitated just inside the door, letting her eyes grow accustomed to the dim, golden light. The atmosphere in here was thick with the smell of sheep and hot tar and working men's sweat. In the pens, sheep bleated in panic, their tiny hooves beating a restless tattoo against the hard-packed earth. As Amanda watched, one of the shearers—a tall, thin man with narrow, stooping shoulders and a dirty blond beard, nicked the wrinkled neck of the ewe he held clamped between his knees. He swore and threw up his head to shout, "Tar boy!" Liam came on the run, a bucket of molten tar ready to dab on the cut. From the distant wool room came the thump of the wool press, joining with the whirl of the grinding wheel, the click of the shears, the soft swish of the fleeces, hitting the board...

And the deep, rich cadence of O'Reilly's laugh.

"There's Papa!" said Missy, tugging her hand. "Look, he's shearing today."

Amanda had already seen him. He stood at the far end of the board, half-turned away from them so that he hadn't seen Amanda and Missy come in. It was hot in the shed, and like many of the men he'd stripped off his shirt. Amanda let her hungry gaze rove over his naked, sweat-streaked shoulders and back. He stretched slowly, flexing tired muscles, then reached over to snag a wether out of the central pen and upend the sheep onto its backside in one smooth, practiced motion. The sheep let out a startled *baah*, then slumped resignedly on its rump, looking for all the world like an old man sitting down for a rest.

O'Reilly tightened his knees on the wether and bent gracefully at the waist, the long, thin blades snapping continuously in his hands as he swept the shears around the animal's neck, down its flank.

Amanda felt her breathing grow shallow and rapid as she watched. He was so big and strong and masculine. The muscles beneath his smooth, sweat-slicked skin flexed and bunched as he worked; the veins of his bare forearms bulged. She had never thought of a man's body as beautiful, but O'Reilly was beautiful. His shoulders were broad and corded with muscle, his back long and lean as it tapered down to a narrow waist. His every movement was agile, controlled, and unbelievably gentle. She thought she could stand there and watch him forever.

The fleece tumbled to the board in one continuous piece. O'Reilly eased the pressure of his knees, and the wether scrambled to its feet naked but free. O'Reilly straightened. And saw her.

Across the length of the shearing shed,

their gazes met and locked, and it was as if something shimmered in the hot air between them. She could see his sides heaving as he sucked in air. His dark, taut body was wet with sweat, his lean face dripping, his golden hair plastered dark against his head. Without taking his gaze off her, he hooked his shirt off the railing of the nearest pen and wiped his face with it as he strolled toward her.

He stopped in front of her. "You came," he said, still breathing heavily, something warm and disturbing lighting his eyes.

Amanda watched a bead of sweat form on his tanned forehead and trickle down his temple to disappear into his hair. She knew a forbidden urge to reach out and touch him, there, and had to swallow hard and lace her fingers together behind her back. Turning half away from him, she watched Hannah swoop up a fleece and carry it to the wool-rolling table. "Yes," she said, her voice as light and airy as she could make it. "Missy wanted me to see how it's all done."

"Mm-hmm." A dimple flashed in his cheek, and she knew he wasn't fooled one bit.

She should not have come, she thought with something like a panic. By coming to see him, by so obviously, so betrayingly watching his body while he worked, she had crossed some sort of invisible line that she had carefully observed for weeks now.

And they both knew it.

That afternoon, Amanda went for a ride by herself.

She normally rode with Missy, but the after-shearing races and dance were now just days away, and Missy was busy "hulping" Ching make gingerbread cookies.

"You go and leave her with me," said Ching, giving Amanda a wink over Missy's bowed head. "I no can do without my helper."

So Amanda saddled Calypso and followed the track that ran southeast along the creek bed. The mare's hooves thudded dully in the dust as Amanda squinted at the shimmering horizon. It was the beginning of November now, still spring. But the sky above her burned a searing blue, the sun was dazzling, the air hot and dry.

She rode to where the creek had cut a rocky gorge through a bank of low hills. There she pulled up and slid out of the saddle. In the shade of the red cliffs, patches of grass still grew, and she eased Calypso's cinch and tied the mare to a deadfall where it could graze. Then she climbed onto the flat-topped rock that jutted out over what had once been a deep, fair-sized water hole but was now only a small, tranquil pool.

She had been here before, with Missy, but she had always wanted to return alone. In some ways this spot reminded Amanda of Cadnowie; it had that same sense of almost supernatural harmony. It was why she had come here today. She felt restless, edgy. In need of peace.

Sitting on her haunches, she wrapped her arms around her bent knees and sucked in a deep breath scented with the heavy oils of the bush, then let it out again in a long sigh. There was something about these windblown, timeless ranges that struck a wild, lonely chord deep within her that she hadn't even known still existed. This country was like O'Reilly, she thought; both the man and his land frightened her and disturbed her and attracted her, all at the same time.

She kept remembering the way he had looked in the woolshed that morning, his chest naked and shiny with sweat, his muscles bulging, his eyes hot with desire. Just the thought of it was enough to send the hunger flashing through her again, tormenting her.

Reaching up, she tore off her hat and tossed it aside, then yanked the pins out of her chignon and shook her head to let her hair tumble free about her shoulders. She loosened her cravat, too, and unfastened the top buttons of her riding habit.

She felt abandoned, wicked. Needy. If she had never allowed Grant to touch her all those years ago, she wondered, would she still be like this? Yearning for O'Reilly's touch, for his kiss?

She closed her eyes and lifted her face to the hot spring sun and the wild wind. She imagined what it would feel like to strip off her

291

clothes and lie here, caressed by the fingers of the sun-warmed breeze. She undid two more buttons, then stilled. A feeling of anticipation came over her, of subtle, fine-tuned awareness. She knew even before she opened her eyes that O'Reilly was there.

She lowered her head and looked at him. He sat tall and easy in the saddle, one wrist resting on the pommel as the chestnut shifted weight from one side to the other. She thought he must have been there, watching her, for some time.

"Mr. O'Reilly," she said, her voice surprisingly calm and clear, although her heart thudded wildly beneath the unbuttoned jacket of her habit.

She watched him urge the horse around the edge of the water hole toward her. On the near side of the creek bed he stopped, and a forbidden thrill of excitement and fear shot through Amanda as she watched him swing out of the saddle and loop the reins around a scruffy bottlebrush.

The wind gusted, sighing through the overhead branches of the gums and fluttering the tawny hair that hung over his collar. He braced his hands on the edge of the flat rock and swung up beside her as graceful and agile as a wild animal on the prowl. He landed on the balls of his feet, his knees bent, his moleskins pulling taut over the muscles of his thighs.

"Ching told me you'd ridden out alone," he said, his gaze capturing and holding hers.

The air between them throbbed with things known but unsaid.

"And so you followed me."

"Yes."

He suddenly seemed too near, too intimidatingly masculine to bear. She swung her head away to watch a pair of vivid green-and-red rosellas fluttering through the lower branches of a gum across the creek.

She heard his boot heels scrape over the rock as he eased himself down beside her. "I remember my grandfather had a water hole with a big flat rock beside it," he said, "very similar to this, in the hills behind his house in Tasmania. It used to be one of my favorite places when I was about four or five."

She cast a quick glance at him. "Was your grandfather really transported for stealing a horse?"

A wicked smile curled his lips, taking her breath away. "Sure was. I remember one time when I was a lad, he showed me his scars. The ones on his back, from the cat-o'-nine-tails. And the marks left by the shackles on his ankles and wrists."

He paused. She waited, hoping he would go on, and after a moment, he did. "He served seven years. But after that, he got his certificate of freedom, took up a run, and had the most amazing luck finding sheep and cattle to stock it."

"In other words, he stole them."

He let out a huff of laughter. "Well, let's put it this way: if he did, he never got caught. He

293

found a free Irishwoman willing to marry him, and had himself a half-dozen children by her, so that by the time my mother's family came out a few years after Waterloo, ol' Patrick O'Reilly was one of the most prosperous men on the north end of the island."

"So he was respectable by then."

"Oh, no." Something about his expression hardened, and he lowered his head until his hat brim hid part of his face. "The O'Reillys were never that. Not to the likes of my mother's family. The Beaumonts were so poor when they first got here, they lived under canvas for more than a year. But they were still *gentry*, and my mother was a *lady*. My father was just convict's spawn."

"But your mother didn't care."

"When she was eighteen, she didn't. My father was a handsome devil, and he knew how to make my mother laugh." Amanda watched his throat work as he swallowed. "Then they left Tasmania to take up a new run in Victoria. She didn't laugh so much anymore."

He breathed. She could see his chest lifting against his shirt, and her heart ached for him, ached for the pain she knew he was feeling. He was no longer looking at her, but sat with his head lifted, his gaze fixed on something in the distance.

"Does your sister look like her?" Amanda asked quietly.

"Hetty?" He brought his gaze back to her face. "Yeah, she does. Hannah takes after her a bit, too. Although she has more the look of Katherine."

His wife's name hung in the air between them, like something unwanted and oppressive. To push it away, she said, "What about your brothers? Where are they?"

He took off his hat and tossed it onto the rock beside his thigh, then leaned back to brace his weight against his outstretched arms. "Luke still has my father's old station down in Victoria. But John died of pneumonia about ten years ago, in Bendigo."

She saw the tightening of his jaw, and the shadows shifting, deep in his blue eyes. "I'm sorry," she said. She rested her chin on her knees, letting her gaze drift over the red cliffs on the far side of the creek. The lower part of the rock had been worn away by the ebb and flow of the water hole through the aeons, until it formed an indentation almost like a shallow cave. Looking at it now, her eyes began to pick out patterns in the gloom.

"Are those handprints, painted on that rock?" she asked.

"That's right. They're Aboriginal rock paintings. The spirals, too. You see them a lot around here."

"I didn't realize the natives had any kind of painting."

He grunted. "A lot of folks assume that because the Aborigines see themselves as a part of the land, and because they don't have much interest in accumulating personal possessions, then they must exist at a level little better than that of animals. But the way I see it, a people's culture consists of a lot more than things."

When she didn't say anything, he nodded toward the low branches of a nearby coolabah tree where the trilling song of some unseen bird came in staccato bursts from out to the shadows. From the far side of the creek bed came an answer, loud and shrill.

"Hear that?" he asked.

"Yes," she answered slowly.

"The Aborigines call them deereerees. When they chatter like that, the blacks say they're hurling insults at each other, telling one another their grandmothers died in forks of trees."

A surprised gurgle of laughter bubbled up from within her. "Is that a great insult?"

"Well, wouldn't you think it was?"

She swung her head to look directly at him. "You're unusually friendly with the Aborigines, aren't you?"

He shrugged. "They interest me. And the more I learn about them, the more I find to admire. This is a hard land. Just surviving here is something anyone can be proud of."

She let her gaze run over him, over the worn blue work shirt pulled tight across his broad chest by the way he sat, down to his lean, knife-slung hips and the scuffed toes of his leather boots. She felt her need for him, her love for him, swell within her, hot and painful and sad.

"I don't understand what draws people to

this place," she said. "It's too wild. Too raw. Too frightening."

"I don't think it's something anyone can explain. The Flinders either speaks to you—calls to the wildness that heats your blood and the loneliness that howls in your soul—or it doesn't."

They stared at each other. Brilliantly colored cockatoos chattered, and larks trilled their sweet songs from the upper boughs of the red gums and wattles. A dragonfly hovered over the pool, its wings fluttering as the warm wind blew softly around them. O'Reilly's eyes were a fierce, hungry blue. And she realized that they had focused on her mouth.

He shifted his weight, his hand coming up as he leaned forward. He laced his fingers through her free-flowing hair, cupping the back of her head in his palm. "Amanda," he said softly. "I want to kiss you."

Her chest suddenly felt unbearably tight and she sucked in a deep, painful breath, trying to ease it. She could see the want in his face, feel the tension in the fingers that curled around her neck. His head dipped, her lips parted. She waited, unable to move, her gaze caught by his.

She watched his mouth twist up into a funny smile. "Only problem is, I promised I wouldn't," he said. "Which means, you're going to have to kiss me."

CHAPTER SIXTEEN

O'Reilly watched Amanda's throat work as she swallowed, painfully. "I can't," she said.

He let his hand trail down her neck to the open jacket of her riding habit. "I watched you here, this afternoon. I watched you take down your hair and open this tight collar." He ran his finger down between the juncture of her clavicles, and felt her shudder.

"The woman you once were—the woman you still want to be—is awake, Amanda. She's in there, ready to burst out of this drab cocoon you've wrapped around her. But you're going to have to free her yourself."

He saw the torment in her eyes. Saw her head jerk sideways in denial.

And knew she couldn't do it.

He brought both hands up to cradle her face between his palms. "I think it's time we talked about him."

O'Reilly saw her eyes widen with alarm, then shift sideways so that she was no longer looking at him. "I don't know what you mean."

He let his gaze travel over the thin bridge of her nose, her high, pale cheeks, her trembling, vulnerable mouth. "I'm talking about the man who took your virginity."

She flung back her head, her face tight with strain, her fists coming up to slam against his chest. The attack caught him by surprise, knocking him backward. *"No,"* she screamed, her hands blindly pounding his shoulders, his arms. "There was no one. Do you hear me? *No one.*"

He caught her wrists, yanking her forward until her weight fell against him and he could roll with her and pin her flat on the rock. She tried to rear up, so he covered her with the length of his body. She heaved against him, her breasts pressing into his chest, her belly thrusting against the ridge of his erection.

She went utterly still as the significance of their position dawned on them both.

"Did he force you?" O'Reilly asked, his breath coming in quick pants. She strained against his hold, refusing to look at him, so he raised her wrists high above her head and brought his face to within an inch of hers. "Is that why you're so afraid? Look at me, Mandy; listen to me. I won't hurt you. I promise I won't do anything you don't want me to. If you're afraid—"

"No." He watched her face crumple, her eyes squeeze shut against the tears that welled up anyway. "No, damn you. He didn't force me." She let out a hoarse, ragged laugh that clutched at his heart. "He didn't force me. But I wish to God he had. If he had, then I wouldn't have to live with the knowledge of what I did to myself."

He let go of her wrists, easing his hands down her arms to smooth the tangle of hair away from her face, his fingers gently freeing the fiery strands that stuck to her wet cheeks. He realized his hands were shaking. "So you gave yourself to a man you loved. Is that so wrong?"

She opened her eyes and looked up at him, the gray of her irises dark and luminescent with pain. "Yes. Because he didn't love me, you see." Her beautiful lips curled up into a bitter smile. "Oh, he said he did, of course. He said he loved me and was going to marry me. Only we had to wait. Until he finished university. Until he was of age. Until he could talk to his father."

O'Reilly watched the sad smile fade. "I was so much in love. And I wanted him so badly. So when he said the words I wanted to hear I...gave myself to him. It never occurred to me to doubt him."

She paused, her nostrils flaring as she sucked in a breath. "He didn't even have the courage to tell me the truth himself. I read about his engagement in the paper. It said the arrangement was of long standing; the announcement was only delayed because the bride-to-be had been in mourning."

"Amanda. You don't need to tell—"

She jerked her head. "It was all a lie, you see. Everything he told me, everything he promised me, from the very beginning. He knew I wouldn't give myself to him any other way, so he told me what I wanted to hear. And I believed him. Because I wanted to. I was such a gullible fool."

"How old were you?"

"Seventeen."

Christ, he thought. So young. So vulnerable. He slid his thumbs across her pale cheeks, gently wiping her tears. "And you've been punishing yourself ever since, haven't you?"

She didn't say anything, just swallowed hard. He felt his jaw tighten in anger at the thought of how she'd been hurt, but he kept his voice gentle. "What do you think, Amanda? That because some lying bastard seduced the loving, trusting child you once were, you have to spend the rest of your life hiding your beautiful body beneath ugly dresses? And covering this wonderful hair as if it were something to be ashamed of?"

He fingered a curl that lay against her breast and heard her suck in her breath in an audible hiss. "Because of that man," said O'Reilly, "you've spent the last ten years doing everything you possibly could to convince the world you're no longer the vibrant, sensual woman you once were." He lowered his head until his lips hovered just above hers. "And pretending to yourself that you don't ever want to feel desire or know pleasure again."

He felt her hands clutch at his upper arms, her fingers digging into the flesh beneath his shirt. "Please don't do this to me," she said, her pupils dilating until her eyes looked black.

"Kiss me, Amanda."

"No. Please..." But against his chest, her breasts shuddered with her uneven breaths. He heard her moan. Felt her hands slide up his shoulders to tangle in his hair. He watched her lashes flutter. His mouth was only a sigh away from hers.

And she lifted her head and kissed him.

Her lips were soft and sweet and yielding, and the desire he had been fighting to hold in check

301

surged through him hot and demanding and damned near unstoppable. He groaned, grinding the length of his hard, wanting body against hers, covering her mouth with his. Her lips opened beneath his insistent pressure, and he captured her face between his hands, holding her head steady as he deepened the kiss, sliding his tongue past her lips and teeth, filling her, stroking her, letting his tongue tell her mouth what his body wanted to do to hers.

She whimpered and arched against him, tore at the back of his shirt to jerk it free of his trousers and slide her hands over the bare skin beneath it. Her touch seared like fire, igniting him almost to the breaking point. "Ah, Christ, Amanda," he said on a heavy expulsion of breath.

Her head fell back when his mouth left hers, and he dropped his kisses to the bare arch of her neck. Her skin was soft as petals, her scent as sweet as hyacinths and as arousing as musk. He rubbed his open lips against her wildly throbbing pulse point. Ran his tongue down to where the swell of her breasts showed at the open neck of her riding habit. He swore impatiently and tore at the remaining buttons. Shoving the green cloth aside, he pushed her corset out of his way and opened her chemise to bare her breasts to his hands and his mouth and his hot gaze.

Sighing with wonder, he felt her palms cupping his head, guiding his mouth to her plump, dusky nipples. He flicked his tongue over one and watched it harden, then lifted his gaze to her face as he sucked the aroused tip into his mouth.

She jerked and gasped, her head coming up so she could watch him. He bathed her nipple with his hot tongue while gently kneading her other breast with his hand. Her neck arched, her eyes closed. She squirmed beneath him, thrust her pelvis against him and rubbed, rubbed...

He felt the convulsive tremors begin deep within her, felt them sweep her body, felt her fingers spasm in his hair. And knew that she had found her release.

He had never known a woman to respond so quickly and easily to a man's touch. He watched with awed wonder as ecstatic rapture flooded her face. Watched her closed eyes spasm, her features contort, then still. Slowly, her eyes fluttered open and met his. For a long moment, they stared at each other, each breathing heavily, each trying to come to terms with the unexpected intimacy of what had just happened between them.

Still holding her gaze with his own, he slid back up her body to take her mouth in a long, wet, trembling kiss that went on and on. He released her mouth slowly, reluctantly, coming back to brush her lips with his own one more time before he raised himself on his elbows and looked down at her.

"I want you to come to my bed tonight," he said, his voice husky with arousal.

Her eyes widened and her lips parted, but she didn't say anything.

He tangled his fingers in her loose hair and stole another hot, deep kiss. "I want you," he said, his lips moving against hers. "I want to make love to you."

"I know," she said, her gray eyes calm and solemn. "I want you, too."

He felt a surge of hope. "Then you'll come?"

"I can't."

He didn't realize he'd been holding his breath until he let it out in a painful sigh. He rolled off her to come to a sitting position a few feet away, his head bowed, his chest heaving as he sucked in air. His body was heavy with want, shaking with desire. He knew if he'd kept touching her, kept kissing her, he probably could have brought her to the point that she'd have given herself to him, right here, right now, because the passion had been that strong for both of them. But he didn't want her that way, even if he couldn't exactly say why.

He swung his head to look at her. She had sat up, too. She had already buttoned her habit, and now she was busy winding up her hair. Except that her hands were shaking so badly, half of it had fallen down already.

"Is it because of Katherine?" he asked quietly. "Is that why you won't come? Because I've never divorced?"

Her hands stilled, but she kept her head bent. "No." She reached for one of the pins she'd assembled in a small pile on the rock beside her. "I suppose it should matter, but for some reason, it does not. She has been gone from

304

your life for so long. And while divorce may be legal, the consequences are always... unpleasant, particularly when children are involved. I can understand why you have never done it."

She raised her head then and looked at him. Her cheeks were flushed, her eyes over-bright, her lips red and swollen from his kisses, her breasts rising round and full. She looked lush, ripe. Ready. At the sight of her, he felt his desire roar through him again. It was all he could do to keep from pressing her back down on that bloody rock and shoving up her riding habit to take her here, now, with the sun hot on her white naked thighs and the air fresh and free around them. The urge to do it was so intense, he almost shuddered with the need for self-control.

He forced himself to look away from her. "Is it because of Mary, then? Because if it is, you should know that I haven't been to town to visit her since you arrived." He stretched out his leg and winced. "Although it might have been better for both of us if I had."

She surprised him by laughing, then sobered almost at once. "No. It has nothing to do with Mrs. McCarthy. It's because..." She stared out over the pale, sun-seared hills, and he thought he heard her sigh. "It's because you are a part of this land. And I am not."

He went quite still. "What are you afraid of? That if you share my bed, and let your life become tangled up with mine, you might be tempted to stay?"

"Yes."

He reached out and took her hand, entwining his fingers with hers. "Our lives are already tangled. You realize that, don't you?"

Her hand spasmed in his. "Yes," she said softly. "But if I come to your bed, and what we do there should happen to make a baby..." She eased her hand from his hold. "Well, that's an entanglement we won't be able to break."

"Why not?" he asked harshly, standing up. "Katherine broke it easily enough. As did my mother."

"I'm not like them."

"How do you know?" He stared down at her. Hating her. Wanting her. "You've only been here less than three months."

"I'm not like them," she repeated.

"We'll see."

Missy peeked her head over the edge of the long trestle table spread with her mother's second-best damask cloth and weighted down with plates of cold chicken and turkey, wine truffles and custards, and dozens of other wonders, all carefully covered with net tents to keep out the flies.

Ching had been cooking for three days now, getting ready for the scores of people coming to Penyaka for the after-shearing races and dance. They'd been arriving all morning—miners from Blinman and Brinkman, station families from as far away as Wilpena

Pound and Arkaba. Some of them had come from so far away they'd traveled all of yesterday, just to get here. And none of them had come empty-handed: baskets of apples and fresh bread and jars of quandong jam and barrels of cider and jugs of syrup and cordials were steadily added to the overflowing tables on the veranda, or loaded into carts to be taken down to the shearing shed for the races.

"Why do I have to do it?" Missy whispered to Liam, who crouched just out of sight around the corner of the house.

"Because if you get caught, Ching will just shake his head at you and laugh. But he said if he caught me messin' with any of the food for the party again, he'd come after me with his cleaver."

Ordinarily, threats like that wouldn't have carried much weight with Liam. Except that just that morning, Ching had caught him stealing one of the apple turnovers cooling on the kitchen windowsill, and the Chinese cook had been so put out he'd actually *thrown* the cleaver at Liam. The heavy, sharp blade had sunk into one of the posts of the kitchen stoop, right above Liam's head, with a lethal *thwunk*. Liam had been walking timid around the cook ever since.

Missy made a face at her brother, but she knew if she didn't do what he wanted her to, he'd get that mean, hard look on his face that scared her, and he'd call her a chicken and a baby and all kinds of other names that made her want to cry. She figured she could probably take that—at least, Miss Davenport had said she needed to learn not to let it bother her when Liam and Hannah called her names, so she'd been trying. Only Missy had a feeling Liam wouldn't just call her names; he had a nasty way of twisting her arm that left it red and sore for hours.

She threw a quick glance at the kitchen, then grabbed a whole plateful of jam tarts and ducked between the open French doors behind her. She was halfway across the dining room when Liam passed her, lifted the plate from her hands, and sprinted toward his room. "Liam!" she cried, chasing after him as fast as her short legs would carry her. "At least let me have one!"

Liam didn't break stride. But one of the tarts came sailing through the air. Missy just managed to catch it as Liam's door slammed shut.

She was dawdling on the front veranda, finishing the last of the jam tart, when Mary McCarthy and her son, Tad, drove up in a rattly old-fashioned spring cart with cracked, faded black upholstery and a tired old buckskin mare between the shafts.

Licking her telltale sticky fingers, Missy retreated back through the open front doorway, but she stuck her head around the opening so she could still watch. She liked Mrs. McCarthy. Whenever Missy went into Brinkman with Papa, Mrs. McCarthy always gave her a big, shiny peppermint stick. But Missy hated Tad. He'd punched her in the nose once and made it bleed, and she hadn't even done anything to him. He'd hit her simply because he couldn't get his hands on Liam, and he wanted to pay Liam back for saying Mary McCarthy would spread her legs for any man in the Flinders, as long as he had a charming smile and a big prick.

Missy squirmed at the memory. She hadn't known what it all meant, of course. So as soon as her nose stopped bleeding, she'd asked Papa. Papa had threatened to wash her mouth out with soap if he ever heard her say anything like that again, and he'd taken his razor strop to Liam for saying it in the first place. And then Liam had caught Tad behind the Brinkman Inn, and even though Tad was three years older than Liam, Liam had still managed to twist his arm so hard, it'd broken. That had been six months ago. Liam figured the score was even. But Missy suspected Tad didn't think so.

"Mary." Papa's deep, laughing voice sang out across the garden. "It's about time. I was beginning to think you weren't comin'."

Papa had been standing by the wisteria, talking to Miss Davenport. But when the cart pulled up at the gate, he left Miss Davenport and went to give Mrs. McCarthy a hand down from her seat.

Papa liked Mary McCarthy, too, same as Missy. He liked her a lot. Missy had asked him once if he liked Mrs. McCarthy enough to marry her. But Papa just laughed and tweaked her curls and told her neither he nor the widow was the marryin' kind. Missy thought it was a funny thing to say, since Papa and Mrs. McCarthy had both been married once, which seemed to indicate they were the marrying kind after all. But it'd relieved her just the same. Missy wouldn't have minded having Mrs. McCarthy for a new mama. But it woulda meant having Tad as a stepbrother, and Missy figured she couldn't abide that, so she was glad it wasn't going to happen.

She knew Mrs. McCarthy was older than Papa, but it was hard to tell how much older, because Aunt Hetty said the bush was hard on a woman's complexion. Missy wasn't sure what a complexion was, but she thought it was probably a grown-up's word for a woman's face, because the few times Aunt Hetty had visited them, she never stuck her nose out of the house without a heavy veil on, and she spent hours rubbing funny-smelling creams into her skin.

Looking at her now, Missy supposed Mary McCarthy was pretty, in a way. Her hair was so dark, it was almost black, and she had dark-brown eyes that always seemed to laugh at whatever they saw. She was a tall woman, almost as tall as Papa, and tough as jerked beef. She'd spent so many years throwing around bags of grain and lifting heavy barrels that her arms were as hard and strong as most men's.

But that didn't stop her from taking Papa's hand and letting him help her climb down from the cart, as if she didn't do it all the time by herself. Even when she was standing solid on her own two feet, Papa still held her hand,

and he smiled at her and sort of leaned toward her in a way that, for a moment at least, seemed to shut everyone else out. Then he said something to her in a low voice, something that must have been funny, because his dimples flashed and she laughed and reached out to playfully slap him on the cheek.

Missy could see Tad, still sitting on the bench of the cart and staring down at his mother. Tad was tall and dark-haired and wiry like his mother, but he wasn't pretty like her, and at the moment he had an awful scowl on his face. It had something to do with the time Papa spent alone with Mrs. McCarthy in her house, but Missy didn't understand it, and the threat about the soap meant she kept her mouth shut and didn't ask.

Something—a small sound, or maybe it was just a slight movement—made Missy glance back at Miss Davenport. She still stood by the wisteria, right where Papa had left her. She looked small and fragile and a little sad, standing there alone like that. Like Tad, she had a funny look on her face. Not sulky, like Tad. But there was still something about the way she stared at Papa and Mrs. McCarthy that reminded Missy of Tad. Her face looked pinched, like something was hurting her. She sucked in a deep breath and took a step forward, and Missy thought she meant to walk over and meet Mrs. McCarthy. Only instead, she did something strange.

Smoothing her hair with both hands, as if to make sure it wasn't messed up, she turned her back on Papa and Mrs. McCarthy and swung away to the left, to where Mr. Whittaker stood talking to some of the mining people from Brinkman.

Mr. Whittaker had just got back from Adelaide yesterday. He'd been away so long that Miss Davenport had been afraid he wouldn't get back in time for the dance, and she'd been really glad to see him when he rode up this morning.

Papa hadn't, though. It wasn't that he hadn't been friendly to Mr. Whittaker, because of course he had. It was just that, as he stood watching Miss Davenport go with Mr. Whittaker to see to the stabling of his horse, Missy had heard Papa muttering something.

Something about how he wished they'd have finished the shearing a few days earlier.

The horse races were scheduled to be held in the late afternoon, in the fields behind the woolshed.

But first came other, less serious events. Some were typical athletic competitions, such as one might see at any fair in England. But most were peculiar contests that involved things like men rolling down hills in barrels, or trying to run with pumpkins balanced on their heads.

Amanda turned her back on the field of laughing, half-drunken men trying to catch their tumbling pumpkins, and stared out over the crowd of unfamiliar people who had assembled for O'Reilly's after-shearing festivities.

312

She wished Christian hadn't left her here alone while he went in search of refreshment; without his solid, very English presence at her side, she felt out of place, adrift. A dusty wind tugged at her skirts and slapped her bonnet strings against her cheek and left her with a strange, restless feeling she didn't understand.

She didn't belong here. She didn't belong in this raw, wild, disturbing land. She didn't belong someplace where rough, hard-drinking, hard-swearing men in worn white moleskin trousers and high boots mingled freely and unconcernedly with ladies in silk dresses and gentlemen in high-buttoned frock coats and celluloid collars. Where men raced across sheep paddocks with pumpkins on their heads and dances were held in woolsheds.

"Frightfully sorry to have taken so long." Christian's well-bred English voice sounded behind her. "But I have, at last, returned."

She swung around to find him triumphantly bearing two mugs of cider. She was so glad to see his familiar, pleasant face that she laughed. "My dear Mr. Whittaker, I was beginning to fear you'd decided to emulate the indigenous practice, and gone walkabout."

He handed her one of the deliciously cool mugs and grimaced. "Peculiarly irrational practice, that. Actually, I was forced to send one of the lads up to the house for a fresh barrel of cider. Some cretin must have dumped at least two bottles of rum into the stuff in the woolshed."

"Probably Hannah and Liam," said Amanda, sipping the cider. It was sweet and tangy and decidedly nonalcoholic.

"Dear me." Mr. Whittaker looked shocked. "Do you think so? Well, at least they won't be able to tamper with this lot. I set Jacko to guarding the fresh barrel, so there shouldn't be any more problems of that sort."

Amanda swallowed a chuckle and swiveled away before her face could betray her. Evidently Mr. Whittaker didn't know that Jacko was the children's favorite accomplice.

The smile faded from her lips as her gaze fell on Patrick O'Reilly, standing in the center of the field. He was one of the rough men in moleskin trousers and worn leather boots. He had his blue cotton shirt open at the neck and his hat tipped back on his sun-streaked hair as he tried to organize some score or so half-grown boys jostling for position in a line. At the sight of him, her stomach clenched and her blood heated treacherously. Just at the sight of him.

"What are those lads doing?" she asked as she watched Liam shove Tad McCarthy hard enough to make the bigger boy stagger. Tad shoved Liam back, and O'Reilly stepped forward and separated the boys just in time to keep Liam from letting fly with his left fist. So the two lads disliked each other, did they? Amanda tried hard not to let the thought please her, but it did. "Isn't it almost time for the horse races to begin?"

Mr. Whittaker slipped two fingers into the pocket of his brocade waistcoat and pulled out a gold pocket watch at the end of a long chain. "No, still an hour yet." He snapped the watch closed and stowed it away again before squinting at the sun-washed field. "That would be the medley race assembling."

"The what?"

"It's a peculiar contest—Irish in origin, I should think. The first fifty yards are run on your hands and feet, the next fifty are run backward, and the final fifty are any way you can, no holds barred."

"That sounds like a recipe for disaster."

"It usually is."

O'Reilly stuck a sheepherder's whistle in his mouth and shouted something around it at the boys. The contestants hunkered over onto their hands and feet.

"Ready, lads? On your mark...set..." The sheer, piercing shriek of the whistle cut across the field. The boys lurched forward like a line of drunken camels.

"Oh, dear," said Amanda, her eyes on the scrambling contestants. "Liam isn't doing very well."

"No. His arms are too short compared to his legs. But just look at Tad McCarthy go."

Legs splayed outward, skinny arms flashing, his bony buttocks thrusting back and forth, Tad McCarthy charged down the field toward the first fifty-yard line.

"Come on, Tad!" Mary McCarthy's deep, throaty voice carried easily above the cheers and encouragements of the other spectators. "Good onya, lad!"

Amanda's gaze shifted from the cat-walking boys to the tall, dark-haired woman punching her fist into the air on the far side of the field. At the sight of her, something burned in Amanda's chest, something hot and uncomfortable that she realized with a sense of shame was jealousy.

The woman might lack Katherine O'Reilly's rare beauty and ethereal air of breeding, Amanda thought, and years of hard work and exposure to wind and sun might have thickened and tanned her skin, and set squint lines in the corners of her eyes and laugh lines around her mouth; but she was still a handsome woman. A woman strong enough and tough enough to take whatever this country could throw at her, and still survive.

As Amanda watched, the widow moved over to stand beside Patrick O'Reilly and rest one hand, casually, on his arm. O'Reilly's gaze left the field and he smiled down at the woman beside him, his dimples deepening as a look passed between them, a look not meant to be seen by others.

For Amanda, it was as if the shouts and cheers of the crowd, the flashing arms and legs of the running boys, all disappeared. She was conscious only of the sun beating down on her from out of the hard blue sky and of the wind, gusting wild and lonesome across the dry grass as she stared at Patrick O'Reilly.

Her love for him might be unwanted, but it seemed to grow stronger, run deeper, with every passing day. It wasn't something she could control, however much she might wish she could. She wasn't even certain for how much longer she could control herself. Every night after she put out her lamp, she now found herself lying awake beneath her covers, her thoughts on the man in the room across from her own. It was as if she could hear his voice, calling to her, tempting her. *Come to my bed tonight...*

"Now they change. See?" Christian Whittaker's gently modulated voice broke through her thoughts. "Liam is good at this next bit."

Amanda's attention snapped back to the race. The boys were running upright now, but in reverse, their backs to the finish line, their elbows and heels pumping wildly as they churned backward, kicking up a cloud of dust that hung thick in the air.

Tad McCarthy led the field by a good five yards, followed by two other boys strung out behind him, then Liam. But Liam was gaining on the others rapidly. He might lack the McCarthy boy's height, but his legs were long, and he was as lithe and agile as a well-bred greyhound. While the other boys stumbled and flailed about awkwardly, Liam streaked backward down the field as if he were born to run in reverse.

He passed the two other boys easily, but Tad had set up a formidable lead over the first third of the course. If he could hold his own in this part, he was bound to win in the final sprint.

"Come on, Liam," Amanda whispered, straining forward. "Run." She might have had her problems with the boy in the past, but

317

things had eased between them since the didgeridoo incident, and she suddenly, desperately wanted him to beat Tad McCarthy. She wished she could hoot and wave her arms like the other men and women in the crowd, but of course she would never do anything so undignified and ungenteel. So she clenched her fists at her sides and whispered again, "Come on, Liam."

She saw the McCarthy boy's face darken with rage and determination as he watched Liam steadily gain on him. For Amanda, the race had narrowed down to these two boys; as far as she was concerned, the other lads on the field might as well have ceased to exist. Tad's mouth hung open as he sucked in air, his skinny, gangly arms and legs working hard. He kept swiveling his head back and forth, trying to keep his eye on where he was going, so that he wouldn't waver too far from a straight line. But he couldn't seem to stop himself from throwing wild glances back at the lean, brown-haired boy closing on him fast.

Like Tad, the other boys kept craning around, trying to watch where they were going. But Liam must have sighted on some distant point he used to keep his bearings, because he flew backward in a smooth, unbroken line, his brows drawn together in intense concentration. The distance between the two boys shortened to a couple of yards, then one. By the time they crossed the second fifty-yard line, Liam and Tad ran shoulder to shoulder.

They swung around at the same time, chests

heaving, faces strained and sweat-streaked, arms and legs reaching forward to swallow the remaining distance in a final, wild sprint. Only, as they turned, Liam lurched sideways. Whether he did it deliberately or by accident, Amanda couldn't tell. The two boys collided with an audible smack of lean, hard flesh and bone.

Tad fell so hard, he practically did a complete somersault on the parched ground. Liam broke stride and pitched forward, falling on one knee. He flung out his hands to break the fall and, with a great heave, pushed himself back up off the ground. He was away again almost at once, but not before a blond-headed boy with a compact, powerful body streaked past him.

His face grimacing with effort and concentration and pain, the blond boy lunged through the tape. Whistles and horns sounded, the crowd cheered. Liam hurtled across the finish line three seconds behind the winner, followed closely by Tad.

"Oh," said Amanda, choking on disappointment. "He came so close. But at least he came in second."

"Jolly good race," agreed Mr. Whittaker.

"Come on, Miss Davenport," shouted Hannah, running past with Missy by the hand. The cheering crowd surged forward, and Amanda allowed herself to be swept out onto the field to where Liam stood bent over, his head bowed, his hands braced on his knees as he sucked in air.

She saw Tad McCarthy step forward. Liam straightened up, and the two boys stared at each other, both still breathing hard, chests heaving, nostrils flaring. She thought for a moment they would shake hands. Then Tad's fist flashed out, catching Liam high on the cheek.

The force of the impact was great enough to lift Liam off his feet and send him flying backward. He hit the ground, hard.

And he didn't get up.

CHAPTER SEVENTEEN

"He tripped me out there." Tad McCarthy yanked away from the two men who'd grabbed him. "The bastard deliberately tripped me."

Amanda watched O'Reilly hunker down beside his son's limp body.

"Liam!" Missy cried. Amanda caught her just in time to keep the little girl from throwing herself at her unconscious brother.

"What's wrong with him?" asked Amanda, holding Missy in front of her, her arms looped around the little girl's shoulders. She was aware of Hannah, silent but wide-eyed and anxious beside them.

"He hit his head on a rock when he fell," said O'Reilly, sliding his fingers, tenderly, beneath the boy's head.

Liam stirred and moaned softly. His eyelids fluttered open, closed, then opened again.

O'Reilly laid a hand on the boy's chest, restraining him when he would have struggled up. "Rest easy for a minute, son." He glanced around at the assembled crowd. "Anyone got some water?"

A canvas bag appeared, passed from hand to hand. O'Reilly twisted off the top and slipped one arm under Liam's shoulders to raise the boy's head. "Here, drink this."

Liam drank deeply.

"That's enough for now." O'Reilly folded his handkerchief into a pad and soaked it with water. Without turning his head, he handed the bag to Hannah. "Think you're ready to sit up?" he asked Liam.

Liam nodded. O'Reilly eased himself behind the boy until Liam was half sitting, half leaning against O'Reilly's leg.

"You got yourself a nasty bump there." O'Reilly pressed the soaked pad to the swelling at the back of the boy's head. "But other than that I think you'll be right, mate."

"He might have a concussion," said Mary McCarthy, crouching down beside father and son. "It would be best if he went up to the house and rested awhile."

O'Reilly's head swiveled around to meet the widow's concerned brown eyes. "You're probably right."

Her arms still around Missy, Amanda felt a bittersweet ache burn like tears in her throat as she watched another one of those wordless, intimate interchanges pass between the two.

Liam jerked and would have scrambled up

if his father's arm hadn't tightened around him, holding him down. "I can't go to the house now," said Liam, his voice rising. "I'm riding Fire Dancer in the first race."

O'Reilly's lips tightened in a firm line. "You're not riding anything, son. Not after a blow to the head like that."

"Bloody hell, you can't do this to me! Just because that bloody—"

"Whoa there, boy," said O'Reilly. "You better watch your language before you shock Miss Davenport here." He surprised Amanda by throwing her a grin as he slipped his other arm beneath Liam's knees and rose gracefully to his feet, the boy held easily against his chest. "Now I'm going to put you in the cart and drive you back up to the house. And you're going to stay there, in bed, until I say you can get up. Or that bump on your head will be the least of your worries. Do I make myself understood?"

Liam's swirling green-brown eyes met his father's determined blue stare.

It was Liam's gaze that faltered and fell. "Yes, sir."

"I'll come and stay with the lad," said Mr. Whittaker, starting forward. "You'll be needing to get back down here to see to the horse races."

"Thanks, Christian," said O'Reilly, heading for the cart that stood in the shade cast by the woolshed. "I'd appreciate it."

"Do you think I should go, too?" asked Hannah, still clutching the water bag.

"Probably not," said Amanda as she watched Mary McCarthy stalk over to where Tad stood alone, his head bowed, the toe of one scruffy boot digging a hole in the dusty paddock. "I'd have offered to go myself but, in my experience, boys Liam's age detest having females hover around them when they're hurt."

Hannah gave a gentle, shaky laugh. "You're right. Liam doesn't like me making a fuss over him." Her gaze followed her father and brother off the field. The faint smile faded from her lips, and she swallowed hard. "Miss Davenport?"

"Yes?"

"Do you think Papa would let me ride Fire Dancer in the race? In Liam's place?"

Instinctively, Amanda opened her mouth to say it wouldn't be proper; that it was indecent for a girl even to think about riding, astride, in a public race. But something about the needy, hopeful light she could see shining in Hannah's wide brown eyes stopped her.

For Hannah, this race would be an unexpected chance to show her father just how competent and capable she was, to make him proud of her. Only there was more to it than that. Because it occurred to Amanda, looking at the girl's tightly drawn face, that this race also offered O'Reilly an opportunity. An opportunity to show his daughter that however strained their relationship might be—and for whatever reason—he still loved her. Loved her and trusted her and respected her.

Amanda chewed her lower lip and regarded the girl beside her thoughtfully. "Can you do it, Hannah? I know you're a good rider, but—"

"I can do it. I know I can."

"Papa always says Hannah's the best horse-woman he's ever seen," put in Missy, looking up at her governess.

Amanda drew in a deep breath, torn. She remembered the sight of Hannah galloping her black horse, bareback, across the hills near Cadnowie. But controlling a big, spirited stallion like Fire Dancer in a race in front of a cheering crowd was something else again.

Hannah's hopeful, pleading gaze met Amanda's. "Papa would let me do it if you said it was all right. Will you talk to him for me?"

Amanda hesitated only a moment. Then she gently laid one hand on the girl's thin shoulder. "I'll talk to him."

O'Reilly was just leaving the homestead when he spotted Mary and Tad McCarthy coming up through the garden. He leaned against the doorjamb and fished his pipe out of his pocket, waiting for them.

"Go on into the parlor. I'll be there in a moment, Thadeus," said Mary as they reached the veranda. "I want to talk to Mr. O'Reilly."

Hiding his grin, O'Reilly shifted to one side so the boy could get past. Mary called the boy Thadeus only when she was really peeved at him.

Tad hesitated, then shoved through the front door into the parlor, his shoulders slumped, his footsteps dragging.

"How's Liam?" Mary asked, sinking down on one of the benches that lined the house wall, out of the sun.

O'Reilly looked up from loading tobacco in his pipe and smiled. "Mad as hell about not being able to race Fire Dancer."

Mary laughed. "I guess he's all right, then."

O'Reilly reached over to strike a match against the worn wood of one of the veranda posts. "He's got a hard head."

"Like his father."

O'Reilly grunted around the stem of his pipe while Mary gave him a considering look and said, "Care to tell me what's goin' on between you and that pretty little English governess of yours?"

O'Reilly choked, forgot he still held a lit match in his hand, and burned his fingers. "Bloody hell." He dropped the match and stuck his stinging fingers in his mouth. "You don't miss much, do you?" he said, shaking his hand.

"Nope. Although you were both tryin' so hard not to look at each other, I doubt anyone else noticed."

He eyed her thoughtfully. "Not jealous, are you, Mary?"

The creases beside her eyes deepened. "No more'n you're jealous of Ian Stanley and Michael Tate."

O'Reilly leaned back against the post and

drew on his pipe. Michael Tate was the manager of Three Springs Station, on the other side of Brinkman. Like O'Reilly, Tate had been one of Mary's lovers for years. But the other man he'd never heard of. "Who the hell is Ian Stanley?" he asked.

Mary tipped back her head and looked up at him. "A foreman with the Brinkman Mining Company. You invited him to your shindig today."

"Did I? Guess I can't be too jealous, then."

"I didn't think you would be." She loosened the pin that steadied her chip straw hat and took it off to use its broad brim as a fan. "Tell me somethin', O'Reilly: if I up and decided to marry one of the other men I see from time to time, how would you feel about it?"

"Why, I'd be happy for you, of course. I really would be. You know that." He sucked on his pipe. "Why? You plannin' to settle down with this Stanley?"

"Me?" Mary flapped her straw hat back and forth, and grinned. "Nah. I'm happy with my life the way it is. I just wanted to make sure you understood there'd be no hard feelings on my part, if you ever decided to settle down yourself."

"Christalmighty." O'Reilly straightened up with a jerk. "I hope you're not suggesting I'm thinking about *settling down* with Amanda Davenport."

"No? Well, I hate to tell you this, O'Reilly, but women like your Miss Davenport aren't usually comfortable with the kind of arrangements I like."

"Hell, I know that."

Mary stopped swinging her hat. "Then what exactly are you doin', O'Reilly? Or do you even know?"

O'Reilly knocked his pipe against the post and stared down at the hot ashes before grinding them beneath the sole of his boot. "I thought I did. It started out as...oh, I don't know, some kind of a joke. It just got outa hand."

"Did it?"

He swiveled around to look down at her and smiled wryly. "Maybe you're right. Maybe that was just an excuse. Although after what my mother did to my father, and Katherine did to me, you'd think I'd be smart enough to steer clear of pretty women with English accents and snooty attitudes."

"I didn't know your mother, of course. But from what little I've seen of Miss Davenport, I must say she doesn't remind me much of Katherine."

O'Reilly shifted around to stare unseeingly out over Katherine's garden while his mind resurrected the image of his uninhibited, self-absorbed wife. "You're right, in a way. Amanda Davenport and Katherine are about as different as two women can get...except for their accents, and the fact that they both hate the Australian bush."

Behind him, he heard Mary stand up. "Then you better think long and hard about what

327

you're doing, Patrick O'Reilly." She moved forward to rest her hand, companionably, on his arm. "Because if Miss Davenport hates the bush, then she's never gonna to be happy here. And whether she leaves or stays, you're both gonna end up gettin' hurt."

O'Reilly laid his hand over Mary's and met her frank brown eyes. "It's been good between us, Mary. Fun and uncomplicated."

"Yeah." She smiled sadly. "But we both know it hasn't been as good as it can get. Which is probably why it's been so fun and uncomplicated."

He swiveled around to rest his hands, lightly, on her waist, and kiss her cheek. "Know something, Mary? You're a very wise woman."

"Nah. I'm just a woman." She gave his shoulder a light punch. "Go on now. You better get back down to the woolshed and see about those horse races. Tad and me'll stay up here with Christian and Liam for a while."

Halfway back down to the woolshed, O'Reilly was surprised to meet Amanda, coming up the dusty cart track toward him. "Somethin' wrong?" he asked.

The climb to the house was steep enough that he could see her chest rise and fall with each labored breath as she paused beside him. She pressed the back of one white-gloved hand against her damp forehead, then frowned down at the resulting gritty smudge before saying, "There is something I wish to discuss with you."

She'd been so ostentatiously avoiding him

328

ever since that afternoon on the big flat rock that he tipped his hat back on his head and stared at her through narrowed eyes. "What's on your mind?"

He watched her hesitate, and felt a smile tug at the corners of his mouth. Whatever it was, she wasn't overly eager to spit it out. "It's about"—she sucked in a deep breath—"the horse race. Who will ride Fire Dancer, now that Liam is unable to do so? You?"

O'Reilly laughed. "At my weight? Not if I want the horse to have a fair chance at winning. I was thinkin' about gettin' Jacko to do it."

"Oh?" She looked off across the dry creek bed to where a couple of kangaroos grazed with slow, graceful hops. "Is he a good rider?"

O'Reilly studied her half-averted face, his eyes narrowing in suspicion. She was up to something, but he'd be damned if he could figure out what. "Good enough."

"As good as Hannah?"

If it'd been anyone other than Amanda who'd asked that question, he'd have suspected her of angling to convince him to let Hannah ride in the race. But surely Miss Don't-Say-That, Don't-Do-This, Don't-Touch-Me-There Davenport wasn't suggesting...

"You care to explain that question?" he asked slowly.

Her head swung around to meet his gaze squarely. "Hannah wants to ride in the race. And I think you ought to let her."

He crossed his arms over his chest and leaned into her. "Oh you do, do you?"

He watched her nostrils flare on a quickly indrawn breath. "Yes, I do."

"You think I ought to let her ride in a horse race? In front of all those people? Wearing those trousers you're always carrying on about?"

Her gaze flickered away from him again, and he knew the scheme didn't sit well with her. But for some reason he couldn't begin to understand, she was determined to push it.

"She's wearing trousers now. Your guests have all seen her."

"They haven't seen her astride that big bloodred stallion."

The flush in her cheeks deepened, but she pushed on anyway. "Is Hannah as good a rider as Liam?"

"Better." He propped his backside against a big old gum that had blown down at the side of the track a couple of years ago and now lay, pale and fading. "And it's not just because Hannah's older. I told you, she's one of the best riders I've seen in my life. It's a gift some people are born with, and she has it."

"So you'll let her race?"

O'Reilly let his breath out in a little huff. "I didn't say that. It's too dangerous. She could get hurt."

"But..." He heard the confusion in her voice. "You just said she's a better rider than Liam, and you were willing to let him do it."

"Liam's a boy."

"What does that have to do with it?"

"I can't believe you just said that. I'd have expected you of all people to agree that it has everything to do with it."

"Well I don't." She gave him that thin-nosed, disdainful look she did so well. "Not in this instance."

"Christ." He pushed away from the fallen tree and straightened up. "This is exactly the kind of *instance* in which it does matter. I might be willing to let Hannah wear her trousers, and I might teach her how to dip sheep and muster cattle, and I'll even let her learn to read Virgil if she wants to." He saw her eyebrows shoot up. "Yes, I know about that. But there's absolutely no reason or justification for me to let her run the kind of risks she'd face in that race."

"Yet you'd let Liam?"

"Damn it, Amanda. It's different with Liam, and you know it. Liam's a *boy*. Boys grow up and have to become men. Which means you can't coddle them, can't protect them too much—no matter how much you might want to. You need to let them challenge themselves. Face danger. Let them spread their wings and try to fly. Even if it means they might fall and hurt themselves."

Her lips parted in a sad smile that tugged oddly at his heart. "You think girls don't yearn to fly free, too?"

Whatever annoyance he'd felt melted away beneath an onslaught of unwanted emotions. He reached out one hand to rub his knuckles, very gently, against her petal-soft cheek. "Do

331

you yearn to fly free, Amanda?" he asked hoarsely. "Then why don't you just let yourself go?"

He felt her tremble, saw a glimmer of what might have been tears in her fine gray eyes. "I didn't come here to talk about myself."

She would have turned away, but he dropped his hand to her shoulder, stopping her. "Maybe not. But we need to talk, you and I. We need to talk about a lot of things."

Her gaze met his, and held it. The moment stretched out, taut, pregnant with meaning and emotion. He felt the hot, golden sun pouring down on them. Heard the quick intake of her breath and the buffeting of the wind that blew the worn gray ribbons of her bonnet across her lips.

He reached up, gently, and smoothed the tattered ends down, his fingertips lingering against her strong chin.

A loud burst of cheering and horn-blowing from down by the woolshed brought his head around. She slipped quickly out of his grasp to stand stiffly, hugging herself, her arms crossed at her chest, her hands gripping precisely where he'd touched her, her eyes huge in a pale, drawn face.

"It must be almost time for the race," she said. "Will you let Hannah ride?"

"You don't give up, do you?"

"Not when it's this important."

He shoved his fingertips beneath his belt and rocked back on his heels. "Why is it so important?"

332

"Because Hannah doesn't believe you love her."

He jerked. "That's the stupidest thing I've ever heard. Why would she think a fool thing like that?"

He saw Amanda hesitate, and knew she was keeping something back. "Because of the way you treat her."

He stared at the tiny woman before him. "What's wrong with the way I treat Hannah?"

"Everything." She leaned forward, her forehead knit with concern. "Don't you see? You neither *coddle* her the way you do Missy—"

"Hannah doesn't want to be coddled. She never has. Even as a toddler, she never wanted to be held, or hugged, or kissed. She's not like Missy—"

"Nor do you allow her to *fly free*, the way you do Liam."

"*Bloody hell*. She's a *girl*."

"She's a girl who is desperate to prove herself to you. Desperate to make you proud of her. Desperate for some sign from you that you love her."

"That's ridiculous. Of course I love her." He jabbed one finger into the air in front of her nose. "It's because I love her that I don't want her to get hurt."

"She's already hurting." Amanda's voice broke, and he watched her swallow hard. "More than you'll ever know."

He pushed out his breath in a long sigh. "You don't want her to ride in this race either, do you?"

Her trembling smile answered him. "No. But my reasons aren't good enough to stand in her way."

"Well, come on, then," he said, cupping his hand beneath her elbow to draw her down the track with him. "We'd better hurry."

The course was a long one: two miles altogether, starting just beyond the gums on the far side of the dry creek bed, then stretching out into the valley, around an upthrust of splintered red rock on a rise about half a mile out, then back and around the loop again. The jumps had been formed of sheep hurdles, and there was a small creek bed, too, that would have to be jumped.

Standing in the shade of a big old river gum, O'Reilly carefully tied his handkerchief to a stick, conscious of Amanda standing beside him, anxiously surveying the assembling field of horses and riders. Her teeth worried her bottom lip and she'd gone a bit white, as if she were already regretting whatever impulse it was that had led her to talk him into this.

"Are you familiar with any of the other horses in the race?" she asked.

"Some." He nodded to where the riders struggled to bring their mounts into line. "See that dark bay there? The one with the young Aboriginal stockman on him? He's from Arkaba. I've seen him run before. He's fast, but he's not reliable." O'Reilly clamped one end of the stick between his knees to steady it. "The gray with the white blaze I don't know, but the way he keeps tossing his head and sidling isn't a good sign for anybody who's got money on him."

Her gaze snapped to his. "Do you mean to tell me people are gambling on the outcome of this race?"

He gave her a deliberately devilish grin and tightened the knot. "Some people, Miss Davenport. But I wouldn't bet on that glossy black stallion with the four white socks, if I were you. He's from Wilpena Pound. And while I'll allow he's showy enough, he's too long in the back and short in the leg for my taste." He nodded to the fourth horse in the field. "That big white mare's the one to watch. It belongs to Hannibal Cox."

She studied the mare with interest. "Isn't that the gentleman from the run to the east of here? The man who originally brought Fire Dancer from New Zealand?"

"That's right. I hear he's not too happy about the fact I ended up with Fire Dancer. He's been bragging that Cox's Lady there can beat my stallion any day of the week. That's his son, Richard, riding. He might be only fifteen, but he's a tough little bastard, and a damned good horseman."

He expected her to make some comment about his language, only she didn't. She just stood staring at the assembling horses, her hands clenching and unclenching in front of her as she watched the carrot-headed, freckle-faced Cox boy, with his washed-out gray eyes and small mouth, pull his big white mare into line beside Fire Dancer.

"Hey!" he called to Hannah. "What you doin' here? Ain't you supposed to be over in the wool-shed, handin' out pies and cordials with the rest of the ladies?"

The other boys in the race all laughed, and a few of the spectators, too. Hannah was leaning over to adjust her stirrup leather. At the sound of the boy's sneering voice, she froze for the briefest instant. O'Reilly saw her fingers tighten around the buckle, then slowly relax again. She straightened up, gathered her reins, and stared straight ahead.

O'Reilly felt a warm glow of pride as he watched his daughter ignore the boy's continuing taunts. Liam would have been off his horse in a flash, ready to pull the Cox boy down into the dust and bloody him. But Hannah was too smart to let herself be distracted or irritated in any way. Her attention was focused inward, gathering her forces for the contest ahead.

O'Reilly held the stick out to Amanda. "Whenever you're ready, Miss Davenport."

She met his smiling gaze with a start of surprise. He saw her hesitate, then reach for the makeshift flag. For one moment, their hands both grasped the stick as it passed between them. O'Reilly let go and stepped back.

She raised the flag high. A tense, expectant hush fell over the crowd. Then the flag dropped.

The horses broke away in a bunch. All

except the gray, which had swung around and was facing backward at the crucial moment. Its rider, swearing viciously enough to bring bright color to Amanda's cheeks, yanked the horse's head about and brought his crop down with a resounding whack. The gray bolted forward.

The other horses streaked across the field together, clattering safely over the first hurdle, their hooves chipping at the hard, dry earth.

"Up here," said O'Reilly, taking Amanda's arm as they ran with the rest of the noisy, cheering crowd to a nearby high bank. "We'll be able to see better."

As they topped the bank, the horses cleared the second hurdle, then soared over the small creek bed, the first four all still in a bunch. But by the time they reached the turning, they were strung out in a ragged line. Hannah was in third place, behind Cox's white mare and the dark bay from Arkaba. The nervous gray had already passed the showy black, and was coming up on the three leaders fast.

"Come on, Hannah," whispered Amanda, clenching her little white-gloved fists in front of her. "Move up."

"She's holding him back," said O'Reilly, his eyes narrowing as he watched the horses pour over the next hurdle. "Cox is pushing that mare too hard. She won't last the whole two miles at that pace. And neither will the dark bay."

The spectators on the bank jumped and yelled themselves hoarse as the racers swept past in front of them. The very earth seemed to quiver beneath the thudding hooves as the horses streamed over the nearest hurdle. They stretched out over the flat, then turned sharply at the creek, heading back out across the plain, an overlapping ribbon of flashing hooves and sweating horseflesh and straining riders.

As they thundered past the bank again, Hannah eased Fire Dancer up past the dark bay, into second place. But she was still a good three lengths behind the Cox mare.

All around them, the crowd cheered and yelled and swayed back and forth in a frenzy of excitement. All except Amanda. O'Reilly felt her fingers dig into his arm. He glanced down at her tense, anxious face and rigidly stiff body, and wondered if she even realized she was clutching him so desperately. He watched her strain forward, and knew she wanted to yell and hop around like everyone else. A wave of sympathy swept over him. She was so obviously held back. Held back by her own damned hide-bound ideas about the kind of behavior fitting and proper for an English gentlewoman.

Let go, Amanda, he wanted to say. *Let go and jump up and down and scream and shout like the rest of them. The way you want to. The way you need to.*

But she couldn't.

A ragged cheer arose from the crowd as the horses swept around the broken rocks on the distant rise for the second and last time. Looking up, he saw the white mare still in the lead, Fire Dancer pacing it three lengths behind,

338

the dark bay and the nervous gray hard on his heels. The showy black lagged far behind.

"Now, Hannah," O'Reilly said quietly. "Let him go."

As if she heard him, Hannah leaned low over the big stallion's neck. His stride reached out, accelerating. Hannah's fluid, lithe body seemed to flow into the muscular strength of the stallion, until it was as if the girl and the horse moved as one, were one.

Fire Dancer's flashing legs churned up the distance, gained steadily on the white mare, left the dark bay and the gray far behind. When they lifted over the next hurdle, Hannah was only two lengths behind Richard Cox. By the time they closed on the last jump, Cox's lead had narrowed to less than a length.

And then, just when it looked as if Hannah were set to ease into the lead for the final jump and the home stretch, Fire Dancer stumbled. Hannah pulled him up, but they were too close to the last hurdle. Cox sailed over it easily, but O'Reilly could see the tense awareness on Hannah's face as she realized she was coming at the jump all wrong.

She hauled in rein, but it was too late. The big bay lifted into the air a stride too soon.

"Oh, my God," Amanda cried. "She's going to fall." Amanda lunged forward, as if she could physically stop it from happening. O'Reilly caught her around the waist and held on. "Hannah," she whispered, clutching frantically to the arm he wrapped around her. *"Oh, Hannah."*

O'Reilly's arms tightened around her warm body, hugging her close, his gut churning, his heart thudding painfully. If Hannah fell now, the others would all smash into her. She'd be horribly injured.

Or killed.

To O'Reilly, it seemed as if the big, bloodred stallion soared through the air in slow motion. He had always admired his daughter's horsemanship, but he realized now that he'd never fully appreciated just how gifted she truly was. Just when he was convinced the stallion would come down in disaster, she somehow managed to collect him in midair. His stride lengthened out, and they cleared the last hurdle with a jarring but safe landing.

Ahead of her, flat out in a wild gallop, Richard Cox risked throwing a glance over his shoulder at the horse thundering up behind him. His lead narrowed to a length again. Half a length. His elbows pumped like jack handles, his whip rose and fell unmercifully. But his horse was spent.

"Hannah!" yelled O'Reilly, his fist punching into the air. "That's my girl!"

And then whatever it was that had been holding Amanda back, broke away. *"Hannah!"* she cried, jumping up and down in wild abandon beside O'Reilly. "Come on, Hannah. Come on, you can do it! *Come on. Come on.*"

A sonnet of bloodred, rhythmic muscle moving poetically beneath the light, sure hands of a dark-haired slip of a girl, the stallion swept past Cox's Lady. Together, Hannah

340

and Fire Dancer streaked across the finish line, winning easily by two lengths.

Amanda, all her prim, proper decorum totally forgotten, swung around in O'Reilly's arms and laughed up at him with such unself-conscious happiness, it stopped his breath. "She won! Hannah won."

Wordlessly, he stared down into Amanda's radiant face, at her full lips trembling with emotion, at her fine gray eyes glistening with tears of joy. Around them, the shouting, bustling crowd streamed down the bank toward the foam-flecked, steaming horses and their heaving riders. But O'Reilly's gaze stayed locked with Amanda's as his feelings for her swelled inside him, warm and filling and exciting. Laughing, he closed his hands on her waist and lifted her up into the air, high up, spinning around and around with her in a dizzy, triumphant circle.

She gave a wide-eyed gasp of surprise and clutched wildly at his shoulders. But then her head fell back in delight and her laughter mingled with his, spontaneous and uninhibited and exuberant as for one stolen moment, Amanda soared free.

CHAPTER EIGHTEEN

Memory of where they were returned to Amanda far too quickly.

She could not believe she had allowed O'Reilly to display such familiarity toward her in public. "*Mister* O'Reilly," she said with a horrified gasp as she stared down into his handsome, laughing face. "Please put me down. You are making a spectacle of me."

He let her slide slowly down the length of his long, hard body, but he didn't let her go. "Relax, Mandy," he said against her ear. "No one's looking."

She was excruciatingly aware of the heat of his lean, muscular body pressed against hers. She batted his hands from her waist and jerked away from him to follow the crowd rushing down the slope. "You mustn't call me Mandy in public," she hissed at him. "It is not proper." She fussed with her skirts and straightened her bonnet and did anything she could think of to avoid looking at the man keeping pace with her.

"Do you *always* have to be proper, Amanda?"

"Of course."

"Why?" He grabbed her arm and pulled her around to face him again. "What happens if you're not? What happens if you just let go like everyone else and have a bit of fun? Are you afraid people will think you've stopped being a proper, precious bloody Englishwoman? Is that what really scares you about this country?

The way it makes you feel? The way it makes you want to behave?"

She knocked his hand from her arm. *"Don't!"* she cried, meaning not just *don't touch me* but also *don't say these things to me.*

They stared at each other, eyes wide. Down by the empty creek bed, a magpie broke into song, its joyous melody joining with the sound of Hannah's high, light laughter.

"There's Hannah," Amanda said, swinging away to walk stiffly to where the girl was just sliding down from the back of the big stallion.

Hannah spotted Amanda and her father through the crowd and started forward, Fire Dancer's reins still clutched in her hand. "Did you see me, Miss Davenport?" she asked, her cheeks flushed, her chest heaving with the effort of the hard ride, her eyes glowing with pride. "Did you see, Papa?"

Amanda smiled and nodded, but she held back, letting Hannah's father be the first to congratulate her.

Amanda had expected O'Reilly to sweep his daughter into his arms in an exuberant display of affection and pride. She watched, stunned, as he simply sauntered over to casually clamp one arm around Hannah's shoulders and pull her against his side in a rough hug. "Good onya, mate," he said, as if she were Liam, or even just one of the stockmen.

A wave of indignation swept over Amanda. How *could* he treat Hannah's win so casually? Didn't he know how much this meant to the girl? Couldn't he have done something, said something to show how proud he was of her?

Then Amanda saw Hannah's glowing face, and she understood.

Australian men never called a female *mate*. It was a man's word, a word reserved exclusively for other males. A word that somehow embodied all the comradeship, all the pride, all the quiet strength, all the exclusivity that was part of being a man.

O'Reilly probably couldn't have said anything that would have gratified Hannah more.

Patrick O'Reilly's after-shearing dance was unlike any ball Amanda had ever attended.

It wasn't just the venue—the woolshed. Or the band, which consisted of a redheaded Irish miner with an accordion and a skinny, gray-whiskered fiddle player Amanda recognized as Ichabod Hornbottom, the proprietor of the Brinkman Inn. The main problem was that the number of men present outnumbered the women by about five to one.

If they wanted to dance, most of the men had to dance with each other. That might have been all right, except that when the men weren't dancing, they spent their time clustered around the long refreshment tables set up just outside the great eastern doors. Every once in a while they'd stagger back into the golden light of the woolshed, reeking of tobacco and rum and laughing so hard, they had to hold each other up as their wayward feet tried to follow the instructions of the caller guiding the dancers through the rounds. When a couple of children playing tag darted across the dance floor, four all-male couples trying to pivot in a square collided into one another and toppled over like skittles.

Amanda choked on a laugh and quickly raised one white-gloved hand to hide her smile.

"Appalling," muttered an outraged female English voice to her right. Someone else *tssk*ed audibly. Amanda cleared her throat and carefully schooled her features.

She formed one of a row of sedate English governesses who sat, stiff and disapproving, on a line of wool bales shoved up against the wall to form a makeshift bench. She had told the children she would not dance tonight, and she meant it. But as the fiddle wailed faster and faster, her rebellious feet picked up the beat and began tapping surreptitiously beneath her drab skirts.

She rested her hands on her knees to still them.

Across the room, she could see Christian Whittaker talking to some of the managers from the Brinkman mine. He was dressed in neat gray pin-striped trousers and a matching coat with a burgundy brocade vest over a striped shirt, and she found his familiar, respectable appearance both calming and reassuring. He was such a comfort. When she'd told him of her decision not to dance, he'd assured her that he understood her sentiments exactly. One could always rely on Mr. Whittaker, Amanda thought, to act the perfect gentleman.

Unfortunately, O'Reilly was no gentleman.

"That's the stupidest bloody thing I've ever heard," he'd announced, hands on hips, when he found out.

"*Mister* O'Reilly," she'd hissed, quickly glancing around to see if he'd been over-heard.

"Why the hell won't you dance with me?"

"I told you. I do not think it appropriate for me to dance at all."

"Oh you don't, do you? Well, I'll tell you what's inappropriate." He jabbed one finger into the air before her nose in a way that was becoming a habit with him. "It's inappro-priate for one of the few pretty young women in a room full of men to announce she's going to sit against the wall all night like some dried-up old hag who gave up on having a life twenty years ago." He flung his hand out in the direction of the line of stern-faced, faded governesses.

"*Mister* O'Reilly." But the protest was more obligatory than real, because inside, her heart gave a little leap of pleasure. So he thought she was pretty, did he? It was difficult to force her face into a frown. "I am here as a gov-erness, not a guest. I belong with those women."

He pursed his lips and blew out a long sigh. "Don't you understand? No one is making those damn women sit there. They're the ones who decided it's not proper for them to have any fun."

"Quite rightly."

"Who says?"

"Not who, Mr. O'Reilly. What. Something called propriety. Custom."

"English custom, maybe. Not Australian."

"But I, sir, am English." And with that, she spun about on her heel and stalked over to join that depressing line of desiccated, lifeless gentlewomen.

Suppressing a sigh, Amanda tilted back her head against the rough stone wall and half closed her eyes until the interior of the woolshed was only a blur of golden light and bare timber and stone and the whirling, laughing, gaily clothed splashes of the dancers.

She knew the building had been thoroughly scrubbed in preparation for the dance, but the scents of the shearing lingered still, she decided, faintly detectable beneath the ladies' perfume and the gentlemen's hair oil and the hot press of dancing bodies. She imagined that if she tried, she could almost catch the faint echo of clicking shears and bleating sheep beneath the swish of the ladies' satin gowns and the stomp of the men's boots and the cheerful, energetic wailing of the fiddle and accordion.

A querulous but well-bred English voice intruded upon her thoughts. "One would think the least they could do is provide us with decent seats."

Amanda swiveled her head to look at the lady who sat beside her, stiffly sharing the same wool bale. Miss Iantha Thorndike was governess to the Browne family of Wilpena Pound. A spare woman with a long face and eyes as tiny as a ferret's, she'd kept her mouth crimped into a pained scowl for so many years that it now seemed little wider than her thin nose. Her dress was a dull brown, the same dull brown as her hair and her beady little eyes. In age, she could have been anywhere between thirty-five and fifty-five. Looking at her, Amanda found it difficult to believe that this severe, joyless woman had ever been really young.

"It is so *typical* of life in the colonies, is it not?" continued Iantha, taking Amanda's silence for agreement. "This strange mixture of refinement and roughing it which one finds here. In England, of course, as governesses, we would never have been invited to attend a ball. But then again, in England no one would think of expecting a gentlewoman to sit on a *wool bale*, of all things."

Amanda stared at the arrogant, mean-souled Englishwoman beside her and felt a rush of unexpected antipathy, mingling with a right-eous urge to leap to the defense of the man who had provided the wool bales, and the music, and the endless flood of food she'd noticed Miss Thorndike enjoying all day long.

"Actually, they smell better than the parlor sofas," said Amanda, her tongue pressed against her cheek in an effort to keep a straight face. "I'm afraid Liam's dog sleeps on them most of the time."

"Hhmm." Iantha contracted her dried-up mouth like a pale raisin. "I suppose one must learn to expect almost anything when dealing with such a collection of parvenus and mush-rooms." She threw a speaking glance toward the dance floor, where a boisterous Irish jig was in progress. "Oh, there are a few ladies and gentlemen from good families, of course. But as for the rest! One grows so *tired* of the pervading vulgarity of mind and general want of intellect and breeding that most squatters betray." Iantha leaned in closer and lowered her voice. "I have heard that Mr. O'Reilly actually employs *black savages*. How *trying* it must be for you."

Black savages. It was an expression Amanda had used herself. But for some reason, hearing Iantha Thorndike condescendingly refer to Jacko and Sally and Pinba in that way suddenly made Amanda understand fully, for the first time, exactly why O'Reilly hated that phrase so much.

"True," said Amanda. "But he does ask them to put on their clothes when they come up to the house itself."

Iantha's eyes widened in horror. "Do you mean they are actually allowed on the station in a state of...of *nudity?*" She splayed one hand across her chest, as if to hide her own meager bosom from view.

Watching her, Amanda felt the faintest stirrings of pity for this narrow-minded, unhappy woman. Whatever breasts Iantha might once have had were now as withered as an old maid's dreams: dried up, shriveled away, as if from disuse. No babe had ever suckled at them. And a woman such as Iantha Thorndike

349

had surely never allowed any man to let his hands wander there.

Conscious of a rising sense of distress, Amanda threw a quick glance down the row of faded English gentlewomen who lined the wall. Hands clasped in laps, identically gowned in shades of gray or brown, they sat sour and disapproving, their fading brown or blond hair scraped back into identical tight knots that were like parables of their wasted, virgin lives. Had any of these women ever ached for the touch of a man's hands on her breasts? Amanda wondered. Had they once yearned to know what it would feel like to have a man's hot mouth kiss them, there? Had they ever burned with the need to feel a man press his hard heat between their willing thighs? Looking at that row of pinched, severe faces, it was impossible to tell.

Is that what I'm going to look like in another ten years? Amanda thought desperately. *Or...*
Or do I look like that already?

Panicked by the thought, she turned away, her gaze searching the twirling dancers, seeking out the tall, lean figure of Patrick O'Reilly.

He looked almost respectable tonight, with his peg-leg trousers and midnight-blue satin vest and crisp white shirt. Except that his tawny hair was still too long, so that it curled reprehensibly against the collar of his fine coat. And there was nothing staid or respectable about the way his blue eyes sparkled, or the devilish smile that brought the dimples to his smoothly shaven, suntanned cheeks.

She watched him kick up his heels in an energetic Irish jig, and smiled when she noticed that hidden beneath the cuffs of his fine trousers he still wore his scuffed brown leather riding boots. The fiddle squealed through the tune, the accordion scrambling to keep up as the music whirled away, faster and faster.

O'Reilly jumped and spun, his feet flashing, his lean, taut upper body unbelievably controlled. Around him, the other dancers stopped to applaud and roar their encouragement. Lamplight glinted on his tumbled, sun-shot hair, on his sweat-sheened, flushed cheeks as he danced and danced and danced.

Amanda sat breathless, her heart filling with her love for him as she admired again the beauty of his healthy body and thrilled to his strength and the irresistible lure of his powerful masculinity. Heat glowed within her. Heat and need and a growing, insistent fear that she might never know what it felt like to take his hard, hungry body deep inside her. The fear that one day, ten years from now, she would find herself sitting against some wall, her hands clenched in her lap, her face sour and pinched with regret as she watched a young man dance.

And realized what she had missed.

The night pressed down hot and still, and so quiet the laughter and music from the woolshed must have carried out over the empty, rolling plains for miles.

O'Reilly stood beyond the rectangular splash of golden light thrown across the hard ground by the open eastern doors. He'd come out here for a smoke, but in the end he'd just wandered off with his pipe in his pocket, his thoughts on Amanda.

He hated seeing her sitting there against the woolshed wall, hated the very idea that she should consider herself a part of that pathetic row of shriveled-up, living mummies. He'd watched her surreptitiously tapping her toes beneath her skirt, noticed the way her sad eyes followed the dancers around the floor like a hungry calf looking for its mama. She *wanted* to dance, he was sure of it. She didn't think she should, and she was probably even a bit afraid of the prospect of letting go and enjoying herself after all these years. But she wanted to.

Problem was, how to get her to do it? She was such a damn stubborn woman.

Swearing softly to himself, he was fishing in his pockets for his pipe and tobacco pouch when something caught his eye. Something that looked like the beruffled bottom of his younger daughter sticking out from beneath the refreshment table dedicated to the gentlemen.

Stuffing his pipe back in his pocket, he sauntered up to the table, turned around as if he meant to use it as a prop for his backside, swooped down to grab a handful of ruffled skirt, and tugged.

Missy came out backward, her arms spinning like weather vanes in a high wind in an attempt to maintain her balance. Out of the corner of one eye, he caught a flash of white cut by black suspenders and reached out with his other hand to nab Liam by the back of his collar.

"Hold on a minute there, you two varmints." He swung them around to face him as Hannah quietly slunk from behind the side of the woolshed and ranged herself on the other side of Liam. The girl might be more headaches than a cartful of rotgut whiskey, but she'd never been one to let the others take the fall alone for something she'd been a part of, too.

"Look," he said, resting his hands on his hips as he stared down all three of them at once. "I'm not even going to ask what the hell you kids were up to out here."

His offspring exchanged guarded sideways glances of relief.

It was all he could do not to laugh. "What I want to know is, why aren't you in bed?"

"Miss Davenport said we could stay up till midnight if we were good," volunteered Liam.

"You don't look to me as if you were bein' good."

"Please, Papa," pleaded Missy, turning those big blue charmers on him. "You wouldn't tell, would you?"

He gave them a considering look. "Well," he said slowly, drawing out the suspense. "That depends."

"On what?" demanded Hannah suspiciously.

He grinned back at her. "On how open you three are to bribery and corruption."

Missy's forehead crinkled. "What's brib'ry and cor-cor—"

O'Reilly swung the little girl up onto his hip. "Missy, you need some serious educating here."

Missy scrambled up onto the empty wool bale beside Miss Davenport. Missy was feeling pretty proud of herself, because Papa had selected her for the starring role in what he called an *impromptu play*. Or something like that. He'd picked her because he said she could charm the stripes off a ring-tailed possum when she turned it on full blast.

It was a bit of a shock to discover that Papa knew she could turn her smiles and tears on and off whenever she wanted to, and that she wasn't above doing it for her own ends. But she decided that as long as it continued to work, she didn't need to worry about it too much.

"Miss Davenport," she began, only to have to stop when Miss Davenport gently touched her hand, hushing her.

A long-faced governess with a mouth like a dried-up dead worm, who sat on Miss Davenport's other side, was talking.

"...and of course one of the most trying aspects of life here is the total lack of improving conversation," the woman was saying. "I mean, all they ever talk about is *sheep*."

"Oh?" Miss Davenport raised her eyebrows as if in all innocence. "Don't the Brownes run any cattle at Wilpena Pound?"

Missy giggled, but the woman with a worm for a mouth just looked confused. "Yes. I suppose they do. Why?"

"Excuse me one moment," said Miss Davenport, turning. "Did you want something, Missy?"

Missy gave Miss Davenport her biggest, brightest smile. "Liam and Hannah want to know why you aren't dancin'."

Miss Davenport glanced over to where Liam and Hannah were systematically searching the crowds of men hemming the dance floor. "I already explained that, remember?" she said. "I'm here as your governess. It wouldn't be proper for me to dance."

"But Miss Tucker is dancing, and she's a governess." Missy nodded toward the pretty young woman with blond curls and a high complexion who was dancing with Papa.

A sad, hurting look dampened Miss Davenport's pretty gray eyes as her gaze followed Papa and Miss Tucker, but the worm-mouthed woman *tssk*ed in disapproval and said, "Susan Tucker. *She* was born in *New South Wales*."

"I don't understand," said Missy.

Worm Mouth frowned at her. "She is not English."

"Don't English ladies know how to dance?"

Worm Mouth's eyes boggled out, as if she'd accidentally swallowed a real worm. "Don't be impertinent, child."

Missy felt a spurt of irritation. This wasn't going to work at all, not with that horrible old woman pouring out her sour vinegar at every other word. Missy glanced over to where Hannah and Liam had finally located Mr. Whittaker and corralled him between them. Papa had told them to use Mr. Whittaker only if they really needed to, but Missy decided they were definitely going to need all the help they could get.

Twisting sideways with her hand behind her back, she frantically motioned to her sister and brother to come up.

Miss Davenport turned to talk to the nasty governess. "I hear Wilpena Pound is well watered and forested, almost like a park. Tell me, do you ride?"

Worm Mouth shrugged. "It is true the land is not as dry and desolate as what one sees in most other areas of the Flinders. But as to riding... Well, what is the point of riding without a destination? There are no settlements or other homesteads within comfortable riding distance."

At that moment, Hannah and Liam strolled up with Mr. Whittaker pinned between them. He looked kinda uncomfortable and bemused, as if he didn't know what he was doing there but couldn't figure out how to get away.

Hannah waited patiently, her head tilted to one side, until Worm Mouth stopped to draw breath. Then she pounced. "Miss Davenport enjoys riding. Don't you, Miss Davenport?"

Miss Davenport smiled at Hannah. Hannah was wearing her usual moleskins and a red shirt. But she had pulled her hair back with a red satin ribbon for the dance, and the way Miss Davenport was beaming about it, you'd have thought Hannah had decked herself out in hoops and lace.

"Yes. Although until recently I haven't had as much opportunity to ride as I did when I was a girl." She looked a bit wistful when she said it, as if she were remembering something that had once made her happy. Except remembering it now seemed to make her sad.

Mr. Whittaker cleared his throat. "I must admit, I personally have never understood the attraction of riding as a form of recreation. More an unavoidable means of transportation, to be endured rather than enjoyed, I say."

Behind him, Liam rolled his eyes and made a face, but Missy remembered what they were supposed to be doing, and leapt at the chance to pipe up and ask, "Don't you like to dance, either, Mr. Whittaker?"

Mr. Whittaker smiled down at her and said in that peculiar tone of voice some grown-ups reserve for small children, dogs, cats, and other presumably slow-witted creatures, "Why yes, of course."

"Then why aren't you dancing?"

He managed to keep the smile in place, although it slipped a bit, and Missy noticed his cheeks got red. "Well, err..." He looked flustered, and the coloring in his cheeks deepened.

"Yes, why aren't you dancing?" asked Hannah.

"Well, actually, it is because of Miss Davenport here," he finally said with a hearty

357

kind of bluffness that didn't quite ring true. "It didn't seem right, somehow, for me to dance when *she* has decided she should not participate."

He threw Miss Davenport an apologetic look, and she smiled back at him so warmly that Missy had to stop herself from scowling at Mr. Whittaker.

"It doesn't seem fair for you to miss out on the dancing, when you like it so much," Missy said slowly.

"No, really, I assure you I'm not actually very fond—" began Mr. Whittaker.

"Yeah," said Hannah, turning to Miss Davenport. "I think you should dance with him."

Miss Davenport was so startled, she almost jumped. "It really would not be proper—"

"But he likes it so much. And he won't dance unless you do," said Missy, giving her governess her best big-eyed, soulful look.

Miss Davenport sighed. "Missy, you don't understand—"

"Come on, Miss Davenport," said Hannah, seizing the governess's hand and giving it a tug. "Dance with him."

"But Hannah—"

Missy grabbed Miss Davenport's other hand and jumped up to help Hannah pull. It seemed to Missy that Miss Davenport wasn't really as reluctant to dance as she tried to pretend she was. She certainly came up off the wool bale easily enough. "You embarrassing children, the man hasn't even asked me for this dance!"

Liam gave Mr. Whittaker a nudge, and he

stepped forward right on cue and bowed to say, "If you would do me the honor, ma'am, I would be privileged."

Miss Davenport laughed. "After such an effort on the children's part, I really don't see how I can refuse." She put her hand on Mr. Whittaker's arm and let him lead her off to join the nearest square for the country dance that was just forming.

Liam and Hannah exchanged triumphant grins and went off to tell the fiddle player that Papa wanted them to make the *next* dance a waltz.

But Missy lingered beside old Worm Mouth, who was leading the other governesses in a chorus of *tssk*ings and exaggerated head-shakings. "Excuse me, ma'am?" said Missy, assuming her Innocent Child face. "Do you have a hanky I could use? I seem to have lost mine."

The Wilpena governess hesitated a moment, sighed, and handed over a neatly pressed square of white linen.

"Thank you." Missy reached down to wipe at a spot of dirt on the side of her shoe. "You see, I stepped in some dog doo outside, and it does smell so."

She wadded up the handkerchief and handed it to the governess, along with her best smile. Then, trying to whistle through the gap left by her newly missing front tooth, she wandered away to wait for the waltz. She and Liam and Hannah had done their part.

The rest was up to Papa.

CHAPTER NINETEEN

It was only one dance.

Surely she could be forgiven for indulging herself just this once, Amanda thought, as she scrambled to keep up with the nasal-voiced caller. She told herself that as soon as the music ended, she would rejoin that depressing line of aging Englishwomen and properly rot with them for the rest of the night. But for now...now, she was going to enjoy herself.

She'd forgotten how much she loved to dance. The rush of wind and giddy blur of lights as she spun from one partner to the next, her hands clapping, her feet flying, her heart racing, her hair coming down. She felt young and vitally alive, as if she had suddenly awakened from a long sleep to find the world a wonderful, joyous place.

But all too soon, the fiddle squealed to an abrupt halt and the dance was over. "Oh, that was too short," she said, holding onto Christian's arm as she gasped for breath. "But wonderful."

"Wonderfully exhausting." Christian puffed his ruddy cheeks and blew like a sorely pressed steam engine. "I think I'd rather go head to head with Hermes than stagger through another round."

Amanda laughingly squeezed his arm, just as a deep male voice behind her said, "I thought you weren't going to dance."

She spun about to discover O'Reilly staring

down at her through narrowed, hooded eyes. "It was the children," she said quickly, her heart giving an odd little *thump-bump.* "They maneuvered us both into this." She pressed one hand to her pounding chest and tried very hard to sound nonchalant. "I was just about to rejoin the other governesses—"

"Oh no, you don't." She had managed to take only one step before O'Reilly's strong arm snagged her waist and hauled her back to face him. "Excuse us, Christian?"

"What are you doing?" Amanda's voice ended in an embarrassing squeak as O'Reilly drew her up against his big, male body. He smelled pleasantly of brandy, the warm night air, and himself, and it was so delicious to be this close to him that she swayed toward him dangerously. She felt the pressure of one of his strong hands, riding low on the small of her back, urging her even closer as his other hand swallowed hers.

"I'm dancing with you."

"But this isn't a waltz—" she began, just as the fiddle sailed into a rendition of "The Russian Prince."

"Yes, it is," he said, and spun her expertly onto the dance floor.

Her head fell back, her fingers digging into the hard muscles of his shoulder as she stared up into his lean, smiling face. "It was you. You put the children up to this. Didn't you?"

His dimples deepened in a way that made her feel hot and breathless. "Yes."

She threw a quick glance at the brown-

and-gray line of governesses, fluttering and *tut-tutt*ing like a row of ruffled biddy hens. "You do realize that every governess from within a hundred and fifty miles is sitting over there right now condemning me as disgustingly ill-bred and common?"

His palm pressed her closer, guiding her into a sensuous circle that left her heart soaring and her breath shallow. He met her gaze, his expression unexpectedly serious. "Do you really care, Mandy?"

She loved it when he called her Mandy. She felt his strong hand tighten around hers, felt his breath warm against her cheek, felt her heart take wing and soar free. "Only in one sense," she said, still holding his gaze.

"What's that?"

"I feel sorry for them. They're so miserable. Yet they don't have to be."

He hugged her to him and laughed, and she laughed with him. Their laughter mingled together, joined with the wail of the accordion to rise up to the rough-hewn rafters. Then her laughter died away, slowly, as she lost herself in looking at him. At his flashing blue eyes and reckless smile. She moved her hand over his shoulder, felt his body warm and hard beneath her touch. She sucked in a deep breath of wonder, then another, and it was as if the shearing shed spun around her, enveloped her in the throbbing beat of the music and the golden glow of the lamplight and a kaleido-scope of brilliantly colored silks and satins and bright, happy faces.

She took it all in, with her heart and her soul and every sensitive inch of her being, and she felt oddly complete—filled with an inner glow of love and happiness and peace, a sense of rightness, of belonging, that was so different from the loneliness she had always carried deep within her. And she thought, *I've never felt like this before.* And then she thought, *I want this. I want this forever and ever and ever.*

The laughter and music from the woolshed followed the three tired children and two adults as they walked together up the moonlit track to the homestead. The night was warm, the wind a gentle caress that whispered through the gum trees along the creek.

"Sing something, Papa," murmured Missy, snuggling sleepily against O'Reilly's shoulder.

He looked down at the little girl in his arms. "What would you like, darlin'?"

"How about 'The Morning Dew'?" suggested Liam, walking ahead with Hannah.

"All right." O'Reilly shifted Missy's weight and began to sing, letting the night breeze carry his voice away over the pale hills. " 'Come listen you lads and ladies so true, I'll tell you a tale of the sweet morning dew, that freshens the green dells each soft Irish morn, in the land of bright moonlight in which I was born.' " He took a deep breath to start the chorus, glanced down at Amanda walking companionably beside him, and abruptly closed his mouth.

"Sing the rest of it, Papa," Missy said, lifting her head when he paused.

He grinned at Amanda. "I don't think I should."

"Come on, finish it, Papa," called Hannah.

"Yes, do," said Amanda, smiling up at him.

She wasn't going to like it, but he shrugged his shoulders and said, "You asked for it." Tipping back his head, he raised his voice again. " 'Sing hey and ring the bell, for it's to Botany Bay I sail. God rot the bloody English and send them all to—' "

Amanda's fingers clapped down over his mouth. "You were right. You shouldn't."

He laughed softly against her hand.

And felt her tremble.

"Why'd we have t'come back t'the house?" Missy demanded as Amanda tugged the little girl's dress over her head. "All the other children are still down at the woolshed."

"And falling asleep on the wool bales," said Amanda, slipping off the child's shoes and stockings and petticoat.

"I'm not sleepy," Missy insisted, even as her mouth stretched into a big yawn.

Amanda eased the little girl's nightgown down over her outstretched arms. "Well, I am."

"That's because you danced with Papa all night."

Amanda felt hot color flood her cheeks as she smoothed the covers up beneath Missy's chin. "I'm tired because it's late," she said,

364

or started to say, when she noticed that the little girl's eyelids had fluttered closed, and her lips parted with her slowed, even breathing. "Good night, darling," Amanda whispered, and gently kissed her cheek.

"Miss Davenport?" Hannah's voice came to her from the other side of the room.

Shadows danced over the walls as Amanda picked up the chamberstick and went to perch on the side of Hannah's bed. "I thought you were asleep."

Hannah's hair spread over her pillow like a dark wave. In the candlelight, she looked pale and very pretty. "I wanted to thank you." Her hands moved restlessly over the edge of her sheet; she did not meet Amanda's gaze. "For what you did this afternoon."

"You're welcome." Impulsively, Amanda reached out to smooth the girl's hair back from her forehead. "You were magnificent. I was very proud of you."

Amanda was afraid the girl would flinch from her touch, but all Hannah said was, "Papa was proud of me, too, wasn't he?"

"Yes, he was." Amanda squeezed the girl's hand and let it go. "Good night, Hannah."

Hannah tilted her head to stare up at Amanda with dark, wise eyes. "He's been...different since you came here. I think he likes you. I mean, really likes you. The way a man likes a woman."

"*Hannah.*" Amanda stood up so fast, she almost put out the candle, and had to shield the flame with her cupped hand to coax it back to life.

"Know something else?" Hannah continued, her mouth curling up into a grin.

Amanda paused at the door. "What?"

"I think you like him, too."

"Good night, Hannah," Amanda said repressively.

Hannah's soft laughter follow her out the door. "Good night, Miss Davenport."

Amanda could hear the low murmur of masculine voices from Liam's room as she carried the chamberstick to her own bedroom. She set the candle on her dressing table, meaning to tidy her hair. But the snap of the front door closing brought her head up with a jerk.

She flew across the room, yanked open the French doors, and burst outside to be brought up short by the sight of O'Reilly standing at the near end of the veranda, one outflung arm braced against a post, his back to her as he stared at the darkened garden. He had taken off his jacket and vest; she could see his white shirt glowing faintly in the moonlight.

He spun to face her, and she saw the flare of something in his eyes before he hooded them. Behind him, the strange southern sky arced so gloriously clear and crowded with stars it sparkled.

"I was afraid you'd left already." She sounded winded—she *felt* winded, as if she had been running.

He stared at her. There was a look about his face—sharp, almost predatory—that she had never seen before. It frightened her and excited her at the same time. But when he spoke, his voice was soft. "Your hair is coming down."

Wordlessly, she raised her arms, her elbows spread wide, and began removing the pins from the thick coil she wore loosely twisted at the nape of her neck. Her hair tumbled heavily to her shoulders, curled around her breasts. He watched, his eyes darkening with heat and desire, as she shook her head, loosening the coil. Then she dropped her arms to her sides, and waited.

"Come here," he said.

The warm night wind blew around him, fluttering his fine dress shirt, molding it against his lean, working man's muscles. She went to him, and the same wind caught at her hair and billowed it out around her. She could feel her heart thumping painfully in her breast, feel her skin shivery with a sensitivity so exquisite it ached. She kept walking until she could stare right up into his wild, hot eyes. She could feel his intense sexual energy swirling around her, calling to her at a level she only dimly understood.

He furrowed the fingers of both hands through the hair at her temples, held her face between his palms, ran a thumb along the crest of her cheekbone. Her breath came in little pants, her lips parted, her breasts rose and fell rapidly. She was trembling with her need for him, trembling with awe at the boldness of what she was doing.

She reached for him, but his hands slipped down to grip her shoulders and hold her away from him. "No. Wait," he said, his arms fixed and hard, his voice harsh, ragged. "I want you, Amanda. I want to carry you into your room and lay you down and bury myself inside you. So if you let something start here tonight, you gotta understand where it's gonna end."

She laid her spread hands against the solid muscles of his upper chest. She could feel the heat of his body, feel the rapid pounding of his heart. "I want you, too," she said. "And I can't fight it anymore."

"Amanda..." He still held himself stiff, but beneath her hands, she could feel his chest rise as he drew in a shuddering breath. "I'm not right for you. I—"

"I know what you are." Shaking with her desire for him, desperate with her need to touch him, she stroked her hands over his chest, his shoulders, his neck. "I've fought the way I feel about you for so long. But not anymore." She looked deep into his tortured blue eyes. "I love you."

"Oh, God..." His fingers dug into her shoulders almost painfully as he hauled her up against the hard length of his body. Silver moonlight played over the taut, aroused planes of his face. He caught his fists in her loose hair; his breathing became rapid, urgent. She saw his eyelids flutter closed, heard him groan deep in his throat. Then he brought his mouth slamming down on hers.

It was a wild, hungry kiss, full of all the raw passion and violent need he had kept restrained in the past. She curled her fingers around the back of his neck, drawing his head down to her as she opened her mouth beneath his, welcomed him, tasted his hot sweetness.

He groaned again and thrust his tongue deep inside, stroking her, claiming her as his. She felt his hands slide down to pull her hips up against his pelvis. She arched against him, achingly aware of the hard length of his erection pressing intimately against her stomach. Her entire body quivered with a gnawing, empty need that was an agony. The need to be touched. To be filled.

He swung her around, thrusting her back against a veranda post to trap her between the rough wood and his male body. His hands found her breasts and she cried out, squirming with the piercing pleasure of his touch as he lifted their fullness, kneaded them with rough desperation. His mouth lost hers and she whimpered impatiently, rising on tiptoe to seek his lips, recapture his mouth. She was aflame, drowning in fire, lost in a world of sensation, of the exquisite interplay of tongues and lips, of roaming hands and sensitive flesh, of need and heat and want. She was aware of nothing but the man in her arms and the black, star-studded silence of the night. The bush-scented wind swirled around them, wild and free and hot.

Wanting to put her hands on his naked flesh, she tugged at the tail of his shirt, pulled it loose from his trousers so that she could feel the smooth, hot skin of his back. As if driven by the same need, he sought the buttons at the front of her dress. But they were small and numerous, and his fingers clumsy with need. Swearing impatiently, he hooked his fingers in the high neck and ripped.

"Hell," he said in an awed voice, as if surprised by what he'd done. "I'm sorry."

She laughed softly. "It doesn't matter. I've decided I hate this dress."

"I'll replace it with a new one," he said, and she heard the smile in his voice. "Only, I'll make sure it's cut low enough to show me at least a hint of *these*."

She sucked in her breath as his impatient fingers shoved aside the cloth of her dress and pushed down her corset and chemise so that he could cradle her naked breasts in his hands. The night air felt cool and wicked, skimming over her bare skin. But his hands were hot. Hot and sure.

Amanda's head fell back, an incoherent sound of pleasure torn from her lips. She felt his mouth trail down her neck, felt the softness of his lips, the wetness of his tongue as he kissed and licked his way downward, sinking to one knee at her feet. She cried out with expectation and need, bucking against him as he closed his mouth over the aroused peak of first one breast, then the other. He wrapped one arm around her waist, his hand splayed against her bottom, trying to hold her steady, but she squirmed helplessly, whimpering with want, swirled away in a mindless fever of desire. Her fingers spasmed in his hair, holding his head to her breast. But it wasn't enough. She wanted, wanted, wanted—

He tore his mouth from her taut, quivering nipple, his breath washing hot over her wet, exposed breasts, his body racked with his own shuddering need as he rose to his feet, his hardness rubbing suggestively against her. He stared down at her, his eyes glittering in the moonlight, his face almost cruel with the intensity of his arousal. His hands fisted in her skirts, ready to shove them up and take her, right there, against the veranda post beneath the open sky.

Then his mouth slanted up in a devilish smile that brought a dimple to one cheek, and he leaned his forehead against hers. "Christ," he said, his breath coming in ragged pants as the starched cloth of her skirts slipped from his fingers. "Do you have any idea how many people there are roaming around this station tonight? I think we need to find somewhere more private."

Her laugh turned into a gasp of surprise as one strong arm caught her behind the knees, the other cradling her back as he swept her up against his chest. She wrapped her arms around his neck, held him close. His long, swift strides covered the length of the veranda to where she had left her French doors swinging open to the night. He turned sideways, easing them both through the opening before kicking the panels shut with his booted foot.

The candle dipped and flared in the draft, sending golden light shimmering up whitewashed walls and throwing dark shadows across his face. He released her slowly, letting her body slide down his, his gaze fixed on hers.

She felt suddenly, unexpectedly shy as the wild exuberance of that abandoned, wind-washed, moonlit kiss on the veranda gave way to the pregnant, sheltered intimacy of her room. He stood before her, so large and male, his shirt untucked and half pulled open. The sight of his tanned, muscled chest reminded her vividly of what they had already done. And what was coming next.

She brought up a shaking hand to draw together the torn edges of her dress, but he nudged her fingers aside. "No. Let me look at you," he said hoarsely, and pulled apart her ripped bodice to expose her naked breasts. She felt herself tremble, even as her nipples tightened into two erect nubs.

He stared openly at her, his eyes glowing. She felt the heat of his gaze on her, sending a tingling warmth rippling through her to add to the heaviness pooling between her legs. His hands moved to cover her breasts, and they both watched as he lifted her fullness, her skin so white and fine beneath his dark, callused fingers.

"I've been wanting to do this since that first day, when I met you up in Brinkman," he said with a low, breathy laugh that ended in something like a sigh. "You have such beautiful breasts. So full and firm."

She laid her palms over his, increasing the pressure of his hands as they moved in erotically slow, undulating circles. "You did touch me that day, remember?" she said.

He brought his gaze to her face and smiled. "I remember. Only it wasn't your breasts I touched." He reached down to grip her bottom bawdily. "It was this."

She chuckled and leaned into him, pushing aside his open shirt so that she could splay her hands against his bare chest. "I wanted you that first day, too," she admitted, watching her palms glide across the taut, golden skin of his chest. "I saw you standing there with your open shirt, and I thought you looked so strong and beautiful, so much a man, it frightened me. Then later, when you put your hands on me to hoist me into the wagon, I felt touched by fire. Scorched."

She let her fingers drift down to unfasten the few remaining shirt buttons, and sighed. "*I've* been wanting to do *that* for months now." She would never get tired of touching him, she thought. She loved the rippling flat tautness of his stomach, the bulging muscles of his chest. She eased his shirt off his powerful shoulders, heard the whisper of fine linen falling to the floor as she caressed his smooth back. "I used to watch you working around the station with your shirt half-unbuttoned. Sometimes I'd have sworn you did it deliberately, to tempt me. Torment me."

"I did," he admitted, nuzzling her hair with his chin.

Her head fell back, her gaze seeking his. *"You knew?"*

His dimples flashed beguilingly. "I knew."

"But—"

He caught her words with his kiss. A light, teasing kiss that quickly grew hotter, hungrier, more needy and demanding. He slanted his lips urgently across hers. She twined her fingers in his sun-streaked hair, pulling him closer as she opened her mouth beneath his. His tongue thrust inside her, deep, hot, demanding. Their breath came in ragged gasps, their bodies straining against each other, their hands coursing up and down, touching, learning, arousing, possessing. But it wasn't enough.

He tore his mouth from hers. In the flaring light of the candle she could see the passion in his face, the hot yearning. "Take your clothes off," he said harshly, his chest heaving with the strain of drawing air. "I want to see you naked." His hands tightened around her waist to set her away from him as he sank down on the edge of her bed and tugged off first one boot, then the other.

But his gaze never left her.

She stood before him, conscious of his eyes upon her, of the hot color surging into her cheeks. With trembling fingers she undid the remaining buttons of her dress and lifted it over her head, letting the ruined, ugly striped satin fall where it would. She unfastened her red petticoat and took it off, then her crinoline. And all the while he sat on her bed and watched her, his face half in shadow, the warm candlelight playing over his naked shoulders and chest.

She paused.

"Keep going," he said, his voice low and smoky, his eyes bright, his face taut with leashed hunger.

She unbuttoned her corset cover and eased it off her shoulders, the fire within her burning brighter and brighter, hotter and hotter. She could feel his desire for her, see it in his face, in the tense expectancy of his body. And she thrilled to the knowledge that she had this power over him, this ability to make him want her so badly.

With deliberate, provocative slowness, she untied her garters one at a time, rolling her stockings down her leg, easing off first one shoe, then the other. And heard the hiss of his quickly indrawn breath.

"Take off your pantalets next," he said huskily.

Her fingers hesitated at her waistband, but only for an instant. Delicious shivers coursed up and down her spine. She felt wonderfully wicked and naughty as she unbuttoned her drawers and shoved the smooth cotton over her bare hips and down her thighs, and let it go.

The room was so quiet, she could hear the candle gutting in its melted wax, and the sound of their strident, aroused breathing.

"Come here," he said.

Wearing only her corset and chemise, she went to him, and his powerful arms closed around her. He splayed his hands over the cheeks of her naked bottom and drew her forward until she stood within the V of his spread thighs, her hands on his shoulders.

She felt the warm night air, caressing her bare skin. Felt the heaviness of moist heat collecting between her legs. Felt his hard fingers, digging intimately into the curves of her buttocks.

"God, I've wanted you," he said on an almost painful expulsion of breath. Tightening his knees around her, he brought up both hands and began rapidly to flick open the hooks of her corset. She was small enough that she had never needed to resort to tight lacing; she simply drew in her stomach, and the fastenings came open easily.

"There," he said with a sigh of satisfaction as he stripped away her stays and tossed the stiff garment aside. "I've been wanting to get you out of that damned thing for a long time now." She chuckled softly as he untied her chemise and yanked that off as well. Then they both fell silent as his hands came back down to rest on her bare hips.

She stood naked before him, shy, excited, quivering with expectation, her heart thrumming wildly. His hungry gaze roved over her, his eyes hooded, sleepy. "You are so beautiful," he whispered. "More beautiful even than in my dreams."

She ran her fingers through his hair, her elbows spread upon his bare shoulders. "I dreamt about you, too," she admitted.

"God." He drew her closer. "Why did we wait so long to do this?"

She felt his lips on her neck, nibbling at her flesh, trailing kisses up the line of her jaw, across her cheek until he found her mouth, which opened beneath his. He wrapped his arms around her waist, drawing her with him as he fell back. The mattress sighed and bent beneath their weight as he hugged her to him, then rolled with her until she lay flat on her back beneath him.

Heat coursed through her as he bore her down and she took the weight of his hard man's body, pressing intimately against her, his bare chest flattening her breasts. She gazed up into his glittering blue eyes. Watched his eyelids slowly close as he dipped his head and kissed her.

She gave herself to the hot, sweet meeting of lips and tongue, the entwining of bodies. Sighing with pleasure, she ran her hands down his back, reveled in the bulging play of hard muscle beneath the satiny surface of his skin. Her thumb snagged in the waistband of his trousers and she tugged at them impatiently. But they were still fastened.

Keeping his mouth locked with hers, he raised his hips and reached between them with one hand to fumble with his trousers. He swore softly.

"Be right back," he said, his lips moving against hers. He started to stand up, but came back to brush her mouth with his again. Once, twice more, before pulling away.

She lay watching, fascinated, as his strong hands unbuckled his wide brown leather belt, then went to work on his buttons. He swore again, wincing as if in pain, then sighed with relief as the long, thick shaft of his sex sprang free.

He lifted his head and watched her face as he shoved his trousers down, baring the tight curve of his buttocks and the leanly muscled line of his legs to her gaze. She was intensely aware of her own nakedness, spread out before him. Of the size and power of his male body, and what was about to happen between them.

The mattress dented again as he straddled her, his sex nestling intimately in the crevice between her thighs. He took most of his weight on his own knees and calves, easing back on his bent toes as he placed his dark, working man's hands over her naked breasts, his brows drawing together in a frown as he gazed down at her. "Are you afraid?" he asked softly.

"A little," she admitted.

"Do you want me to stop?"

She shook her head, deliberately running her fingers up and down his hard, outstretched arms. "No."

"Don't be afraid," he whispered gently. "We'll go slow. And I won't do anything you don't want me to."

And then he began to move his hands in a slow, expert pattern of arousal, palming her fullness, taunting her nipples until the fire within her leapt to new, almost unbearable heights. She whimpered and arched up against him, and he leaned forward, his hair brushing her shoulder, his hard chest pressing against her belly as he brought his mouth down to trace the curves of her breasts with his tongue and suck her nipples into his hot, wet mouth.

"Oh, God," she cried, squirming beneath him, consumed by heat, racked by torturous tremors of desire. Her fingers twined in his hair, guiding his head first to one breast, then the other. But it wasn't enough, wasn't enough.

As if he knew what she needed, his hand slid down across her belly, his weight shifting as he brought his knees between hers, shoving her legs wide. Then his fingers parted her, rubbed against the center of her desire, slipped inside her. She cried out, arching her neck, her shoulders lifting off the bed as she flew out of control, hurtling straight to a wild, throbbing, shattering release...

That wasn't enough. That inner, wanting emptiness was still there. Her fingers wrapped around his wrists, clutching him, her gaze meeting his. "I need you," she said in a broken whisper. "I need you inside me. Now."

He reared up, his big, dark body looming over her, his nostrils flaring as he sucked in air. "Amanda," he said in a strident whisper. Her dim gaze fastened on his face, hard now with his own need and driving hunger. He slipped his hands beneath her buttocks, lifting her, fitting her against his smooth, hot tip. "Take me," he said. "Take me inside you."

He was so big and hard, he probably would have frightened her if she hadn't wanted him so badly. She watched as he eased himself inside her, stretched her, filled her with his heat and his strength and his hardness. Slowly, slowly, until he was buried to the hilt.

"You're so tight," he said hoarsely. "So tight and wet and hot." She felt him shudder, then lie still within her for a moment. His hands sought hers, found them, lifted them above her head, their fingers entwined, as he lowered the length of his body to hers. She gazed up at the ardent features of his face, and felt her love for him so intensely, it hurt.

"Feel me," he whispered. "Feel me inside you."

"I feel you."

"You're a part of me now, Mandy. And I'm a part of you." His hands slid down the inside of her arms to smooth her tangled hair away from her forehead and cheeks. "There's no going back from this night. Not to the way we were before."

"I told you," she said, looking deep into his eyes. "I love you."

He raised himself on his out-thrust arms, easing some of his weight off her chest as he began to move inside her, the dimples in his cheeks flashing wickedly as he smiled. "Say it again," he told her.

"I love you."

He thrust into her, harder, deeper, his smile becoming something fierce. "Again."

She gasped. "I love you."

She clutched at his hot, sweat-slicked back, breathed in the gentle scent of his warm body as her legs came up and wrapped around his rhythmically undulating hips. She held him to her, drew him deeper and deeper into her as he pumped harder, faster, each rasping drag, each powerful thrust taking her higher and higher, until she was incoherent, wild with the exquisite sensation of what he was doing to her.

He dipped his head, his mouth finding hers, his kisses catching the mounting cries of pleasure she hadn't even realized she was making. She was frantic with an unbearable onslaught of sensation, striving, straining toward a peak that hovered achingly within reach, tormenting her, tantalizing her, before it exploded over her in a shattering crescendo of noiseless sound and blind colors that went on and on and on in waves of rapturous ecstasy.

Her vision had only just begun to clear when she felt his own tremors start, deep inside her. She saw his back arch, his muscles clench, his features contort as if with pain. He gave one last, violent thrust. And then, right before he shouted in triumph and fell forward upon her, she heard him say it.

"I love you, too, Amanda."

CHAPTER TWENTY

O'Reilly stood at the French doors of Amanda's room, one half of the slightly parted curtain clutched in his hand as he stared out at Katherine's garden, just visible now in the faint light of early dawn. An ache built in his chest. He sighed, trying to ease it, but it didn't help.

A whisper of cloth, the light padding of a woman's bare feet on polished floorboards brought his head around. He caught a glimpse of flame-colored hair, felt soft hands creep around his sides as Amanda pressed herself against his back and hugged him close. He smiled.

"Good morning," he said, covering her entwined small hands with his own large one.

"You're up early."

"I couldn't sleep."

She rubbed her smooth cheek against his bare shoulder. "What are you looking at?"

"Katherine's garden."

She didn't say anything, but he thought he felt her tense against him. He suddenly wanted to see her face, and turned in her arms so that he could look down at her.

She was beautiful in the cool blue light of morning, her skin pale, her vivid hair loose about her shoulders. She had pulled on her embroidered sapphire Chinese wrapper, and he marveled at the unexpected quickening in his loins as his palms roamed over the swell of her hips, the curve of her waist, the silk sliding seductively beneath his touch. He'd spent most of the night making love to this woman, over and over again. And still he wanted her. Wanted her with a hunger he knew might mellow with the passage of time, but was never going to go away.

Yet as intense as it was, that raw, physical

hunger was still the lesser part of what he felt for her. And it was the other part of what was between them—the deep, soul-exposing love—that scared the hell out of him and left him feeling vulnerable and defenseless.

She tilted back her head, her brows drawing together as she searched his face. "What are you thinking?" she asked.

He ran one finger along the line of her collarbone, where it showed above the plunging neck of her wrapper. She was so tiny, so finely made. She didn't belong out here, and he knew it was wrong of him even to be thinking of asking her to stay. "I'm wondering if this was a mistake."

She went quite still in his arms. "Do you think it was?"

He turned away from her to stare, once more, at the garden. "I've been standing here, trying to imagine our future together. But all I can see is the past."

"We can't see the future," she said quietly. "We can only know what we want now."

He glanced back at her. "What do you want, Amanda?"

She stared up at him, her lips parted, her breasts rising and falling gently with her breathing. He saw the shadows that darkened her clear gray eyes, saw her throat work as she swallowed, and knew she was feeling afraid and vulnerable, too. But she was braver than he was, he thought, because she answered him simply, honestly.

"You."

"Aw, Mandy..." He gathered her to him again, nestling her head in the hollow of his shoulder, his fingers combing through her hair. "I come with a lot of baggage. Three children—"

"I love your children already," she said, her breath warm against his skin. "You know that."

"I know. But you don't love this place. And this place is my life. It's a part of who I am."

In the silence that followed, he could hear the sweet, piercing song of a magpie, greeting the rising sun. Her hand crept up to curl around his wrist. "I don't...hate it the way I used to."

"Katherine didn't hate it at first either."

He was surprised by the violence with which she pushed away from him, her hair flying about her shoulders, her eyes huge in a white face. *"Damn you,"* she said on a harsh, grating expulsion of breath. She wrapped her arms around her waist, hugged herself close as she faced him. *"I am not Katherine.* I'm not Katherine, and I'm not your mother, and it's not fair for you to judge me by what they did simply because the three of us happened to share the same accent and the same place of birth."

A tense silence descended on the room, ringing with the echo of her loud, angry words. They faced each other across a distance vaster than that measured by the floorboards; he made no attempt to draw closer to her.

"I'm not judging you, Amanda," he said

384

quietly, his arms hanging loose at his sides. "I'm just scared to death because I let myself fall in love with you. And I'm even more afraid to start thinking we might have a future together, because I know what it would do to me if I let myself believe in that, and then lost you."

Her hand made a swift, jerking motion through the air. "Either one of us could die tomorrow."

"I know. But death is different. It hurts when the people we love die, because we know we'll never see them again. But the love doesn't die. Their love for us, our love for them, it...stays with us."

She looked at him through wide, dark eyes that suddenly filled with the glitter of unshed tears. "Did you love Katherine?"

"Yes. It was a young love, but it was very real, very intense—at first."

"So, what happened?"

"We grew apart." He shrugged. "She never did like it here, and it wasn't long before she started hating it—and blaming me for bringing her here. For not being able to give her a better life right away. But it wasn't just her fault. I started to see things in her that I didn't like, and I wasn't very...tolerant."

"Did you still love her when she left?"

"Of course. We'd had three children together—lived six years of our lives together. She was my *wife*. I hadn't given up on her. And it hurt like hell to discover that she had given up on me."

The light was stronger now, spilling warm and golden across the garden as the sun crested the horizon. She swung abruptly away to go stand beside her dressing table, her back stiff and straight. "Is that why you never divorced her? Because you're still in love with her?"

"No. What I told you before was the truth; I never divorced Katherine because of scandal, for the children's sake. And now it's just one more bloody thing we need to deal with, isn't it?" He walked up behind her and put his hands on her rigid shoulders, nuzzled her hair with his chin. She quivered beneath his touch, but she didn't turn to look at him.

"I want to marry you, Amanda, and I'll do whatever it takes to make that possible. As soon as I get back from taking this mob south..."

He heard her draw in a deep breath of air that shuddered in her chest. "I wish you didn't have to go."

Her voice sounded oddly strained, husky. He wrapped his hand around her upper arm and pulled her about so that he could see her.

"Aw, Jesus," he said, at the sight of her tearstained cheeks. "Don't cry, darlin'." He brushed her face with the backs of his hands, catching her glistening tears with his fingers. "Why are you crying? I love you." He stared down at her, feeling helpless and slightly lost. "Is it something I said?"

Her eyes widened, and she surprised him with a watery gurgle of laughter even as she buried her face against his chest. "O'Reilly," she said on a rushing breath. "You love me, but you don't trust me."

He could feel her tears, warm and wet against his bare skin. They made him feel inept, clumsy. He threaded his fingers through her hair, surprised to realize that his hands were shaking. "I want to, Amanda. I am trying."

She tilted back her head to look up at him, and he saw her throat work painfully as she swallowed. "How long will you be gone?"

"Not long. I'm hoping I won't have to go much farther south than Melrose." He bent to brush his lips against her temple. "But things are going to get bad here, Amanda. Summer is starting, and it's not likely we'll get any rain now until March or April. In the next few months, I think you'll probably see the worst of what you'll be getting yourself into, if you stay here and marry me."

She tightened her jaw. "I'm not as weak as you think me."

"I know how strong you are." He let his hands ease down to stroke her shoulders. At his touch, a gentle sigh escaped her lips, and he began to knead the tense muscles at the base of her neck. "I know how strong you are," he said again. "But I also know what this country can be like for a woman, and how different it is from what you're used to. And I haven't forgotten the things you said when you first came here, how desperate you were to get back to England. Are you really sure you could bear it, never seeing home again?"

At his words, a deep, inescapable pain darkened her eyes. He saw it, and it scared the hell out of him.

"It would hurt," she admitted softly. "But it would be nothing compared to the pain I would feel if I had to leave you."

She captured his hand and cradled it against her cheek with a sigh. "Love shouldn't have to be this hard," she said, her voice wistful and a bit sad.

He nudged her chin up with the heel of his hand. "It'll be good," he said, dipping his head so that his lips moved against hers. "You'll see. It'll be good."

He left a week later.

He was so busy—seeing off all the guests who had congregated for the after-shearing festivities, loading the wool on the drays that would haul the bales to port, mustering the sheep for the drive—that she barely saw him that week. And then he was gone.

December passed. Long, sun-seared days of relentlessly clear skies and parching winds that sucked the remaining life from the land. In January, the drays that had taken the wool bales to the port came back. The men said conditions in the south were a lot drier than anyone had expected. They said O'Reilly figured he might have to drive the mob he was trying to save down to Clare—maybe even all the way to Adelaide.

Amanda gazed out over the dying land. And waited.

But as January neared its end, she knew a swelling of uneasiness she could no longer ignore. He'd been gone too long. She noticed the men, looking at each other, watching the horizon, and knew they were worried, too.

On this particular hot, breathless Thursday afternoon, Liam was reading Latin with Christian Whittaker while Missy went off to help Ching in the kitchen, and Amanda retreated to her room, to work on the new dress she was making herself. But it was too hot to sew. Too hot to do anything but stare at the cruel blue sky and wonder why O'Reilly had been gone so long.

A familiar, lilting melody floated through the still house, picked out by a sure hand on the piano. Amanda lifted her head, listening, puzzled. She recognized the tune; it was "Greensleeves." And she was very sure that she had never seen it among the sheet music in the dining room.

She walked quietly through the empty parlor to stand in the shadow of the doorway. Hannah sat at the piano, her hands now still on the keys.

"My mother used to play that song when she was sad," Hannah said without looking up. "Right before she left, she played it all the time. I remember lying in bed at night, hearing her play it, over and over again."

Amanda stayed where she was, afraid to draw too near. She had come to realize long ago just how vulnerable Hannah was beneath the tough, prickly front she showed the world. But Amanda had never seen the girl this open, this exposed. "You miss her, don't you?"

Hannah nodded, her head bowed. "It's funny, isn't it? I hate her, because she went away and left us. Because she didn't love me enough to take me with her. Yet...I still miss her."

Amanda rested one hand against the wooden door frame, her heart twisting with empathy for this lonely, hurting child. "Your mother only went to Victoria at first, didn't she? To her parents? Perhaps she didn't mean to stay away forever. Not at first."

Hannah's chest lifted on a shuddering breath. "Before she met that Frenchman, you mean? Maybe. But it doesn't really matter, does it? Because when she met him, she decided she loved him more than she loved us. And she left us for him."

Amanda didn't say anything. Privately, she had come to the conclusion that Katherine O'Reilly was probably a spoiled, selfish woman, who had never loved anyone as much as she loved herself. But Amanda wasn't about to say that to Katherine's daughter.

"Liam was only three years old when she left," Hannah said. "I still remember him waking up in the night, crying for her. Papa used to sit by the fire and hold him, for hours. Sing to him. Tell him stories about his shearing days. I was always awake, too. But I didn't cry. And I never let Papa hold me."

Hannah's hands slipped down to her lap, her fingers splayed, taut, against the worn cotton of her moleskins. "At first he tried, but I would just wiggle out of his arms. Eventually, he stopped even trying. I remember telling myself that if I didn't let him hold me, if I didn't let myself love him, then it wouldn't hurt if, someday, he left me, too."

Hannah lifted her head to show Amanda a tear-streaked face. "I'm scared, Miss Davenport. What if something has happened to Papa, and he doesn't come back? He's been gone so long. I don't want to lose him, too."

"Oh, Hannah..." Unable to hold herself back any longer, Amanda went to enfold Hannah in her arms. She was afraid the girl would push her away. Instead, Hannah rose up to meet her.

"I'm scared, too," Amanda admitted in a broken voice as they clung to each other.

Perhaps, she thought, as she felt Hannah's arms tighten convulsively around her, she should have lied and told the girl her fears were groundless, that there was nothing to worry about. But Amanda had too much respect for Hannah's intelligence to even attempt it. Hannah was growing up.

She felt a sob shudder through the girl's slender body, and realized with a slight sense of shock that Hannah's head was level with her own. In another six months, Amanda thought, Hannah would probably tower over her. The girl was growing up, and she was going to be tall.

Like her father.

Later, Amanda went outside and stood in the garden. She could feel the gritty sweat trickling down her forehead as she stared at the blackened stalks and curled, dead leaves that were all that was left of the beautiful white rose that had once scrambled up the veranda post to riot over the homestead's roof. Tears welled in her throat. She tipped back her head and blinked up at the hard sky. The endless summer sun poured down on her, relentless, merciless. Deadly.

If O'Reilly were here beside her, she thought she could probably take anything this land threw at her. But he wasn't here, and she missed him desperately. Memories of his hard, male body haunted her. She ached for his touch, for his kiss. For the sight of his smile and the sound of his voice, for the gentle, reassuring warmth and strength of his presence. A dozen times a day, something would happen to make her wish she could tell him about it. Her triumph the day she trimmed Hannah's hair. Missy's progress with her letters. The funny thing Liam said when Campbell startled them all by taking a bath and changing his clothes. All the little joys and traumas of life she wanted to share with him.

But he wasn't here.

Swiping at her damp face with her forearm, she swung away from the veranda to walk slowly through the withered ruins of Katherine's garden. It was breaking Chow's heart, killing the garden like this. First, he'd stopped watering only the annuals. But as the creek-bed water hole he used for irrigation sank lower and lower with each passing day, he'd had to let the perennials die, too. Now the bushes and the trees were dying, and if it didn't rain soon, he was going to have to use well water to keep the fruits and vegetables alive.

Unless the wells all ran dry, too.

Amanda paused at the enclosure wall and looked out over the barren landscape, shimmering in the afternoon heat haze. There was nothing left anymore. Just red sand and naked rocks; no grass, little brush, dying trees. She felt the hot, dry wind whip around her, loosening her hair, slapping her skirts against her legs. She imagined she could smell the death the wind carried, hear the echoing groans of the thousands of animals dying out in the bush.

Sometimes, it seemed to her that the only living things left moving, the only things prospering in this living hell of a drought, were the crows. She could hear them out there, flapping their wings and cawing, day and night. *Caaww, caaww.* Sometimes she thought she might go mad, listening to the hot wind and that ceaseless, macabre crowing.

And, sometimes, she found herself afraid. Not just that something awful had happened and O'Reilly was never coming back. But afraid that when he did come back, he would look into her eyes and *know*. Know that as much as she had grown to love this wild, desolate land, she still feared it—feared it more than ever before, because now she had seen what it could do.

The closing of a door brought her head around. She watched Christian step out from beneath the veranda and squint up at the harsh sun before he walked toward her. He'd grown thinner in the last few months—gaunt and careworn, like the rest of them. This was to be his last visit to Penyaka. The Brinkman mines were closing, and in just a few days he would be leaving, driving south to Adelaide to catch ship for home. At the thought, she felt a fierce pang of sorrow, accompanied by a twist of envy that shamed her. And scared her.

He came up to her and she gave him a bleak smile that he didn't even try to return. His serious gaze met hers, and held it. "Come south with me, Amanda," he said, for they had slipped into using each other's first names long ago. "You can't stay here. Not anymore."

She swung to face the dying Ranges, her fingers gripping the stone wall before her. "I can't leave, Christian. You know that. I can't leave these children."

"I think you should take them to Adelaide, too. To their aunt."

"But O'Reilly—"

Christian came to stand beside her and put his hand over hers. "I honestly think when he comes back and sees how bad things are, O'Reilly's going to want you out of here, himself. Besides—" He bit back what he'd

394

started to say. But she knew what he was thinking. That something might have happened to O'Reilly. That he might not come back at all.

They stood together, watching the wind lift eddies of dust off the valley floor to swirl up and around, then dissipate in the furnacelike air. After a moment, she said, "This wind is so hot. Do you think there's another dust storm coming?"

By now Amanda knew all about dust storms. About how they began with a vivid brown cloud on the horizon that seemed to rise up as it approached. About how it just kept getting hotter and hotter, until the temperature reached 120 degrees and still kept climbing.

She knew how the sky would become overcast and thunder would rumble, but there would be no rain. How the wind would rise, filling the air with thick red sand until anyone unfortunate enough to be caught out in it could see barely two feet in front of his face. The wind would blow faster and faster, and the dust would just keep getting thicker and thicker, choking the life out of every living thing in its path.

In an attempt to escape it, the magpies and bronze-winged pigeons and diamond sparrows would overcome their fear of men and crowd into the outbuildings and under the verandas of the house—anywhere they thought they might find shelter. When the storm finally ended, Amanda would take down the rags and towels she used to cover the cracks around the homestead's doors and windows. But she hated to go outside, she hated to find the tiny, lifeless bodies of the bush birds littering the wind-scoured yard.

"The windstorms usually come out of the north," Christian said, twisting to squint into the light of the sinking sun. "As long as the wind stays from the west, we should be all right."

She nodded, her gaze focused on a persistent pall of dust that hugged the valley floor. "Someone's coming," she said. She was always scanning the horizon, always looking for O'Reilly's return. But this was a wagon, not a man on horseback. And it was coming, not from the south, but out of the northeast.

She'd grown accustomed to people stopping at the station for a night or two. At first, they were mainly swagmen—drovers and shepherds who'd lost their jobs when the stations they used to work for had laid off men, or closed down completely. But lately, there'd been families, too. Tilted carts pulled by dying bullocks or horses, driven by men and women with the hollow-eyed look of those who have given up all hope of ever enjoying life and are simply trying to endure it.

Sometimes, those driven off the land by the drought had no livestock left alive. They came on foot, seeking food and water that was always freely given. But sometimes they didn't make it to the house; Penyaka's stockmen would bring in tarp-wrapped bodies and Amanda would supervise their burial in the little cemetery across the creek bed.

"Looks like a family," said Christian, watching the wagon lurch toward them. "God preserve us. When will this end?"

He walked with her to the front gate where they stood together and waited. It was only a small cart, pulled by two gaunt horses and driven by a scrap of a boy that Amanda at first took to be no more than twelve, until he drew close enough that she could see his face. Then she realized he was more likely fifteen or sixteen, only underfed and work-worn. Beside him walked a tall, brown-haired man with thin, sloping shoulders and tattered clothes.

"Good afternoon," Amanda said. "And welcome. Come in and have some tea. One of the men will see to your horses."

The man pulled off his dusty hat to reveal a pale complexion and deep shadows under his eyes. "Thank you, ma'am, but we've a sick child in the cart here. If we could just camp in the shade of the trees there, and if you'd let us have some water, and maybe some chlorodyne if you've got it, for my baby girl—"

"What's wrong with her?" Amanda asked, starting forward. She reached the back of the cart where she caught a brief vision of a tiny, fair-haired child lying beside a weeping, distracted woman. Then the mingling odors of vomit and feces and blood hit Amanda in the face, and she reeled backward.

"Oh, goodness," she said, gasping. "We must get her in the house at once."

"But Amanda," said Christian, backing

away with his handkerchief to his nose. "It may be typhoid."

Amanda whirled to face him. "Would you have me leave a child out here to die?"

"No, but—"

She spun back to the father. "Bring her into the house. And Christian"—she glanced at him—"perhaps you could ask Ching to heat some water?"

He nodded and hurried off.

She worked quickly. The mother was practically incoherent with exhaustion and grief and her own sickness, and the father and brother had been sick, too. But with Chow's help, Amanda soon had the little girl cleaned up and tucked into the guest bedroom. Amanda dosed her with chlorodyne and meadowsweet tea, but the child could keep nothing down.

"She must have a doctor," Amanda whispered urgently to Christian when she found him pacing the parlor floor. It was late now; the children were asleep. "If we can't stop this purging—and soon, that child will die."

Christian regarded her anxiously from the far side of the room. She noticed that ever since she'd touched the child, he'd been careful not to come too close to her. But he hadn't left, either, and she was grateful to him for that. "There's a doctor in Edeowie," he said. "I can go for him."

Amanda brushed the loose hair out of her face with the back of her hand. "How far is that?"

"Forty miles."

"My God." Amanda's hopes sank like a crushing weight in her chest. "You'll never get there and back in time. Isn't there anyone closer?"

"No. It'll have to be him." Christian reached for his hat. "If I leave right away—"

"Wait." She stretched out her hand to stop him, then curled her fingers and dropped her arm to her side when he flinched. "No, Hermes will never make it. We'll send one of the men. Can you arrange it? Tell him to choose a fast but sturdy horse. With any luck he can be back with the doctor tomorrow."

Amanda stood for a moment, her hand on the door frame as she watched Christian hurry off. *If only O'Reilly were here,* she thought, then pushed the painful, useless wish out of her mind and went to sit beside the weakening child.

She was a pretty little girl, Amanda thought, staring down at the child as the hours of the night stretched out. Soft lamplight played over pale blond hair, big gray eyes, a fine-boned face, pinched now with misery and dehydration. She was only six years old, the father had said. Missy's age.

Amanda lifted her gaze to the exhausted mother, dozing fitfully in a chair on the far side of the bed. The woman couldn't be more than thirty-five, but she looked old, her once-blond hair streaked with gray, her shoulders hunched with despair, her face set in sad lines. Unconsciously, Amanda's hands slid down to press against her own empty womb, and she knew a terrible fear for the future, for her own unborn children, who would live their lives—and die—in this wild, strange place.

It was such a cruel land, she thought. Cruelly treacherous and dangerously, frighteningly isolated. Shaking off the thought, she reached for the little girl's fretful hand and held it comfortingly.

Amanda sat beside the child for hours, wiping her damp face, coaxing her to take sips of cool chamomile tea, then holding the basin for her when the spasms hit again. Amanda tried to stay awake, but at some point during the long night she must have nodded off. Her head jerked, and when she raised it, she found herself staring into the child's open, sightless eyes.

"Dear God," Amanda whispered, covering her slack mouth with her hand. "No. Oh, no." Glancing at the still sleeping mother, Amanda felt the tears well in her eyes to run silently down her cheeks, and knew she did not have the strength to wake this poor woman and tell her that her little girl was dead. She felt too defeated, too hollowed out inside by waves of sorrow.

Then rage rushed in, blinding and hot. Standing, she went to jerk back the curtains from the French doors and stare out over the ruined, moonlit garden and the dark, looming bulk of the Flinders Ranges beyond.

From the beginning, this land had frightened her. Attracted her, stirred her, and moved her, but frightened her, nonetheless. Now she had grown to love it. Yet what she felt for this place was still fierce.

And fierce love is always so close to hate.

Patrick O'Reilly reined in at the top of the hill and let his gaze rove slowly, achingly over the heat-cracked rocks and parched earth of the dying land sprawled out before him.

Hell, he thought bitterly, *it's not dying. It's dead.*

He touched his heels to the chestnut's flanks and let the tired horse amble down the hill toward the homestead lying bleak and quiet in the shimmering, suffocating afternoon heat. The loose dust from the track billowed up around the horse's plodding hooves to hang heavy in the hot, lifeless air.

He was alone. Of the men he'd taken south with him, some had hired on at the stockyards in Port Augusta, where they'd sold some of the sheep. He'd left a couple of shepherds with the mob in the pasturage he'd finally managed to rent all the way down in The Coorong. The rest had decided to stay in Adelaide, rather than brave the drought again. There wouldn't have been much for them to do here, anyway. Not on a station stripped of three-fourths of its livestock.

Easing the horse down the hill, O'Reilly let his gaze rove over the scattered buildings. He felt a sudden lightening in his heart, a racing of his pulse at the thought of finally seeing Amanda again. Seeing her. Holding her. Touching her...

Sometimes it seemed to him as if there hadn't been a single minute, night or day, during the last two months when he hadn't thought of her, hadn't wanted her. He'd carried south with him a hundred different images. Of Amanda, kneeling in a bed of thyme, her cheeks flushed, her head thrown back as she laughed and laughed and laughed. Amanda clutching his arm, her lips parted in a silent prayer as she watched Hannah ride Fire Dancer to victory. Amanda with her eyes squeezed shut, her face flooded with rapture as he drove his hard body into her welcoming softness.

Amanda hugging Missy close and whispering, "I'll stay, darling."

He swung out of the saddle at the homestead gate, his gut twisting sickeningly as he took in the desiccated ruin of Katherine's garden. God in heaven; the place looked as if it had been blasted by hell. Deserted. For one heart-stopping moment he wondered if things had got so bad here in the two months he'd been away that they'd all left.

That she'd left.

The sickening, soul-destroying, unthinkable thought had barely formed when he heard a distant cry.

"Father."

He lifted his head to see Liam pelting up the hill from the barns, one elbow cocked as he held his hat clapped to his head, the other arm pumping. "Father." The boy flung himself against O'Reilly's chest with something like a sob. "You're back."

For the next twenty minutes, O'Reilly was surrounded by laughing, clinging children, a couple of wildly gesturing Chinese men, and a painfully sober Campbell, all talking at once.

"Why were you so long?"

"We thought you were dead!"

"Tonight, I fix very special dish for supper, just for you."

"Did you find a pasture for the sheep, Papa?"

"If it keeps up like this, boss, the wells are all gonna run dry."

He heard Amanda's name mentioned enough times to be certain that she hadn't left, but she didn't appear to join the noisy group in the parlor, either. Finally, he held up his hands and said, "Wait a minute here. Where is Miss Davenport?"

It was Liam who answered. "I think she said she was going to plant some aloe on that child's grave, and then go for a ride."

O'Reilly swung around to stare at his son. "What child's grave?"

"Some people come through here, two, three day ago," said Chow. "People from small run to north. They have little girl, but she very sick. Miss Davenport try to help. Only little girl die."

"Miss Davenport's been pretty upset about it," put in Missy. "I offered to go riding with her, but I think she wanted to be alone."

O'Reilly felt an inexplicable surge of dread pumping through him. "Is she all right?"

Hannah looked at him strangely. "Why wouldn't she be?"

After that, it was another half hour before he managed to detach himself from his enthusiastic family and employees, and head down the path to the cemetery.

The air hung heavy and uncomfortably close. He heard a chorus of fluttered cacklings from the chook house as the hens sought their perches early, and when he passed the hay barn, a couple of sheepdogs lying panting in the shade snarled and snapped at him. The smell of dust was bitter in his nostrils. He picked up his pace.

Penyaka's cemetery had grown in the last couple of months, he noticed, as he worked his way across the rocky creek bed. He could see fresh mounds of bare red earth within the weathered gray wood of the post and rail fence. As he neared the gate, he spotted the simple cross marking a heartbreakingly tiny grave where someone had recently planted a young aloe.

He stood beside the grave, his hat in his hands, his head bowed. He felt the wind gust hot and dusty around him as he wondered about all the things that must have happened in the last two months to the woman he'd ridden away from. She had nursed this unknown child, then buried it and obviously grieved for it. He glanced around the lonely, windblown cemetery and felt it again, that sense of uneasiness, of dread, tearing at his gut. What kind of effect had all this had on her, he wondered, on her plans to stay here and marry him? The Flinders Ranges had always been hard and dangerous. Now they had become deadly.

He settled his hat back on his head. She was out riding, Hannah had said. Out riding alone, because she was upset. Riding and thinking about...what?

The wind gusted again, spraying grit against his back. He swung around, his eyes narrowing as he stared at the ugly bank of clouds billowing on the northern horizon. The storm rolled across the sun-bleached sky, thunder shaking the parched earth. Only there was no rain in these clouds, just a deadly pall of dust that seemed to glow with a ghastly red and brown light of its own.

"Bloody hell," he whispered, and took off in a run for the stables.

CHAPTER TWENTY-ONE

Amanda sat on the flat rock overlooking what she'd come to think of as her water hole. Although it wasn't a water hole anymore, just an expanse of drying, cracking mud. She had her arms wrapped around her updrawn legs,

405

her cheek resting against her knees, her eyes closed. The rock beneath her felt solid, and warm still from the sun. The hot, thick air seemed to press down upon her, crushing her body, sucking the breath from her. Yet she felt as if she were drifting.

For ten years she had known who she was— or at least who she had decided to become. Then she had found herself cast adrift in this raw, untamed land, and after years of denying what she wanted, of denying *herself*, she had felt it again—all those restless stirrings and wild yearnings she thought she had suppressed.

She felt the way she had felt as a young girl, when she had *wanted*. Wanted so many things, so desperately. To be free to study and discuss the kinds of things with which women weren't supposed to concern themselves. To be loved by a handsome, virile young man, not tied to someone like a lifeless, unimaginative vicar. To be the woman she knew she'd been born to be, not the creature everyone expected her to be.

It was exciting, but also frightening. If only O'Reilly were here...

Calypso's nervous neighing brought Amanda's head up. "What's the matter, girl? Hmmm?" She slipped off the rock to rub the shivering mare's velvety black nose. "What has you so fidgety all of a sudden?"

A hot blast of wind slammed into her, heavy with grit that stung Amanda's eyes. She swung her head away, her eyes squeezing shut with pain. When she opened them again, it was to stare to the north where thick, ugly brown clouds roiled like something alive, rushing forward, blotting out the sun to cast an ugly shadow over the parched valley.

"Oh my God."

She yanked Calypso's reins from the low-growing native myrtle and pulled herself into the saddle just as another ferocious rush of hot, sand-laden wind peppered her cheeks and brought a gum branch crashing down into the rocky creek bed beside them. The mare jumped and whinnied nervously, her head tossing, her nostrils flaring.

"It's all right, Calypso," Amanda crooned, touching her heel to the mare's flank. "We're going home."

Iron-shod hooves clattered over loose stones as she urged the jittery horse upstream toward the homestead. But as Amanda nervously watched the dust storm hurtle across the valley toward them, she knew they would never make it in time. It had been a mistake to leave the shelter of the gorge, she realized sickeningly, but it was too late to turn back now.

She quickly ripped a strip off her petticoat to tie around her nose and mouth, then urged the mare on, faster. They were still a good two or three miles east of the woolshed when the full force of the storm hit.

It came at her like a roaring, dirty brown tidal wave that engulfed her in a choking blanket of stinging sand. She could see nothing but dust, smell nothing but dust, breathe nothing but dust. The only sound was the howl of the wind and the rattle and smash of storm-tossed debris.

Twigs, dead leaves, small branches ripped loose by the gale tore at her clothing, cut the mare's black hide. Wide-eyed, terrified, Calypso snorted and sidled, pulling at Amanda's aching arms as she fought to hold the horse on the path. Thunder rumbled around them, shaking the earth until it seemed to Amanda that she could feel the tremors in her very soul.

A loud crack ripped through the thick, foul air. Amanda flung up her head and jerked the mare sideways just in time to keep from being swiped by the trunk of a falling wattle. Sheared-off limbs rained down around them, but she didn't dare pull away from the creek; she needed the ghostly, barely discernible line of towering river gums to guide her home through the blinding swirl of confusion. Then a thick branch slammed down on Calypso's withers. The mare reared up in terror and bolted.

Bracing one hand halfway to the poll, Amanda immediately pulled up hard on the other rein, bending the horse's neck and muzzle until the mare was pulling against its own neck. Thrown off balance, Calypso turned sharply. But before Amanda had brought the mare completely under control, the black stumbled into a pit of sand and her legs shot out from under her.

Squealing, the mare pitched forward onto her nose and rolled. Flung sideways, Amanda flew through the air to slam facedown against the ground. She heard Calypso scramble to her feet, felt the earth tremble beneath pounding hooves as the horse cantered into oblivion. Then there was only the wind and the dust.

Amanda lay on her stomach, her weight propped on her forearms, her head bent as she gasped in pain, fighting to draw the breath back into her aching chest. Wincing, she rolled over and stared into the swirling, choking, all-enveloping cloud of hot sand.

A funny sound popped out of her mouth, like an erupting bubble of panic. She swallowed hard, forcing it down.

The first thing she had to do was find her way back to the creek, she decided. She was fairly certain the horse had not crossed the rocky bed when she bolted, which meant Amanda must still be somewhere south of the creek. And since she knew the wind was blowing out of the north, all she had to do was walk into the storm until she hit the creek, and then turn left.

Setting her jaw, Amanda struggled to her feet, then stumbled as the full howling, stinging fury of the wind grabbed her, flung her around, sent her flying backward. She dropped back to the bare, rocky ground and began to crawl.

Sharp stones tore the skirt of her riding habit, slashed her hands. She paused long enough to rip off strips of thick green cloth and wrap them around her bleeding palms. Then she pushed on.

With her head bowed against the dust-laden wind, she didn't even see the gum-lined creek bed, only felt the change to smooth, water-polished stones beneath her lacerated hands and knees. Looking up, she spotted a big old coolabah tree and dragged herself toward it, collapsing with something like a sob behind its wide, sheltering trunk.

Her eyes ached, her throat was parched, her lips cracked, her hands were slick with blood. Her arms and legs trembled, her lungs burned from the effort to draw breath out of the hot, dust-laden air. Wrapping her arms around her waist, she hugged herself as choking spasms convulsed her body, doubling her over.

"I am not going to die here," she said aloud, gasping. "Not here." She hated this drought too much to let it defeat her. And she loved O'Reilly too much to die without seeing him again.

And then he was there. A tall, masked man on a gray horse looming up out of the swirling darkness.

"But he rides a chestnut," she said as he scooped her into his arms, holding her close to his strong, protective body. She clutched at him, her hands clenching fistfuls of cloth. She felt the familiar hard muscles beneath his heavy duster and rough shirt. Heard his breath expel in an almost painful-sounding sigh as he kissed her hair, her ear, her eyelids.

"Amanda," he whispered hoarsely, saying her name over and over again. "Dear God, I thought I'd lost you."

And then she knew that he was safe, and she was safe, and they were going home.

He didn't notice when she first opened her eyes.

He was lounging awkwardly in her straight-backed bedroom chair, his long frame curled sideways so that the dim light from the oil lamp on the round wooden table fell on the accounts he was studying.

After bringing her home that afternoon, he had helped her to bathe, then tucked her into bed and held her until she slept. But that had been hours ago. It was late now. The house lay quiet around them, and except for the dim circle of light cast by the lamp, the bedroom was in darkness.

She made no sound when she awoke. Yet he sensed her gaze upon him, and when he turned his head, he found her watching him, her cheek resting against the pillow, her eyes wide and still.

He put aside his papers and went to stand beside her bed, his heart pounding almost painfully in his chest as he stared down at her. She looked so delicate, so fragile lying there, that it scared him. "How do you feel?" he asked softly.

She smiled up at him. "Battered. How do I look?"

He gave her a crooked grin. "Worse."

She raised a bandaged hand to her face and winced. She had one cut over her right eye, another on her cheek, and her nose was

411

bruised, as if she'd landed on it when the mare rolled. "It's not fair," she said. "I wanted to look beautiful the first time you saw me again. I even have a new dress that I made up from a bolt of material I bought at Mary's. I was going to rush in here and put it on as soon as I saw you coming. It's a brilliant green satin with a shockingly low-cut bodice and—"

He pressed his fingers to her lips. "You will always be beautiful to me, Amanda. Always. Even when we're both old and gray." The words were simple, but he meant them. Sinking down on the edge of the bed, he took her hand in his. "Are you well enough to talk?"

She nodded.

For a long time, he said nothing, just let his eyes fill with the sight of her. The way her long, fire-licked hair spilled over the pillow. The gentle curve of her full, wonderful mouth. The way her gray eyes deepened with concern as she studied his face, waiting.

He dropped his gaze to their entwined hands. "I can't imagine what it's been like for you here the last couple of months," he said. He ran his thumb over the back of her hand, and she shivered the way she always did when he touched her. "Things were bad before I left, but now...Penyaka looks like a desert. A desert strewn with the bodies of countless animals. Sheep, cattle, horses, kangaroos, birds—they're all dying out there. Riding back here—"

His voice caught, and he had to swallow hard

412

before he could go on. "Riding back here, I kept thinking about you. Worrying about how this bloody drought was going to affect things between us. I started wondering if maybe you'd changed your mind—no, let me finish," he said, when she would have interrupted him. "I was afraid maybe you'd decided that you couldn't stand living here, that you wanted to go back to England. But then..."

He swung his head away to stare at the glowing lamp. "After a while, I realized I was only thinking about myself. About what I want. About what would be good for me." He brought his gaze back to her face. "This land is in my blood, Amanda; it's a part of who and what I am. But you're English. When you first came here, nothing was more important to you than getting back to England. You might be willing to stay here for my sake, and if things were as good as I know they can be, then I'm selfish enough that I'd ask it of you. But I love you too much to ask it of you now."

Her eyes were two unfathomable pools, her lips parted as if she were afraid to breathe. "What exactly are you saying?"

He curled his hand against her cheek. His fingers were so calloused, her skin so smooth and fine. "I'm saying I want you, Amanda. I want you in my life, beside me, always. I want you as my wife. I want you to have my babies. I want to grow old with you. But this bloody drought..."

He let his breath ease out slowly, painfully.

"Campbell says the mines are closing. That Christian's leaving for Adelaide at the end of the week. I want you to go with him and take the children to Hetty. Stay in Adelaide until it's over. Until the drought breaks and this land is livable again, or until, God help us, the drought breaks me. But I want you and the children out of this hell."

She looked at him, her nostrils flaring, her face white. "Why?"

He stood up to pace the room. "What do you mean, why? Jesus Christ." He swung around to face her. "You saw what happened to that family whose child you buried. Things are already worse here than I ever thought they could be. I want you out of this, and I want my children out of it."

She pushed herself up into a sitting position. "It's because you still think I'm like them, don't you? You think I'm like your mother and Katherine. You think that if I stay here, now, through this, it will all get to be too much for me and I'll decide I can't take it, and I'll leave."

He stared at her, nonplussed. "It's not the main reason, but... Ah, hell, Amanda. How can I help but worry about it?"

She thrust her legs over the side of the bed and came to him, sliding her arms around his waist to hug him close, her cheek pressed to his chest. "I love you, O'Reilly. When are you going to get that through your thick Aussie skull?"

He laughed softly, and she tilted back her head to look up at him wonderingly. "What's so funny?"

He put his hands on her shoulders and rubbed the tight muscles of her neck. "Do you realize you've never used my first name?" he said. "It's Patrick, you know."

He watched her lips curl into a smile that made his chest ache. "You've always been O'Reilly to me."

"Huh," he grunted. "Except when you're mad. Then I become *Mister* O'Reilly."

She chuckled, and his gaze focused again on her mouth, with its full lips and white, even teeth. He tangled his fingers in her hair, and her laughter died away as his head dipped toward her. He wanted so desperately to kiss her, to taste her, to lay her down and bury himself inside her.

He jerked his head up and sucked in a deep breath to steady himself, his thumbs rubbing restlessly back and forth over the line of her cheekbones. "There's something you need to know, Amanda. On my way back up from The Coorong, I stopped in Adelaide. It seems that once Katherine has been gone for seven years, I'll basically be free to remarry. But it's only been six and a half years now, and it might be better if we..."

His voice trailed off as she looped her arms around his neck and leaned into him in a way that flattened her full breasts against his chest. She was wearing only her nightgown,

415

and the material was very thin indeed. He was suddenly, achingly aware of her naked body beneath the nightdress.

"Better if we...what?" she asked in a husky voice as she looked up at him.

"Better if we...waited—" He sucked in his breath with an audible hiss as she tilted her pelvis forward and rubbed her belly against his painfully straining erection.

She raised herself on tiptoe, bringing her lips so close to his, they almost touched. Against his will, his hands slid down to her hips to hold her warm, sweet body close to his. "I've waited for you for over two months," she said, staring deep into his eyes. "I don't want to wait any longer."

He sighed, his hands roaming feverishly up and down her back, her hips, her sides. He was so desperate to touch her, to feel her, to hold her, to make love to her. "Ah, Christ, Amanda. I am trying to be honorable. The last thing I want to do is get you with child when I'm not in a position to marry you yet. I promised myself—"

She bit his earlobe. "Don't turn into a gentleman on me now, O'Reilly. Not when I want you to be a degenerate Australian."

"But you're covered with bruises and cuts from getting caught in that bloody storm. I don't want to hurt—"

"I am not made of porcelain." She nibbled at his neck, her hands spreading fire as she rubbed her palms over his shoulders, his chest. "I'm a flesh-and-blood woman, and

I've spent the last two months waiting for you. *Aching* for you."

With a laughing groan, he snagged his hands in her hair, bringing her head back. Her lips were parted with desire, her eyes dark with love. For him. It was still a wonder to him, that she loved him, that she wanted him. Wanted him with a wildness that surprised and delighted him, and loved him with an intensity that awed and humbled him.

"God, Amanda," he whispered. "I've missed you so." He covered her mouth with his in a kiss that was meant to be gentle but soon blazed up into something hot, frantic. They clutched at each other, their lips and tongues twining as if they could make themselves one flesh. Her lips were soft and sweet, her mouth hot. He thrust his tongue past her teeth, loving the feel of her, the taste of her, the little breathy, erotic noises she made deep in her throat as she strained against him.

Reaching down, he cupped her buttocks to lift her hard up against him. She squirmed, rubbing herself against him, and he grabbed fistfuls of her nightdress and shoved it up around her waist so that he could spread his hands over the naked flesh of her bottom.

"O'Reilly," she said with a gasp, her warm breath flowing over his mouth. She lifted one slim white leg up to curl it around his hip, and he let his hands drift over the bare skin of her thigh, seeking the tender folds at the secret entrance to her body.

He touched her, there, and she gasped

again and flung her head back, arching against the support of the arm he held braced about her waist. "Oh, if you only knew how I've ached for your touch," she whispered.

Her skin was so soft there. So soft and hot and sensitive. He moved his fingers, exploring, stroking as he bent his head to lay his open mouth against the creamy column of her throat. "Tell me," he said, moving his mouth lower, to where the placket of her nightdress opened to reveal the upper curves of her full breasts. "Tell me what you want."

She bracketed his face with her hands. "You. I want you. Please... I want you."

He raised his head and looked down at her. Her lips were parted, and swollen from his kisses, her eyes wide and dewy with passion, her glorious hair a fountain of fire that flowed over them both. "Ah, Amanda. I love you so. I've missed you so. I've wanted you so."

He let her leg slide to the floor and backed her up until they tumbled together across the rumpled sheets of her bed. She laughed, wrapping her arms around his neck and rolling with him until he landed on top of her. He braced himself above her on one outstretched arm, and for a long moment, they lay still, simply gazing into each other's eyes. Then she grasped his shirt and yanked it free from his waistband. "I want you naked," she said, in a rough, smoky voice that seemed to flow into his blood like a fever.

Standing up, he stripped off his shirt and sent his boots flying, never taking his gaze from where she lay sprawled across the bed before him, watching him, the hem of her night-gown hiked up wantonly about her hips to reveal her slim white legs and the faintest hint of a fiery triangle. He shoved down his trousers and peeled them off, then straightened to stand tall and naked before her. He saw her eyes widen, and grinned as he stretched out his hand to tug at her rucked-up nightdress. "You next."

Wordlessly, she reached down, her arms crossed, to gather the worn linen in her hands and draw it up slowly, wriggling her hips to free the gown from her weight and expose a flat belly, then her full, rosy-tipped breasts, puckered now with arousal. Another tug, and she lay before him, naked and inviting.

"You're beautiful," he said on an awed expulsion of breath as he lowered himself beside her. He let one hand rove over the pale mounds of her breasts, then leaned forward, using his tongue to draw a slow circle around a dark nipple before sucking it into his mouth.

Her head tipped back and her eyes squeezed shut, her lips parting in a soft cry of pleasure. He made love to her breasts, first one, then the other. He explored her body with his hands, with his tongue, stroking, sucking, nibbling at her throat, her chin, kissing her eye-lids, her breasts again, then lower, across her belly and down.

He felt her fingers tangle in his hair, her hips bucking up as he moved between her thighs. "I love you," he said, letting his hot breath wash over her wet flesh. "I love you, love you."

419

She writhed beneath the touch of his tongue and fingers, made small keening sounds of yearning that aroused him almost beyond bearing. Then he felt the tremors start, deep within her. Felt her hands clutch at his shoulders, trying to draw him up to her. "Now," she said, her head lifting off the pillow, her gaze meeting his. "Please."

He eased himself up the length of her slim body, trying to be careful, but she rose up to meet him eagerly, her mouth seeking his, clinging to him as if she were starving for him. A powerful animal desire roared through his blood: a primitive, wholly masculine urge to posses her, to join his body to hers and make her his.

"Yes," he said, the word a harsh gasp as he felt her open her thighs beneath him, her hand reaching down to guide him home. *Home,* he thought, as he clenched his buttocks and thrust his hips forward, pressed his hot, hard flesh against her yielding entrance, pressed, pressed, until he finally eased himself fully inside her.

He groaned and lay still for a moment, feeling his body stretching her, filling her. She was so hot and wet and tight around him, and he loved her so much. He drew himself partway out of her slowly, then thrust in again, and she arched her back and sighed.

"Ah, how I have wanted you." Her breath was warm against his neck, her hands spread against his naked chest.

He meant to be gentle, to keep the rhythm

easy. But his desire for her roared through him, sucking him out of control. "I'm sorry," he said, bracing himself on his outstretched arms so he could watch her face as he speared into her, again and again, harder and harder. "It's been so long. And I've wanted you so very much."

She stared up at him, her eyes wide and glazed with passion, her skin damp and flushed, her hands clutching his sweat-slicked upper arms as she wrapped her legs around his hips and drew him in, deeper and deeper, faster and faster. He bent his head, his mouth capturing hers for a long, hot, sucking kiss. Then he felt her nails dig into his shoulders and she flung back her head, her teeth sinking down on her lower lip to keep herself from screaming. He felt the tremors start deep within her, so powerful and clenching that it pulled him over the brink into a climax so shattering, he thought for one endless, rapturous moment that he had died and found eternity, and that it was an everlasting ecstasy.

He made love to her all night long.

Sometimes the pace was slow and erotic, at other times fast and passionate. Toward dawn, she fell asleep in his arms. But still he lay awake, prolonging the pleasure of holding her, of watching her face while she slept, of letting his heart fill to the aching point with his love for her.

The sweet morning call of a lark outside the

French doors awakened her. She stirred sleepily, her eyelids fluttering open to find him staring down at her in the dim light, his elbow bent, his head propped on his fist.

He watched the joyful smile that blazed across her face at the sight of him. And again he felt blessed that she could love him so. Blessed, and terribly afraid that he might lose that love—lose her.

"It's nice to open my eyes and find you in my bed." She stretched her arms up to loop them lazily around his neck.

He rubbed his nose against hers. "You, Miss Davenport, are a shockingly wanton woman."

She yawned. "Yes, I know. Isn't it wonderful?"

He laughed softly, rolling onto his back as her hands traveled downward, stroking his chest, his belly, before dipping lower. He sucked in a quick, startled breath.

"Why, *Mister* O'Reilly," she said, her smile becoming saucy as her hand moved up and down that part of his anatomy that was always willing to rise at her beckoning. "What have we here?"

"Something you want, perhaps?" He reached for her hips, meaning to draw her up on top of him. But she was already moving to straddle him, her knees digging into the mattress beside his hips, the covers falling from her bare shoulders as she rose above him.

"I might have a use for it," she said, then closed her eyes and sucked her bottom lip between her teeth as she slowly lowered herself, taking his length deep inside her.

He put his hands on her breasts, lifting them, stroking them, as she rose up, and sank down, rose up, and sank down, timing her gentle undulations to the lift and drag of his hips. "Does it fit your requirements, ma'am?" he asked, his voice a bit rough now as he picked up the tempo, his buttocks clenching and unclenching.

She braced her outstretched arms against his chest to steady herself. "I believe I find it...more than adequate."

He laughed softly, but it was a breathy laugh that turned into a whispered sound of pleasure as she moved faster and faster, riding him, riding him, until they were both straining, and the only sound in the room was the harsh soughing of their breath in and out, and the slap of their bodies coming together.

"*Oh, God, Amanda,*" he cried, lunging up to explode with such force, it seemed as if he were flying into a million pieces. He felt her inner muscles clench around him, saw his own stunned wonder mirrored in her face before she collapsed against him.

He tightened his arms around her, holding her to him. He kissed her hair, her dampened forehead, rubbed his hands over the sweat-slicked skin of her bare back. It took a long time for the pounding of his heart to begin to slow and his ragged breathing to even out. He felt his love for her swell within him, so deep and raw, it almost hurt. "I don't know how I'm going to bear being away from you again," he said, pressing his lips to her temple.

She lifted her head and stared down at him, her gaze wide and still. "You still want me to take the children to Adelaide."

He smoothed the tangled hair from her brow and cupped her cheek. "I want you out of this, Amanda. You, and the children." He searched her pale, strained face. "Please."

He expected her to argue with him again. But all she said was, "All right. I'll do it."

She rested her cheek against his chest, her head turned so that he could not see her face. But she didn't hide quite fast enough, because he got a good look at the expression in her eyes. He saw the fear and uncertainty she'd managed to hide from him until now.

And the relief that flooded in to replace it when she said she would take the children and go.

"But I don't want to go to Aunt Hetty's house," Missy said as O'Reilly swung her up into the wagon. "She makes me wear shoes. And *gloves*."

He laughed softly, even though it hurt so much to send them all away like this that he felt as if something were dying inside him. "Don't worry, pumpkin." He hugged her to him more fiercely than he'd intended. "It won't be for long. Just until the first good rain. Then I'll come get you."

"But it hasn't rained for yonkers."

"Then it ought to rain soon, don't you think?"

She didn't say anything, just wrapped her small arms around his neck and held him close in a surprisingly grown-up silence of grief. He kissed the top of her golden head and forced himself to let her go.

The sound of horses' hooves brought his head around. Liam reined in his roan gelding and, without dismounting, reached down to grasp O'Reilly's hand. "Good-bye, sir," he said, only the tight set of his lips and the strength of his grip betraying just how much effort it was costing the boy to control an unmanly urge to cry.

O'Reilly felt the morning breeze gusting warm and lonely around them. "Good-bye, son," he said, his own voice sounding uncomfortably thick. "Take good care of those horses, you hear?"

"Yes, sir." Liam stared off across the pale, dried hills, turning golden now with the rising sun. His teeth worried his lower lip, as if he had something to add but was having a hard time pushing the words out. At last, he said, "I wish you'd let me stay."

"I know."

Their gazes met and held for a moment before Liam's veered away again. O'Reilly watched the boy's throat work as he swallowed. Then he ducked his head and wheeled the roan toward where Jacko waited, the dog Barrister at his side.

"Papa?"

O'Reilly turned to where Hannah stood beside her horse, and found himself hesitating awkwardly. He wanted to hug her, the way he'd hugged Missy. But then he thought maybe she wouldn't like that, and maybe he should just shake her hand, as he'd done with Liam. Ever since that day when Katherine had finally arrived at Penyaka and presented him with a fretful daughter already one and a half years old, he had never quite felt at ease with this child, never quite been sure of himself with her the way he had with his other children.

He was still trying to make up his mind when Hannah threw herself against his chest. "Good-bye, Papa," she said, her voice muffled against his shirt. "Please be careful."

He closed his arms around her, holding her close. "I will, baby," he said. And he knew then that Amanda was right, that Hannah was growing up. Growing up enough to realize just how dangerous it would be for him, staying here. Growing up enough to realize that she might not see him again.

He helped her mount, then watched her ride to where Jacko and Liam waited with the mob of horses they'd be driving. Along with his family, O'Reilly was also moving Fire Dancer and the other breeding stock south, to be put out to pasture in the Adelaide hills. If he survived this drought, he thought, as the mob started off down the track, he was going to open up runs in different parts of the country—Victoria, New South Wales, even Queensland—so that he could move his stock easily whenever the rains failed in one area or another. If he survived this drought...

His swung back to Amanda, who had come out of the house again and was now busy tucking away the hampers of food Ching had packed for them. She was wearing the same ugly brown dress she'd had on the first time he'd seen her, standing on that dusty, wind-blown street in Brinkman. Remembering that day now, it was a wonder to him how far they had come, how much things had changed.

And yet, when he looked at her, he still saw a tiny, fragile-seeming woman with pale skin and fine bones and an air of rarefied gentility that seemed all wrong for this harsh, hostile environment.

As if she sensed his gaze upon her, she turned her head. He saw her lips part, her nos-trils flare as she sucked in a deep breath. He saw the pain and longing and fear that were his own, mirrored in her eyes, and for one shameful moment, he was glad of it. Glad to know that she was hurting, too.

He still wasn't unshakably certain of her love for him. He thought she loved him enough to wait for him in Adelaide. But that didn't mean she loved him enough to overcome her hatred and fear of this country. To stick with him through the worst this land could throw at a man and a woman, and not come to hate him, too. He kept remembering the look he'd seen in her eyes the morning she said she'd go, and it scared the hell out of him.

If he'd been sure of her—really sure—he'd

have asked her to come back to him after she saw the children safely settled with Hetty. Even now, the temptation to ask it of her was so strong that when she walked up to him, he couldn't trust himself to say anything for a long moment; he simply stared down into the deep, shifting gray oceans of her eyes.

"We're ready," she said.

He nodded. They'd already said their good-byes in private, in the pale, hushed hours of early dawn. He had held her naked body close to his, made slow sweet love to her. And told her that he'd love her forever.

But there was one thing he'd deliberately waited until now to say, when he knew she wouldn't be in a very good position to argue about it. "I want you to take this," he said, pressing a thick wallet into her open hand. "You'll be needing it."

Her fingers closed automatically around the leather. She glanced down at it, then up at him, her eyes widening when she realized how much he'd given her. "There's far more here than we could ever need for the journey. Would you like me to give what's left to your sister?"

He shook his head. "No. I have an account set up in Adelaide that you'll have access to. If you need anything—either for yourself or the children—there's money in the bank. Not a lot, but enough that you won't need to worry about going without."

"Then why this—"

"This is for you, Amanda. If something should happen to me, there's enough here to get you back to England and help you get reestablished. Especially if you—"

She pressed the fingers of her free hand to his lips, silencing him. "Nothing's going to happen to you."

He closed both his hands around her small one, holding it to his mouth so that he could kiss her curled fingers. His gaze locked with hers. "Something might."

"But—"

"Promise me, Amanda. Promise me that if something happens to me, you'll use this to get back home."

Her face was white, pinched by some emotion he couldn't begin to name. And it occurred to him, looking at her now, that as much as he loved this woman, he didn't entirely understand her yet. It was a thought that excited him, but it scared him, too. He could feel the fierce golden sun beating down on them. Hear the wind gusting, rustling the dry leaves of the dying gum trees. Hear the heavy pounding of his heart as he waited for her answer.

As if she'd been holding it, she let her breath out in a low, keening sound that was like an ache given voice. "All right. I promise. But nothing's going to happen to you."

He felt something shift inside him. He wasn't sure if it was a letting go of the fear that she wouldn't agree to let him do this for her, or if it was a swift thrust of sadness at the reminder of how much she had given up when she had turned her back on England and decided to stay in Australia and marry him.

He hadn't meant to kiss her, or even hug her, in front of the men, in front of the children. But he couldn't seem to stop himself from reaching for her, from holding her one last time.

His arms slid around her, pulling her slender body up against his hardness. He needed her close to him. Needed to smell her starchy muskiness, to feel the silken richness of her sinfully bright hair slip through his fingers one more time as he bracketed her face with his hands. He gazed deep into her beautiful, luminescent eyes...

And then he was kissing her. Kissing her as if he were starving, as if he could devour her and keep her with him. Kissing her open mouth, her suddenly tearstained cheeks, her trembling eyelids. "God, I love you," he whispered, a shudder ripping through him as he pressed his forehead to hers. "Wait for me, Amanda. And when this is all over, come back to me. Just...come back to me."

She spread her fingers over his cheek, her lips hovering next to his. "I'll wait, O'Reilly. And I'll be back. We'll all be back. You'll see. You'll see."

O'Reilly squinted up at the shimmering hot ball of the sun, hanging low on the horizon like something malevolent, something fierce and deadly that refused to go away. "Shit," he said, swiping at his sweaty forehead with his arm. Then he remembered his shirt was covered with mud, and he said "shit" again, before hunkering down beside the dead ewe at his feet.

She'd been alive a minute ago, when he'd dragged her out of the water hole she'd got herself bogged in. But the strain had been too much for her; as soon as he'd set her on solid land, she'd given one panicked little bleat and rolled over dead.

It seemed to O'Reilly as if he spent most of his time these days pulling dead or dying sheep out of the few water holes that were left. The poor dumb creatures would drag their bony carcasses across the bush to drink, then find themselves too weak to stagger away from the deadly grip of the water hole's trampled, muddy edges.

He straightened, his gaze drifting back to the hazy horizon. It was probably just dust, he thought, hanging heavy in the thick, oppressive air. But he kept an eye on it as he swung into the saddle and turned his tired horse's head toward the homestead. They all spent a lot of time watching the horizon these days. This was bushfire weather. It wasn't even a question anymore of if, but more like when, and where.

Amanda and the children hadn't been gone for more than a few days when he'd seen the glare of fire reddening the sky to the east. He'd mounted up every man he could spare and ridden hard to help the neighboring stations fight the flames. But with the bush this dry, there'd been no stopping the fire. Before the wind changed direction and drove the flames back onto charred ground, the fire had burned at least half of Bungowie Station and a good portion of Hannibal Cox's run, including the homestead and all the outbuildings.

Cox's wife and two sons had managed to survive by hiding deep in a cave where the nearby creek cut through a gorge, but Hannibal Cox and three of his men got caught in a blind canyon along with a mob of about five thousand sheep. Now, whenever the wind blew from the east, O'Reilly thought he could still smell the stench of roasted flesh and charred wool riding on the hot, sour air.

Lifting his head, he pressed his lips into a thin line as he watched the sun slip reluctantly behind the purple reaches of the Ranges. It would be dark soon, but he kept the gray gelding at an easy walk. He was in no hurry to get home. He'd almost reached the point that he hated that silent, empty house, hated the thought of spending another night alone with a book, or sitting on the veranda with Campbell, throwing back more drinks than was good for either one of them.

He'd thought at first that with time, it would get easier to bear, this living hell of having Amanda and the children gone. But as days turned into weeks and the weeks piled up, one on top of the other, the ache inside him seemed only to grow, until there were moments when he wanted to go stand out in the dying garden and howl at the moon like some bloody dingo.

The station buildings loomed ahead of him, dark and solid in the fading light. He pulled up at the homestead gate and watched the setting sun pour like melted honey over the ruin of Katherine's garden. He'd always hated that garden; now the sight of it like this, all withered and beaten, made him sad.

He turned the gray over to one of the men and went up the garden path to the darkened house. On the veranda, he paused to draw water from the cooler and was just lifting the mug to his lips when a voice said, "I must admit, Patrick, you're looking very healthy for a ghost."

O'Reilly spun about in a crouch, the mug clattering to the stone flagging as his hand flashed to the knife he always wore sheathed on his wide belt. "Bloody hell, Bagshaw," he said, straightening when he recognized the bulky figure lounging on a bench against the house wall. "You tryin' to get yourself killed or something?"

Mr. Errol Bagshaw, the local magistrate out of Melrose, raised a glass of what smelled like O'Reilly's best brandy to his lips and *tssk*ed over the rim. "My, my, my. Aren't we jumpy?"

"There's some pretty desperate characters roaming the bush these days."

"How true, how true." Bagshaw shook his head sadly, his long, greasy gray hair swishing back and forth against his shoulders. The Englishman was fat and sloppy and usually a good two months overdue for a bath, but O'Reilly liked the man anyway. He was quick, and he was clever. And he was also a lot softer-hearted than most people realized.

Picking up the mug with one swipe, O'Reilly sauntered over to lean against the rough stone wall of the house. "You bring the whole bottle out here, or just that glass?"

Bagshaw smiled wide enough to show his teeth and held up the half-empty brandy bottle.

"Much obliged," said O'Reilly, taking the bottle from the magistrate's slack grasp to splash two fingers' worth into the tin mug. He knocked it back with a shudder, then poured some more.

"You don't drink like a dead man, either," said Bagshaw.

O'Reilly paused with the mug raised halfway to his lips. "What the hell is all this about me being dead?"

"Vulgar, unfounded rumor, evidently. Word has it your run was wiped out by a bushfire a while back, and you and some of your men were turned into mutton chops. I was in the area, so I thought I might as well swing by here and see the damage for myself. I must admit I was a bit surprised to discover the home-stead still standing." He grunted as he leaned forward to retake possession of the bottle. "And truly astounded—but gratified, of course—when your men told me you are as yet numbered among the living."

"It was the Cox run that burned, not mine," said O'Reilly, the fine brandy tasting foul on his lips. "Hannibal Cox and some of his men got caught when the wind changed and swung the fire around on them."

"Ah, so that's the way of it."

O'Reilly set aside the rest of his brandy unfinished and jammed his fingertips beneath his belt. "What made you think it was me, anyway?"

Bagshaw sighed as if he bore all the cares of the drought-devastated Flinders on his plump shoulders. "The tale was carried to Melrose by a couple of bullockies, who had it from Tie-Ping."

"You mean that Chinese hawker?" O'Reilly grunted. "Hell, according to my cook, Tie-Ping can't even speak Cantonese properly, let alone English. How the hell did they get the tale out of him?"

"Obviously not with a great degree of accuracy. I gather the bullockies identified you—or rather, thought they did—by your ownership of a blood bay stallion the hawker kept going on about."

"You mean Fire Dancer?"

"That's the one."

O'Reilly shoved away from the wall to go stand at the veranda's edge and stare out at the gathering twilight. It would be a dark night. There was no moon, and the thickening haze obscured most of the stars. "Hannibal Cox is the man who originally brought the stallion in here from New Zealand," said O'Reilly over his shoulder.

Bagshaw pushed himself up from the bench with a mighty heave that tore a hoglike grunt from someplace deep in his ample belly. "That'll explain it. Now," he said, grunting again as he reached down to recapture both his glass and the brandy bottle, "do you suppose that excellent Chinese cook of yours has supper ready yet? I told him as soon as I arrived that I would be staying."

O'Reilly swung around, surprised into a grin. "I assume you told him to get the guest room ready, too?"

"But of course, my dear lad," said the fat man with a gentle laugh. "Of course."

After dinner, O'Reilly pulled a gaming table and two chairs out onto the veranda, and challenged Bagshaw to a game of chess. O'Reilly won the first game easily enough, but he knew from experience that Bagshaw was only warming up. They were forty-five minutes into the rematch and O'Reilly was carefully studying the board, when Bagshaw said in a deceptively conversational tone, "You remember those bullockies I told you about? The ones who had it you were dead?"

O'Reilly grunted, his gaze still fixed on the game.

"They were on their way down to Adelaide."

"So?" said O'Reilly.

"Your family is in Adelaide, aren't they?"

Wordlessly, O'Reilly lifted his gaze to the fat man's face. He was half out of his chair before Bagshaw said, "Sit down, son. You can't go anywhere on a night like this." He nodded to the darkness beyond the light thrown by the coal oil lamp and the smoking chrysanthemum leaves that kept away the mosquitoes. "It's blacker than a crow's backside out there tonight. If you don't want to break your horse's leg and your own neck, you're going to have to wait until dawn."

"Bloody hell," murmured O'Reilly, sinking back down into his seat to shove his knight into position almost randomly.

Reaching forward, Bagshaw edged the white queen to the left and showed his teeth in another one of those wide smiles. "Checkmate."

"Easy, boy," crooned O'Reilly as he settled the saddle on the horse's back. The chestnut gelding snorted and shivered its hide as O'Reilly reached for the cinch. The dawn was still only a faint rosy blush on the eastern horizon, but he was damned if he was going to wait any longer.

Four weeks. Those damned bullockies had left Melrose at least four weeks ago, Bagshaw had said. And if they'd got to talking on the way to someone heading south on a fast horse..."Bloody hell," he swore, pulling the cinch tight. For all he knew, Amanda could already be on a ship bound for England. He'd *told* her to go, hadn't he? Made her *promise* she'd go if something happened to him. "Bloody hell," he said again, reaching for his bridle. "Bloody, bloody fool."

He was leading the gelding out of the stables when he caught sight of a flash of white, coming down the hill from the homestead. He paused, puzzled, as he watched Mr. Errol Bagshaw, clad in a nightshirt and nightcap and with a blanket folded diagonally around his fat shoulders, materialize out of the darkness.

"For God's sake, Bagshaw, what are you doing out at this hour?" O'Reilly demanded as he swung into the saddle. The leather creaked loudly in the stillness of the coming dawn.

"I forgot to tell you something I heard when I was up near Blinman yesterday," said the magistrate, panting. "It seems Costner Creek got sixty hours of rain not long ago. There's been some flooding downstream already. Just watch out, will you?"

A surprisingly cool wind swept up from the valley, bringing with it the smell of dust. O'Reilly gathered his reins. "I'll be careful," he said, as the wind gusted again, filling the air with a sound not unlike the clatter of a handful of pebbles thrown against a cliff face.

Bagshaw glanced around, puzzled as the faint pattering sounded on the roof of the stables and the drooping wattles and gums down by the creek bed. "What *is* that noise?"

Something wet hit O'Reilly on the cheek. He tilted back his head to stare up at the starless sky above. "It's rain," he said. "It's bloody raining."

And then the sky opened up, and it poured.

CHAPTER TWENTY-TWO

Amanda found the children in the hayloft, above the stables at the back of their aunt's East Terrace mansion.

It had been two days since one of Henrietta Radwith's acquaintances had brought them word of the devastating bushfire that had destroyed Penyaka. Two days since they'd been told that Patrick O'Reilly and three of his men had died in the flames.

Sick with dread and uncertainty, yet refusing to believe it could be true, Amanda and the children had waited to be told it was all a mistake. Then, that afternoon, Christian Whittaker had come to tell Amanda that he'd met a couple of bullockies who'd just trailed down from the Flinders. The men had confirmed the news.

Suddenly desperate to be with the children, and afraid they'd somehow already heard about the bullockies in that mysterious way children have, Amanda went in search of them.

The atmosphere in the loft was thick with the scent of dried grass and horses, the light dim and dusty. She paused at the top of the ladder, her gaze shifting from one to the other of O'Reilly's three, silent children. Missy's cheeks were tear-stained, her eyelids red and swollen, her lips trembling. But Hannah and Liam were stony-faced, almost angry.

"I gather you heard what Mr. Whittaker came to tell us?" Amanda said.

Missy blurted out, "We still don't believe it," then burst into tears again.

Amanda sucked in a deep breath. It felt as if her heart were splintering into countless cutting shards of glass inside her breast. She had carried this agony within her for three days now. She had managed to bear it only because the pain was to some extent numbed by disbelief.

If he was truly dead, no one would have had to tell her. She was certain of that. She would have sensed it, felt it. She and O'Reilly were too close to each other, too well in tune with each other's feelings and thoughts, for him to have met his death in such a horrible way, without her knowing his pain. Even as she had sat listening to Christian telling her about the bullockies, she had still found herself thinking, *There must be some mistake.*

Yet she was aware of a small voice, somewhere deep within her, that kept whispering that she might be wrong, that it was possible she was refusing to believe he was dead simply because she could not bear to accept the truth. Now she looked at his children, and said, "May I come up?"

Hannah only stared at her, but Liam nodded his head.

Her hooped skirts awkwardly clutched in one hand, Amanda clambered up the rest of the ladder to the rough planking of the loft floor. Using a bale of hay as a seat, Amanda pulled

Missy into her lap and hugged O'Reilly's little girl close. "Let me hold you, sweetheart," she whispered. "I need to hold you."

Missy wrapped her arms around Amanda's neck and hugged her back so tightly it almost hurt. "You're not going to stop us, are you?" Missy asked, her tears wetting Amanda's shoulder through the cloth of her dress.

Amanda knew a quick, warning rush of apprehension that cut through her grief. "Stop you from doing what?" Her gaze flicked to Hannah and Liam. The two older children exchanged guarded glances, then stared pointedly away from each other, their faces carefully composed and blank.

"What is it?" Amanda demanded, looking from one child to the other. "What were you plotting before I came up? I know you, Liam and Hannah O'Reilly, and you never look this innocent unless you've something to hide."

In the silence that followed, Amanda could hear Henrietta Radwith's horses moving restlessly in their stalls below. "If you—" She broke off in sudden comprehension. "Dear God. You were going to try to get back to Penyaka, weren't you?"

With a sudden, violent motion, Hannah pushed away from the pile of hay and went to stare out the loading door, her shoulders rigid, her jaw tight.

"You were, weren't you?" Amanda said again.

Hannah braced one arm against the opening's

frame, but she didn't turn around. "I don't believe he's dead," she said, staring out over the tops of the gum trees in the nearby parklands. "I don't care what those bullockies said. I still don't believe Papa is dead."

Whatever Amanda's own doubts, she wasn't so irresponsible as to encourage the children to build up false hopes. "I know it is difficult to accept, Hannah," she said, her voice sounding tired. "But—"

Hannah whipped around, showing Amanda a white, strained face. "Do *you* believe he's dead, Miss Davenport? Really believe it?"

Amanda met the girl's wide, frank gaze. And couldn't lie. "No," she said on a painful expulsion of breath. "No, I don't. But a part of me is afraid that I'm wrong, that I'm simply finding it difficult to accept the truth, and that he is dead."

"If we go to Penyaka and I see his grave, then I'll believe it," said Liam.

"I'm sorry, but I can't let you do this. Your father wanted me to bring you children here to Adelaide to keep you safe. I can't let you go back up there."

"But we have to," said Hannah. "Don't you understand?"

Amanda let her breath out in a long, hurting sigh. "Yes. I do understand." And she knew now what she must do. "I'll go myself," she said.

"You, Miss Davenport?" said Missy, staring up at her.

Amanda's arm tightened around the little

girl's shoulders, but she kept her gaze on Hannah and Liam. "If I went to Penyaka—if I talked to the people there, and saw your father's grave, would you accept it? For now? Until the situation improves and you can go there yourself?"

Hannah stared at her across the dusty length of the loft. And for the first time in days, Amanda saw a ripple of emotion pass over the girl's face. "And if Papa really is dead, will you go back to England?"

It wasn't until Hannah asked the question that Amanda realized just how little thought she had given to her own future. She had been so *sure* that O'Reilly wasn't dead, that her future still lay with him, with these children, at Penyaka. "I don't know," she answered honestly. "Why?"

It was Liam who answered. "Missy said she heard you promise Papa that you'd go back to England, if...anything happened to him."

Amanda felt as if something were squeezing her chest, stopping her breath with panic and pain. She thought about saying good-bye to these three children. About leaving this sun-seared, untamed land and returning to her old life in England.

And she knew she could not do it. If it turned out that she was wrong—if she truly had lost the man she loved, then she didn't want to lose these children, too. She knew she had no legal claim to them, but she and Henrietta Radwith had come to respect each other in the weeks Amanda had been in Adelaide, and she didn't think O'Reilly's sister would stand in her way.

"I'm not going back to England," Amanda said, her voice firm. "I want to stay here with you. I promised your father I'd go home, but...Australia is my home now. It's where I belong."

It wasn't until she'd actually said it that Amanda realized it was true. Here she had a family, and she had a home.

She was where she wanted to be.

"I have spoken to the captain of the *Atlas*," Christian told Amanda the next day as they strolled through the parklands opposite Henrietta Radwith's East Terrace mansion. "He says he can hold a cabin. But the ship sails next week. You must make up your mind what you're doing."

"I have made up my mind," said Amanda. The rustle of her skirts startled a pair of lorikeets chattering in an emu bush beside the path; the birds took flight, two streaks of vivid emerald touched with flashes of sapphire and ruby. She turned her head, watching them.

"Good God," said Christian, stopping to gaze at her. "You're not going."

She swung to face him. "No, I'm not. I can't."

She saw the dismayed concern flash in his gentle brown eyes before he quickly veiled it. He was a good friend, she thought, reaching out to clasp his hand. They'd become especially close on that hard trip from Penyaka down to Adelaide. They'd spent many an evening together, sitting beside a crackling, eucalypt-scented fire and staring up at the starry southern sky while they talked. She had told him, shyly, about her future plans with O'Reilly, and Christian had told her of the young cousin he thought he might marry on his return to Oxfordshire. Since their arrival in Adelaide, he had been busy, winding up the company's affairs, getting ready to sail. But he'd kept in touch often, and since the news of what had happened at Penyaka, he had visited every day.

"But O'Reilly is dead," Christian said now, his fingers tightening around hers. "What is the point of staying?"

"First of all, I still can't accept it." She curled her free hand into a fist and pressed it to her chest. "If he were dead, I would know it. I'd feel it. Here."

A muscle bunched in Christian's ruddy cheek, twitching one side of his mustache. "Are you sure, Amanda? Are you sure it's not just because you don't want to believe it?"

"Perhaps," she said softly. "But I can't simply take someone's word for it. Don't you see? I must *know*."

Christian's gaze shifted uncomfortably away from her. "Short of going up there to find his grave for yourself, I don't see how that's possible."

"But that's exactly what I plan to do. There's a German missionary and his wife leading a small group up north. They've agreed to take me with them. They leave on Wednesday."

"Go back up there?" Christian's gaze flew to hers, his voice rising uncharacteristically in alarm. "In this drought? You must be mad."

"No." She shook her head. "Just in love."

He sighed and swung away from her, as if trying to master his feelings. "You do realize that the *Atlas* is the only ship in the harbor at the moment bound for England? I've checked; there's not another expected for months. Once we sail, you'll be stranded here for goodness only knows how long."

"It doesn't matter. I've decided I won't be returning to England."

"*What?*" Christian spun back around to stare at her, his jaw slack, his eyes bulging. "Not go back to England? You mean, stay *here*? Forever?"

For the first time since they had heard the heartbreaking, soul-destroying news about O'Reilly, Amanda felt a smile tug at her lips. "Dear Christian. Don't sound so horrified. I want to stay here. I want to be with the children, but... It's more than that."

Lifting her face to the gentle, wattle-scented breeze, she let her gaze drift to the blue-green hills that stretched away toward the north. "There was a time when I thought I'd never say this, but I actually like it here. I like feeling the golden warmth of the sun on my face, and looking up at a sky so clear and blue and endless, it almost hurts to see it.

There's something about this land—it's so ancient, so strange, so wild. And yet so peaceful and honest." She brought her gaze back to his puzzled face. "I like it here," she said again. "But more importantly, I like *myself* here. And I'm afraid that if I went back to England, I'd end up going back to being the person I was before—the person I don't want to be anymore." She laughed softly. "Does that make sense?"

"Probably not," said Christian. "But as long as it makes sense to you, that's all that matters." He took her hand again and pulled it through the crook of his elbow. "Come, let's finish our walk, shall we?"

"I'm going to miss you," she said quietly, strolling beside him.

"Yes, I shall miss you, too. If you ever need anything—anything at all—"

She squeezed his arm. "Yes, I know. And thank you."

By the time O'Reilly reached Brinkman, the creeks had already begun to run.

At first, they were only trickles of water, their surfaces covered with dust, creeping like slowly awakening fingers from one shrunken waterhole to the next. But as the rain continued to pound down, the dry, hard earth could not absorb the water fast enough. Thick red rills appeared, joining together, washing with a roar into creeks that swelled and swirled with all the debris of the drought.

Dawn brought little light to the storm-washed landscape. The clouds hung thick and low: roiling black masses that rumbled and split with fire and sent sheets of rain hurtling at the parched landscape. O'Reilly slogged on. Rain poured off his hat, soaked through his clothes, ran into his eyes, dripped off the edge of his nose. The chestnut's hooves made sucking, plopping noises in the rain-splattered mud, and twice it slipped in the muck and almost went down. O'Reilly swore at the delay, gritted his teeth as the cold wind bit him to the bone, and pulled the gelding in to a walk.

If it had been up to O'Reilly, he would probably have ridden on through the night. But by four o'clock, when he spotted smoke curling from the stone chimney of a rain-washed shepherd's hut on a distant hill, the chestnut was exhausted. O'Reilly reluctantly left the track and stopped for the night.

The shepherd and his hut keeper provided O'Reilly with a warm meal for his belly, hay for his horse, and the chance to dry his clothes in front of a roaring fire. But the next night he had to make do with the burned-out ruins of an abandoned station. The roof leaked and the wind howled through the broken walls, and O'Reilly was up and in the saddle again before daybreak.

He rode determinedly on, his mind eased by a decision he'd reached at some point during the long, cold night. He'd already known that if he arrived in Adelaide to discover

Amanda gone, then he was willing to go to England after her. But he'd now resolved that—even if she was still in Adelaide—he was going to tell her that he was willing to go to England with her. If she didn't think she could face the prospect of spending the rest of her life in Australia, then they would both make their home someplace else. He loved this land, loved it like his own life. But he loved Amanda more.

Dawn was barely a pale hint through the heavy gray clouds when he pulled up at the top of a rise and looked down on the flood-swollen torrent at the base of the hill. "Bloody hell," he said, wiping the rain from his face with his soaked forearm. He studied the four or five wagons huddled together on the near bank, trying to decide which way they'd been headed before they'd made camp, but it was impossible to tell if they'd been stopped by the storm-fed creek or had crossed too late last night to go any farther.

A forlorn wisp of smoke testified to someone's pitiful attempt to coax forth enough of a fire to cook breakfast. O'Reilly eased the chestnut down the steep hill to the camp, hoping whoever it was had at least managed to brew up a pot of hot coffee or tea. That creek looked mighty cold.

He could see the fire now, partially sheltered by canvas rigging, and the big, sturdily built man with a long, straw-colored beard and clean-shaven upper lip who was tending it. At the sound of the chestnut's hooves splashing through the mire, the man looked up, showing

449

a lined but pleasant face that split into a smile. "Guten Morgen."

"G'day," said O'Reilly, his stirrup leather creaking as he lifted in the saddle, easing his aching, cold-cramped muscles.

"It is a good day to spend in a varm, dry bed, I think."

"Yeah. You see one around here?"

The man laughed. "No. My own bedding got soaked through last night, when we crossed the river, so I vas not tempted to linger." He reached to lift a blackened pot from the hissing fire. "Would you like some coffee?"

"Much obliged." O'Reilly swung out of the saddle to hold his hands out to the flames. "So you crossed the creek last night, did you?"

"Creek? You call that a creek?" The German handed O'Reilly a steaming mug of coffee and hunkered back down beside the fire. "In my country, we call that a river."

"Thanks," said O'Reilly, wrapping his numb fingers around the hot mug and taking a sip of the scalding black liquid. "I suppose it'd be called a river here, too, if it looked like that all the time. But if you'd come through a few days ago, you could have driven right across the bed without even gettin' your wheels muddy."

"That is what the *englische* woman we have with us said. I would have made camp on the other side last night, but she said the vater was rising, and we had best cross while we could." He shook his head. "She vas right. We could never have crossed if we had waited until this morning. It would be suicide."

"Yeah. Well, thanks for the coffee," said O'Reilly, setting down the empty mug and collecting his reins.

"*Lieber Gott.*" The German straightened up to face him. "You are going to cross that river? Now?"

"No worries, mate." O'Reilly swung into the saddle. "You just keep your horse's head upstream and relax and let him drift over. It's only if you pull him up suddenly or don't sit still or try to turn that he's liable to roll on you."

The German shook his head. "This is a hard country you have. First drought. Now flood."

"Don't forget the bushfires," said O'Reilly with a grin. And he nudged the gelding forward into the swirling reddish-brown water.

She heard his voice in her dream, heard the clipped Australian cadences and the light, self-depreciating tone she loved. In her bedroll in the Herbolts' wagon, Amanda moaned softly as sleep—and the dreams of O'Reilly it always brought her—slipped away from her.

She sat up, shivering in the damp, chill air. "First drought. Now flood," she heard Mr. Herbolt say.

And O'Reilly answered, "Don't forget the bushfires."

"O'Reilly," she whispered. "Dear God, it's him."

Hope flared within her, brilliant and breath-taking. She tried to damp it down, terrified of disappointment even as she threw back the covers and leapt to her feet. "O'Reilly!" she screamed, lunging toward the cart's tailgate. Her foot hooked Frau Herbolt's outflung arm and Amanda went down, whacking her knee on a trunk and slamming her elbow against an iron pot.

"Vat is it?" Frau Herbolt sat up with a start, her nightcap slipping over one eye.

"*Auf Wiedersehen*," called Herr Herbolt.

"He's leaving." Amanda scrambled to her feet. "No! *Wait*."

She threw herself over the endboard, barely conscious of the loud rip that sounded as her nightdress caught on a peg. Then her bare feet hit the cold, slippery mud and shot out from beneath her before she could do more than scrabble to grab a handhold.

Her bottom slammed against the sodden ground with a teeth-jarring thud that sent the breath *whoosh*ing out of her. Gasping for air, she thrust both hands into the mire and pushed herself up, going down again on one knee before she was on her feet and running for the creek, the mud squishing up between her toes.

She could see him now, in the dim, storm-tossed light of dawn. A tall man astride a big chestnut already up to its withers in the swirling waters. As she watched, the horse's head thrust forward and it began to swim.

She slid down the bank to the water's edge,

heedless of her bare feet and legs, heedless of her torn nightdress, heedless of the cold rain pelting down on her and the wind whipping her loose hair around her face. "*O'Reilly!*" she screamed, her voice a thin wail lost in the roar of the rain and the boom of the creek and the howling of the wind.

She felt a man's brawny arm close around her, yanking her back as a beefy palm slapped across her mouth. "No, my child," Herr Herbolt said, shouting to be heard over the raging floodwaters. "He can't come back now—he's already in the middle of the current. If he tried to turn that horse now, they'd both drown."

Her eyes rolled sideways until she could see the bearded face and gentle brown eyes of the man who held her. She nodded solemnly, so he would know that she understood.

He let his hand fall slowly. "You know this Australian?"

"Yes." Rain ran down her face as she gasped for breath, her chest rising and falling, her heart pounding. "He's the one I told you about— the man they said died in the fire."

"Then by God's mercy he will not drown in this flood," said the German.

Amanda wished she had the man's quiet faith. Her stomach felt as if it had wedged up in her throat, choking her. Reaching out one cold-numbed hand, she gripped Herr Herbolt's strong arm as they stood together, side by side, their gazes fixed on the swimming horse and its rider. The rain washed over them in

icy, windblown sheets chased by flashes of lightning and the ominous rumble of thunder.

Above them, the cloud-filled sky slowly
paled with the coming day, showing them a
red-brown river that heaved and churned and
seemed to rise higher and higher with each
passing moment. Broken tree branches and
entire uprooted gums swirled dangerously in
the churning, frothing flow, sending waves
rolling out to slap against the flooded banks
and lap at Amanda's bare feet.

"He's being swept downstream," she said,
shivering uncontrollably.

"Yah. He is letting the current carry him
across."

"There." Amanda strained forward as the
chestnut seemed to heave up out of the water.
"He's touched bottom again." Then the horse
staggered and lost its footing, and Amanda had
to bite her lip to keep from crying out. Man
and horse plunged down, lost for a moment
in the turmoil of swirling thick mud, only to
reappear again, scrambling up on the far
bank, wet but whole.

"Thank God," whispered Amanda. "He
made it. He's safe."

The man on the horse reached to pat the
chestnut's streaming wet withers, leaning
forward as if he were saying something to
the frightened, shivering animal. Then he
wheeled about to look back at the floodwaters
he had conquered.

Even from this distance, Amanda saw his head
come up. Saw his gaze fix on the bedraggled,

barefoot woman who stood at the water's edge, her nightdress ripped half off, her hair hanging about her shoulders like a limp red rag. He stiffened.

"*No*," she screamed as he urged his mount forward again. "*Don't come back!*"

But the chestnut hesitated only an instant before, shuddering, it plunged straight into the churning, deadly waters.

CHAPTER TWENTY-THREE

O'Reilly kicked his feet free of the stirrups and willed his body to relax as the icy waters swirled up around his thighs to lap at his groin. He held the chestnut's head pointed upstream, but beyond that he just let the horse drift across and concentrated on keeping his own weight as still and evenly balanced as possible.

She was running now, her slim white legs flashing, her arms pumping as she dashed along the bank to keep him in sight while the current swept him downstream. Her bare feet splashed through the shallow water, kicking up a spray that soared through the air behind her. Rain slashed down at her. The wind whipped at her glorious flame-colored hair and plastered the thin wet cloth of her ripped gown to the naked body beneath. She looked magnificent, wild, free.

And he wanted her.

He wanted to lay her down in the water's edge and take her there, with the rain pouring down on them and the wind howling around them. He wanted to bury himself inside her and listen to her breath catch and watch the rapture spill across her face. He wanted to hold her in his arms and cover her with kisses and never, ever let her go.

He still couldn't believe that she was here. He certainly didn't understand why she was here. He only knew that she was here, that she hadn't gone back to England, that her eyes were wide with terror for him even as her lips quivered with what could only be joy. And he felt a sweet warm ache flood through him at the realization that this joy, this terror, this abandoned dash through the stormy dawn was for *him*. For love of him.

"*O'Reilly.*" Her voice floated to him over the rush of the water and the roar of the wind and the pounding of the rain. "O'Reilly, you mad, degenerate *Australian*. Are you trying to *kill* yourself?"

He laughed then, feeling the chestnut's hooves strike solid ground. With a mighty heave, the horse lunged and scrabbled up onto the bank, muddy water running off both man and beast in noisy rivulets that splashed onto the stony ground. She was still running toward him; O'Reilly spurred the gelding to meet her, and leaned down to catch her around the waist and scoop her up onto the pommel before him.

"Amanda," he said on a joyous expulsion of breath as she flung her arms around his neck, pressed her trembling body to him. "Amanda. Dear God, Amanda."

She was wet through, her body shaking with the chill and the need to draw air into her gasping lungs. "They told me you were dead." She kissed his chin, his cheek, his neck. Her hands skimmed over his shoulders, his back, his chest, as if she would touch every inch of him. "They said you were dead. But I didn't believe it. I knew it couldn't be so. I knew. I knew."

He snagged his fist in her wet, tangled hair, tilting her face so that he could stare down at the rain-drenched curve of her cheek, the swell of her full lips. She smelled wonderfully of roses and morning rain and herself.

"I was afraid you'd left," he said, his voice husky with emotion, his head dipping until his lips hovered over hers. "Left Australia and gone back to England." He brushed his open mouth against hers, hugged her even closer. "Riding down here, I made up my mind about something, Amanda. I decided I want to go back to England with you, if that's what it takes to make you happy. If you—"

She pressed her fingers to his lips. "I don't want to go back to England." Her solemn gray eyes locked with his. He saw no uncertainty, no fear there now. Only love, and the deep conviction of commitment. "I want to stay here. Always."

He smothered her mouth with his. The horse

shifted restlessly in the water's edge as the rain poured around them. But O'Reilly knew only the sweet, frantic pressure of her lips, slanting against his, opening beneath his. She clung to him, her fingers digging into his shoulders as the kiss went on and on.

"*Lieber Gott*," said a booming voice.

O'Reilly flung up his head to see the German missionary some hundred feet away, splashing through the shallows toward them. Then O'Reilly's gaze fell to the woman in his arms, and he began to laugh. "What in God's name are you *doing* here, anyway?"

"Looking for you," she said, her smile wide and breathtaking.

"And the children?"

"They're safe with your sister."

He stared off across the swirling floodwaters. "We'll have to go get them."

Her hold on him tightened, as if she thought he meant to charge back through the creek right then and there. "Not yet," she said.

He grinned down at her. "No. Not yet. We'll have to get a message through to them somehow, but right now, I intend to find someplace warm and dry and private, where I can spend the next week doing absolutely nothing except showing you how much I love you."

Her hands curled around his neck, pulling his mouth back down to hers as she said in a sultry purr, "How about two weeks?"

He covered her mouth with his. "God, I love you," he said, his lips moving over hers. "So much. So much."

EPILOGUE

Morning was Missy's favorite time of day. Especially September mornings, when the air smelled cool and sweet, and the sun streamed golden warm out of a vivid blue sky.

Sucking in a deep, joyous breath of spring, Missy wrapped one elbow around a veranda post and spun about, admiring the way her starched yellow satin skirts swirled around her. True, her pointy-toed shoes pinched her feet, but Hannah had warned her that because it was Papa's wedding day, Missy had better keep her shoes on. And since Hannah was actually wearing a *dress* for the occasion, Missy decided she'd better do what she was told, or risk a painful thump between her shoulder blades.

The lilting strains of Ichabod Hornbottom's fiddle drifted across the veranda to mingle pleasantly with the happy trills of the Irish miner's accordion, coming from somewhere down by the gate. The garden was noisy and crowded with people—bushmen tugging at uncomfortably tight shirt collars, women preening in silk and lace, children squealing and running every which way. Everyone from miles and miles around had come for the wedding, which was why it was being held outside, in the garden. Papa had talked about maybe having it in the woolshed, but Miss Davenport said she thought it would be nice to be married in the garden.

With the coming of spring, the garden was bursting with new life, and thick with the sweet scent of roses and the heady blossoms of the apple and plum trees that had made it through the drought a year and a half ago. After the rains finally came, Chow and Miss Davenport had worked hard, cutting things back and replanting, so that the garden now looked as pretty as it ever had. Different, but still nice, maybe even nicer, because along with the flowers she knew from England, Miss Davenport had also planted things like striped mint, and emu bushes, and yellow buttons—Australian plants, that coaxed the bush birds and butterflies to come right up to the house.

Humming quietly in time with the fiddle, Missy switched elbows and twirled around the post again, until she could see Papa where he waited under the heavily scented purple-and-white umbrella of the wisteria arbor. He seemed relaxed, his thumbs hooked casually on the pockets of his fine new trousers, his head tipped back, laughing at something Liam'd just said. It was Liam, beside him, who looked unusually serious, almost nervous.

Then the sound of the French doors of Miss Davenport's room opening onto the veranda brought Papa's head around. The smile still lingered on his lips, but it changed somehow, softening into a look so tender that Missy felt tears prick her eyes and tickle her nose, even though she couldn't quite have said why, because she certainly wasn't sad.

Hannah came out first. Her thick, dark hair framed her face in neat glossy ringlets and, like Missy, she wore starched yellow satin and white lace. It was amazing how pretty Hannah could look when she dressed like a girl—not that Missy would ever tell her that, of course. Besides, from Hannah's triumphant smile and high color, Missy was fairly certain her sister knew it, anyway.

Hannah was being disgustingly bossy about the wedding, just because she was maid of honor and Missy was only the flower girl. She'd even insisted on holding on to Missy's basket of rose petals, and only handed it to her now with a harshly whispered "Stop spinning around. Be careful you don't spill all the petals out of the basket at once. And for heaven's sake, pay attention."

Missy closed her fist over the basket's handle and made a face at her big sister. She didn't think Hannah had any reason to act so puffed up and important. After all, Hannah was only maid of honor, while Mary McCarthy was the matron of honor, which surely meant she was more important.

"Imagine having your groom's former paramour stand up next to you at your wedding." A voice that sounded suspiciously like Iantha Thorndike's tittered suggestively as Mary McCarthy, also pretty in yellow satin, followed Hannah out into the sunlight.

Missy craned her head around, looking for

the worm-mouthed governess, but saw only a sea of smiling, expectant faces, shiny now with the first traces of sweat as the sun rose higher in the sky.

"*Missy,*" hissed Hannah.

Yanked back around by her sister's firmly guiding hands on her shoulders, Missy stepped off the veranda and took her place in front of Hannah. She wasn't exactly certain what a *paramour* was. But Miss Davenport and Mary McCarthy had become really good friends lately, and Missy couldn't see why Mrs. McCarthy shouldn't be in the wedding, just because she and Papa used to spend so much time alone together in the middle of the afternoon.

Missy was still trying to figure it out when a man's voice said, "Sure then, she's beautiful, isn't she now?" and Missy's new mama stepped out of the shadows.

Splendid in cream silk embroidered with yellow rosebuds, Amanda Davenport paused at the edge of the veranda, her lips parted with excitement, her smiling gaze fixed on the man who waited for her at the end of the path. A circlet of cream and yellow sweetheart roses crowned the glorious, flame-colored hair that floated in a loose aurora of fire about her shoulders. In comparison, her fine-boned face looked radiant but pale, her figure still slight and fragile-seeming, despite the noticeably swelling burden she carried beneath the graceful folds of embroidered silk.

"It's due before Christmastime, according

to what I hear," said Iantha Thorndike, her precise English voice carrying clearly in the sudden hush.

Missy glanced about angrily, but Miss Davenport only laughed softly, her hand coming up, briefly but unselfconsciously, to touch her bulging stomach.

It was because of the baby, Missy knew, that Papa had been desperate to get his *dee-vorce*, and quickly. Missy didn't quite understand what the problem was, but it seemed that *dee-vorces* weren't very easy to get in South Australia. So Papa and Miss Davenport had been really happy when they found out that Missy's real mama had *dee-vorced* Papa a long time ago, in France or England or America, so that she could marry a Russian count, or German prince, or some such person. Liam was hoping for the Russian count, but Missy had decided she'd rather have a prince, even if he was sure to be a Lutheran, like Hannah said.

"Missy!"

Jerked back to attention by a sisterly finger poked between her shoulder blades, Missy stepped forward, the leather soles of her shoes tapping against the flagged path in time to the surprisingly stately melody coming from Mr. Hornbottom's violin. She remembered to hold tightly to the basket so that it didn't tip. She remembered to walk slowly, so that she didn't get too far ahead of everyone else.

The only thing she forgot to do was to throw the rose petals.

But nobody seemed to notice. As they

reached the wisteria arbor, a light breeze soughing through the gums down by the creek sent sweet, lilac-colored blossoms cascading down upon yellow satin and rose-strewn cream silk. Missy's new mama said her vows clearly, precisely. It was Papa whose voice was hushed with awe and an almost trembling kind of joy.

Then Reverend Townsend said, "You may kiss the bride."

The bride stood still, almost shyly waiting for her groom's touch. His hands came up, his fingers sliding into the fiery cascade of hair that framed her face. Their gazes locked and held, and it seemed to Missy as if, for these two, in that moment, there was no one else in the garden, no one else in the universe.

"You're mine now," he said softly. "Forever."

A smile touched the bride's lips as she lifted her face to her husband. "I've always been yours."

His head dipped. Missy turned away...

Just as a loud bellow floated across the garden from the direction of the kitchen.

"*Li-am.*" Hannah rounded on her brother, her hands closing into threatening fists that did serious damage to the bridal bouquet she still held. "You promised you wouldn't play any tricks during the wedding."

"And I didn't," said Liam gaily, his swirling green-and-gold eyes bright with devilry and merriment.

Ching's voice, rising and falling in curses that lost none of their impact for being uttered in Mandarin Chinese, broke off suddenly in another howl of rage.

"Then what is that all about?" demanded Hannah.

Liam grinned. "I didn't say anything about the reception."

AUTHOR'S NOTE

A ruggedly beautiful landscape of raw, brittle red ridges and unexpectedly lush and peaceful water holes, the Flinders Ranges today still preserve much of the wild grandeur and indescribable majesty that first awed strangers to Australia almost a century and a half ago.

The killing drought described in this book was real. Unfamiliar with the harsh cycle of flood, fire, and drought that dominates this ancient land, the first European settlers in the Flinders paid a heavy price for their ignorance. The overgrown tombstones and crumbling stone walls of their abandoned homesteads, mines, and ghost towns are still visible today, mute testimony to their suffering and loss.

Yet those who learned to understand the land were able to survive and even prosper. While Patrick O'Reilly and his family are, alas, products of my imagination, the descendants of many of the strong, self-sufficient settlers who inspired this tale can still be found today in the wild reaches of South Australia's outback.

A note about language: I have tried to give the flavor of nineteenth-century Australian speech without reproducing it exactly. Oddly enough, some words or phrases that Australians today think of as "American" were actually in use in nineteenth-century Australia but have since been dropped. Other words, such as *pom* or even *Australian*, more correctly belong to the late nineteenth century, but I have used them because they most clearly and familiarly express the meanings I wished to convey. Also, while Australian novels often use *yer* to convey the Australian pronunciation of the word *you*, this practice makes sense only if one understands that Australians typically turn their *r*'s into *a*'s. I have therefore used *ya*—although many Australians would read that as *yer*, since they also have a tendency to turn their *a*'s into *r's!*